Ruth Rendell

THE LAKE OF DARKNESS

THE VEILED ONE

ARROW

This edition published by Arrow in 1999
an imprint of The Random House Group
20 Vauxhall Bridge Road, London SW1V 2SA

Papers used by Random House UK Ltd are natural
recyclable products made from wood grown in
sustainable forests. The manufacturing process conform
to the environment regulations of the country of origin.

A catalogue record for this book is available
from the British Library

Printed and bound in Great Britain by
Cox & Wyman Ltd, Reading, Berkshire

ISBN 0 09 187009 7

THE LAKE OF DARKNESS

For Don, again

Nero is an angler in the lake of darkness. . . .

King Lear

I

Scorpio is metaphysics, putrefaction and death, regeneration, passion, lust and violence, insight and profundity; inheritance, loss, occultism, astrology, borrowing and lending, others' possessions. Scorpians are magicians, astrologers, alchemists, surgeons, bondsmen and undertakers. The gem for Scorpio is the snakestone, the plant the cactus; eagles and wolves and scorpions are its creatures, its body part is the genitals, its weapon the Obligatory Pain, and its card in the Tarot is Death.

Finn shared his birthday, November 16, with the Emperor Tiberius. He had been told by a soothsayer, who was a friend of his mother's that she had met in the mental hospital, that he would live to a great age and die by violence.

On the morning of his birthday, his twenty-sixth, one of Kaiafas's children came round with the money in a parcel. He knocked on Finn's door. Someone downstairs must have let him into the house. They didn't know it was his birthday, Finn realized that, it was just a coincidence. He undid the parcel and checked that it contained what it should contain, two thousand five hundred pounds in ten-pound notes. Now it had arrived he had better get on with things, he might as well start now.

It was too early to go up to Lena. She liked to sleep late in the mornings. Not that she would mind his waking her on his birthday, she would like it, she would expect it almost, but he wouldn't just the same. He tucked the money safely away and went downstairs.

Finn was very tall and thin and pale. He was near to being an albino but saved by the watery grey colour which stained the pupils of his eyes. It was remarkable that eyes of such an insipid shade should be so piercing and so bright, like polished silver. His hair, when he was a child, had been white-blond but had now faded to the neutral greyish beige of cardboard. He had a face that was quite ordinary and unmemorable but this was not true of his eyes. Under a longish PVC jacket he wore blue denims, a check Viyella shirt, a black velvet waistcoat, and round his neck one of those long scarves which Greek women wear, black and triangular and sewn along one side with small gold coins. He carried a tool box of laminated blue metal. Finn had a smallish head on a thin, delicate-looking, neck and his wrists and ankles and feet were small, but his pale hands were almost preternaturally large with an extravagant span.

His van, a small, pale grey, plain van, was parked in front of the house in Lord Arthur Road. You might call it Kentish Town or Tufnell Park or Lower Holloway. There were some curious houses, mini-Gothic with step gables, fat Victorian red brick, great grey barns with too many bays for grace or comfort, and small, narrow, flat-fronted places, very old, and covered in a skin of pale green peeling plaster. Finn wasn't interested in architecture, he could have lived just as easily in a cave or a hut as in his room. He unlocked the van and got in and drove up past Tufnell Park Station, up Dartmouth Park Hill towards the southernmost part of Hampstead Heath.

It was nine-fifteen. He drove under the bridge at Gospel Oak Station, up into Savernake Road which skirted Parliament Hill Fields, and on the corner of Modena Road he parked the van. From there he could keep the house that Kaiafas owned under observation. He sat at the wheel, watching the three-storey house of plum-coloured brick.

The Frazers were the first to go out. They left together, arm in arm. Next came Mrs Ionides, five minutes afterwards. Finn didn't care about them, they didn't count. He wanted to be sure of Anne Blake who quite often took a day off and had told Finn she 'worked at home'.

However, she emerged from the front door at exactly nine-thirty and set off the way the others had for the station. As a trusted handyman, Finn was in possession of a key to the house in Modena Road and with this he let himself in. His entering as the agent or servant of the landlord was perfectly legitimate, though some of the things he intended to do there were not.

Kaiafas's sister had the ground floor flat and the Frazers the next one up. The Frazers had accepted two thousand pounds from Kaiafas and had agreed to move out at the end of the month. Mrs Ionides would do anything Kaiafas told her and now he had told her she must go back to nurse their aged father in Nicosia. With vacant possession, the house would sell for sixty, maybe seventy thousand pounds. Kaiafas had asked estate agents about that and he had watched prices rising and soaring as houses just like his had been sold. The one next door, identical to his, had fetched sixty in August. The house agent smiled and shook his head and said that had been vacant possession, though, hadn't it? Kaiafas had told Finn all about it, that was how he knew.

He let himself into Mrs Ionides's hall and thence into her living room where one of the window sash cords had broken a day or so ago. He fitted a new sash cord and then he went upstairs to see what could be done about the coping over the bay window that Mrs Frazer said let water in. This occupied him until lunchtime.

He had brought his own lunch with him in an earthenware pot. Not for him the black tea and hamburgers and chips and eggs and processed peas of the workmen's café. In the pot was fruit roughly cut up with bran and yoghurt. Finn ate a piece of dark brown bread and drank the contents of a half-pint can of pineapple juice. Pineapple was not only his favourite fruit but his favourite of all flavours.

After lunch he sat cross-legged on the carpet and began his daily session of meditation. Presently he felt himself levitate until he rose almost up to the ceiling from where he could look through the top of the Frazers' window at the bright green escarpment of Hampstead Heath rising against a cold, sallow, faintly ruffled, sky.

Meditation always refreshed him. He could feel a wonderful

sensation of energy streaming down his arms and crackling like electricity out of his fingertips. His aura was probably very strong and bright but he couldn't see auras like Lena and Mrs Gogarty could, so it was no good looking in the glass. He took his tool box and climbed the last remaining flight of stairs. Unlike the Frazers and Mrs Ionides, Anne Blake had given no permission for Kaiafas or his agent or servant to enter her flat that day, but Kaiafas made a point of retaining a key. Finn unlocked Anne Blake's front door, went in and closed it after him. The hall walls were papered in a William Morris design of kingcups and water hawthorn on a blue ground and the carpet was hyacinth blue Wilton. Anne Blake had been living there since before Kaiafas bought the house, ten or twelve years now, and she wouldn't leave even for a bigger bribe than Kaiafas was giving the Frazers. She had told Kaiafas she wouldn't leave for twenty thousand and he couldn't make her and the law was on her side. He could have the flat, she said, over her dead body.

Finn smiled faintly in the dimness of the hall.

He opened the cupboard between the bathroom door and the door of the living room and took out a pair of lightweight aluminium steps. They were so light that a child could have lifted them above his head on one hand. Finn took them into the bathroom.

The bathroom was small, no more than eight feet by six, and over one end of the bath, in the ceiling, was a trapdoor into the loft. But for this trapdoor, Finn would have had to choose some other method. He set up the steps and then he went into the bedroom. Here was the same blue carpet, the walls painted silver-grey. There was no central heating in the house in Modena Road and each tenant had his or her own collection of gas and electric heating appliances. Anne Blake had an electric wall heater in her kitchen, a gas fire in her living room, a portable electric fire in her bedroom and no heating at all in her bathroom. Finn plugged in the portable electric fire, switched it on, and when he saw the two parallel bar elements begin to glow, switched it off again and unplugged it.

He climbed the aluminium steps and pushed up the trapdoor, a torch in his left hand. The loft housed a water tank and a good deal of the sort of discarded equipment which has become unusable but which cannot quite be called rubbish. Finn had been up there before, once when a pipe had frozen and once to get out on to the roof itself, and he had a fair idea of what he would find. He was observant and he had a good memory. He trod carefully on the joists, shining his torch, searching among the corded bundles of the *National Geographic* magazine, the ranks of glass jars, aged Remington typewriter, rolls of carpet cut-offs, flat-iron and trivet, chipped willow pattern dinner plates, until he found what he was looking for. An electric ring.

There was no plug on its lead. It was dirty and the coiled element had some kind of black grease or oil on it. Finn brought it down the steps and set about attaching a 13-amp plug to it. When this was plugged in, however, nothing happened. Never mind. Mending something like that was child's play to him.

The time had come to check up on her. He didn't want her coming home because she was starting a cold or her boss had decided to take the afternoon off. She had been unwise enough to tell him where she worked that time he had been in to mend the pipe, just as she had also told him she always took a bath the minute she got in from work. Finn never forgot information of that sort. He looked up the number in the phone book and dialled it. When he had asked for her and been put through to some extension and asked to hold and at last had heard her voice, he replaced the receiver.

An old, long-disused gas pipe ran up the kitchen from behind the fridge into the loft. This Finn intended to utilize. He cut a section out of it about six inches from the floor. Then he returned to the loft, this time with a 100-watt light bulb on the end of a long lead. He soon found the other end of the gas pipe and proceeded to cut off its sealed end. While he worked he reflected on the cowardice of human beings, their fears, their reserve.

Finn had a sense of humour of a kind, though it was far from that perception of irony and incongruities which usually goes by the name, and he had been amused that Kaiafas, in all their dealings, had never directly told him what he wanted doing. It was left to Finn to understand.

'Feen,' Kaiafas had said, 'I am at my wits' end. I say to her, Madam, I give you five thousand pounds, five thousand, madam, to quit my house. Please, I say, I say please on my knees. What does she say? That it is a pity I ever come away from Cyprus.'

'Well,' said Finn. 'Well, well.' It was a frequent rejoinder with him.

A look of ineffable slyness and greed came into Kaiafas's face. Finn had already guessed what he was after. He had done jobs for Kaiafas and others before, the kind of thing a professional hit-man does in the course of his work, though nothing of this magnitude.

'So I think to myself,' said Kaiafas, 'I make no more offer to you, madam, I give you no five thousand pounds. I give it to my friend Feen instead.'

That had been all. Finn wasn't, in any case, the sort of person to invite confidences. He had merely nodded and said well, well, and Kaiafas had fetched him another pineapple juice, handing over the key to the top flat. And now the first instalment of his fee had come . . .

He had inserted a length of electric flex into the pipe from the loft end, its frayed tips protruding ever so little from the cut-out section behind the fridge but apparent only to a very acute observer. The other end of the flex reached as far as the trapdoor and with a further two yards to spare. Finn was more or less satisfied. Once he might have done the deed without all this paraphernalia of wires and gas pipe and trapdoor, without clumsy manual effort. He looked back wistfully to his early teens, his puberty, now a dozen years past, when his very presence in a house had been enough to begin a wild poltergeist activity. It was with a yearning nostalgia that he remembered it, as another man might recall a juvenile love – bricks flying through windows, pictures falling from the walls, a great stone out of the garden which no one could lift suddenly appearing in the middle of Queenie's living room carpet. The power had gone with the loss of his innocence, or perhaps with the hashish which a boy at school had got him on to. Finn never smoked now, not even tobacco, and he drank no alcohol. It wasn't worth it if you meant to become an adept, a man of power, a master.

He checked that in the electric point behind the fridge there was a spare socket. A certain amount of the black fluffy dirt which always seems to coat the inside of lofts had fallen into the bath. Finn cleaned it with the rags he carried with him until its rose-pink surface looked just as it had done when he arrived. He replaced the aluminium steps in the cupboard and put the electric ring into a plastic carrier bag. It had been a long day's work, for every minute of which Kaiafas was paying him handsomely.

The Frazers would return at any moment. That was of no importance provided Finn was out of Anne Blake's flat. He closed her front door behind him. By now it was dark but Finn put no lights on. One of the skills in which he was training himself was that of seeing more adequately in the dark.

The air was strangely clear for so mild an evening, the yellow and white lights sparkling, dimming a pale and lustreless moon. As Finn started the van he saw Mrs Ionides, dark, squat, dressed as always in black, cross the street and open the gate of the house he had just left. He drove down Dartmouth Park Hill, taking his place patiently in the traffic queueing at the lights by the tube.

The house where Finn lived was a merchant's mansion that had fallen on evil days almost from the first, and the first was a long time ago now. He climbed up through the house, up a wider staircase than the one in Modena Road. Music came from behind doors, and voices and cooking smells and the smell of cannabis smoked in a little white clay pipe. He passed the door of his own room and went on up. At the top he knocked once at the first door and passed, without waiting, into the room.

It was a room, not a flat, though a large one and it had been partitioned off into small sections, living room, bedroom, kitchen. Finn had put up two of the partitions himself. You entered by way of the kitchen which was a miracle of shelving and the stowing of things on top of other things, and of squeezing a quart into a pint pot. In the living room, nine feet by eight, where a thousand little knick-knacks of great worth and beauty to their owner were displayed upon surfaces and walls, where a gas fire burned, where a small green bird sat silent in a cage, was Lena, consulting the pendulum.

'Well,' said Finn, going up to her and taking her free hand. They never·kissed. She smiled at him, a sweet vague smile as if she couldn't quite see him or was seeing something beyond him. He sat down beside her.

Finn could do nothing with the pendulum but Lena had great ability with it, just as she had with the divining rod. This was very likely one of the consequences of what those people at the hospital called her schizophrenia. The pendulum was a glass bead suspended on a piece of cotton and when Lena put it above her right hand it revolved clockwise and when she put it above her left hand it revolved widdershins. She had long since asked it to give her signs for yes and no and she had noted these particular oscillations. The pendulum had just answered yes to some questions which hadn't been revealed to Finn, and Lena sighed.

She was old to be his mother, a thin, transparent creature like a dead leaf, or a shell that has been worn away by the action of the sea. Finn thought sometimes that he could see the light through her. Her eyes were like his but milder, and her hair which had been as fair as his, had reverted to its original whiteness. She dressed herself from the many second-hand clothes shops in which the district abounded, and derived as intense a pleasure from buying in them as a Hampstead woman might in South Molton Street. Mostly she was happy, though there were moments of terror. She believed herself to be a reincarnation of Madame Blavatsky, which the hospital had seized upon as a casebook delusion. Finn thought it was probably true.

'Did you buy anything today?' he said.

She hesitated. Her dawning smile was mischievous. It was as if she had a secret she could no longer keep to herself and she exclaimed with shining eyes, 'It's your birthday!'

Finn nodded.

'Did you think I'd forgotten? I *couldn't*.' She was suddenly shy and she clasped her hands over the pendulum, looking down at them. 'There's something for you in that bag.'

'Well, well,' said Finn.

In the bag was a leather coat, black, long, double-breasted, shabby, scuffed, and lined with rotting silk. Finn put it on.

'Well,' he said. 'Well!' It was like a storm trooper's coat. He fastened the belt. 'Must be the best thing you ever got,' he said.

She was ecstatic with pleasure. 'I'll mend the lining for you!'

'You've had a busy day,' he said. The coat was too big for the room. With every movement he made he was in danger of knocking over little glass vases, Toby jugs, china dogs, pebbles, shells and bunches of dried flowers in chutney jars. He took the coat off carefully, with reverence almost, to please Lena. The green bird began to sing, shrill and sweet, pretending it was a canary. 'What did you do this afternoon?'

'Mrs Urban came.'

'Well!'

'She came in her new car, a green one. The kind of green that has silver all mixed up in it.'

Finn nodded. He knew what she meant.

'She brought me those chocolates and she stayed for tea. She made the tea. Last time she came was before you put up the wall and made my bedroom.'

'Did she like it?'

'Oh, yes!' Her eyes were full of love, shining with it. 'She *loved* it. She said it was so compact.'

'Well, well,' said Finn, and then he said, 'Ask the pendulum something for me. Ask it if I'm going to have a good year.'

Lena held up the string. She addressed the pendulum in a whisper, like someone talking to a child in a dark room. The glass bead began to swing, then to revolve clockwise at high speed.

'Look!' Lena cried. 'Look at that! Look what a wonderful year you'll have. Your twenty-seventh, three times three times three. The pendulum never lies.'

2

On the broad gravelled frontage of the Urbans' house, were drawn up the Urbans' three cars, the black Rover, the metallic green Vauxhall and the white Triumph. In the drawing room sat the Urbans, drinking sherry, oloroso for Margaret, amontillado for Walter and Tio Pepe for Martin. There was something of the Three Bears about them, though Baby Bear, in the shape of twenty-eight-year-old Martin, was no longer a resident of Copley Avenue, Alexandra Park, and Goldilocks had yet to appear.

Invariably on Thursday evenings Martin was there for dinner. He went home with his father from the office just round the corner. They had the sherry, two glasses each, for they were creatures of habit, and had dinner and watched television while Mrs Urban did her patchwork. Since she had taken it up the year before as menopausal therapy, she seemed to be perpetually accompanied by clusters of small floral hexagons. Patchwork was beginning to take over the house in Copley Avenue, chiefly in the form of cushion covers and bedspreads. She stitched away calmly, or with suppressed energy, and her son found himself watching her while his father discoursed with animation on a favourite subject of his, Capital Transfer Tax.

Martin had a piece of news to impart. Though in possession of it for some days, he had postponed telling it and his feelings about it were now mixed. Natural elation was mingled with unease and caution. He even felt very slightly sick as one does before an examination or an important interview.

Margaret Urban held out her glass for a refill. She was a big, statuesque, heavy-browed woman who resembled Leighton's painting of Clytemnestra. When she had sipped her sherry, she snipped off a piece of thread and held up for the inspection of her husband and son a long strip of joined-together red and purple hexagons. This had the effect of temporarily silencing Walter Urban, and Martin, murmuring that that was a new colour combination, he hadn't seen anything like that before, prepared his opening words. He rehearsed them under his breath as his mother, with the artist's sigh of dissatisfaction, rolled up the patchwork, jumped rather heavily to her feet and made for the door, bent on attending to her casserole.

'Mother,' said Martin, 'wait here a minute. I've got something to tell you both.'

Now that the time had come, he brought it out baldly, perhaps clumsily. They looked at him in silence, a calm, slightly stunned silence into which gratification gradually crept. Mrs Urban took her hand from the door and came slowly back, her eyebrows rising and disappearing into her thick, blue-rinsed fringe.

Martin laughed awkwardly. 'I can't quite believe it myself yet.'

'I thought you were going to tell us you were getting married,' said his mother.

'Married? Me? Whatever made you think that?'

'Oh, I don't know, it's the sort of thing one does think of. We didn't even know you did the football pools, did we, Walter? Exactly how much did you say you'd won?'

'A hundred and four thousand, seven hundred and fifty-four pounds, forty-six pence.'

'A hundred and four thousand pounds! I mean, you can't have been doing the pools very long, you weren't doing them when you lived here.'

'I've been doing them for five weeks,' said Martin.

'And you've won a hundred and four thousand pounds! Well, a hundred and five really. Don't you think that's absolutely amazing, Walter?'

A slow smile was spreading itself across Walter Urban's

handsome, though somewhat labrador-like, face. He loved money; not so much the possession of it as the juggling with it, the consideration of how to make it multiply, how (with subtle and refined legality) to keep it from the coffers of the Inland Revenue, and he loved the pure beauty of it as an abstraction on paper rather than as notes in a wallet. The smile grew to beaming proportions.

'I think this calls for some sort of congratulation, Martin. Yes, many congratulations. What a dark horse you are! Even these days a hundred thousand is a large sum of money, a very *respectable* sum of money. We've still got that bottle of Piper-Heidsieck from our anniversary, Margaret. Shall we open it? Wins of this kind are free of tax, of course, but we shall have to think carefully about investing it so that you don't pay all your interest away to the Inland Revenue. Still, if a couple of accountants can't work it out, who can?'

'Go and get the champagne, Walter.'

'Whatever you do, don't think of paying off the mortgage on your flat. Remember that the tax relief on the interest on your mortgage repayments is a concession of HM Government, of which a single man in your position would be mad not to take advantage.'

'He won't keep that flat on, he'll buy himself a house.'

'He could become an underwriting member of Lloyd's.'

'There's no reason why he shouldn't buy a country cottage *and* keep the flat.'

'He could buy a house and have the maximum twenty-five thousand mortgage . . .'

'Do go and get the champagne, Walter. What *are* you going to do with it, dear? Have you made any plans?'

Martin had. They weren't the kind of plans he considered it would be politic to divulge at the moment, so he said nothing about them. The champagne was brought in. Eventually they sat down to the casserole, the inevitably overdone potatoes and a Black Forest cake. Martin offered his parents ten thousand pounds which they graciously, but immediately, refused.

'We wouldn't dream of taking your money,' said his father. 'Believe me, if you're lucky enough these days to get your hands on a tax-free capital sum you hang on to it like grim death.'

'You don't fancy a world cruise or anything?'

'Oh, no, thank you, dear, there really isn't anything we want. I suppose you'd really rather we didn't tell anyone about it, wouldn't you?'

'I wasn't thinking of telling anyone but you.' Martin observed his mother's look of immense gratification, and this, as much as anything, prevented him from adding that there was one other person he felt obliged to tell. Instead he said, 'I'd rather keep it a secret.'

'Of course you would,' said Walter. 'Mum's the word. You don't want begging letters. The great thing will be to live as if nothing whatsoever out of the way had happened.'

Martin made no reply to this. His parents continued to treat him as if he had earned the hundred and four thousand pounds by the expending of tremendous effort or by natural genius, instead of the merest chance. He wished they had felt able to accept a present of some of it. It would somewhat have eased his conscience and helped him over the guilt he always felt on Thursday nights when he had to say good-bye to his mother and go home. She was still, after nine months, inclined to ask plaintively if by now rhetorically, why he had seen fit to move out of Copley Avenue and go far away to a flat on Highgate Hill.

Into this flat, 7 Cromwell Court, Cholmeley Lane, he now let himself with the feeling of deep satisfaction and contentment he always had when he entered it. There was a pleasant smell, a mixture, light and clean, of new textiles, furniture polish and herbal bath essence. He kept all the interior doors open – the rooms were impeccably neat – so that when you walked through the front door the impression was rather as of entering the centrefold of a colour supplement or *House and Garden*. Or so he secretly hoped, for he kept such thoughts about his flat to himself, and when showing it to a newcomer merely led him through the living room to exhibit from the picture window the view of London lying in a great well below. If the visitor chose to comment on the caramel Wilton, the coffee table of glass set in a brass and steel frame, the Swedish crystal or the framed prints of paintings from the Yugoslav naïve school, he would look modestly pleased but that was all. He felt too deeply about his home publicly to enthuse, and along with his gratitude to goodness knows whom, a certain fear about tempting Providence. There were times when he dreamed of its all being snatched away from him and of his being permanently back in Copley Avenue.

He switched on the two table lamps which had white shades and bases made from blue and white ginger jars. The armchairs were of rattan with padded seats and the sofa, or French bed as the furniture shop man had called it, was really only a divan with two bolsters at the back and two at the sides. Now he had won that large sum of money he would be able to replace these with a proper suite, perhaps one in golden-brown hide.

From the coffee table, between the ashtray with the Greek key design round its rim and the crystal egg etched with the goat for Capricorn – his birth sign – he picked up and studied the list he had made on the previous evening. On it were four names: Suma Bhavnani, Miss Watson, Mr Deepdene, Mr Cochrane's sister-in-law. Martin inserted a question mark after this last, he wasn't sure of her eligibility for his purpose, and besides he must find out what her name was. Some doubt also attached to Mr Deepdene. But about Suma Bhavnani he was quite sure. He would call on the Bhavnanis tomorrow, he would call on them after he had seen Tim Sage.

Martin went over to the window. The temples and towers of London hung black and glittering from the sky like the backdrop to some stage extravaganza. He pulled the cord that drew together the long dark green velvet curtains and shut it out. Tim Sage. For days, ever since, in fact, he had heard that he was to benefit from a fifth share in the Littlewoods' Pool first dividend, he had avoided thinking about Tim Sage, but he was going to have to think about him now because tomorrow Tim was coming into the office to talk about his income tax. It would be the first time he had seen Tim for a fortnight and before three tomorrow he had to decide what to do.

What to do? He had suppressed that remark to his mother about being obliged to tell one other person, but that was because he had been unwilling to hurt her, not because he was in doubt as to the right way to act. As soon as he allowed himself to think of Tim he knew without a doubt that Tim must be told Indeed, Tim ought to have been told already. Martin's gaze travelled speculatively over towards the gleaming dark green telephone. He ought to phone Tim now and tell him.

Martin's father always said that one should never make a phone call after ten-thirty at night or before nine in the morning – except, that is, in cases of emergency. This was hardly an emergency and it was ten to eleven. Besides, Martin felt strange about phoning Tim at home. He had never done so. From Tim's own veiled accounts, his home was a strange one, not to mention his domestic arrangements, and who, anyway, would answer the phone? Tim didn't live in a place like this where everything was open and above-board as well as immaculate in a more literal sense.

He turned his back on the phone and switched off the ginger. jar lamps. On second thoughts he helped himself to a small whisky from the glass, brass and steel cabinet. It would be silly to phone Tim now when he was going to see him tomorrow. As he drank his whisky he reflected that, of course, it was because he was going to see Tim tomorrow that he hadn't troubled to phone him before.

Martin was a well set-up, healthy man of medium height with rather too broad shoulders. In an overcoat he looked burly and older than his age. He had a big square forehead and a strong square chin but otherwise his features were shapely and refined, his nose being short and straight and his mouth the kind that is sometimes called chiselled. His dark brown curly hair was already beginning to recede in an M-shape from that broad and prominent forehead. He had greeny-blue eyes, a curious shade, very bright and clear, and even white teeth for the attainment of whose regularity Walter Urban had paid large sums to orthodontists in Martin's early teens.

Following in his father's footsteps, he always wore a suit to work. To wash the dishes he put on an apron. Martin wouldn't have worn an ordinary apron, that would have been ridiculous, but the joke kind made of oilcloth was trendy and amusing and perfectly suitable for men. His mother had given him this one which was orange and brown and represented a gigantic facsimile of a Lea and Perrins Worcester Sauce label. He changed the sheets on his bed, a regular Friday morning task, but he did no other housework because Mr Cochrane was due at half-past eight.

That his cleaner was a mister and not a missus was due to the Sex Discrimination Act. When Martin put his advertisement in the *North London Post* he had been obliged by law not to state that he required female help, and when Mr Cochrane turned up, similarly obliged not to reject him. He was lucky to get anyone at all, as his mother pointed out.

Mr Cochrane usually arrived just after the postman and before the newspaper delivery, but this morning the newsboy must have been early – it was unthinkable for Mr Cochrane to be late – and Martin had already glanced at the front pages of the *Post* and the *Daily Telegraph* before his help rang the doorbell. Always at this moment he wished that he was about to admit a large motherly charwoman, an old-fashioned biddable creature who, if she didn't exactly call him sir, yet might treat him with respect and show some consideration for his wishes. He had read about such people in books. However, it was pointless to indulge in day-dreaming with Mr Cochrane outside the door and likely to appear outside the door every Friday for the next ten years. He liked his jobs, of which he had several, in Cromwell Court.

Martin let him in.

Mr Cochrane was about five feet two and spare and wiry with a little scrap of dust-coloured hair fringing a bald pate. His face was exactly like a skull with lampshade material stretched tightly over it and ornamented with a pair of bifocals. He carried the cleaning gear that he didn't trust his employers to provide, about with him in a small valise.

'Morning, Martin.'

Martin said good morning. He no longer called Mr Cochrane anything. He had begun by calling him Mr Cochrane and had been called Martin in return, whereupon he asked his christian name which Mr Cochrane, flying into one of his sudden rages, had refused to give. It was about this time that a neighbour and fellow-employer told him of his own experience. He had suggested that Mr Cochrane call him by his surname and style, to which he had received the reply that it was a disgrace in this day and age to expect an elderly man, a man nearly old enough to be his grandfather, to call him Mr, it was sheer fascism, as if he, Mr Cochrane, hadn't done enough kow-towing all his miserable downtrodden life. He had been, apparently, a manservant to some more or less aristocratic person in Belgravia. A butler, said one of Martin's neighbours who also employed him, but this Martin didn't believe, for to him butlers were less real a bygone race than dodos.

As a cleaner, he was wonderful. That was why Martin, and presumably the others, kept him on in spite of the familiarity of address and the rages. He cleaned and polished and scrubbed and did ironing all at high speed. Martin watched him open his suitcase and take out of it the khaki canvas coat – like an ironmonger's – he wore for work, the silver-cleaning cloths and the aerosol can of spray polish.

'How's your sister-in-law?' said Martin.

Mr Cochrane, wearing red rubber gloves, had been taking the top of the stove apart. 'She'll never be better till she gets another place, Martin. The blacks were bad enough and now they've got the pneumatic drills.' He was a ferocious racist. 'She'll never be better stuck up there, Martin, so you may as well save yourself the trouble of enquiring. Three hours' pneumatic drills in the mornings she gets and three hours in the afternoons. The men themselves can't keep it up more than three hours and that tells you something. But it's no use moaning, is it, Martin? I say that to her, I say to her, what's the good of moaning at me? I can't do nothing, I'm only a servant.'

'What's her name?'

'Whose name?' said Mr Cochrane, wheeling round from the sink in the sudden galvanic way he had. 'You're always wanting to know folks' names. My sister-in-law's name? What d'you want to know that for? It's Mrs Cochrane of course, naturally it is, what else would it be?'

Martin forebore to ask the address. He thought that, from Mr Cochrane's persistent descriptions of the North Kensington block of flats and its geographical location, he could discover it for himself. If he still wanted to. Ten minutes in his cleaner's company only made him feel there must be many far more deserving candidates for his bounty than the Cochrane family – Suma Bhavnani, Miss Watson, Mr Deepdene. He pocketed the list lest Mr Cochrane should find it and pore over it paranoidly.

As usual he left for work at ten past nine, taking the route by way of the Archway and Hornsey Lane. Sometimes, for the sake of variety, he drove up to Highgate Village and down Southwood Lane across the Archway Road into Wood Lane. And once or twice, on beautiful summer mornings, he had walked to work as he had done on the day he met Tim in the wood.

The offices of Urban, Wedmore, Mackenzie and Company, Chartered Accountants, were in Park Road, in the block between Etheldene Avenue and Cranley Gardens. Walter Urban was the expert on matters relevant to the Inland Revenue, Clive Wedmore the investment specialist, while Gordon Tytherton had all the complexities of the Value Added Tax at his fingers' ends. Martin didn't specialize, he called himself the general dog's-body and his room was the smallest.

He knew he would keep at this job for the rest of his life, yet his heart wasn't in it. Although he had tried, he had never been able to sum up that enthusiasm for manipulating cash in the abstract which his father had, or even to understand the fascination which the stock market exerted over Clive Wedmore. Perhaps he should have chosen some other profession, though the leanings and longings he had had while still at school had been hopelessly impractical – novelist, explorer, film cameraman. They were not to be seriously considered. Accountancy had chosen him from the first, not he it. Sometimes he thought he had passively let himself be chosen because he couldn't bear to disappoint his father.

And the safety of it, the security, the respectability, satisfied him. He wouldn't have cared for a job or a life style such as Tim's. He was proud of the years of study which lay behind him, of the knowledge acquired, and always determined not to let a lack of enthusiasm lead to omissions or oversights. And he liked the room he had here which looked out across the tree tops to Alexandra Park, the park and the trees which he had known as a child.

Martin had no clients to see that morning and no phone calls to make or receive. He spent nearly three hours unravelling the zany and haphazard accounts of a builder who had been in business for fifteen years without paying a penny of income tax. Walter looked in to beam on him. The news of the pools win was making him behave towards his son much the way he had done when Martin got his A-levels and then his degree. After he had gone, Martin asked Caroline, who was their receptionist and whom Gordon and he shared as secretary, to bring in Mr Sage's file.

He opened it without really looking at the statements and notices of coding and Tim's own accounts which lay inside. In just over two hours' time Tim would be sitting there opposite him. And he hadn't made up his mind what to do. That firm decision of last night had been – well, not reversed, but certainly weakened by the sight of the *North London Post*. He had to decide, and within the next couple of hours.

Martin usually had lunch in one of the local pubs or, once a week, at a Greek place in Muswell Hill with Gordon Tytherton. Today, however, he drove alone up to the Woodman. It seemed the right and appropriate place in which to be for the solving of this particular problem.

It was far too cold, of course, and far too late in the year to take his sandwiches and lager out into the Woodman's garden. There, in summer, one was made very aware, in spite of the thunderous proximity of the trunk road roaring northwards, of the two woods that nestled behind these divergent streets. To the north was Highgate Wood, to the east Queen's Wood where, walking under the pale green beech leaves, he and Tim had encountered each other on a May morning. Now, in November, those groves appeared merely as throngs of innumerable grey boughs, dense, chill and uninviting.

But Tim . . . Was he going to tell Tim or was he not? Didn't he have a duty to tell him, a moral obligation? For without Tim he certainly wouldn't have won the hundred and four thousand pounds, he wouldn't have done the pools at all.

3

Martin had first known Tim Sage at the London School of Economics. They had been friendly acquaintances, no more, and Tim had left after a year. Martin hadn't seen him again until that morning in Queen's Wood, eight years later.

It was the kind of morning, misty and blue and gold and promising heat to come, when the northern reaches of London look as if Turner has painted them. It was the kind of morning when one leaves the car at home. Martin had walked over Jackson's Lane and into Shepherd's Hill, entering the wood by the path from Priory Gardens. The wood was full of squirrels scampering, its green silence pierced occasionally by the cry of a jay. Underfoot were generations of brown beech leaves and above him the new ones, freshly unfolded, like pieces of crumpled green silk. It had been a strange experience, even rather dramatic, walking along the path and seeing Tim appear in the distance, over the brow of the hill, the idea that it might be Tim gradually deepening to certainty. When they were fifty yards apart Tim had run up to him, stopping sharply like a reined-in horse.

'It has to be Dr Livingstone!'

Why not? Journalist meets explorer in a wood . . .

It was odd the amount of emotion there seemed to be generated in that moment and the intensity of pleasure each felt. They might have been brothers, long separated. Was it because the meeting took place on a summer's morning and under the greenwood tree? Was it the unlikelihood of the wood as a meeting place? Martin had never quite been able to understand why this chance encounter had brought him a sensation of instant happiness and hope, and why there had come with it a prevision of lifelong friendship. It was almost as if what he and Tim had experienced for each other, spontaneously and simultaneously, had been love.

But with the utterance of that word to himself Martin had felt both excited and very frightened. Before parting from him, Tim had briefly put an arm round his shoulder, lightly clapping and then gripping his shoulder, the sort of thing a man may do to another man in comradely fashion but which no man had ever done to him before. It left him feeling confused and shaken and two days later, when Tim phoned, it took him a few seconds to find his normal voice.

Tim had only wanted to know if he could consult him as an accountant. He was worried about the tax he had to pay on his freelance earnings. Martin agreed at once, he couldn't help himself, though he had mental reservations.

It was a maxim of Walter Urban's that one man cannot tell if another is attractive. He can only judge in respect of the opposite sex. Martin thought about this and it troubled him. In his case now it wasn't true, and what kind of a man did that make him?

Tim was very handsome, beautiful even, except that that wasn't a word one could use about a man. He had an actor's beauty, dashing, rather flamboyant. One could imagine him as a duellist. His hair was black, short by current standards (though not so short as Martin's), and his eyes a vivid sea-blue. There was something Slavonic about his high cheekbones and strong jaw and lips that were full like a woman's. He was tall and very thin and his long thin hands were stained leather-coloured down the forefingers from nicotine. He had been smoking in the wood and he lit a Gauloise the moment he entered Martin's office.

Tim's affairs were in considerably less of a muddle than Martin was accustomed to with new clients. It impressed him that, as he studied the columns of figures, Tim was able to repeat them perfectly accurately out of his head. He had a photographic memory. Martin promised to arrange things so as to save him money and Tim had been very gratified.

Were they going to see each other again, though? Were they going to meet socially? Apparently, they were. Martin could no longer remember whether it was he who had phoned Tim or the other way about. But the upshot had been a pub lunch together, then a drink together one Friday evening, encounters at which Martin had been uneasy and nervous, though extraordinarily happy as well, with a curious tremulous euphoria.

After that Tim had become a fairly frequent visitor at the flat in Cromwell Court, but what Martin had dreaded during their first few meetings had never happened. Tim had never touched him again beyond shaking his hand, never tried to take him in his arms as had sometimes seemed so likely, so imminent, just before their partings. Yet Tim must be homosexual, for what other explanation could there be for his obvious fondness for him, Martin? What else could explain why he continued to find Tim so attractive? For he did find him attractive. He had wrenched this confession out of himself. Normal men probably did find certain homosexuals attractive if they were honest with themselves. Martin was sure he had read that somewhere, in a book about the psychology of sex probably. The fact was that he liked watching Tim, listening to the sound of his deep yet light voice, as one might like watching and listening to a woman.

It came to him at last that what he really wanted was to *fight* Tim, to engage with him, that is, in some kind of wrestling match. Of course it was quite absurd. He had never done any wrestling and he was sure Tim hadn't. But he thought a lot about it, more, he knew, than was good for him, and such a wrestling figured sometimes in his dreams. It was part of these fantasies that in real life he should actually provoke Tim to a fight, and that might not be so difficult for, in spite of his affection for Tim, he knew he wasn't really a nice person. Long before the wrestling fantasy began, he had seen in Tim signs of ruthlessness, egotism and cupidity.

Tim lived in Stroud Green. To this address Martin had

sent business letters but he had never phoned Tim on his private number and he had never been there. This wasn't for want of being asked. It was the way Tim had looked and the tone he had used when asking which had set Martin so determinedly against ever visiting those rooms or flat or half a house or whatever it was. Tim had said to come and see his 'ménage', smiling and raising his somewhat satanic eyebrows, and at once Martin had understood. Tim was living with a man. Martin had never actually been in company with two men living together in a sexual relationship but he could more or less imagine it and the fearful embarrassment he would feel in such a situation.

He had returned a polite refusal – he always had an excuse ready – and after a time Tim seemed to understand, for there were no more invitations. But had he really understood? Martin hoped Tim hadn't thought he wouldn't come because he disliked the idea of slumming down in Stroud Green.

Tim seemed impressed by the flat in Cromwell Court. At any rate, he listened and admired when Martin showed him some new item he had bought and he enjoyed sitting on Martin's balcony on summer evenings, drinking beer and admiring the view. Martin, like his father, often mixed business with relaxation, and it was on one of these evenings when Tim had expressed his envy of those who own their homes, that he suggested he too should buy a flat. He should do so as much for the tax relief on a mortgage as for security.

'With your income and the increasing income you're getting from these short stories, I'd say you can't afford not to.'

'My income, as you call it,' said Tim, lighting his twentieth cigarette of the evening, 'is the lowest rate the NUJ allows the *Post* to pay me. *You* know what my income is, my dear, and I haven't got a penny capital.' Martin almost shivered when Tim called him 'my dear'. 'The only way I'd ever get the money to put down on a house is if I won the pools.'

'You'll have to do them first,' said Martin.

The blue eyes that could sometimes flame were lazy and casual. 'Oh, I do them. I've been doing them for ten years.'

31

That had surprised Martin. He had supposed doing football pools to be an exclusively working class habit. He was even more surprised to find himself agreeing to do them too, just to have a go, what had he to lose?

'I wouldn't know how to start.'

'My dearest old Livingstone,' said Tim, who sometimes addressed him in this way, 'leave it to me. I'll work out a forecast for you. I'll send you a coupon and a copy and all you've got to do is copy the same one every week and send it off.'

Of course he had had no intention of copying it out and sending it off. But it had come and he had done so. Why? Perhaps it seemed unkind and ungrateful to Tim not to. Martin supposed he had been to a great deal of trouble to work out that curious pattern on the chequered coupon, a pattern which he found himself religiously copying out each successive week.

Five times he had filled in and sent off that coupon, and the fifth time he had won a hundred and four thousand pounds. He had won it on the permutation Tim had made for him. Tim, therefore, was something more than indirectly responsible for his having won it. Shouldn't he then have gone straight to the phone as soon as the news came to him, to tell Tim?

Martin drove back to Park Road by way of Wood Lane. The wood was a crouching grey mass on either side of the road, crusted underfoot with brown leaves. If he had taken the car that morning in May or if he had walked along Wood Vale instead of Shepherd's Hill or if he had been five minutes earlier or five minutes later, he would never have met Tim and therefore never have won that huge sum of money. In an hour's time he would once more be confronting Tim. Tim was coming at three.

The purpose of his visit was to bring his tax return for the previous financial year and the fees statements from the various magazines which had used his stories. It wouldn't have crossed Martin's mind to keep the news of his win from Tim if Tim hadn't been a journalist. Once tell Tim and the story of his acquisition of wealth would be all over the front page of next week's *North London Post*. Suppose he asked Tim not to use it? It was possible Tim might agree not to, but Martin didn't think it likely. Or, rather, he thought Tim would give a sort of half-hearted undertaking and then drop a hint to another reporter. And this story would be even better when he began on his philanthropy . . .

Martin thought deeply about any major action he took, and about a good many minor ones too. He meant to conduct his life on a set of good solid principles. To perform every action as if it might form the basis of a social law, this was his doctrine, though he couldn't of course always live up to it. Plainly, he ought to tell Tim. He owed Tim thanks, and no consideration that publicity would make life uncomfortable for him for a few weeks should be allowed to stop him. Suppose he received a few begging letters and phone calls? He could weather that. *He must tell Tim*. And perhaps also – a new idea so alarmed him that he was obliged to stop scrutinizing Mrs Barbara Baer's investments and lay the file down – *offer* him something. It might be incumbent on him to offer Tim some of the money.

Tim received the lowest possible salary the National Union of Journalists permitted his employers to pay him. He couldn't buy a house because he had no capital. Ten thousand pounds would furnish a deposit for Tim to put down on a house, and ten thousand, Martin thought, was the sum he ought to give him, a kind of ten per cent commission. He found the idea not at all pleasing. Tim wasn't a deserving case like Miss Watson or Mrs Cochrane. He was young and strong, he didn't *have* to stay working on that local rag. At the back of Martin's mind was the thought that if Tim wanted to get capital he shouldn't smoke so much. He had an idea too that Tim was a fritterer. It would be awful to give Tim ten thousand pounds and then find he hadn't used it to get a home for himself but had simply frittered it away.

Martin continued to present the two sides of this question to himself until three-fifteen. Tim was late. His inner discussion had led to nothing much, though the notion of telling Tim had come to seem rash almost to the point of immorality. At twenty past three, Caroline put her pale red Afro round the door.

'Mr Sage is here, Martin.'

He got up and came round the desk, thinking that if Tim asked, if he so much as mentioned the football pools, he would tell him. But otherwise, perhaps not.

Tim was never even remotely well dressed. Today he was wearing a pair of black cord jeans, a dirty roll-neck sweater that had presumably once been white, and a faded denim jacket with one of its buttons missing. Such clothes suited his piratical looks. He lit a Gauloise the moment he came into the room, before he spoke.

'Sorry I'm late. A court case that rather dragged on.'

'A story in it?' said Martin, using what he hoped was the right terminology.

Tim shrugged. His shoulders were very thin, and his hands and his narrow, flat teenager's loins. He looked hard like an athlete until he coughed his smoker's cough. The only soft fleshy thing about him was his full red mouth. He sat down on the arm of the chair and said, 'Humanity treads ever on a thin crust over terrific abysses.'

Martin nodded. He was struck by what Tim had said. That was exactly how he had felt that morning while recalling all the chances there had been against the meeting in the wood happening at all. 'Is that a quotation?'

'Arnold Bennett.'

'Humanity treads ever on a thin crust over terrific abysses . . .' Of course there weren't inevitably abysses, sometimes only shallow ditches, Martin thought. Novelists were very prone to exaggeration. 'Let's have a look at all this bumf then, shall we?' he said.

'I've had a demand for nearly five hundred pounds tax. That can't be right, can it?'

Martin got out Tim's file. He had a look at the demand. Tim wanted to know if he could get an allowance for the use of his car and if a library subscription he had taken out was tax-free. Martin said no to the car and yes to the subscription and asked Tim some questions and said he would lodge an appeal with the inspector against the five hundred demand. There wasn't really anything more to say, as far as business went. Tim was on his second cigarette.

'And how's life been treating you, love?' said Tim.

'All right,' said Martin carefully. It was coming now. He felt nervous, he couldn't imagine saying it, couldn't bear to think of Tim's initial disbelief, his dawning wonder, his gleeful congratulations. He said in a tone that sounded in his own head artificially bright, 'I had that carpet laid in the flat, the one I told you I thought I'd have.'

'Fantastic.'

Martin felt himself redden. But Tim's expression was quite serious, even interested and kind. 'Oh, well,' he said, 'I don't lead a very exciting life, you know.'

'Who does?' said Tim. He sat silent for a moment. It seemed to Martin that his silence was *expectant*. Then he stubbed out his cigarette and got up. Martin found that he had been holding his breath and he let it out in what sounded like a sigh. Tim looked at him. 'Well, I mustn't keep you. I've having a party tomorrow week, Saturday the twenty-fifth. Any chance you might be free?'

This caught Martin unprepared. 'A party?'

'Yes, *you* know,' said Tim, 'a social gathering or entertainment, a group of people gathered together in a private house for merry-making, eating and drinking et cetera. A feast. A celebration. In this case we shall be celebrating my thirtieth birthday, thirty misspent years, my Livingstone. Do come.'

'All right. I mean, of course I will, I'd like to.'

'The place is unsavoury but the food won't be. About seven?'

Martin felt a lightness and a relief after Tim had gone. He hadn't asked. He hadn't so much as mentioned football or gambling, let alone the pools, and he had hardly mentioned money. Probably he had forgotten ever having introduced

Martin to the pools. How absurd I've been, thought Martin, telling myself he would be bound to ask and I would be bound to reward him. As if I could give money to Tim, as if I could ever offer it. All the time Tim had been there he had felt as if he were walking on that fragile crust over that chasm and yet he hadn't really, the ice had been inches thick and perfectly safe to skate on.

Caroline came in with a request from Clive Wedmore for the Save as You Earn literature he had lent Martin the day before.

'Mr Sage is very attractive, isn't he?' said Caroline. 'He reminds me of Nureyev, only younger.'

He wouldn't be much good to you, my dear, were the words that sprang immediately into Martin's head. The vulgarity of this thought was enough to make him blush for the second time that afternoon. 'Be a good girl and take that ashtray away, would you?'

'It smells like being in France.'

She bore the ashtray away, sniffing it appreciatively as if it had been a rose. Martin wrestled with the builder's tax for another hour or so and then he set off down Priory Road to the tobacconist and newsagent's kept by the Bhavnanis. He felt rather excited. He tried to put himself in Mrs Bhavnani's shoes, imagining how she was going to feel in five minutes' time when she understood that someone cared, that someone was going to give her son life and health and a future. Possibly she would cry. Martin indulged in a full-blown fantasy of what would happen when he made his offer, only breaking off when he remembered that one should do good by stealth and so that the right hand knoweth not what the left hand doeth.

It was an old-fashioned little shop. When he opened the door a bell rang and from the back regions appeared Mrs Bhavnani in a green sari with a bright blue knitted cardigan over it. Her face looked dark and wizened and full of shadows in contrast to these gay colours, and when Martin said he wanted to speak to her privately it grew grim. She turned the sign on the shop door to *Closed*. Martin stammered a little when he explained to her why he had come. She listened in silence.

'You are a doctor to operate on Suma?' she said.

'No, no, certainly not. It's just that – well, my mother told me about him and what I'm saying is that if it's a fact you can get this operation on his heart done in Sydney – well, I could help pay for things.'

'It will cost a lot.'

'Yes, I know that. I mean, *I* could pay. I *will* pay. I'd like you to let me pay for you and him to fly to Sydney and for your accommodation there and for the operation, that's what I mean.'

She looked at him, then lowered her eyes and stood passively before him. He knew she didn't understand. Was her husband in? No, not at present. Martin asked the name of their doctor.

'Dr Ghopal,' she said, 'at Crouch End.' The dark mournful eyes were lifted once more and Mrs Bhavnani said, as if he were some importunate intruder, as if that munificence had never been offered, 'You must go now, the shop is closed, I am sorry.'

Martin couldn't help laughing to himself, and at himself, once he was out in the street. So much for the philanthropist's reward. Of course it would have been far more sensible and businesslike to have got Dr Ghopal's name in the first place and to have written to him rather than make that romantic direct approach. He would write to him tonight. He would also, he thought as he began to drive home, make the preliminary manoeuvres in his project for using half the money. Suma Bhavnani was merely a sideline. The really serious business was his scheme for giving away fifty thousand pounds.

He could concentrate on that, now that Tim Sage was off his conscience.

4

Dear Miss Watson,

   I don't know if you will remember me. We met last Christmas at the house of my aunt, Mrs Bennett. I have since then been told that you have a housing problem and that when your employer goes to live abroad next year, you expect to be without a home. The purpose of this letter is to ask if I can help you. I would be prepared to advance you any reasonable sum for the purchase of a small house or flat, preferably not in London or the Home Counties. You could, if you would rather, regard this sum as a long-term loan, the property eventually to revert to me by will. I should then be able to look on this money in the light of an investment. However, please believe that my interest is solely in helping you solve this problem and I hope that you will allow me to be of assistance.
   Your sincerely,
      Martin W. Urban.

Dear Mr Deepdene,

   You will not have heard of me, but I am a friend of the Tremletts who, I believe, are friends of yours. Norman Tremlett has explained to me that the local authority which is your landlord intends to pull down the block of flats in which you are at present living and to re-house you in a flat which will be of inadequate size to accommodate your furniture, books, etc. The purpose of this letter is to ask if I can be of any help to you. I would be prepared to advance you any reasonable sum for the purchase of a small house or flat preferably not in London or the Home Counties. If you would care to get in touch with me as soon as possible we might meet and discuss this, whether you feel you can accept the money

as a gift or would prefer to think of it as a lifetime loan, whether
you feel able to consider living outside London, and so on.
Yours sincerely,
      Martin W. Urban.

Dear Mrs Cochrane,
      You may have heard of me through your brother-in-law. He
has told me that you are suffering considerable hardship owing to
your housing conditions and are anxious to move. The purpose of
this letter . . .

Martin had found these letters very difficult to write. He
abandoned temporarily the one to Mrs Cochrane because he
still hadn't found out her address. Dr Ghopal must have had
his letter by now, though he hadn't yet replied to it. It was
pleasant to think of the incredulous delight of those two
elderly people when the post came on Monday morning. They
would understand without resentment, wouldn't they, what he
meant by asking them to choose homes away from London? If
he was to benefit four or five people he couldn't rise to London
property prices. He posted the letters on his way to have his
usual Saturday lunchtime drink with Norman Tremlett in the
Flask.

Dr Ghopal phoned him at the office on Monday morning. He
would be seeing Mrs Bhavnani that day and then he hoped to
be in touch with the great heart surgeon in Australia. The
accented voice that always sounds Welsh to English ears cracked
a little as Dr Ghopal said how moved he had been by Mr
Urban's more than generous offer. Martin couldn't help
feeling gratified. His mother had said Suma was reputedly good
at his school work. Suppose, as a result of his, Martin's, timely
intervention, the boy should grow up himself to be a famous
surgeon or a musician of genius or a second Tagore?

Gordon Tytherton came in in the middle of this daydream to
say that he and his wife had a spare dress circle seat for 'Evita'
on Saturday night and would Martin like it and to come with
them? Martin accepted with alacrity. He passed the rest of the
day on the crest of a wave and it was some time before it

occurred to him that perhaps he ought to have asked for Dr Ghopal's discretion in the matter of the source of the money. Still, you could hardly imagine a doctor, a general practitioner, telling the press a thing like that. He thought very little more about it until Thursday when, as he came in from lunch, Caroline told him Mr Sage had phoned and would call back.

Had Tim found out, maybe from the Bhavnanis? Not that Martin had said anything about the source of his wealth to Dr Ghopal, but Tim was no fool. Tim would put two and two together. If Tim wanted a story for the *Post* tomorrow this would be just about his deadline, Martin calculated. He pictured the headlines in thirty-six point across the front page . . .

'If he does call back, tell him I'm not available, will you?'

'What, even though you're really here?'

'I'll be too busy to talk to him this afternoon.'

Caroline shrugged and pouted her shiny, blackberry-painted mouth. 'OK, if that's the way you want it. He's got a lovely voice on the phone, just like Alastair Burnet.'

Whether Tim had phoned again Martin didn't bother to enquire. It would now, in any case, be too late for this week's *Post*. He went alone to the house in Copley Avenue, his father having an engagement with a client in Hampstead, and on an impulse told his mother about his fifty thousand pound charity and his offer to Suma Bhavnani. She listened, drinking oloroso, and Martin could see that she was torn between admiration for his magnanimity and a natural maternal desire to see him spend the whole hundred and four thousand on a house for himself.

'I suppose I shouldn't ask why,' she said.

It would have been embarrassing to give his reasons, that life had been extraordinarily kind to him, that he felt he owed the world a living and a debt to the Fates. He didn't answer, he smiled and lifted his shoulders.

'What does Dad say?'

'I haven't told him – yet.'

They exchanged a glance of veiled complicity, a glance which implied that while they could they would keep this, to him highly disconcerting, information from Walter Urban. Martin refilled their sherry glasses. Later, after they had eaten, Mrs Urban said:

'You know, when you said what you were going to spend that money on I couldn't help thinking of Mrs Finn.'

'Who's Mrs Finn?'

'Oh, *Martin*. You remember Mrs Finn. She was my cleaner. It must have been – oh, while you were still at school, when you were a teenager. A very thin, fair woman, looked as if a puff of wind would blow her away. You must remember.'

'Vaguely.'

'I've made a point of keeping in touch with her. I go there regularly. She lives in such a dreadful place, it would break your heart. A room smaller than this one divided into *three*, and where the bathroom is, goodness knows. I was dying to spend a penny last time I was there but I didn't dare ask, there are such strange people in the house, it's a real warren. There's a son who's a bit backward, I think, and he's got a room downstairs. He's a plumber or a builder's labourer or something. Of course, Mrs Finn herself has had mental trouble. The misery and squalor they live in, you can hardly imagine it.'

There was a good deal more of this and Martin put on a show of listening attentively but he felt that, since Mrs Finn had a son whose responsibility she was, she hardly qualified for his bounty. Besides, he had two elderly women on his list already. Wouldn't it be better to complete it with perhaps a young couple and a baby?

It surprised him that he hadn't yet heard from either Miss Watson or Mr Deepdene. There was nothing from them in the morning. Mr Cochrane and the newspapers arrived simultaneously and Martin leafed quickly through the *North London Post,* looking for a story about Suma Bhavnani or, worse, about Suma Bhavnani in connection with himself.

'I said it was a nice morning, Martin,' said Mr Cochrane severely, putting on his ironmonger's coat. 'I said it was considerably warmer than it has been of late. I suppose you don't think it's worth answering the pleasantries of a mere servant.' His eyes bulged dangerously in their bony sockets.

'I'm sorry,' Martin said. The newspaper made no mention of the Bhavnanis or himself. Its front page was devoted to the murder of a girl in Kilburn, a story which carried Tim's by-line. 'It *is* a nice day. You're quite right, it's a lovely day.' He saw that he had just managed to deflect Mr Cochrane's incipient rage. It was like looking at some kind of meter on which, when oil or water is poured into the appropriate orifice, a needle oscillates, wavers and finally sinks away from danger level. 'How's your sister-in-law?'

'Much the same, Martin, much the same.' Mr Cochrane, applying silver polish to the tea and coffee spoons, seemed to brood with suspicion on this question. When Martin came back with his overcoat on he said sharply, 'I don't know what accounts for your interest, Martin. She's not a nubile young lady, you know, she's not one of your pin-up girls. Just a poor old woman who went out into service when she was fourteen. You wouldn't trouble to pass the time of day with the likes of her, Martin.'

If it hadn't been for the fact that he knew that Mr Cochrane, by the time he left at noon, would have made the flat more immaculate than even the house in Copley Avenue, would have ironed with exquisite finesse seven shirts, cleaned three picture windows and polished a whole canteen of cutlery, Martin would have booted him out on the spot. He only sighed and said he was off now.

'Good-bye, Martin,' said Mr Cochrane in the tones of a headmaster taking end-of-term farewell of a pupil whose conduct has been idle, slovenly, violent and rude.

It was rare for Mr Cochrane to leave him messages but if he did his notes were in the same disapproving and admonitory style as his conversation. Martin found one waiting for him when he came home just before six.

Dear Martin,

A Mr Sage phoned 2 mins after you left. I said I was only the cleaner and could not account for you going off so early like that.

W. Cochrane.

Martin screwed the note up and threw it into the emptied, and apparently actually polished, wastepaper bin. As it struck with a faint clang the side of this, in fact, metal container the phone began to ring. Martin answered it cautiously.

'How elusive you are,' said Tim's voice. 'You have quite an army of retainers to protect you from the press.'

'Not really,' said Martin rather nervously. 'And what can I – er, do for the press now it's found me?'

Tim didn't answer that directly. There was a silence in which Martin guessed he must be lighting a cigarette. He braced himself for the question and was very taken aback when Tim said, 'Just to remind you you're coming over here tomorrow night, love.'

Martin had forgotten all about the party. It had gone so far out of his head that he had accepted Gordon's invitation to the theatre. Suddenly he realised how much he hated, and had always hated, Tim calling him 'love'. It was much worse than 'my dear'. 'I'm sorry,' he said. 'I'm afraid I can't. I've arranged to do something else.'

'You might have let me know,' said Tim.

Martin said it again. 'I'm sorry,' and then, rather defensively, 'I didn't think it was necessary for that sort of party.'

If it were possible to hear someone's eyebrows go up, Martin felt he would have heard Tim's then. 'But what sort of party, Martin?' the drawly, now censorious, voice said. 'This is going to be a dinner party. Surely you understood that when I said to come at seven? Just eight of us for dinner.' There was a long, and to Martin awful, pause. 'It was to be rather a special celebration.'

'I'm sure my not being there won't spoil the evening.'

'On the contrary,' said Tim, now very cold. 'We shall be desolate.'

The receiver went down. No one had ever hung up on Martin before. He felt unfairly persecuted. Of course he had always refused in the past to go to Tim's but this time, if it had been made plain to him from the first that this wasn't going to be a noisy drunken get-together in uncomfortable darkened rooms, he wouldn't have forgotten about it and he would have gone. If Tim was asking him to dinner, why hadn't he told him so when he had invited him last Friday? Martin felt a sudden, almost fierce, dislike of Tim. When he heard from the tax inspector he would write him a formal letter, not phone this time. He had had quite enough of Tim for the time being. Let a few weeks go by, then maybe at Christmas he'd give him a ring.

But that night he dreamed of Tim for the first time for many weeks. They were in the house in Stroud Green which Martin, in waking reality, had never visited. Tim had spoken of it as unsavoury and in the dream it was more than that, Dickensian in its grotesque squalor, a series of junk-crowded rat-holes that smelt of rot. He and Tim were arguing about something, he hardly knew what, and each was provoking the other to anger, he by a kind of contrived pomposity, Tim by being outrageously camp. At last Martin could stand it no longer and he lunged out at Tim, but Tim parried the blow and together, clutching each other, they fell on to a deep, red, dusty, velvet settee that filled half the room. There, though still locked together, elbows hooked round each other's necks, it was impossible to continue struggling, for the red velvet which had become damp and somehow soggy, exerted an effect of sucking and seemed to draw them into its depths. Or to draw Martin into its depths. Tim was no longer there, the red velvet was Tim's mouth, and Martin was being drawn down his throat in a long devouring kiss.

It was the kind of dream from which one awakens abruptly and to a kind of rueful embarrassment. Fortunately, it was half-past eight when Martin awoke as he could hardly have remained comfortably in bed after visions of that sort. Once recovered, he saw the day floating invitingly before him, a rather-better-than-usual Saturday. It was warmish, a damp, misty November day with the sun like a little puddle of molten silver up there over the dome and cupolas of St Joseph's, jade green and gleaming in that sun's pale glow.

By lunchtime the mist had melted and the sun brightened

and Martin wondered whether to walk to the Flask for his drink with Norman Tremlett. It took him about a quarter of an hour to walk there, two or three minutes to drive – but walking there meant walking back too. He often thought of that in the weeks to come, that if he had decided to walk he wouldn't have been there when the doorbell rang and he would never have met Francesca. Why hadn't he? There had been no reason but laziness. A spurt of energy had prompted the walk that led to his meeting Tim, laziness had cancelled the walk which would have prevented the meeting with Francesca. He felt there must be some significance in this, though he was never able to say what it was.

He thought his caller must be Miss Watson. She had never called on him before, but he had never offered to buy her a home before, and he was convinced it must be she. He opened the door, a kindly and welcoming smile already on his lips.

Outside stood a boy holding a bunch of enormous bright yellow incurved chrysanthemums. The boy had thick smooth black eyebrows and big dark brown eyes and very pink cheeks. He was wearing jeans and a kind of tunic of dark blue cotton or canvas and a close-fitting woolly cap that covered all his hair.

He said, 'Mr Urban?' in a voice that sounded to Martin very like a woman's.

'Yes, that's right,' said Martin, 'but those can't be for me.'

'You are Mr Martin W. Urban and this is 12 Cromwell Court, Cholmeley Lane, Highgate?'

'Yes, of course, but I still can't . . .'

'They certainly are for you, Mr Urban.' The woolly cap was suddenly snatched off to release a mass of long glossy wavy hair. The hair was dark brown and nearly two feet long and its owner was definitely a woman, a girl of perhaps twenty. She had a rather earnest voice and she spoke slowly. 'It's really warm today, isn't it? I don't know why I put this on. Look, you can see on the label they're for you.'

He forced himself to stop staring at her hair. 'Please come in, I didn't mean to keep you standing there.' She came in rather shyly, it seemed to him, hesitated between the open doorways, not knowing which to enter. 'In here,' he said. 'People don't send flowers to men unless they're ill, do they?'

She laughed. In here, where the big window made it very light, he was a little taken aback to see how pretty she was. She was tallish and very slim and delicately made and with a beautiful high colour in her face, a rose-crimson that deepened with her laughter. How awful if he had betrayed to her that at first he had taken her for a boy! It was her slimness, those strongly marked eyebrows, her earnest look, the boyishness, in fact, about her which only made her more attractive as a woman. He was suddenly aware of the strong, aggressive, bitter scent of the chrysanthemums.

'Is there a card with them?' He took the flowers from her and found the card, wired on to the bunch of coarse damp stems. The message on it was printed, the signature an indecipherable scrawl. '"Thanks for everything,"' he read aloud, '"I will never forget what you have done".'

'The name is just a squiggle. I expect whoever it is came into the shop and wrote that themselves.' She looked distressed. 'Could it be Ramsey or Bawsey? No? I could try and check if you like.'

He was standing by the window and he could see the van she had come in parked on the drive-in to the flats. It was a dark blue van lettered on its side in pink: Floreal, 416 Archway Road, N6.

'Is that your shop on the corner of the Muswell Hill Road? I pass it every day on my way to and from work.'

'On weekdays we don't close till six. You could call in on Monday.'

'Or I could phone,' said Martin. It would be difficult to park the car, one of the worst places he could think of. Was it his imagination that the girl looked slightly hurt? You're twenty-eight, he told himself, and you're fussing like some old pensioner about where you're going to park a car two days hence. He could put it in Hillside Gardens, couldn't he? He could walk a hundred yards. 'I'll come in about half-past five on Monday,' he said.

From the window he watched her drive away. The mist had gone and the puddle of sun and the sky had become leaden. It was twenty-five to one. Martin put on his jacket and went off to the Flask to meet Norman Tremlett. When he got back the first thing he had to do was put those flowers in water. He didn't know anyone called Ramsey or Bawsey or anything like that, he didn't think he knew anyone who would send him flowers.

There were far too many chrysanthemums for one vase, there were too many for two. He had to use a water jug as well as the Swedish crystal vase and the Copenhagen china jar with the spray of brown catkins on a blue ground. Fleetingly, he thought of not putting them into water at all but of taking them with him as a gift for Alice Tytherton. And have Alice think he had chosen them? It seemed awful to say so but they were very ugly flowers. Martin had always believed that flowers were beautiful, all flowers as by definition, and his feeling about these slightly shocked him. But it was no use pretending. They were very ugly, hideous, more like vegetables than flowers really, like a variety of artichoke. You could imagine them cooked and served up with butter sauce.

He began putting them into water and in doing so looked again at the card. Not Ramsey – but, yes, surely, Bhavnani! What more likely than that Mrs Bhavnani should send him flowers as a token of her gratitude. As an Indian she wouldn't know it wasn't the custom in England to send flowers to men, and she might see flowers with different eyes too. The eye of an oriental might not see these great spherical blooms as monstrous and coarse. But if she were the sender, it was an oddly colloquial message she had sent: 'Thanks for everything. I will never forget what you have done.' And why would she come all the way to the Archway Road when there was a flower shop in the same block as her own in Hornsey? It was just as likely that Miss Watson who lived in Highgate, in Hurst Avenue, was the mysterious donor.

His living room was transformed, and somehow made absurd, by an embarrassment of chrysanthemums, chrome yellow, incurved, smelling like bitter aloes. All the time he was arranging them Martin had been searching his memory for what incident in the past that scent brought back to him. Suddenly he knew. A dozen years ago and chrysanthemums arriving for his mother from some friend or recent guest. Those chrysanthemums had been fragile-looking, pale pink with frondy petals, but the smell of them had been the same as these. And what Martin remembered was going into the drawing room where a pale frail woman called Mrs Finn was crying bitterly because she had dropped and smashed a cut-glass vase. The pink flowers lay about in little pools of water and Mrs Finn wept as if it were her heart and not a vase which had broken.

The extraordinary things one remembers, thought Martin, and evoked by so little. He could still see Mrs Finn as she had been that afternoon, weeping over the broken glass or perhaps over her own cut finger from which the blood fell in large dark red drops.

5

His window gave on to the back of a house in Somerset Grove. There were strips of untended garden between and tumbledown sheds and even a greenhouse in which all the glass was broken. But unless he looked down all he could see was the yellow brick back of the other house, its rusty fire-escape and its bay windows. In one of these bays a woman stood ironing.

Finn stared at her, exercising his powers on her, trying to bend her to his will. He bore her no malice, he didn't know her, but he willed her just slightly to burn her finger on the iron. Pressing his body against the glass, he concentrated on her, piercing her with his eyes and his thought. He wanted her to feel it in her head, to stagger, bemused, and graze her trembling hand with the burning triangle.

The iron continued to move in steady, sweeping strokes. Once she glanced up but she didn't see him. All magicians long to discover the secret of making themselves invisible, and Finn wondered if he had found it. He stared on, forcing his eyes not to blink, breathing very deeply and very slowly. The woman had set the iron up on end now and was folding a rectangle of something white. He could have sworn she brushed the tip of the iron with her hand, but she didn't wince. And now, suddenly, she was staring back at him with indignation, looking at him full in the face. If he had been invisible he was no longer. He saw her move the ironing board away from the window to another part of the room and he turned back to what he had been doing before, screwing the cover back on the hotplate.

His room was on the second floor. It contained a single mattress, a three-legged stool and a bookcase. There had once been more furniture but gradually, as he mastered himself and his energies increased, he had disposed of it piece by piece. He hung his clothes from hooks on the wall. No curtains hung at the window and there was no carpet on the floor. Finn had painted the ceiling and the walls a pure, radiant white.

He had no means of cooking anything but he seldom ate anything cooked. On the floor stood a stack of cans of pineapple and pineapple juice and in the bookcase were the works of Aleister Crowley, *Meetings with Remarkable Men* and *Beelzebub's Tales to his Grandson* by Gurdjieff, Ouspensky's *A New Model of the Universe*, and *The Secret Doctrine* of Helena Blavatsky. Finn had picked them up in second-hand bookshops in the Archway Road.

As he was coiling the flex round the hotplate and putting it into a carrier bag, Finn heard Lena pass his door and go on up the stairs. She had been out all the morning at a shop in Junction Road called Second Chance, spending two ten-pound notes Finn had given her from the initial Anne Blake payment. Her movements were uneasy. He could tell by ear alone, by the sound of her feet on the stairs, her footsteps pattering across the landing, whether she was happy or afraid or whether there was a bad time coming. There hadn't been a bad time for nearly two years now. Finn looked on her strangeness quite differently from the way most people did, but the bad times were another matter, the bad times had been brought into being by himself.

He took off the white cotton robe he wore for studying or meditating or just being in his room and hung it on one of the hooks. Finn had no mirror in which to see his long body, hard and white and thin as a root. The clothes he put on, jeans, a collarless grandad shirt, the velvet waistcoat and the scarf with the coins on, had all been acquired by Lena, as had the pearl-handled cut-throat razor with which he now began to shave. He could see his face reflected in the window pane which, if he stood back a little, the opposing brick wall made into a passable looking glass. Nevertheless, he cut himself. Finn, with no pigment anywhere except in those water-grey pupils, sometimes thought it strange his blood should be as red as other people's.

Lena's tiny living room was draped all over with her purchases, a mauve silk dress with a fringe round the hem, a man's grey morning coat, a bunch of scarves, a pair of lace-up can-can girl's boots, and several little skirts and jumpers. The budgerigar, temporarily manumitted, surveyed all this array from its perch on an *art nouveau* lamp standard. In a day or two Lena would sell all these clothes to another shop, retaining perhaps one garment. She nearly always lost by these transactions but sometimes she made a tiny profit. When she saw Finn she recoiled from him, alarmed, inordinately distressed as always by even a pinhead drop of blood.

'You've been cut!' As if it had been done to him by someone else.

'Well, well,' said Finn, 'so I have. Let's cover it up, shall we?'

She gave him a lump of cotton wool that might have come out of a pill bottle or been the bedding of a ring. Finn stuck it on his chin. It smelt, like Lena's clothes, of camphor. She had brought in with her, he saw to his annoyance, a local paper, the *Post*, and he knew at once the cause of her uneasiness. Her eyes followed his.

'There's been a girl murdered in Kilburn.'

He opened his mouth to speak, guessing what was to come. She came up even closer to him, laid her finger on his lips, and said in a hesitant, fearful voice:

'Did you do it?'

'Come *on*,' said Finn. 'Of course I didn't.' The bird flew down and clung to the hem of the mauve dress, pecking at its fringe.

'I woke up in the night and I was so afraid. Your aura had been all dark yesterday, a dark reddish brown. I asked the pendulum and it said to go down and see if you were there, so I went down and listened outside your door. I listened for hours but you weren't there.'

'Give it here,' said Finn. He took the paper gently from her. 'She wasn't killed in the night, see? She wasn't killed yesterday. Look, you read it. She was killed last Wednesday week, the fifteenth.'

Lena nodded, clutching on to his arm with both hands as a person in danger of drowning clutches on to a spar. The bird pecked little mauve beads off the dress and scattered them on the floor.

'You know where we were that Wednesday, don't you? The day before my birthday it was. All afternoon and all evening we were in here with Mrs Gogarty, doing planchette. You and me and Mrs Gogarty, OK? Panic over?'

Ever since the Queenie business, which had also marked the onset of her trouble, Lena supposed every murder committed north of Regent's Park and south of Barnet to have been perpetrated by her son. Had supposed it, at any rate, until Finn proved it otherwise or someone else was convicted of the crime. From time to time there came upon her flashes of terror in which she feared his arrest for murders committed years ago in Harringay or Harlesden. It was for this reason, among others, that Finn intended to make his present enterprise appear as an accident. Had he known what he was doing in those far-off days, had he not been so young, he would have done the same by Queenie and thus saved poor Lena from an extra anguish.

'Panic over?' he said again.

She nodded, smiling happily. One day she might forget, he thought, when he took her with him to India and they lived in the light of the ancient wisdom. She had begun rummaging through the day's horde of treasures, the budgerigar perched on her shoulder. A cushion, falling out, was caught between an octagonal table and a wicker box. Few objects could fall uninterruptedly to the floor in Lena's flat. She surfaced, grasping something yellow and woollen.

'For you,' she said. 'It's your size and it's your favourite colour.' And she added, like any mother who fears her gift won't be appreciated as it should be, 'It wasn't cheap!'

Finn took off his waistcoat and pulled on the yellow sweater. It had a polo neck. He got up and looked at himself in Lena's oval mirror with the blue velvet frame. The sleeves were a bit short and under the left arm was a pale green darn but that only showed when he lifted his arm up.

'Well, well,' said Finn.

'It does suit you.'

'I'll wear it to go out in.'

He left her noting down her new stock in the book she kept for this purpose. Finn had once seen this book. When Lena couldn't describe a garment she drew it. He went down into his own room and collected his tool box and the hotplate in its carrier and his PVC jacket. It was just gone two. He went in the van but not all the way, leaving it parked in a turning off Gordonhouse Road at the Highgate end.

Finn had waited to do the deed until after the departure of the Frazers. They had moved out the previous Friday. Sofia Ionides always spent Monday evening baby-sitting for her brother and his wife in Hampstead Garden Suburb. Finn didn't mind being seen entering the house in Modena Road, but he would have preferred not to be seen leaving it. By then, however, it would be dark. What most pleased him was the turn for the worse that the weather had taken. From Saturday afternoon it had grown steadily colder, there had been frost this morning, and as he drove up Dartmouth Park Hill a thin snow had dashed against the windscreen. If the weather had stayed as warm as it had been on Saturday morning he might have had to postpone his arrangements.

Anne Blake's flat was clean and tidy and very cold. One day, Finn thought, when he had developed his theta rhythms, he might be able to generate his own bodily heat, but that day was not yet. It would be unwise to use any of Anne Blake's heating appliances, he must just endure it. He attached a 13-amp plug to the flex which protruded from the gas pipe behind the fridge and plugged it in to the point next to the fridge point. Then he put up the steps and climbed into the loft, carrying the hotplate. Up there it was even colder. Finn joined the flex on the hotplate to the flex, some five or six yards of it, that came out of the gas pipe. Down the steps again to test if it worked. It did.

Watching the coiled element on the electric hotplate begin to glow red, Finn checked over his plan for the perfect accident. She would come in at six, turn on the heaters, including the electric fire in her bedroom, maybe have a drink of some sort, then her bath. She might bring the electric fire into the bathroom or she might not, it mattered very little either way. Finn would be lying up in the loft on the joists between the trapdoor and the water tank. When he heard her in the bath he would lift up the trapdoor and drop the hotplate down into the water. Electrocution would take place instantaneously. The hotplate he would then dry and replace among the glass jars and the *National Geographic* magazines. Once more broken and unusable, what more suitable place for it? When all the arrangements of flex and plug had been dismantled, nothing remained but to plug Anne Blake's bedroom electric fire into the bathroom point, switch it on and toss it into the bath water. Accidental death, misadventure, the fire had very obviously (a complaisant coroner would say) slipped off the tiled shelf at the end of the bath.

Finn felt no compunction over what he was about to do. There was no death. He would simply be sending Anne Blake on into the next cycle of her being, and perhaps into a fleshly house of greater beauty. Not for her, this time, the human lot of growing old and feeble, but a quick passage into the void before giving her first cry as a new-born child. Strange to think that Queenie too was a child somewhere now, unless instead her unenlightened soul still wandered aimlessly out there in the dark spaces.

Clambering across the loft, he peered out through a gap between roof strut and tile to watch the fluttering snow. In the wind on the top of Parliament Hill grey trees waved their thin branches as if to ward off the cloudy blizzard. The sky was the hard shiny grey of new steel.

It was because he was at the extreme edge of the roof, lying down to look under the eaves, that he was able to hear nothing in the depths of the house below him. Soft-soled shoes treading the carpeted stairs made sounds too low to reach him. He heard nothing at all until there came the scrabbling of a key in the front door lock.

Finn might just have managed to pull the steps up in time and close the trapdoor but he wouldn't have been able to push the fridge back against the kitchen wall or remove his open toolbox from the middle of the kitchen floor. She had come home more than two hours early. He came across the loft and looked down through the aperture in the ceiling as Anne Blake opened the bathroom door and stood looking up, startled and annoyed. There were snowflakes on her bushy dark grey hair.

'What on earth are you doing up there, Mr Finn?'

'Lagging the pipes,' said Finn. 'We're in for a freeze-up.'

'I didn't know you had a key, it's the first I've heard of it.'

Finn didn't answer, he never went in for pointless explanations. What now? She would never have her bath with him up there, otherwise he might have proceeded as planned. He must try again tomorrow. Nevertheless, it wouldn't be quite safe to leave that mysterious lead proceeding from the gas pipe still plugged in. Finn descended. He wrenched off the plug, went back into the loft and disconnected the hotplate. It would be a good idea actually to lag those pipes, an excuse for being in the roof again tomorrow. He would go down and tell her he would return tomorrow with fibreglass wrap for the pipes.

Finn put the hotplate with the iron and trivet, packed up his tool box and came down the steps, pulling the trapdoor closed behind him. He was sitting on the side of the bath, about to close the lid of the box when, across the blue and yellow papered hall, through the open doorway to the bedroom, he saw Anne Blake crouched down, her back to him, as she struggled to pull open the lowest drawer of a tallboy. Lying on the top shelf of the box was the largest and heaviest of his hammers. How easy it would be now! In just such a manner had he struck Queenie down.

He shut the box, slipping the hammer into his right-hand pocket. Then the box was on the bathroom floor and Finn was moving swiftly across the blue carpet towards her.

6

She was on her feet, clutching to her the two or three garments
she had been groping for in the drawer, before Finn had so
much as entered the bedroom. He stood still on the threshold
and she seemed to find nothing untoward in his looks or his
behaviour. She said rather ungraciously:

'Have you finished whatever you were doing up there?'

Finn nodded, fixing her with his pale eyes. He knew she was
uneasy in his presence, but there was nothing new in that, most
people were. Quite alone in the house with him for the first
time, she was probably afraid of rape. Finn smiled inwardly.
He wasn't much interested in sex. It was more than a year
since he had had anything to do with a woman in that way, and
then it had been very sporadically.

He put the steps away and got into his jacket. It was still
only four-thirty, but twilight. Anne Blake had turned some
lights on and gone into the kitchen. The gas fire, just lighted,
burnt blue in the living room grate. Finn still had the hammer
in the pocket of his jeans. He went into the kitchen to tell Anne
Blake about coming back tomorrow with the fibreglass and
while she talked to him, asking him what right Kaiafas had
to a key to her flat and scolding him about knocking over
something when he moved her fridge, he closed his hand
round the hammer handle and thought, how easy, how easy . . .
And how easily too he would be found out and caught afterwards, not to mention Lena's terror.

She forgot to ask him to relinquish the key or perhaps she
thought he had better keep it since he was coming back the
next day. It was still snowing when he got down to the street,

but the snowflakes were now the big clotted kind that melt and disperse as soon as they touch a solid surface. Finn walked along Mansfield Road and under the railway bridge at Gospel Oak and got into the van.

Immediately, it seemed, he had closed the door, the blizzard began. The wipers on his windscreen weren't what they had been and Finn decided to stay put until the snow stopped. It flopped on to the roof and windows of the van and streamed as water down its sides.

After about twenty minutes the snow had almost ceased but there was a big build-up of rush-hour traffic headed for Highgate West Hill. Finn couldn't stay parked where he was and he couldn't turn round, so he started the van and drove back the way he had walked. It was dark now but the street lamps were all on, and as he passed the end of Modena Road he saw Anne Blake leaving the house, holding a pagoda-shaped umbrella in one hand and a plastic carrier in the other. She turned in the direction of Hampstead Heath.

Finn turned right at the next turning into Shirlock Road and came out into Savernake Road by the great porridge-coloured pile of All Hallows' Church. Anne Blake had just reached the corner of Modena Road and Savernake Road and was now crossing the road towards the footbridge. Finn parked the van among all the other parked cars and vans. The snow had changed to a thin sleety rain.

It was very dark, though not yet half-past five. Finn supposed that Anne Blake had gone to call on some friend who lived on the other side of the railway line in Nassington Road maybe or Parliament Hill. She wouldn't go shopping that way. Besides, the carrier had looked full. He debated whether to go back into the house in her absence. She would very likely be absent for a couple of hours.

He wondered if she had had her bath. There had been quite enough time for her to have had it, but would she go out into the cold immediately after having had it? She might intend to have it immediately she got in. It would only take him a few minutes, say ten, to reconnect those plugs. But if she had already had

57

her bath he might find himself stuck up there in the loft all night.

Perhaps a dozen people, coming singly or in pairs, had appeared from the approach to the footbridge while he sat there. Its only use really was to take one on to the Heath or into the streets to the east of South End Road. No one living here would use Hampstead Heath station when Gospel Oak was just as near. She hadn't gone to the station.

At last Finn got out of the van, crossed the road and let himself once more into the house in Modena Road. The rain had begun lashing down by the time he got there. He went upstairs without turning any lights on, and at the top, he entered Anne Blake's flat in darkness. A street lamp lit the living room and so, with a richer orange glow, did the gas fire which she had left on. She wouldn't have done that, Finn thought, if she had intended to be out for long.

He went into the bathroom and ran his hand along the inside of the bath. It was wet and so was one of the towels that hung on the chromium towel rail. There was no point in his remaining. He padded softly, although there was no one to hear him, across to the bedroom window. The rain was now coming down in the kind of deluge that no one would venture out in unless he had to. Finn had to. He opened one of the doors of Anne Blake's wardrobe. Inside, among her clothes, were two or three garments still sheathed in the thin polythene covers in which they had come back from the dry-cleaners. Finn selected one of these, slipped it off the hanger, and the long black evening dress it covered, and pulled it over his head, splitting its sides open a little way down for his arms to go through. It made a kind of protective tunic, impervious and transparent.

The rain began to let up a little as he came up to Savernake Road. There was no one about. He felt drawn by theHeath, by its wide green emptiness, and he walked up the steps and on to the footbridge. A single lamp, raised up high, illumined the bridge, but you couldn't see the railway line, the walls were built up too high for that. To prevent suicides, thought Finn.

He gazed across the smooth slope of Parliament Hill Fields to Highgate on the horizon, the emerald domes of St Joseph's gleaming colourless and pearly against a sky which the glow of London made velvety and reddish. The backs of the houses in Tanza Road were as if punctured all over with lights but the glittering screen of rain prevented much of that light from being shed on the path. It seemed to Finn that the whole area to the left of the footbridge and immediately above the railway embankment was extraordinarily dark. He could barely see where the turf ended and Nassington Road began.

He came down the steps on the Parliament Hill side of the bridge. A train rattled underneath as he passed. The rain was running in streams down his plastic covering, though now it was lightening again, setting in evidently for a night of torrents with short drizzly remissions. In the dark hollow where the path ran under the trees to link with the end of Nassington Road, Finn picked his way between the puddles. Now he could see why it was so dark. The lamp at the end of Nassington Road had gone out or never come on.

Finn liked the solitude and the silence. The train and its noise had long gone down the deep cutting to Gospel Oak. No one was venturing out into the rain. A strange tall figure in a shining glassy robe, Finn stood under the trees viewing the grey and rain-washed plain, feeling one with the elements, a man of power, a conqueror.

Someone was coming down Nassington Road, he could just hear the footfalls, though they were deadened by the wetness of the pavement. He stepped a little aside, behind the trunk of a tree. He could see her clearly now, passing under the last lighted lamp, the pagoda umbrella up, the carrier in her other hand empty or nearly so. She had waited to leave for home until the rain lifted a little. He could tell she was nervous because the lamp was out. She looked to the left past where he was standing and to the right, towards the bridge, and then she came on into the lake of darkness.

Finn no more intended to move forward and strike than he had intended to move forward and strike Queenie. It happened, that was all. It happened without his volition or his desire in the same way, perhaps, as the stone had moved and the pictures fallen. At one moment he was standing, watching with those night-seeing eyes of his, at the next the hammer was in his hand and he had fallen upon her. Queenie had made terrible sounds. Anne Blake made none but a throaty gasp, falling forward from the knees as he struck her again and again, now using the wide, flat side of the hammer.

In the dark he couldn't tell which of that dark fluid that spread everywhere was water and which blood. He pulled her away from the path and round the side of the nearest tree. There was no pulse, she was dead. Already she had passed into the unknown and was in possession of what was beyond. He almost envied her.

There was no Lena this time to come in and witness what he had done. He must keep this from Lena, wash himself clean of all the blood that so terrified her, deny her newspapers. Finn picked up Anne Blake's umbrella and furled it. He felt inside the carrier and found there a small suede handbag in which he found twenty-six pounds in notes, a cheque book and two credit cards. He took these and the money with him.

In the light on the bridge he could tell blood from water by running his fingers down his body and then holding up his hands. The lamplight robbed everything of colour, but the fluid was dark that ran from his hands. Someone was coming from the Parliament Hill side. Whoever it was had passed Anne Blake's body. Finn took refuge at the foot of the switchback slope that was designed for those who didn't want to or couldn't use stairs. Footsteps passed across the bridge and went on towards Savernake Road. The rain had returned now to all the force of its former intensity.

Finn stepped out into it and let it wash him clean.

He also washed the hammer in the rain. Once back in the van, he stripped off his plastic tunic and rolled it up into a ball. Underneath he was perfectly clean and fairly dry. He replaced his hammer in the tool box and fastened the lid. The gas fire would still be on in Anne Blake's flat, might very likely remain on all night, but it wouldn't burn the house down.

The problem was to get rid of the contents of the handbag, particularly the cheque book and the credit cards. Finn drove home. It was still only seven, the rain falling steadily as if, having at last found a satisfactory rhythm, it meant to stick to it. Because of the rain he put the van away in the garage he rented in Somerset Grove, an old coach house with bits of rotting harness still hanging on the walls.

With Lena was Mrs Gogarty, the friend who had predicted for Finn a violent death in old age. The two of them were intent upon the pendulum. A white and pink baby's shawl with a scalloped edge had been thrown over the birdcage. Mrs Gogarty was as fat as Lena was thin, with abundant hair dyed a stormy dark red.

'Well, well,' said Finn, 'you *are* cosy. Can I have a lend of a pair of scissors?'

Lena, looking in the mauve dress and yards of stole like the appropriate one of the Three Fates, handed him the Woolworth scissors with which she picked and snipped at her daily finds.

'He's a lovely boy, your boy,' said Mrs Gogarty, who made this remark every time the three of them met. 'The picture of devotion.'

Finn managed to palm his mother's reading glasses off the top of a chest of drawers where they nestled among some half-burnt candles and incense sticks and pieces of abalone shell. He went down to his own room where he cut up the notes and the cheque book and the credit cards into very small pieces. The tin from which he had eaten pineapple chunks at lunchtime was now quite dry inside. Finn put the pieces of paper and card into the empty tin and applied a match. It took several more matches to get it going and keep it going, but at last Anne Blake's twenty-six pounds and her Westminster Bank cheque book were reduced to a fine black ash. The American Express and Access cards were less destructible, but they too went black and emitted a strong chemical smell.

Re-entering his mother's room, Finn dropped the glasses and trod on them. This made Mrs Gogarty scream out and jump up and down, jerking her arms, which was what she did whenever anything the slightest bit untoward happened. Lena was too much occupied in calming her down to say anything about the glasses, she diverted her with the pendulum as one diverts a child with a rattle.

Finn promised to get the glasses repaired as soon as he could. He would go into the optician's first thing tomorrow, he said. In the meantime, had she noticed the rain coming in over her gas stove? Better put a bowl there, and the first moment he got he'd be out on that roof.

'Devotion itself,' gasped Mrs Gogarty.

The pendulum rotated, widdershins and swiftly.

7

The snow, which had been falling for most of the afternoon, had changed to rain when Martin drove across the Archway Road and began searching for a place to park. Southwood Lane was hopeless and so was the narrow congested curve of Hillside Gardens. He finally left the car in one of the roads up behind Highgate Police Station and walked back to the cross-roads, wondering if he might be too late to catch Floreal open, although it was only ten to six.

During the weekend he had asked himself several times why he should bother to call at the shop when he was sure it must have been the Bhavnani family who had sent those flowers. Anyway, did it matter particularly who had sent them? Of course, if he knew he could write a note of thanks or phone. Dr Ghopal had phoned the office during the afternoon to say that the great heart specialist was preparing to operate in the week immediately preceding Christmas. No further time should be wasted when a condition like Suma's was in question. Would Martin buy the air tickets himself and arrange an hotel for Mrs Bhavnani? Martin had agreed to do this, but he had felt unable to make enquiries about the flowers, especially as he was going to see the pretty dark-haired girl that evening.

He saw her when she was still on the other side of the road outside the post office. She was taking in boxes of cut flowers and poinsettias in pots from the pavement. He waited for the lights to change and then crossed the street. The shop, which was very small, had a red bulb in one of its hanging lights, and the orangey glow, the mass of fresh damp glistening foliage, the red velvet long-leaved poinsettias, gave to the place a festive air, Christmassy, almost exciting. It was dark and bleak outside. The shop was alight with reds and yellows and jungle greens, and the girl stood in the middle of it, smiling, her arms full of carnations.

'Oh, I was so sure you wouldn't come!'

She checked herself, seeming a little embarrassed. The colour in her cheeks had deepened. It was as if – he couldn't help feeling this – she had actually looked forward to his coming and had then resigned herself to – disappointment? She turned away and began putting the carnations in water. He said in a voice he recognised as typically his, a hearty voice he disliked:

'Did you happen to find out who was the kind person who sent my bouquet?'

It was a little while before she turned round. 'There, that's all done.' She wiped her hands on the brown and white checked apron she wore. 'No, I'm awfully afraid we couldn't. You see, the person who came in didn't give her name. She just wrote that card and paid for the flowers.'

'You wouldn't know if it was an old woman or a young one, I suppose, or if she was – well, white or Indian or what?'

'I'm afraid not. I didn't see her, you see. I *am* so sorry.' She took off her apron, went into the little room at the back and reappeared wearing a red and blue striped coat with a hood. 'If you're worrying about thanking them,' she said, 'I'm sure you needn't. After all, the flowers were to thank *you*, weren't they? For something you'd done. You can't keep on thanking people for thanking you backwards and forwards, the next thing would be they'd have to thank you for your thank-you letter.' She added, the pink once again bright in her cheeks, 'Of course it's nothing to do with me, I don't mean to interfere.'

'No, you're quite right.' He went on quickly, 'If you're going to close the shop now – I mean, if you're leaving, can I give you a lift anywhere? I have my car.'

'Well, you can. Oh, *would* you? But you're going home and I have to go to Hampstead. I always go to see my friend in Hampstead on Monday evenings and you've no idea how awful it is getting from here to Hampstead if you haven't got a car. You have to go on the 210 bus and they either don't come at all or they hunt in packs.'

Martin laughed. 'I'll go and get the car and pick you up in five minutes.' To make it as fast as that he had to run. When he pulled up at the lights she was waiting, scanning the street, looking lost.

'You're very very kind,' she said.

'Not at all. I'm glad I happened to mention it.' He was already aware that she was the kind of girl who makes a man feel manly, protective, endowed with virile power. Sitting beside him, she smelt of the flowers she had been with all day. She pushed back her hood and felt in her hair to release some slide or comb which held it confined, and the dark silky mass fell down over her shoulders like a cape.

At Highgate High Street, waiting in the traffic queue to turn up past the school, he turned to speak to her. She had been talking artlessly, charmingly, about transport difficulties between Highgate and Hampstead, how there ought to be a new tube under the Heath, a station called the Vale of Health. He didn't speak. He was suddenly conscious that she was not pretty but beautiful, perhaps the only truly beautiful person who had ever been in his car or sat beside him. Except, of course, for Tim Sage.

She told him her name as they were driving along the Spaniard's Road.

'It's Francesca,' she said, pronouncing it in the Italian way. 'Francesca Brown.'

It turned out that the friend, who had a flat in Frognal, wouldn't yet be home from work. Martin suggested a drink in the Hollybush. The rain was lashing against the windows of the car but Martin had an umbrella on the back seat. He put up the umbrella and held it out over her but, to his surprise and slightly to his confusion, she put her arm through his and drew him towards her so that they were both protected from the rain. There weren't yet many people in the bar. As he came back to her, carrying their drinks, he saw her big dark glowing eyes fixed on him and slowly she broke into a somehow joyful smile. His heart seemed to beat faster. It was eight before either of them realised how much time had passed and even then she lingered for another half-hour.

'Would you have dinner with me tomorrow night, Francesca?'

He had parked the car at the top of Frognal in front of the big houses in one of which Annabel had her flat. Francesca hesitated. The look she turned on him was intense, unsmiling, no longer joyful.

'What's the matter?' he said. 'Is something wrong?'

She said carefully, 'No,' and then in a shy voice but as if she couldn't hold the words back, 'We must meet again, I know that.'

'Then tomorrow?'

Her answer was a vehement nod. She got out of the car. 'Call for me at the shop.'

The grey rain, blown by sharp gusts of wind, swallowed her up. It went on raining most of the night. On the radio at breakfast there was an announcement of a murder that had taken place in Hampstead the evening before. Martin shivered a little to think that while he had been sitting and talking with Francesca, a woman had been murdered less than a mile away, her body left lying out in the teeming rain.

He called for Francesca at the shop at a quarter to six. They had drinks at Jack Straw's Castle and then dinner at the Villa Bianca. Francesca didn't smoke or drink more than a glass of wine and for an aperitif she had orange juice. When the time came for her to go home she wouldn't let him drive her. They were standing by his car, arguing about it, Martin insisting that he must drive her and she declaring in her earnest fashion that she wouldn't dream of allowing it, when a taxi came along and she had hailed it before he could stop her. The taxi bore her away down Hampstead High Street and turned into Gayton Road which was what it would have done whether her home had been to the north of Hampstead or to the east or even possibly to the west. Tomorrow night, he thought, he would ask her point blank where she lived. Why hadn't he done that already? He felt almost ashamed when he reflected that he had spent most of their time together talking about himself while she had listened with the attention of someone already committed to a passionate interest in the speaker. Of course he wasn't used to that kind of companionship. It was laughable to think of his parents or Gordon or Norman Tremlett hanging breathlessly on his words. But it hadn't been laughable in Francesca. It had been enormously flattering and gratifying and sweet and it had made him feel very protective towards her – and it had distracted him from asking her any questions about her own life. However, he would ask her tomorrow.

Not the shop this time but the foyer of the Prince of Wales Theatre. This was the way he had conducted his previous and rather brief, unsatisfactory relationships with girls, dinner one night, theatre the next, cinema the next, then dinner again. What else was there? Francesca looked so beautiful that he blurted out his feelings once they were in their seats.

'You look absolutely beautiful. I can't stop looking at you.'

She was wearing a softly draped dress of rose-coloured *panne* velvet, and round her neck on a ribbon a tiny pink rosebud. Her hair was piled like a Japanese lady's in mounds and coils, fixed with long tortoiseshell pins. The unaccustomed make-up she wore made her seem a little strange, remote, and violently sexually attractive. She winced a fraction at the compliment.

'Don't, Martin.'

He waited until the play was over and they were walking towards his car, parked in Lower Regent Street. Then he said gently and with a smile:

'You shouldn't make yourself look like that if you don't like compliments.'

His tone was light but hers serious and almost distressed. 'I know that, Martin! I know I'm a fool. But I couldn't help it, don't you see? I did want you to think I looked nice.'

'Of course. Why shouldn't you?'

'Oh, let's not talk about it,' she said.

When they were driving up Highgate West Hill he said he was going to drive her home and where did she live? If he would drop her here, she said, she would get a taxi. He pulled into Gordonhouse Road by the Greek Orthodox Church, switched off the engine, turned to look at her.

'Have you got a boy friend that you're living with, Francesca?'

'No, of course not. Of course I haven't.' And she added, 'Not a *boy friend*. Not that I'm *living* with.' He was quite unprepared for what she did next. She opened the car door and jumped out. He followed her, but not fast enough, and by the time he reached the corner a taxi carrying her was starting off up the hill.

That night he asked himself if he could possibly, after only three days, be in love, and decided that he couldn't. But he slept badly and could think of nothing and no one but Francesca until he had phoned Floreal at nine-thirty and spoken to her and been told she would see him again in the evening.

They went to a little restaurant she knew at the top of the Finchley Road. He didn't ask her why she had run away and she volunteered no explanation. After the meal he asked her if she would come back to Cromwell Court with him and he would make coffee. And in saying this he felt shy and awkward with her, for invitations of that kind to girls, he supposed, always carried the implication of a sexual denouement. He had had a secret half-ashamed conviction since last night that she might be a virgin.

She agreed to come. The yellow chrysanthemums were still alive, fresh and aggressive as ever, only their leaves having withered.

'They are *immortelles*,' said Francesca.

After half an hour she insisted on leaving. He helped her into her coat, she turned to him, and they were so close that he brought his face to hers and kissed her. Her lips were soft and responsive and her hands just touched his upper arms. He put his arms round her and kissed her passionately, prolonging the kiss until suddenly she broke away, flushed and frightened.

'Darling Francesca, I couldn't help it. Let me take you home.'

'No!'

'Then say you'll see me again tomorrow.'

'Will you come down with me and find a taxi?' said Francesca.

It was a damp rather misty night, the last of November. From every bare twig hung a chain of water drops. They walked out into Highgate Hill. There were plane and chestnut leaves underfoot, slippery and wet and blackened.

'Shall I call for you at the shop tomorrow?' He had hailed the taxi and it was already pulling in towards them. So many of their dramas, he was later to feel, had been associated with taxis. She shook his hand.

'Not tomorrow.'

'When, then? Saturday?'

She gasped, put up her hands to her face. 'Oh, Martin, never!' And then she was gone.

If his car had been at hand he would have followed that taxi. But it was two hundred yards away in the Cromwell Court car park. He walked back, dizzy with panic, with near-terror, that he had lost her. Because of that kiss? Because he had pressurized her about her private life? He was sitting desolate in his living room when the phone rang. The reprieve of her voice made him sink back with a kind of exhaustion.

'I shouldn't have said that, Martin, I didn't mean it. Only you do understand, don't you, that I can't see you this weekend?'

'No, I don't understand but I'll accept it if you say so.'

'And we'll meet next week, we'll meet on – Tuesday. I'll explain everything on Tuesday and it'll be all right. I promise you it'll be all right. Trust me?'

'Of course I trust you, Francesca. If you say it'll be all right I believe you.' He hadn't meant to say it, he hadn't been quite sure until this moment that he felt it, and it should be said for the first time face to face, but, 'I love you,' he said.

'Martin, Martin,' she said and the phone clicked and the dialling tone began.

It was a strange empty feeling knowing he wasn't going to see her for four whole days. Instead, his parents' house tonight to make up for his absence on Thursday, drinks tomorrow with Norman in the Flask, dinner with Adrian and Julie Vowchurch, Sunday a long gloomy void . . . The postman came early, at ten past eight, bringing the phone bill and an envelope addressed in an unfamiliar elderly hand.

The letter inside was signed Millicent Watson. She addressed him as Mr Urban, 'Dear Mr Urban', though he remembered having been introduced to her as Martin and hearing her call him by his christian name. She hadn't quite understood his letter, she wrote. Was he sure he wasn't mistaking her for someone else? If he was under the impression that she was a client of his firm and had investments, this was not so. She couldn't take on the responsibility of owning property. Moreover, she would never be in a position to repay any money which Urban, Wedmore, Mackenzie and Company might advance her. She had never in her life owed anyone a penny and didn't want to begin now. His letter had worried her a lot, she hadn't been able to sleep for worrying.

Martin was reading this in some dismay when Mr Cochrane arrived. He was carrying a six-foot-long cane with a green nylon brush attached to the head of it. This implement, designed for sweeping the ceilings, had once before been brought into the flat, transported very ill-temperedly by Mr Cochrane on the bus from his home in the Seven Sisters Road. Martin had said he would gladly buy a ceiling brush to save his cleaner so much trouble and inconvenience but Mr Cochrane, getting angrier and angrier, had replied that it made him sick to hear people who had never known the meaning of want, talk of throwing money about like water, spending pounds like pence, Martin would want to buy a dustette next, he supposed, or an electric polisher – and so on.

This morning he omitted any greeting. Positively hurling himself into his ironmonger's coat, he plunged into a rather incoherent account of his sister-in-law's latest dramas – and thereby imparted to Martin information that otherwise would have been hard to get. The green nylon brush rasped and whisked across the ceiling.

'On the verge of total nervous collapse, Martin, according to the doc. He's put her on eight Valium a day – no, I tell a lie – twelve. I was round there at number twenty, up with her half the night, Martin, and I don't mind telling you . . .'

'Number twenty?' hazarded Martin.

'Number twenty, Barnard House. Top of Ladbroke Grove, isn't it? How many times do I have to tell you? Might as well talk to a brick wall. Now mind out or you'll get cobwebs down on that expensive suit. Beautiful, them chrysanths, aren't they? Must have cost a packet. And here today, as you might say, Martin, and tomorrow to be cast into the oven.'

If only that were true, Martin thought, but the yellow chrysanthemums still looked aggressively fresh on Monday morning. On his way to work he posted the now completed letter to Mrs Cochrane. He drove by way of Highgate High Street and Southwood Lane so that he passed the flower shop, but at twenty past nine it wasn't yet open. He waited till ten and then he phoned her at Floreal. The other girl answered, the one who owned the shop. Martin asked to speak to Miss Brown and wondered why he sensed a sort of hesitant pause before the girl said she would fetch Francesca. Again he felt that quickened heart-beat when her voice came soft and serious, faintly apologetic, on the line. Yes, she was going to see him tomorrow, she was looking forward to it, she could hardly wait, only she had to wait, and would he call for her at the shop?

He had lunch with Gordon Tytherton in Muswell Hill. Gordon had invented a new system of taxation. There was, of course, no question of its ever being implemented, it was purely academic, but Gordon was immensely proud of it, being certain that if put to use it would solve all the nation's economic problems. He talked about it all the time. His little short-sighted eyes lit up and occasionally his voice trembled with emotion as might another man's when he spoke of a woman or a work of art. Martin parted from him at the foot of the hill and went into the travel agency where he collected the air tickets for Mrs

Bhavnani and Suma. Should he take them to the Bhavnanis' shop or send them? After a protracted inner debate he decided to send them to Dr Ghopal.

Francesca phoned him at twenty-five to ten on Tuesday morning to say she couldn't see him and not to come to the shop.

'It's not possible, Martin, and something awful's happened! Martin, do you see the *Post*?'

He heard it as the post, the mail. 'What post?'

'The local paper, the *North London Post*. I know you do, I saw it when I was in your flat. Martin, promise me you won't look at it when it comes on Friday. Please, Martin. I'll see you on Friday and I'll explain everything.'

After she had rung off he thought how, if she left her job, he would have no means of knowing where to find her, she would be lost to him. He was in love with someone whose life was a total mystery to him, who might live, for all he knew, in Golders Green or Edmonton or Wembley, with her parents, in a hostel, in her own flat. She was like one of those heroines of a fairy story or an Arabian Nights' tale who come from nowhere, who vanish into a void, and who threaten to disappear for ever if their lover attempts to lift the veil that conceals their secrets.

In her absence, the week passed with a dreary plodding slowness. She dominated his thoughts. Why had she asked for his promise not to look at the local paper? He hadn't given it. Had he done so he would have adhered to his promise but he hadn't and she, strangely enough, hadn't insisted. It occurred to him that the truth might be she really wanted him to see the *Post*, half-feared it, half-desired it, because it was to contain some story about herself, flattering to herself. Francesca was very modest and diffident. Could it be that she was shy of his seeing praise of her? She might have been taking part in some contest, he thought, or succeeding with honours in some examination. And he indulged in a little fantasy in which a photograph of Francesca covered the paper's front page with a caption underneath to the effect that this was London's loveliest flower seller.

The postman and Mr Cochrane arrived simultaneously. Mr Cochrane greeted Martin dourly, said nothing about his sister-in-law, got to work at once on the windows with a chamois leather and soapy water. Martin opened the letter with the Battersea postmark. It was from Mr Deepdene. Here was no misapprehension, no paranoia, no getting hold of the wrong end of the stick. Mr Deepdene wrote that he had never known such kindness in all his seventy-four years, he was overwhelmed, it was unbelievable. At first he had thought of refusing Martin's offer, it was too generous, but now it seemed ungrateful, even wrong, to turn it down. He would accept with a full heart. Martin shut himself in his bedroom, away from Mr Cochrane, wrote a rapid note to Mr Deepdene and put into the envelope with it, a cheque for fifteen thousand pounds. Then he wrote to Miss Watson, asking her to phone him at his office so that they might make an appointment to meet.

The sun was shining on the white frosted roofs that hung like a range of glittering alps beneath his window. It was going to be a fine day, it was Friday, tonight he was going to see Francesca. He stood at the bedroom window, looking down at the white roofs, the long shadows, the occasional spire of whiter smoke rising through the bright mist. Coming across the car park was the paper boy with his canvas satchel. Martin turned away from the window and went into the living room where Mr Cochrane was polishing plate glass and the chrysanthemums were as vigorous as ever. He took the vases out into the kitchen. The big yellow blossoms seemed to look reproachfully at him as he thrust them into the waste bin.

'Wicked waste,' said Mr Cochrane, padding up behind him to empty his bowl of water. 'Not a withered petal on the lot of them!'

The two newspapers had just come through the letter box. Martin picked them up and looked at the *Post*. The front page lead, for the second week running, was the Parliament Hill

Fields murder. This time it was a report of the inquest on Anne Blake, the heading was *Woman Killed for £26* and the by-line Tim Sage's. Martin went through the paper to try and find what had so upset Francesca in anticipation. The *Post* was a forty-page tabloid so this took some time, but he could find nothing, no photograph, no story. It was still only ten to nine. Watched curiously by Mr Cochrane, Martin began again, working this time more slowly and meticulously.

Because he could no longer bear the scrutiny of pebble eyes through distorting bifocals, he took the paper into the bedroom. There, using a red ballpoint, he went through each page like a proof reader, ticking its lower edge when he had cleared it.

He found what he was looking for on page seven, a mere paragraph in a gossip column called *Finchley Footnotes*.

The coming year will be an exciting one for Mr Russell Brown, 35, whose first book is to be published in the summer. This is an historical novel about the Black Death entitled The Iron Cocoon. *Mr Brown, who is an authority on the fourteenth century, teaches history at a north London polytechnic. He lives with his wife Francesca and two-year-old daughter Lindsay in Fortis Green Lane.*

8

'Since this is going to be our last meeting,' said Martin, 'I should have liked to take you somewhere nice.' He glanced round the Greek taverna in the Archway Road where she had insisted on coming. It smelt of cooking oil, and over the glass-fronted case of raw kebabs trailed the fronds of a plastic tradescantia. 'Still, I don't suppose it matters.' An unpleasant thought, among so many, struck him. 'Where does *he* think you are? Come to that, where did he think you were all last week?'

'He had flu,' she said, 'and the doctor said to take a week off to convalesce, so he went to his parents in Oxford and took Lindsay with him.'

'I can't believe you have a child,' he said miserably, 'a child of two.' The waiter came to their table. Martin ordered lamb kebab, a salad, for both of them. She passed across the table to him something she had taken from her handbag. He looked without enthusiasm, with dismay, at the photograph of a dark-haired, wide-eyed baby girl. 'But where is she? What happens to her when you're at work?' It was as if he doubted the very truth of it, as if by questioning her closely, he might break her down and make her confess that she had lied and the newspaper been wrong.

'In a day nursery. I take her there in the mornings and Russell fetches her. He gets home before me.'

'I looked him up in the phone book,' said Martin. 'I take it he's the H. R. Brown at 54 Fortis Green Lane?'

She hesitated momentarily, then nodded. 'His first name,' she said, 'is Harold, only he prefers his second name and Russell Brown sounds better for an author.'

'And I used to wonder all the time why you wouldn't let me take you home. I thought you might be ashamed of your home or even have an angry father. I thought you couldn't be more than twenty.'

'I'm twenty-six.'

'Oh, don't cry,' said Martin. 'Have some wine. Crying isn't going to help.'

Neither of them could eat much. Francesca picked at her kebab and pushed it away. Her deep brown glowing eyes held a kind of feverish despair and she gave a little sob. Up till then he had felt only anger and bitterness. A pang of pity made him lay his own hand gently on hers. She bit her lip.

'I'm sorry, Martin. I shouldn't have gone out with you last week, but I did want to, I wanted some fun. I'm not going to indulge in a lot of self-pity, but I don't have much fun. And then – then it wasn't just fun any more.' He felt a tremor of delight and terror. Hadn't she just admitted she loved him? 'Russell came home on Friday, and on Monday he said he'd had this phone call from the *Post* about his book. I knew they'd put something in the paper and I knew you'd see it.'

'I suppose you love him, don't you? You're happy, you and Russell and Lindsay and the Black Death?' Wretchedness had brought out a grim wit in him and he smiled a faint ironical smile.

'Let's go,' she said. 'Let's go back to your place, Martin.'

In the car he didn't speak to her. So this is what it's like, he thought, this is what it had been like for all those men he had heard of and read about and even known who had fallen in love with married women. Clandestine meetings, deception, a somehow dirty feeling of being traitorous and corrupt. And at the end of it a bitter parting with ugly recriminations or else divorce and re-marriage in some High Street registrar's office to an experience-ravaged girl with a ready-made family. He knew he was old-fashioned. He had been a schoolboy when the word 'square' was current slang, but even then he had known he was and always would be, square. A thickset square-shouldered man with a square forehead and a square jaw and a square outlook on life. Rectangular, tetragonal, square, conventional, conservative and reactionary. The revolution in morals which had taken place during his adolescence had passed over him and left him as subject to the old order as if he had actually spent a lifetime under its regime. He would have liked to be married to a virgin in church. What he certainly wasn't going to do, he thought as he drove up to Cromwell Court, was have an affair with Francesca, with Mrs Russell Brown, embroil himself in that kind of sordidness and vain excitement and – disgrace. They must part, and at once. He helped her from the car and stood for a moment holding her arm in the raw frosty cold.

The place looked strangely bare without the chrysanthemums, as a room does when it has been stripped of its Christmas decorations. He drew the curtains to shut out the purplish starry sky and the city that lay like a spangled cloth below. Francesca sat on the edge of her chair, watching him move about the room. He remembered that last week he had thought there was something childlike about her. That had been in the days of her supposed innocence and it was all gone now. She was as old as he. Under her eyes were the shadows of tiredness and suffering and her cheeks were pale. He glanced down at her hands which she was twisting in her lap.

'You can put your wedding ring on again tomorrow,' he said bitterly.

She said in a very low voice, not much above a whisper, 'I never wear it.'

'You still haven't told me where he thinks you are.'

'At Annabel's, the girl who lives in Frognal, the one I see on Mondays. Martin, I thought we could – I thought we could sometimes meet on Mondays.'

He went over to the drinks cabinet and poured himself some brandy. He held up the bottle. 'For you?'

'No, I don't want anything. I thought Mondays and – and Saturday afternoons, if you like. Russell always goes to White Hart Lane when Spurs play at home.'

He almost laughed. 'You know all about it, don't you? How many have there been before me?'

She shrank as if he had made to strike her. 'There haven't been any at all.' She had a way of speaking very simply and directly, without artifice. It was partly because of this, that, like him, she had no sharp wit, no gift of repartee, that he had begun to love her. Begun, only begun, he must remember that. Caution, be my friend!

'We aren't going to see each other any more, Francesca. We've only known each other two weeks and that means we can part now without really getting hurt. I think I must have been a bit crazy, the way I went on last week, but there's no harm done, is there? I'm not going to come between husband and wife. We'll forget each other in a little while and I know that's the best thing. I wish you hadn't – well, led me on, but I expect you couldn't help yourself.' Martin came breathlessly to the end of this speech, drank down the rest of his brandy and recalled from an ancient film a phrase he had thought funny at the time. He brought it out facetiously with a bold smile. 'I was just a mad, impetuous fool!'

She looked at him sombrely. 'I shan't forget you,' she said. 'Don't you know I'm in love with you?'

No one had ever made that confession to him before. He felt himself turn pale, the blood recede from his face.

'I think I loved you the day I brought those horrible flowers and you said – ' her voice trembled ' – that no one sends flowers to men unless they're ill.'

'We're going to say good-bye now, Francesca, and I'm going to put you in a taxi and you're going home to Russell and Lindsay. And in a year's time I'll come and buy some flowers from you and you'll have forgotten who I am.'

He pulled her gently to her feet. She was limp and passive, yet clinging. She subsided clingingly against him so that the whole length of her body was pressed softly to his and her hands tremulously on either side of his face.

'Don't send me away, Martin. I can't bear it.'

He was aware of thinking that this was his last chance to keep clear of the involvement he dreaded. Summon up the strength now and he would be a free man. But he longed also to be loved, not so much for sex as for love. He was aware of that and then of very little more that might be said to belong to the intellect. His open lips were on her open lips and his hands were discovering her. He and she had descended somehow to the cushions of the sofa and her white arm, now bare, was reaching up to turn off the lamp.

Martin hadn't much experience of love-making. There had been a girl at the LSE and a girl he had met at a party at the Vowchurches' and a girl who had picked him up on the beach at Sitges. There had been other girls too, but only with these three had he actually had sexual relations. He had found it, he brought himself to confess, to himself only, disappointing. Something was missing, something that books and plays and other people's experience had led him to expect. Surely there should be more to it than just a blind unthinking need beforehand and afterwards nothing more than the same sense of relief as a sneeze gives or a drink of cold water down a thirsty throat?

With Francesca it wasn't like that. Perhaps it was because he loved her and he hadn't loved those others. It must be that. He had done nothing different and it couldn't have been any great skill or expertise on her part. She had whispered to him that he was the only man apart from Russell. Before Russell there had been no one and for a long time now Russell had scarcely touched her. She was married and she had a child but still she was nearly as innocent as Martin would have had her be.

She slept beside him that night. At eleven she phoned Russell and told him she would be staying the night with Annabel because of the fog. Martin heard the murmur of a man's voice answering her truculently. It was only the second time in his life he had been in bed all night with a woman. On an impulse he told her so and she put her arms round him, holding him close to her.

In the morning he looked once more at that copy of the *Post* with its cover photograph of the path from the railway bridge to Nassington Road and, on the inside, the paragraph about Russell Brown. It seemed a hundred years since he had first read it, had underlined that emotive name and inserted, after a feverish scanning of the phone book, the number of her house in Fortis Green Lane. He put the paper on top of the neat pile of tabloids on the floor of the kitchen cupboard and the *Daily Telegraph* on the pile of broadsheets. Later, walking up the hill with Francesca – she refused to let him drive her – he called into the newsagent's and cancelled the *Post*. Why had he ever bothered to take a local paper? Only, surely, because of knowing Tim Sage.

Martin hadn't expected to see Francesca again that weekend, he didn't even really mind that, but he had somehow taken it for granted that now they would meet every evening. He was very taken aback when she phoned him on Monday morning to say she wouldn't be able to see him that night, Lindsay had a bad cold, and perhaps they could see each other in a week's time. He was obliged to wait, phoning her every day, very aware of that other life she led with a husband and a little child, yet scarcely able to believe in its reality.

Nothing could have brought that reality more forcefully home to him than Lindsay herself. On the first Saturday afternoon Russell went off to football and she was able to get away she brought Lindsay with her.

'Oh, Martin, I'm so sorry. I had to bring her. If I hadn't I couldn't have come myself.'

She was a beautiful little girl, anyone would have thought that. She was dark like her mother but otherwise not much like her, their beauty being of two very distinct kinds. Francesca had a high colour and fine pointed features, hair that waved along its length and curled at its tips, and her eyes were brown. Lindsay's eyes were bright blue, her skin almost olive, her mouth like the bud of a red flower, a camellia or azalea perhaps, from her mother's shop. Because her straight, almost black, hair was precociously long, she looked older than she was. To Martin it seemed for a moment as if the face beside

Francesca's smiling apologetic face was that of an aggressive adolescent. And then Francesa was stripping off coat and woolly scarf and it was a baby that emerged, a walking doll not three feet high.

Lindsay ran about examining and handling the Swedish crystal. Martin's heart was in his mouth, but he scolded himself inwardly for turning so young into an old bachelor. If he was like this now, how would he be when he had children of his own, when he and Francesca had children of their own? Lindsay began turning all his books out of the bookcase and throwing them on the floor. It surprised Martin that Francesca kissed him in front of Lindsay and let him hold her hand and sat with her head on his shoulder. It surprised and slightly embarrassed him too, for Lindsay had so far only uttered one sentence, though that frequently and in a calm conversational tone.

'I want to see my Daddy.'

Martin looked at Francesca to see how she took this, but even when Lindsay had repeated it at least ten times Francesca only smiled vaguely and she continued to give Martin butterfly kisses. It's because she doesn't mind Russell knowing, Martin thought and he felt elated, it's because she knows now that her marriage is over.

Then a rather curious thing happened.

Martin had been saying rather gloomily that he supposed they wouldn't be able to meet much over Christmas.

'No, but I've got something nice to tell you, darling.' Francesca's eyes sparkled. 'I'll be able to come and stay the whole New Year weekend with you – if you'd like that.'

'If I'd like it! It's the most wonderful Christmas present you could give me.'

'Russell's taking her to his parents in Cambridge for the weekend.'

Lindsay came over and climbed on her mother's knee and put her hand over her mother's mouth and said:

'We'll go home now.'

Martin said, 'I thought you said his parents lived in Oxford.

That week we met, I thought you said he had taken Lindsay to his parents in Oxford.'

Francesca opened her mouth to speak and Lindsay pinched her lips together. 'We'll go home now, we'll go home now,' Lindsay chanted. 'I want to see my Daddy.'

Lifting Lindsay, Francesca stood up. 'I'll have to take her home, Martin, or we could all go for a walk. Oh, don't do that, Lindsay, don't be so *awful*.' She turned on Martin her direct and transparently honest gaze. 'Russell's parents live in Cambridge, Martin. I'm afraid it's you who got it wrong. One always does associate those two places, don't you think? That's why you got confused.'

She wouldn't let him drive them home but insisted on a taxi.

On Saturday, December 16, Mrs Bhavnani and Suma flew to Sydney and Martin, after drinks in the Flask with Norman Tremlett, did his Christmas shopping. He bought six rose bushes for his father, My Choice, Duke of Windsor, Peace, Golden Showers, and Super Star twice, eau de toilette *Rive Gauche* for his mother, a box of handerchiefs embroidered with blue and yellow flowers for Caroline, and for the Vowchurches, who had invited him on Boxing Day, a macramé hanging plant container. Mr Cochrane would get a ten-pound note. There was no one else to buy for, except Francesca.

This was difficult. He had never seen her wear jewellery so presumably she didn't like it. He couldn't buy her clothes when he didn't know her size or perfume since he didn't know her taste. At last he found two cut-glass scent bottles with silver stoppers in an antique shop and paid thirty pounds for them.

On Sunday he had lunch with his parents. Secretly, so that his father shouldn't observe them, his mother showed him the current *North London Post*. The front page lead was headed *Miracle Op for Hornsey Boy* and there was a photograph of Mr and Mrs Bhavnani with Suma, the three of them posed, evidently several years before, in a very Victorian way in a photographer's studio. Mrs Bhavnani, wearing a sari, was sitting in a carved chair with the boy standing at her knees and her husband behind her.

'It's some relative told the paper,' whispered Mrs Urban. 'Look, it says the money was raised by a customer of the shop who wants to remain anonymous.'

Martin saw that the by-line was Tim's. It was a month now since he had seen Tim. Ought he to give him a ring and arrange to see him at Christmas?

He would be going for a drink with Norman Tremlett on Christmas Eve and to supper with Gordon and Alice Tytherton on Christmas night. Christmas was a time when you made a point of seeing your close friends, and Tim had seemed a closer friend than either Norman or the Tythertons. Had seemed. Martin couldn't remember that there had ever, since that encounter in the wood in May, been such a long time go by without their seeing each other. He had read somewhere that we dislike those whom we have injured but that seemed absurd to him. Surely we should dislike those who injure us? Perhaps both were true. Anyway, you couldn't say he had *injured* Tim by not going to his dinner party. No, it was *he* who had taken rightful offence at Tim's sarcasm and reproaches. So what if they had made him come to dislike Tim? Tim was a dangerous companion, anyway, and not likely to get on with Francesca.

Mr Cochrane didn't come on the Friday before Christmas. He phoned, waking Martin up, at five minutes to six in the morning to say his sister-in-law was about to be taken away to what he called a nursing home. He intended to go with her in the ambulance. Martin wondered if this accounted for Mrs Cochrane's failure to reply to his letter. Perhaps. It couldn't, however, explain why Miss Watson hadn't written again or phoned or why he had had no acknowledgement of his cheque from Mr Deepdene.

9

The police came and talked to Finn. He was one of the last people to have seen Anne Blake alive. Her friends in Nassington Road had told them that. Finn said he had left the house in Modena Road at half-past four, soon after she had come in, and had driven straight home. They seemed satisfied, they seemed to believe him. Finn thought how different things might have been if one of the officers, that middle-aged detective sergeant for instance, had happened to have been involved in the investigation into Queenie's death eleven years before. But no one connected the carpenter and electrician of Lord Arthur Road with the fifteen-year-old white-headed boy who had been in the house in Hornsey when another woman was beaten to death. Finn wasn't frightened of the police, anyway. His fear was for his mother.

Lena's reading glasses were ready for her within a week. By that time the Parliament Hill Fields murder had retreated to the inside pages but Finn was afraid of some old copy of a newspaper falling into her hands. Such a one might be stuffed into the toes of a bargain pair of shoes or used to wrap a scented candle. When Lena set off for the shops, made stout by layers of coats and a lagging of stoles, a Korean straw basket in one hand and a greengrocer's net in the other, he watched her with a pang. He couldn't understand the impulse that had made him slaughter Anne Blake out there in the open, when he might so easily have waited till the next day and achieved an accident. How was he going to master others and control destinies when he couldn't yet master himself?

He had waited in daily expectation for the balance of the

payment to come, for one of those olive-faced children to appear with a parcel. It was Christmas before that happened. The eldest boy brought the money wrapped in red paper with holly leaves on it and secured with silver sellotape. Finn's pale glazed eyes and skeletal frame in a dirty white robe frightened him, he muttered something about Dad having had 'flu and now pneumonia, and fled.

Finn peeled off the red paper, not much amused by Kaiafas's idea of a joke. Underneath, before he reached the Mr Kipling jam tart box in which the money was packed, was an inner wrapping of newspaper, the *Daily Mirror*, November 28, with a picture of the path and the grove of trees where Anne Blake had died. Finn tore it to pieces and burnt it as he had burnt Anne Blake's money and cheque book and credit cards.

The money was correct, two hundred and fifty ten-pound notes. No one would come robbing him, he was the last person. They were wary of him in the neighbourhood since he had roughed up those squatters for Kaiafas. Kneeling on the floor, tucking the money into a plastic carrier under his mattress, he heard Lena pass his door. She was chattering away, there was someone with her. Mrs Gogarty, maybe, or old Bradley whose daughter-in-law locked him out of the house while she was at work so that he had to take refuge in the library or with Lena. Finn listened, slightly smiling. She had a host of friends, she wasn't like him, she could love people. She had even loved Queenie . . .

Lena had been over forty when Finn was born. She had never supposed she would have a child and her husband was dying of Addison's disease. The baby she named Theodore after the dead man, which he was destined never to be called except by schoolteachers. For Lena he needed no name, speaking to him summoned a special note into her voice, and to Queenie he was always 'dear'. They went to live with Queenie when Finn was six months old.

Lena couldn't live alone with a baby. She wasn't strong or self-reliant. Queenie was her first cousin and also a widow, a State Registered Nurse who owned her own house and was fat and practical and seemingly kind.

Queenie's house was in Middle Grove, Hornsey, one of a row of neat, narrow houses on three floors under a slate roof. Finn would have liked to sleep in Lena's room but Queenie said that was silly and wrong when there were four bedrooms. Lena had a small pension from Theodore Finn's employers but it wasn't enough to live on and keep Finn on, so later she went out cleaning for Mrs Urban in Copley Avenue, leaving the child at home with Queenie. It was Queenie's aim and desire, though without intentional cruelty, without really knowing what she was doing, to win Finn's love and make him prefer her over his mother. She knew she would be a better influence on him. She read to him out of *Thomas the Tank Engine* and gave him banana sandwiches for tea and wheeled him round the shops, and when people said 'your little boy' she didn't contradict them.

Lena observed it all with speechless anguish. There was no fight in her, she could only contemplate the theft of her son in passivity and pain. But there was nothing to contemplate, for Finn was not to be won. He wavered for a while, half-seduced by the reading and the sandwiches, and then he returned quietly to his mother, creeping into her bedroom at night, finding his way in the dark.

When he was thirteen the poltergeists started. Lena, who was psychic, believed that they were spirits but Finn knew better. Sometimes he could feel the energy coursing through his veins like electricity along wires, charging his muscles and raying out through his finger ends. Lena saw his aura for the first time. It was golden-orange like the rising sun. He was aware of his brain waves, of a surplus of power.

One day all the plates in Queenie's china cupboard rattled down off the shelves and a lot of them smashed. Another time a brick came flying through the kitchen window, and in the same hour the framed photograph of Queenie in her Staff

Nurse's uniform, wearing her SRN badge, fell down off the wall and the glass cracked.

Queenie said Finn was responsible, he was doing it himself, though even she couldn't explain how he had brought into the house a rockery stone no one could lift an inch off the ground. The poltergeists went away soon after he started smoking the hashish and when they were gone he regretted them bitterly, praying for their return to any god or spirit or seer he came across in his reading. But they had deserted him. He decided to kill Queenie.

There were a number of reasons for this. He was afraid of her mockery and alarmed at her distaste for his pursuits. She had burned a book of his about the Rosicrucians. He also wanted to know how it would feel to have killed, and he saw killing as a fire baptism into the kind of life he wanted to lead and the kind of person he wanted to be. Queenie was the obvious choice for victim, ugly, stupid, unsympathetic, one who had never begun to see the light, a young soul. And she had a house which she had said, over and over again, she would leave to Lena. Brenda, her daughter, who lived in Newcastle, she never saw and got nothing from but a card at Christmas. Finn couldn't understand why his mother wanted a house of her own but she did want one, and Finn thought she had a better right to one than Queenie.

He carried the dream of killing her about with him for two years, but when he actually did the deed it happened spontaneously, almost by chance. One night Queenie awakened him and Lena, saying she had heard someone in the house downstairs. It was springtime, three in the morning. Finn went down with Queenie. There was no one there, though a window was open and some money, about seven pounds in notes and change, had been taken out of a tin in one of the kitchen cupboards. Queenie was carrying the poker they used for riddling out the slow-burning stove in the living room.

'Give me that,' Finn said.

'What d'you want it for?'

'Just to try something out.'

She handed it to him and turned her back to look for her rings, the wedding band and the engagement ring, which each night she took off and dropped into a glass dish on the mantelpiece. Finn raised the poker and struck her on the back of the head. She made a terrible sound, an unnerving, groaning wail. He struck her again and again until she was silent and lying in a big, huddled, bloody heap. He let the poker fall and turned round slowly and saw Lena standing in the doorway.

Lena was trembling at the sight of the blood. Her teeth were chattering and she kept making little whimpering whistling sounds. But she took hold of him with her shaking hands and made him wash himself, and she took away his pyjama trousers and his vest, which were all he had been wearing, and stuffed them into the stove among the glowing nuggets of coke. She washed the poker herself. She made Finn put on clean pyjamas and get into bed and feign sleep and then she went out and got the people next door to phone the police. When they came Finn was really asleep, he was never even suspected.

It pushed Lena over the edge of sanity. She had been teetering there for long enough. 'Spontaneous schizophrenia' was what Finn heard a doctor say. That was in the hospital where they had taken her after she had been found going into butchers' shops and crying out that they sold human flesh. She went into the shops and then she walked into the Archway Road and lay down in the middle of the road and cried out to the motorists to kill her.

And they hadn't got the house after all. There was no will, so it went to Brenda who let them go on living there for just six months. Finn never went back to school after Queenie died, and in the depths of the winter after his sixteenth birthday they moved into Lord Arthur Road, she into her top floor warren, he into this room.

He stood inside the door, listening to the ascending steps and to Mr Bradley's thin broken voice croaking over and over, 'God bless your kind heart, my darling, God bless your kind heart.' After a while Finn went down to the street where he phoned Kaiafas at home from the call box on the corner of

Somerset Grove. He needed employment, he hadn't done a job of work since patching up the Frazers' bay.

Kaiafas suggested a meeting at Jack Straw's Castle. That was halfway between their homes, he said, and he coughed piteously into the phone. The meeting was for a long way ahead, two days after Christmas, but Finn couldn't argue, for Kaiafas claimed still to be bed-bound.

The air was charged with frost and the melted snow had frozen again when he went off to Hampstead to keep his date with Kaiafas. Lena wasn't yet back from some trip she had gone on with Mrs Gogarty. There was a waxing moon that hung up over Highbury, greenish white in a fuzz of mist, and a fine snow was falling, tiny hard pellets of snow that burned when they touched the skin. Up on the Heath, the highest you could get above London and still be in it, an east wind was blowing and the broken and re-frozen ice on the Whitestone Pond made it look like a shallow quarry of granite.

The saloon bar in Jack Straw's was half empty. Finn sat down to wait for Kaiafas. He wasn't going to buy himself a drink, wasting money for form's sake. There was only one person in there that he knew and then only by sight. This was the *Post* reporter, a dark man as thin as himself with black hair and a red mouth, whom Finn had often seen conducting a one-man investigation into stories of maltreatment and terrorization of tenants in Lord Arthur Road. The reporter hadn't got very far. The people he interviewed didn't think it worth their while to talk to the police, let alone a newspaper.

Finn watched him. He was talking to a pompous-looking fat man, writing something in a notebook, stubbing out a cigarette. Finn concentrated on him and tried by the power of thought to make him light another cigarette. What hadn't worked on the woman with the iron, worked immediately on the reporter. Finn felt pleased with himself. Then Kaiafas came in. Kaiafas had a wrinkled, seamed face like an old leather bag and eyes like muscatels. When out for the evening he always wore pale-coloured suits of some smooth cloth with a glistening sheen to it. Tonight the suit was silvery blue but Kaiafas had a black sheepskin coat over it with a black fur collar into which he huddled his paler-than-usual face.

'What will you drink, Feen?'

'Pineapple juice,' said Finn. 'The Britvic.'

Kaiafas began to talk of Anne Blake as if Finn had had nothing to do with her death, as if indeed he might not know of her death, but he did so with numerous nudges and winks.

'The rent she pay me, Feen, she could afford have a car, but no, she must go walking in these lonesome places, in the dark. So here we have the result.' Kaiafas had a way of wagging a finger at whomsoever might be his companion. 'She have some good furniture. Antiques. Her sister come and take them all away.' He sounded regretful.

'Well, well,' said Finn.

Kaiafas nudged him. 'An ill wind that blows nobody no good, eh?' He chortled a little which made him cough. Finn didn't ask him how he was, it wasn't the kind of question he ever asked of anyone. 'Another one of those pineapples?' said Kaiafas.

Finn nodded.

'With a drop vodka this time, no?'

'No,' said Finn. 'You know I don't drink.'

'So. Now how about you do a nice decorating job for me, Feen? Paint out the house, do the re-wire and put down a nice bit of carpet I got fall off the back of a Pickford's?'

Finn said he would and drank his second pineapple juice. They talked about it for a while and then Finn left. In Lord Arthur Road he parked the van in the same troughs of frozen grey snow from which he had taken it out. As soon as he entered the house, he knew there was something wrong, he could smell it. He went upstairs in the manner of an animal that keeps climbing though it knows there may be a trap or a predator at the top.

Halfway up the flight between his room and Lena's Mrs Gogarty was waiting for him. She was bending over the banisters so that he saw her white moon face searching for him, hovering over the deep stairwell before he reached his own floor. He came on more quickly and Mrs Gogarty clutched him, holding fistfuls of his clothes. Her face worked, her voice was a croak and she could hardly speak. Mrs Gogarty was afraid of almost everything the natural world held, of enclosed places and open spaces, of spiders and mice and cats, of crowds, of loneliness, of sudden noise, of silence, but she was rather less afraid of insanity than most people are. She had seen so much of it. As they came to the door of Lena's room he managed to get the story out of her.

She and Lena had been to a sale-and-exchange clothes market in Hampstead, in Fleet Road, and coming away from it to catch a bus, had seen a notice attached to a lamp-post which had frightened Lena. Finn wanted to know what sort of notice and Mrs Gogarty could only say over and over, 'The murder, the murder,' but that was enough to make all clear to him. Lena had seen one of the police notices enquiring for information leading to the arrest of the Parliament Hill Fields murderer. No doubt they were posted up all over the area between Hampstead Heath and Gospel Oak stations.

'What happened?' he whispered.

'She shouted out you'd done it. Him? I said, your lovely boy? But words are wind. There weren't so many people, thank God. A taxi came, I got a taxi, but I don't know how I got her in it. I had to hold on to her in the taxi. She's little but she's strong when she's like that.'

'Where is she now?'

'In there,' said Mrs Gogarty, trembling. 'Crouched down like a tiger. She said you'd done the murder and then she said not to send her away. I knew what that meant, I promised not *that*.'

Finn said, 'Wait a minute,' and went down and into his own room. From the back of the bookshelf, behind *Beelzebub's Tales*, he took a glass jar that contained his hypodermic and his ampoules of chlorpromazine. Give her a big dose, fifty milligrams – or seventy-five? Finn had no friends but he had acquaintances who could get him anything. Mrs Gogarty was still outside Lena's door, her face quivering and tears now shining in the corners of her not quite symmetrical blue eyes.

Finn opened the door and walked across the tiny kitchen. He stood in the doorway of the partition he had made. Lena was crouched in the armchair under the budgerigar's cage, her legs flexed under her, her hands up to her head. When she saw Finn she sprang. She sprang at him and at his throat, holding on to his neck and pressing her thumbs in.

Mrs Gogarty gave a little cry and shut the door and subsided against it like a flung cushion. Finn staggered under his mother's stranglehold. He got his hands under her fingers which had become like steel clasps and he forced her arms down and held her turned from him, one hand holding her wrists, the other arm hooked under her jaw. She was champing now, grinding her teeth, murmuring meaninglessly, 'Take me home, I want to go home.' Finn didn't dare let her go. He knew she would attack him again, for she no longer knew who she was or he was or where they were. He said to Mrs Gogarty:

'You do it.'

She came fearfully to take the syringe, but she had seen it done often enough before, had had it done to herself. Finn could have used a straitjacket but he balked at anything of the sort. He held her until the drug made her limp and then he lifted her up and laid her on the bed in the diminutive bedroom.

'The picture of devotion,' mumbled Mrs Gogarty. 'The very picture.'

'Can you get home on your own OK?'

The big white face quivered in a nod.

'Won't mind the dark?'

'It's been dark,' she said, 'since four,' and she held up for his inspection an amulet she wore round her neck. It wasn't on account of marauders or the glassy pavements that the dark menaced her.

Finn covered Lena up and stayed with her through the night. Before dawn he gave her another injection and she lay quiet and almost without breath as if she were already dead. He didn't know what a doctor would have given her and he wasn't going to call one. A doctor would want to have Lena committed and he wasn't having that, besides listening curiously to her ravings about murder.

These began again in the morning. It was far too late for Finn to produce any trumped-up proofs to exonerate himself. She didn't know him. He wasn't her son but the fiend who had killed Queenie and who had killed since then a hundred women. She screamed so loudly that one of the people from downstairs came up and said he was calling the police if it didn't stop.

Finn got hot milk with phenobarbitone in it down her throat. Because it didn't work at once he forced brandy into her. He was terrified he might overdo it and kill her, but he had to silence those cries. They had been through so much together, he and she, fighting the world, exploring the unseen, approaching strange spiritual agents. She cried herself to sleep and he sat beside her, looking inscrutably at that pale twisted face, holding her big veined hand in his big hand, the nearest he had ever got to tenderness with a living creature.

On the Sunday she walked round and round the room, feeling up the walls with her fingertips as if she were blind, lifting every ornament and feeling it and sniffing it. When she was asleep he took the bird and birdcage down to his room. She would kill the bird, twist it to death in her strong hands as she had the last one, and then break her heart over its death. He gave her phenobarbitone every day until her eyes focussed again and rested on him and a voice that was more or less normal came out of her cracked and swollen lips.

'Don't let them take me away.'

'Come on,' said Finn. 'Would I?'

She cried and she couldn't stop. She cried for hours, tossing this way and that, burying her face in her hands, throwing her head back and forward, crying until it seemed that all the madness had been washed away in tears.

10

'Three cheers for the Three Musketeers!' said Norman Tremlett, waving and slightly spilling his gin and tonic.

He had said this every Christmas for the past ten years and probably would say it every Christmas for the rest of his life if given the opportunity. He referred, of course, to himself, Martin and Adrian Vowchurch. Adrian smiled his thin, tolerant, resigned smile at Norman and handed him a dish of Japanese rice crackers. Although these had been available as cocktail snacks almost as long as Martin (and therefore Norman too) could remember, Norman affected to find them an extremely *avant-garde* novelty, examined them clownishly and expressed as his opinion that they were really made out of insects. Everyone knew the Japanese ate insects. His own father had been offered chocolate-covered ants while in Tokyo on a business trip.

Norman always behaved like this at parties. Nobody minded because he was basically so kind and good-natured. He and Adrian and Martin had been at school together and each, in his particular field, had later entered his father's firm. Norman was a surveyor and Adrian a solicitor. Norman, as well as his Three Musketeers joke, sometimes called them the Triumvirate. It gave Martin considerable deep pleasure and a feeling of power to think that his closest friends were his solicitor and his surveyor and he was sure they felt the same about him being their accountant. He handled the Tremlett and Vowchurch financial affairs and when he had bought his flat, Norman had made the preliminary survey and Adrian had handled the conveyance.

Of the three of them only Adrian had so far married. Because of Francesca, Martin felt closer to him this year than he had done for a long time. Adrian had married a girl with a lot of family money and they lived in a smart little house in Barnsbury. They gave the sort of parties Martin liked, not too many people and nearly all people one knew, proper drinks not plonk, not a buffet meal but a real one with courses. There wasn't any loud music or dancing and the guests stood around in groups talking. Martin couldn't help thinking that Tim would probably be having a Christmas party and that it would be very different from this one, dark, noisy and with goings-on it was better not to think of. Finding himself briefly alone with Adrian, Martin said on an impulse:

'There's a girl I'd like to bring to meet you and Julie – next time you have a party.'

'That'll be for Julie's birthday in March,' his thin face taking on the sharp intense look it did when he was pleased. 'It's serious?'

'About as serious as could be.' Martin looked over his shoulder. 'She has to get a divorce, she'll want to . . .' He was breaking their rule about never consulting each other on social occasions. 'Well, I'll get her to come along and see you, shall I?'

Adrian said very sympathetically, 'Anything I can do to help, you know that. And Martin – congratulations, I'm awfully glad.'

Congratulations seemed a bit premature. They had only known each other for a month. But he was sure, he was certain that no one else would ever suit him as Francesca did. And if, before he could get her entirely as his own, there had to be a divorce and sordidness and haggling over property and maybe trouble with his family, well – he must go through it and endure it, knowing it was all worth while with Francesca at the end of it.

Russell was to take Lindsay to Cambridge by train on Friday evening, having first collected her from the nursery. Martin was going to pick Francesca up at the shop. He had wondered several times why he had queried her saying that

Russell's parents lived in Cambridge. Of course she must know where her own parents-in-law lived. It must have sounded to her as if he doubted her, as if he thought she had been lying. When he phoned her at the shop he apologized for what he had said, he couldn't imagine why he had thought they lived in Oxford, he didn't want her to think he was accusing her of any sort of deception. Francesca only laughed and said she had forgotten all about it, she hadn't been in the least upset.

The weather had been growing steadily colder since Christmas, it had snowed and thawed and frozen. Mr Cochrane, wearing a fur hat that made him look like a bespectacled Brezhnev, arrived late for him, at twenty-five to nine, announcing bitterly that he had fallen over on the ice and thought he had broken his arm. However, since he had intercepted the postman and was holding a letter in his right hand and his attaché case in his left, Martin decided he must be exaggerating. Mr Cochrane made a sling for his arm out of his woolly scarf. He didn't mention his sister-in-law beyond uttering the single word 'Terrible!' when Martin asked after her. He made a disgusted reconnaissance of the flat, running his fingers through dust on the woodwork and muttering that some folks were useless when they had to look after themselves. Martin took no notice. He was reading the letter.

Dear Mr Urban,

I am very sad to have to tell you that my father died on December 11. He seemed quite well and in good spirits the previous evening but was found dead in his armchair when the home help came in at nine. Apparently he had just been going through his post and your cheque was found beside him. I am at a loss to know why you should have sent my father a cheque for what seems an enormous sum to me, but I am returning it with apologies for not having sent it back sooner.

Yours sincerely,

Judith Lewis.

Martin was horrified. Had he, in effect, killed poor Mr Deepdene with kindness? It rather looked like it. Mr Deepdene had been seventy-four and perhaps his heart hadn't been very sound, and although he had known the money was coming, the actual arrival of the cheque would be a different matter from hopeful, perhaps doubtful, anticipation of it. Martin imagined him opening the envelope, taking out the brief one-line note, then the cheque, and his aged, tired heart suddenly – what exactly *did* happen in a heart attack? Well, whatever it was, his heart failing and stopping with the wonderful, unbelievable shock of it, his body falling back into the armchair, the cheque fluttering from his lifeless hand . . .

'You want to mind how you go on that ice, Martin,' shouted Mr Cochrane above the vacuum cleaner. 'You want to watch your step, it's very treacherous, look at my arm. I reckon I've dislocated something, put something out, so don't be surprised if I don't turn up next week, Martin.'

The death of Mr Deepdene troubled Martin for most of the day. A client, an up-and-coming country singer, took him out to lunch but he didn't really enjoy himself and he didn't feel he was being very lucid as he tried to explain, over coffee, why the cost of setting up a music room in the singer's Hampstead home might be tax deductible while a swimming pool certainly would not be. He kept imagining Mr Deepdene, whom he saw as small and bent and frail, reading the sum delineated on that cheque and then the pain thundering up his arm and his chest.

Was he wrong to do what he was doing or attempting to do? Was he playing God without the wisdom and experience essential to a god? All he had done with his philanthropy so far, it seemed to him, was to frighten an old woman into insomnia and shock an old man to death. There was, of course, Suma Bhavnani, but for all he knew Suma Bhavnani might have died on the operating table. Yet surely his project was so simple, just to provide homes for a handful of needy people who suffered particularly from London's housing shortage. He wrote a letter of sympathy to Judith Lewis and that made him feel better – or perhaps it was knowing that in an hour he would be with Francesca which made him feel better. Mr Deepdene, after all, might well have had a heart attack whether he had sent him a cheque or not. He was old, past his three score and ten, and it was what people called a lovely way to go, dying like that in the midst of life . . .

Floreal was glowing with flame-coloured light, its window banked with pots of pink cyclamen. Francesca came out to him, wearing the rose velvet dress. She must have just changed, after the other girl had gone, especially for him. If it could be said that Martin disliked anything at all about Francesca, it was her clothes. Most of the time she wore jeans, flounced skirts with hems that dipped, shapeless tunics, 'antique' blouses, shawls, big loose cardigans, scarves with fringes. She dressed like the hippies used to, a pair of scuffed seven-league boots poking out under a skirt of wilted flower-sprigged cotton. These things couldn't spoil her beauty, they merely disguised it. But in the pink velvet her beauty was enhanced, you could see the fragile wand-like shape of her, her tiny waist, her long legs, and the rose colour was exactly that of her cheeks. She put her arms round him and kissed him with tenderness.

As soon as they were in the flat he gave her her Christmas present. The cut-glass bottles with the silver stoppers had come to seem inadequate somehow, so after lunch with the country singer he had bought some *Ma Griffe* cologne with which to fill them. It was odd, but although she admired the bottles and said they were pretty, beautiful really, she'd never seen anything so delicate, he sensed that she was disappointed. He asked her directly but she said no, not a bit, it was just that she hadn't got anything for him and she felt bad about that.

After they had had dinner – steaks which he grilled and a salad which she made – he asked her if Russell would expect her to phone him but she said she and Russell had had a violent quarrel and weren't on speaking terms.

'It was about you, Martin. I told him I was in love with someone else.'

Martin held her hands. She came closer to him on the sofa and laid her head on his shoulder. 'You're going to leave him and get a divorce and marry me, aren't you?'

'I want to, I don't know . . .'

'There's nothing to stop you. I love you and you say you love me . . .'

'I do love you, Martin!'

'You could stay here. We could go up there tomorrow and fetch your things and you need never go back there again.'

She said nothing but put her arms round him. Later, in the bedroom, he watched her undress. She seemed to have no self-consciousness about this, no false modesty, and no desire provocatively to show off. She undressed rather slowly and concentratedly, like a young child. Her body was extraordinarily white for someone with such dark hair and eyes, her waist a narrow stem, her ankles and feet finely turned. She managed to be extravagantly thin, yet curvy and without angularity. He thought of fairy girls in Arthur Rackham drawings – and then, laying her clothes on a chair, she turned her left side to him.

Her upper arm was badly bruised and there was a kind of red contusion on her forearm. But that was as nothing to the bruising on her hip, black and blue and swollen, and all down the side of her thigh to her knee.

'Francesca . . . !'

He could tell she wished he hadn't seen. She tried ineffectively to cover her body with her arms.

'How on earth did that happen to you?' The explanation would never have occurred to him, he had never lived in that sort of world, if he hadn't seen the ashamed misery in her eyes and remembered what she had said about a quarrel. 'You don't mean that Russell . . . ?'

She nodded. 'It's not the first time. But this – this was the worst.'

He took her very gently in his arms and held the bruised body close to his. 'You must come to me,' he murmured. 'You must leave him, you must never go back.'

But on the following day she wouldn't let him fetch her things from the house in Fortis Green Lane. At the end of the weekend she must go home again as they had arranged, she must be home before Russell and Lindsay returned. Martin didn't persist. The last thing he wanted was to spoil the three precious days they had together. On Saturday afternoon they went shopping in Hampstead. Martin had never before been round dress shops with a woman and he found it boring and alarming, both at the same time. Francesca admired extravagantly a coat and dress in grey suede, a pair of tapered pants in cream leather and a dress that seemed quite impractical to Martin, being made of transparent knife-pleated beige chiffon. Francesca didn't notice prices, he knew that, she was naïve about that sort of thing, like a child in a toyshop. It crossed his mind to buy her the coat and dress but then he saw it was three hundred pounds and he didn't have that much in his current account. Besides, what would Russell say – what would Russell *do* – if she brought something like that home with her? In the end, because she looked so wistful, he asked her to let him buy her the little short-sleeved jumper which was the latest thing to catch her fancy. Martin thought fifteen pounds a ridiculous amount to pay for it, but that didn't matter if it made Francesca happy.

They went to the theatre and then to supper at Inigo Jones. Norman Tremlett called in unexpectedly in the morning at about ten-thirty. Francesca had only just got up and she came out of the bathroom in her dressing gown. It was very obvious she had nothing on underneath it. Martin saw with a good deal of pride and pleasure that Norman's eyes were going round in excited circles like a dog's following the movements of a fly. He stayed for coffee. Francesca didn't bother to go and dress. She was quite innocent of the sensation she was causing and sat there talking earnestly about the play they had seen as if Norman were her brother or she wearing a tweed suit and a pair of brogues.

'You're a dark horse,' Norman whispered admiringly as Martin saw him out. 'I never would have thought it of you. D'you often do this sort of thing?'

Deep down, Martin rather loved being treated as a Casanova. But it wasn't right to allow it, it was a reflection on Francesca, on her – well, virtue, if that term still had any meaning today.

'We're going to be married.'

'Are you? Are you really? That's perfectly splendid.' Norman hesitated on the doorstep. 'At the wedding,' he said, 'I suppose – I suppose you'll have Adrian for your best man?'

Martin laughed. 'It won't be that sort of wedding.'

'I see. Right. That's fine. Only if you do need any – well, anyone, you know what I mean – well, you know where to come.'

On New Year's Day, Francesca wore the jumper he had bought her. It showed up the bruises on her arm and she wrapped herself in one of her shawls. At four o'clock she said she ought to go. She would pack her things and go and get a taxi in Highgate High Street. Russell and Lindsay would be home by six at the latest.

'Of course I'm going to drive you home, Francesca.'

'Darling Martin, there's no need, really, there isn't. It's been snowing again and it's bound to freeze tonight and you might have a skid. You don't want to damage your nice car.'

'The taxi might skid and damage nice you. Anyway, I insist on taking you, I'm not going to be put off this time. Russell won't be there to see us arrive if that's what worries you. I'm going to drive you home and if you try to stop me I shall just put you in the car by force. Right?'

'Yes, Martin, of course. I won't argue any more. You're so sweet and kind to me and I'm a horrid ungrateful girl.'

'No, you're not,' he said. 'You're an angel and I love you.'

He had never thought much about the house she lived in but now that he was going to see it, he felt the stirrings of curiosity. He had probably driven along Fortis Green Lane in the past but he couldn't recall it. It was Finchley really, that area, borders of Muswell Hill. While Francesca was packing her case he looked it up in the London Atlas. There was no telling from that whether the district was seedy terraces, luxury suburban or given over to council housing. She came out and he helped her into the blue and red striped coat with the hood.

'If I'd known it was going to be so cold,' she said, 'I'd have brought my fur.' She gave him one of her serious, very young, smiles. 'I've got an old fur coat that was my grandmother's.'

'When we're married I'll buy you a mink. It'll be my wedding present to you.'

He drove up North Hill and into Finchley High Road. Fortis Green Lane ran out of Fortis Green Road towards Colney Hatch Lane. Francesca didn't issue directions, she wasn't that sort of woman. He got the impression, when she was with him, that she was content to let him organize things and steer her life his way. She wasn't so much passive as gracefully yielding. He took a left turn out of Fortis Green Road and they were in the street where she lived.

By now it was growing towards dusk and what daylight remained was clear and blue. Mustard yellow lamps, true opposite in the spectrum to that blue, were coming on in Fortis Green Lane. It was a long wide winding road, disproportionately wide for the small squat houses which lined it. Here and there was a short Victorian terrace, red brick and three storeys high, but the small low houses predominated and eventually took over altogether. They stood in blocks of four, some of brown stucco, some of very pale anaemic-looking brick with small metal-framed windows and shallow pantiled roofs. In their front gardens snow lay on the grass. They weren't bad houses, they weren't slums, but Martin thought he would go to any lengths to avoid living in such a place. He had always, in his heart, despised people who did. Couldn't Russell Brown, who was thirty-five years old and no slouch apparently, a teacher and a writer, have done better for his wife than this? Poor Francesca . . .

Number 54 was the end house of a block, which meant it had a side entrance. It stood on the corner of a side road depressingly called Hill Avenue in which were similar houses stretching away to be lost in the twilight. Their roofs were so low that over the tops of them you could see the branches of trees which Martin guessed must be in Coldfall Wood. He got out of the car and helped Francesca out. There were no lights on in her house. Her husband and child hadn't yet returned. Carrying her suitcase, Martin began to unlatch the small white wrought iron gate.

'You mustn't come in, darling.' She had taken his arm and was looking nervously up into his face.

'Would it matter so much if Russell and I were to meet? We're sure to some day. I'm sure he wouldn't do anything to me.'

'No, but he might do something to me later.'

The truth of this was evident. He had seen the bruises. It wasn't much of a disappointment not seeing the inside of her house. Compared with what he felt about parting from her, not to see her again for perhaps a whole week, it was nothing. He didn't think she would kiss him good-bye with the chance of some neighbour seeing, but she did. Out there in the street she put her arms round his neck and kissed him on the mouth, clinging to him for a moment. But Francesca was like that, too innocent to be aware of the cruelty and malice in other people's hearts.

He got back into the car. She stood there, waving to him, her small bright face made pale by the lamplight, her beautiful hair tucked inside her hood. He turned the car to go back the way he had come and when he looked round again she was gone.

I I

Although Martin had confided to Francesca most of what had happened to him in the past, his present circumstances and his hopes for the future, he hadn't said anything about the pools win. He didn't quite know why he hadn't. Perhaps it was because she was still living with her husband. He had a vague half-formed idea of Russell Brown as a thorough-going villain, in spite of his education and his talents. Suppose Francesca told Russell that the man she was in love with had won a hundred thousand pounds on a football pool? If he knew that, Russell might try to extort money from him. Martin thought he would only tell Francesca after she had left Russell and was living here with him in Cromwell Court.

After that weekend he didn't see her again, as he had feared, until the following Monday. On the afternoon of that day Dr Ghopal phoned to say that the operation on Suma Bhavnani had taken place on January 5 and been a complete success. This news had a tonic effect on Martin. Playing God was possible, after all. At lunchtime he had had a sandwich in the Victoria Stakes with Caroline and she had regaled him with a long sad tale about a young couple who were friends of hers and who were paying sixty per cent of their joint wages for the rent of a furnished flat. They had no children and the girl couldn't have children so they wouldn't get a council place, said Caroline, for five years, if then. The furnished flat was four draughty rooms in Friern Barnet. By telling a few white lies about knowing someone who knew someone who might possibly have an unfurnished flat to let in April, Martin managed to get these people's name and address out of Caroline. That night, after he had taken Francesca to dine at the Cellier du Midi and sent her home to Russell in a taxi, he added this new name to his list. It now read: Miss Watson, Mr Deepdene, Mrs Cochrane, Mrs Finn? Richard and Sarah Gibson. He crossed off Mr Deepdene's name, put a question mark after Mrs Cochrane's. Then he composed a letter to the Gibsons, beginning by mentioning the connection through Caroline Arnold and going on to ask if they would care to meet him one evening in the coming week to discuss accommodation he might be able to offer them. It obviously wasn't a good idea baldly to state in the preliminary letter that he was dispensing money in large quantities. Look what an effect that had had on Miss Watson and Mr Deepdene. Better meet and talk about it face to face, which was perhaps what he ought to have done and could still do with Miss Watson.

He hadn't said any more to Francesca about leaving Russell. He had hoped she would say something. Perhaps she hadn't liked to, she was such a self-effacing girl. Next time he saw her, he would insist on their making definite plans. He went about the flat, thinking what it would be like when she was there all the time. He would buy a three-piece suite, of course, and put that cane stuff in the bedroom. Or they could go out on the balcony, they would be an improvement on his two shabby deckchairs. The bathroom ought to be re-carpeted. Francesca would like that, a white carpet with a long pile. And maybe he should buy a wardrobe – the cupboard was full of his own clothes – and a dressing table.

Mr Cochrane would probably make a terrific fuss once he found out Martin was living with a woman. Martin could just imagine his face and his comments. They could always pretend to be married or, come to that, Mr Cochrane could be told to go and Francesca do the housework. Martin didn't want her to work in that flower shop or anywhere else once she had left Russell.

It could only have been a couple of hours after he got Martin's letter that Richard Gibson phoned. He was forthright and he sounded suspicious.

'Look, Mr Urban, Sarah and I have been badly let down

about this sort of thing before. If you're really making us a firm offer, that's fine and I'm grateful, but if it's just a possibility or someone else is likely to step in and get the place over our heads – well, we'd rather not know. And I'd better tell you here and now, we can't pay key money or a premium or anything, we haven't got it.'

Martin said the offer was firm and there was no question of key money but he'd rather talk about it when they met. Richard Gibson said any evening in the following week would suit him and the sooner the better, so Martin agreed to go up to Friern Barnet on Monday.

He got back early from the Flask on Saturday because Francesca was coming at two. She got there at five past, wearing the jumper he had bought her and smelling of *Ma Griffe*. He began at once to tell her of his plans for the flat when she came to live with him. When was she going to tell Russell? When would she leave? He supposed that she would want to bring a lot of her other possessions as well as clothes and they would have to . . .

'I can't come and live *here*, Martin.'

She spoke in a small nervous voice and she had begun to twist her hands together in her lap. He stared at her.

'What do you mean, Francesca?'

'I've thought about it a lot, I feel awful about it. But it's not possible. How could we live here? It wouldn't be big enough.'

'Not big enough?' He felt stunned. He repeated her words stupidly. 'What do you mean, not big enough? Nearly all the people in the other flats here are married couples. There's this huge room and a bedroom and a big kitchen and a bathroom. What more do you want?'

'It's not what I want, Martin, you know that. It's Lindsay. Where would we put Lindsay?'

He must have been a fool or totally obtuse, he thought, but it hadn't occurred to him that she would be bringing the child with her. To him, Lindsay was a part of Russell, or rather, she and Russell were part of the life lived in Fortis Green Lane. In leaving it behind, Francesca would be leaving behind all that belonged to it, walls, furniture, husband, child. But of course it couldn't be like that, he ought to have known. He ought to have known vicariously, if not from experience, that a mother doesn't desert her two-year-old child. Lindsay would become his child now. The idea was very disturbing. He lifted his eyes to meet Francesca's mournful eyes.

She would never know what an effort it cost him to say what he did. 'She can sleep in here or have a bed in our room.'

'Oh, dear, you do make it hard for me. Darling Martin, don't you see it wouldn't be right for the three of us to be living all crowded together like that.' It was hard to tell when Francesca was blushing, her cheeks were always so pink. 'She'd – she'd see us in bed together.'

'She sees you and Russell in bed together now.'

'He's her father. I can't take my little daughter away from her father and her home and her own room and bring her here where she'll have to sleep in a living room or on a couch or something.' Her lips trembled. When he put out his arms to her she laid her head against his shoulder and held on to him hard. 'Oh, Martin, you do understand?'

'I'll try to, darling. But what alternative do we have? There isn't anywhere else.'

His pride was bruised by her rejection of his home and he thought of the little box she lived in. After she had gone he began to feel angry with her. Did she expect him to leave the flat he was fond of and buy a house or something just to accommodate the child she had had by another man? This thought was immediately succeeded by another, that it was his Francesca, his love, that he was using those harsh words about. They would find a way, of course they would. Once Francesca had told Russell she wanted a divorce it might be that he would leave. Surely that was what husbands usually did? Martin wondered if he could possibly bring himself, say for a couple of days each week, to live in the house in Fortis Green Lane.

He got to Friern Barnet at the appointed time of eight on Monday evening. The flat was as nasty as Caroline had led him to believe, with bare, stained floorboards, the walls marked all over where other people's posters and pictures had hung. It was furnished partly with Woolworth chipboard and plastic and partly with pre-First World War pitch pine. The Gibsons gave him Nescafé and kept saying how surprised they were that he was young. Sarah Gibson was pale and rather big and dark-haired with a face like Elizabeth Barrett Browning, and her husband was fair and upright and looked like a Guards officer, though in fact he turned out to be a hospital porter on thirty-seven pounds a week.

When Martin told them – he found it very difficult to do this, he even began to stammer – that his intention was to give them money to buy a flat, they refused to believe him.

'But why?' Sarah Gibson kept saying. 'You don't know us. Why should you want to give us money?'

Martin said that he had 'come into' a fortune, which was strictly true. He explained his motives. He even described his experiences with Miss Watson and Mr Deepdene. He had wanted to find a young couple, he said.

'OK, that's fine for you, but what about us? We'd be under an obligation to you all our lives, we'd be sort of tied to you. Anyway, you must want something out of it.'

Martin felt helpless. He couldn't think of any more to say and he wished he hadn't come. Then Richard Gibson said:

'If you're really serious, we'd borrow it from you. I mean, we're both teachers only we can't get jobs. We'd borrow it from you and when we get proper jobs we'd start paying it back like a mortgage.'

That wasn't what Martin had wanted but it was the only arrangement the Gibsons would agree to. He said he would have to do it through a friend of his who was a solicitor. His friend, Adrian Vowchurch, would draw up an agreement for an interest-free loan and he would be in touch with Richard Gibson in a day or two. Sarah Gibson sat staring at him, bewildered and frowning.

Her husband, seeing Martin out, said, 'I honestly don't expect to see you or hear from you again. You see, I don't believe you, I can't.'

'Time will show,' said Martin.

He felt angry. Not so much with the Gibsons as with the world, society, civilization, so-called, which must be in a pretty terrible state if you couldn't perform an act of altruism without people thinking you were mad. Sarah Gibson had thought he was schizophrenic, he had seen it in her eyes. He drove down across the North Circular Road and into Colney Hatch Lane, passing very near to Francesca's home. But Francesca wouldn't be there now, it was Monday and she had gone to Annabel's, she had told him so on Saturday.

How much he would love to see her now! Maybe the time had come for him to tell her about the money and how he had come by it, or if not that, it would simply be lovely to be with her and talk to her. He was aware of something he never remembered knowing before he had met her – loneliness. It was nearly nine o'clock. Why shouldn't he go to Annabel's place in Frognal and pick her up and drive her home? He didn't know Annabel's surname but he knew the house she lived in. He had parked outside its gate after their second meeting to say good-bye to Francesca. Would she mind his calling for her? He didn't think so. She had met Norman Tremlett at his flat, now it was time for him to begin meeting her friends.

For all his convincing arguments, he felt apprehensive as he drove across Hampstead Lane. Annabel knew of his existence, he told himself, even Russell knew of it. He wasn't doing anything clandestine or dishonourable, he was simply calling at a friend's house for the woman who was going to be his wife. Young men all over London were doing the same. He drove down past the Whitestone Pond into Branch Hill. A little snow still lay in patches on the brown turf of Judge's Walk. There was mist in the air, a damp icy breath. He drew the car into the kerb at the top of Frognal and crossed the road. As soon as he was alone with Francesca he would tell her he intended to put the flat on the market and buy a house for the three of them. Would she consent to live in Cromwell Court with him until he could do that?

The house outside which he had parked that night in

November was large, almost a mansion, with a front garden full of leafless shrubs and small grey alpine plants dripping over steps and the rims of urns. It appeared to be divided into three flats and Martin was rather taken aback to find that there were no names but only numbers to the bells. He had taken very little notice of the house on that previous occasion but now, looking up at its brown bricks and half-timbering, red shingles and red tiles, seemingly numberless windows of both plain and stained glass, he wondered how any young girl on her own, a friend and contemporary of Francesca's could afford to live in a place like this. Then, because the top storey seemed the smallest and the least grand, he rang the top bell.

After about a minute a woman opened the door. She was probably forty, a good-looking blonde, very well-dressed but for her footwear which was a fluffy pair of bedroom slippers. Martin apologized for disturbing her. Could she tell him in which of the flats someone with the christian name of Annabel lived? He was calling for his fiancée who was a friend of hers. Martin balked a little at calling someone else's wife his fiancée, yet it had the required respectable ring to it.

'Annabel?' said the woman. 'There isn't anyone called that here.'

'There must be. A young girl living on her own.'

'There's myself and my two sons, we have the top floor. Mr and Mrs Cameron have the middle flat. They're elderly and they haven't any children. The ground floor's occupied by Sir John and Lady Bidmead – the painter, you've probably heard of him – and it's them the house belongs to, they own it. I've known them for twenty years and they certainly don't have a daughter.'

It had occurred to Martin while she was speaking that Francesca hadn't actually pointed to this house and said Annabel lived there. It was possible she had meant the house next door. He went next door, a slightly smaller place, semi-detached. An elderly man answered his ring. The owner of the house was a Mrs Frere who occupied the whole of it and whom he referred to as the employer of himself and his wife.

Martin called at two more houses but at neither had Annabel been heard of.

The astonishment he felt softened the edge of his disappointment at not seeing Francesca. He tried to remember what had happened on the evening of November 27. She had got out of the car, turned back to say to him, 'Call for me at the shop,' and then disappeared in the heavy rain. It had been pouring with rain and he hadn't been able to see much but he knew she had asked him to park here, had said that Annabel lived just here.

Was Annabel an invention then? Had Francesca made her up? There came into his mind the confusion over where Russell's parents lived. She had said Oxford that first time, he knew she had. He went up into the flat and without putting a lamp on, sat at the window, looking down over London. He saw spangled towers drowning in mist, he saw them, yet he saw nothing. He closed his eyes. Annabel as a creation to be presented to Russell for an alibi was feasible – but to *him*? What motive could she possibly have had? Perhaps she lived a fantasy life in a fantasy world, he had heard of people like that. Perhaps none of the people she had told him about existed – but that wasn't true, of course they did. Russell got his name in the papers and there was no doubting the fact of Lindsay. He put the lights on and drew the curtains and poured himself a whisky. What was the matter with him that he doubted her like this and questioned the very foundations of her being? She had small fantasies, that was all. She slightly distorted the truth as some people did to make themselves appear more interesting. That night in November she had told him she had a friend living in an exclusive part of Hampstead to impress him, and later she couldn't go back on what she had said. Russell's parents very likely lived in Reading or Newmarket but the two great universities had come into her head as more glamorous and intriguing.

He lay awake most of the night, thinking about her and wondering and sometimes feeling rather sick.

Lately he had been in the habit of phoning her every day, but he let the next day and the next go by without speaking to her. Francesca didn't work on Thursdays. She had told him she spent her Thursdays shopping and cleaning the house and taking Lindsay out. Perhaps she did. He wondered if anything she had told him was true. He went to dinner with his parents, the usual Thursday night Three Bears get-together. His mother said a neighbour of hers had seen him shopping in Hampstead with a very pretty dark girl, but Martin shook his head and said she was mistaking him for someone else.

In the morning he phoned Adrian Vowchurch and explained the arrangement he had come to with Richard Gibson. Adrian gave no sign of surprise at hearing that Martin had fifteen thousand pounds to lend or that he proposed to lend it free of interest. Martin had an appointment with a client at eleven. It was while he was talking to this man that Francesca phoned. He had to promise to call her back in half an hour, and for that half-hour endeavour to quiet his excitement and his fear while he explained to the client how, if he would spend a minimum of thirty days out of the country on business each year, he might get a proportion of his income free of tax. When he was alone his hand actually trembled as he picked up the receiver.

The explanation of the Annabel affair was so simple and obvious that he cursed himself for doubting her and for his three days of self-torture.

'Darling, Annabel moved away just after Christmas. She lives in Mill Hill now.'

'But they hadn't even heard of her in any of those houses I called at.'

Her voice was soft and sweetly indulgent. 'Now you called at the house where the old lady lives?'

'I just said so, and at the next two down.'

'But you didn't call at the fourth down?'

'Is *that* where she lives?'

'Lived, Martin,' said Francesca. 'Oh, Martin, did you really think I'd been lying to you and deceiving you? Don't you trust me at all?'

'It's because we're not really together,' he said. 'It's because I hardly ever see you. Days and days go by and I don't see you. It makes me wonder all the time about what you're doing and your other life. Francesca, if I put my flat up for sale and buy a house for you and me and Lindsay, would you come and live with me just till the sale went through?'

'Martin, darling . . .'

'Well, would you? It needn't be for more than three months and then we could all go and live in the house. Say you will.'

'Let's not talk about it on the phone, Martin. I'm wanted in the shop, anyway.'

He would have sent her flowers but that would have been coals to Newcastle, corn in Egypt. Instead, he took her a box of hand-made chocolates when he went to call for her at the shop on Monday. He parked the car in Hillside Gardens at a quarter to six and walked down through the cold misty dark to the shop. The grey fog in which its orange light gleamed fuzzily gave it the mysterious look of an enchanted cavern. Francesca wasn't alone. Lindsay was with her, perched up on the counter and occupied in pulling the fronds off a head of pampas grass.

'The nursery was closed,' Francesca said. 'Their heating's broken down. I thought of phoning you – but I did want to see you even if it couldn't be for long.'

He held her in his arms. 'You've had a hard day. Come to me and you needn't work, you can be at home with Lindsay all the time. I'll buy us a house.'

'Listen,' she said, 'I had a long talk with Russell. He says he'll divorce me after two years' separation but the trouble is Lindsay. Russell adores her, you have to understand that. And he says – he says – ' her lips trembled and she had difficulty in bringing out her next words, ' – he says that if I – take her to live with you – he'll ask the divorce judge for custody of – of her – and – and – he'd get it!'

'Francesca, I think that's nonsense. Why would he?'

'He knows about these things, Martin. He's studied the law.'

'I thought he was a history teacher.'

'Well, of course he is but he's studied the law as well. He

says he's been as much a mother to Lindsay as I have, fetching her from the nursery and getting her tea and putting her to bed, and he says the judge would see he could look after her on his own, like he often has, and he'd be leading a moral life while I'd be taking her to live in two rooms with my lover!'

Lindsay threw the pampas grass on to the floor and began whimpering. Francesca started to say more about what Russell would do if she took his child to live under Martin's roof, but Lindsay stamped across the counter and pinched her mother's lips together. She said to Martin, though not in a friendly way:

'We're going home in a taxi.'

'Francesca, let me drive you home. You'll never get a taxi out there and the fog's getting thicker.'

'Really, no, Martin.' Francesca struggled and mumbled like Papageno with his padlock. 'Stop it, Lindsay, I'll put you on the floor.'

'But why won't you let me drive you? We'll be there in ten minutes.' Martin hesitated. 'Anyway, think of me, it would give me ten minutes of your company.'

'I want to see my Daddy,' said Lindsay.

'Is it Russell seeing me that worries you? I promise to drop you a hundred yards from the house. How's that?'

'All right, Martin,' said Francesca in the sweet meek voice he loved. 'You drive us home. I don't meant to be ungrateful, it's very very kind of you.'

12

The drive took much longer than ten minutes because of the dense fog. The sky itself, smoky, choking, gloomy white, seemed to have fallen through the dark on to the upper reaches of Highgate. Each car was guided by the tail lights of the one in front, lights that looked as if their feeble glow came through cloudy water.

Lindsay sat on Francesca's knee, helping herself to chocolates out of the box Martin had brought. She liked most of the flavours but not the violet cream or liqueur cherry and when she had taken a bite out of these she pushed the remains into Francesca's mouth. Silver paper went all over the floor of Martin's nice clean car.

Francesca could see Martin was offended at this cavalier treatment of his present but she didn't care about that. He didn't like Lindsay and he showed it, and to Francesca this was so monstrous that whenever she felt like giving the whole business up and just getting out or telling the truth, she thought of how he looked at and spoke to Lindsay and she hardened her heart and went on. He was looking at her like that, now, while they were stopped at a red traffic light. It was the kind of look a polite host gives to a guest's uninvited dog.

'You see, Martin, she'd soon make a mess of your lovely tidy flat.'

'Maybe, but things would be different if we had a house. We could have a big kitchen and a playroom, we'd have a garden. Look, I can see that's valid, what you said about it's not being right to let your child sleep on a couch in the living room. So suppose I put the flat on the market tomorrow and start to look

115

for a house for the three of us and you stay with Russell just until the house is ready to move into. How does that sound?'

'I don't know, Martin.'

'Well, darling, will you think about it? Will you, please, because I ask you and I want it so much? You see, I don't know what else to suggest. You do *want* to come and live with me, don't you?'

It was so cold and foggy and she had a long awkward journey ahead of her. She hadn't the nerve to say no. She touched his arm and smiled.

'Well, then. You won't live with me at the flat and you won't come and stay there with me till we can get a house, so I'm asking you to think about this idea. Will you think about it, darling?'

'I really don't think I'll ever . . .' Francesca started to say when Lindsay clamped a chocolate-smeary hand over her mouth. She didn't have to finish because Martin was parking the car. They had arrived.

She put Lindsay out on to the pavement and got out herself. It was very cold and wet out there, rain penetrating the fog in large icy drops. Martin wanted her to kiss him so she put her head back in through the window and held up to him red lips that a raindrop had already splashed.

'I'll phone you in the morning, Francesca.'

'Yes, do,' said Francesca vaguely. She was holding on to Lindsay with one hand and clasping the chocolate box against herself with the other. Lindsay was pulling and stamping.

'And you'll have come to a decision? You'll decide it's yes, won't you?'

Francesca had more or less forgotten what she was meant to be deciding. Again she said she didn't know but she managed a radiant smile, keeping her options open. Martin drove off waving, though with that hurt look on his face which so exasperated her.

When the car was out of sight she started to walk along Fortis Green Lane in the opposite direction to that which Martin had followed. He had put them down outside number 26 and when they reached 54, Francesca stopped for a moment and looked curiously at the house. It was unlit. On its doorstep was a bottle of milk with a cover over it to stop birds pecking at the cream.

'Mummy carry,' said Lindsay.

'Must I?'

'Must. Lindsay carry sweeties.'

'That's an offer I can't refuse.'

Francesca picked her up and Lindsay gave her a wet sticky kiss on the cheek and waved the chocolate box about. Perhaps it would be a good idea to turn up Hill Avenue? Francesca rejected it and tramped on. The pavement was coated with greyish-black, soupy, liquid mud that splashed up her legs. She realized what she had thought was rain was in fact condensed fog dripping from the tall bushes in front gardens. She felt like one of those women who abound in Victorian fiction, women who are discovered at the beginning of a chapter wandering over heaths or stumbling along city streets at night and in the most inclement weather with a child in their arms. Very likely she looked like one of them too in her lace-up boots and long skirt and woolly shawl wound round her head and her grandmother's old fur coat, spiky and dewed with drops of fog. In spite of the cold and the heavy weight of the·little girl and her own tiredness, Francesca suddenly laughed out loud.

'Not funny,' said Lindsay crossly.

'No, it isn't, you're quite right, it isn't a bit funny. You'll find out when you're grown-up that we don't always laugh just because things are funny. There are other reasons. I must be mad. Why did I let him bring us up here, Lindsay? I suppose I was so utterly pissed-off with seeing that look on his face. One thing I do know, I'm not going to see him any more, I'm not going on with it, this is the end, this is it. And Daddy can go – go jump in a pond!'

'Lindsay wants Daddy.'

'Yes, well, he won't get home till after we do even at this rate, so shut up. I want my Daddy I want my Daddy, you're a real pain sometimes.'

'I want my Daddy,' said Lindsay. She screwed up a chocolate paper and threw it into someone's garden.

'We're going to have a bus ride first. You'll like that, you never go on buses. Come on, hoist up a bit. Can't you sort of sit on my hip?'

Lindsay replied by dropping the box and pinching Francesca's lips together. Francesca picked up the box which was now much splashed with mud and growled through Lindsay's fingers and pretended to bite. Lindsay screamed with laughter, took her hand away an inch and clamped it back again.

'Come on, you crazy kid, we'll freeze to death.'

By now they had come out into Coppetts Road and Francesca was looking about her for bus stops when a taxi, which had perhaps dropped an inmate or a visitor, came out of the gates of Coppetts Wood Hospital with its light on. The driver didn't seem to know the whereabouts of Samphire Road, N4, even when Francesca said it wasn't far from Crouch Hill station, but he agreed to let her direct him. Lindsay started screaming that she'd been promised a bus, she wanted a bus, and she made so much noise that Francesca could tell, by the back of his neck, that the driver was wincing. She stuffed Lindsay with more chocolate to shut her up and then they played the growl and snap game most of the way home. The fare was two pounds which Francesca could ill afford.

The pavements here were even stickier and more slippery than in Finchley. It was a depressed, semi-derelict region to which the taxi had brought them, a place where whole ranks of streets had been demolished to make way for new council building. Acres of muddy ground stood bare between half-dismantled ruins, and some of the streets had become mere narrow lanes running between temporary fences ten feet high. Even in the driest weather the roadways were muddy, smeared with clay from the tyres of tractors and lorries. There was an air of impermanence, of dull, unhopeful expectancy, as of the squalid old giving place to a not much more inviting new.

But Samphire Road was sufficiently on the borders of this resurgent neighbourhood for it and the streets which joined it and ran parallel to it, to be left alone. Samphire Road, with its rampart-like houses of cardboard-coloured brick, its grave-sized front gardens, its ostentatious treelessness, was to be allowed to live out its century undisturbed and survive until at least 1995. Sulphur-coloured lamplight turned the fog into just such a pea-souper as Samphire Road had known in its youth.

Francesca unlocked the front door of number 22, painted, some years before, the shade of raw calves' liver, and let herself and Lindsay through an inner door into the hall of the ground floor flat. Inside it was as cold as only an old house can be which has no central heating, which has been empty for ten hours, and when the month is January. It was damp as well as cold, with a damp to make you cringe. Francesca put lights on and humped Lindsay into the kitchen where she lit the gas oven and switched on an electric wall heater. Breakfast dishes were still stacked in the sink. She unwrapped Lindsay's layers of clothes and then her own layers, spreading her fur coat over the back of a chair to dry. The two of them squatted down in front of the open oven and held out their hands to the pale bluish-mauve flames.

After a while Lindsay said her feet were cold, so Francesca went to look for her furry slippers. In the hall it was as cold as out in the street. There were only two other rooms in the flat, the front room where there were two armchairs and a dining table and a piano and a sofa that converted into a double bed, and the bedroom at the back where Lindsay slept. Francesca drew the curtains across the huge, draughty, stained-glass french windows and lit the gas fire. The gas fire had to be on for at least an hour before she could put Lindsay to bed in that ice box. The slippers were nowhere to be seen, so Francesca went into the other room (known as the sitting room but where no one could have borne to sit between November and April) and found the slippers under the piano. The bed wasn't made. It hadn't been made for several days and it hadn't been used as a sofa more than half a dozen times since Lindsay was born.

Lindsay said, 'Where's my Daddy?'

'Gone to some meeting about historic Hornsey.'

'I'm not going to bed till my Daddy comes.'

'OK, you don't have to.' Francesca made her scrambled eggs and buttered fingers of brown bread. She sat at the table drinking tea while Lindsay plastered chocolate spread on bread and biscuits and even on to a piece of Swiss roll. Lindsay adored chocolate spread, they had had to take sandwiches of it for their lunch. Francesca wiped it off Lindsay's chin and the tablecloth and the wall where a blob of it had landed. She was thinking about Martin. It was like heaven being in the flat in Cromwell Court and in that warm car and eating in the Villa Bianca. She loved comfort and luxury and longed wistfully after them, perhaps, she thought, because she had never known them, had been too busy living to look for them before. That weekend with Martin had shaken her, the warmth and ease, so that, in spite of the boredom, she had actually thought of becoming the girl he thought she was. Not just sweet and obedient and passive and clinging and Victorian, but the girl who was going to get a divorce and marry Martin and live with him for ever . . .

'There's my Daddy,' said Lindsay.

The front door banged and there was a sound of feet being wiped on the doormat. Francesca didn't get up and though Lindsay did, bouncing off her chair, she wasn't going to venture into that freezing passage, not even to greet her long-awaited father. He opened the kitchen door and came in, throwing back a lock of wet hair out of his eyes.

'Hi,' said Francesca.

'Hi.' He picked up the little girl, held her in the air, then hugged her to him. 'And how's my sweetheart? How did you get on in Mummy's shop? I bet they made you manageress.' He sang to the tune of the Red Flag, 'The working class can kiss my arse, I've got the boss's job at last!'

'Oh, Tim,' said Francesca, 'we've had an awful evening out in the sticks. Wait till you hear!'

13

'So I just don't see the point of carrying on with it,' said Francesca. She and Tim confronted each other across the kitchen table and across the greasy pieces of paper and copy of the *Post* which had wrapped the fish and chips brought in by Tim for their supper. The kitchen was now very warm and smoky, the windows running with condensation. Lindsay had been put to bed ten minutes before. 'Can I have another cigarette, please? I can't smoke when I'm with him, it doesn't go with the image and it nearly kills me, I can tell you.'

Tim gave her a cigarette. He frowned a little, pushing out his red lips, but he spoke quite lightly in his usual faintly ironic drawl. 'Yes, but, honey, why suddenly throw your hand in now? Why *now* when everything is going so extremely well? I mean, even in our wildest fantasies we didn't foresee he'd fall for you quite so heavily. Or has he?' Tim's eyes narrowed. 'Maybe mah honey chile wasn't being strictly truthful when she said Livingstone wanted to marry her.'

'Well, I'm not always absolutely truthful, Tim, you know that. Who is? But I don't tell pointless lies. Oh, dear, I nearly came a cropper over Annabel, though, didn't I?' Francesca giggled and her eyes met Tim's blue eyes and she giggled even more. 'Oh, dear. Now we must be serious. What I mean is, I don't see the point of carrying on with it because it's not getting us anywhere. All it'll do is lose me my job. If he takes to coming into the shop after me I'll have to leave to get away from him. What did we think we'd get out of it, Tim? I can't even remember.'

'Of course you can remember. Money. Prospects. Opportunities.' Tim lit a Gauloise. 'And, incidentally, my little revenge.'

'Isn't it a funny thing? He says he loves me and all that but he doesn't exactly confide in me. He's never said a word about winning the pools and I don't believe he has.'

'You don't believe in your Uncle Tim's total recall? I tell you, if I died and they opened me up they'd find the perm on that pools coupon written on my heart. Of course, there's just the weeniest chance Miss Urban didn't send it in. But if Miss Urban *did* send it in then, sure as fate is fate, she's won herself the first dividend, all or part of, the lucky lucky girl.'

Tim always referred to Martin as Livingstone or, when his camp mood was on him, as Miss Urban. Francesca, for reasons she didn't understand but thought might be sick reasons, found the camp mood almost unbearably sexy. Tim, when he was that way, made her go weak at the knees and she didn't want that happening now, she wanted to be serious.

'Well,' she said, 'when you sent those awful yellow chrysanths, you said to get in his good graces and get him to take me out a bit because he'd got wads of money and hadn't got a girl friend. You said he might let me have the money to start my own florist's or at least give me some big presents. But nothing like that's happened. He just fell right in love with me. He's not even that interested in sex – well, not *very*. I mean, you'd have raped me if I'd gone on with you the way I have with him. But he's in love, it's not just wanting to screw me, it's real love. And the only place it's going to get me is living with him in his flat or some house he wants to buy. And what's the use of that? What's the use of going on with it, Tim, if I only get to where I have to run away and hide to avoid living with him?'

'One would think, wouldn't one,' said Tim thoughtfully, 'that Livingstone would have given you something more by now than those very strange decanters or whatever they are. Five grand is nothing, but nothing, to spend on a ring, say, or a bracelet in these inflationary times. What about furs? An' mah honey chile shiverin' in her ole coonskin.'

'He did say something about a mink,' said Francesca, giggling, 'when we're married.' She groped about under the fish and chip papers. 'He did give me some chocolates tonight only Lindsay's gobbled most of them. Here you are.'

'She's a chip of the old block all right, she's only left the nougats and the coconuts.'

'The latest is he wants to sell his flat and buy a house for him and me and Lindsay, so I suppose he must have money.'

'Now she tells me. Francesca, what d'you think Krishna Bhavnani told me today? That it was Livingstone put up the money for his kid's operation.'

'Are you going to put something about it in the *Post*?'

'If you're quitting, yes. If you're keeping on, no. Just as untruths have been known to appear in the *Post*, so have truths sometimes been suppressed.'

Francesca laughed. She came behind Tim and put her hands round his shoulders and stroked the Nureyev face. 'Tim, I could keep it up a little bit longer, I could see him on Wenesday, if you really think it's worth while. Now I know about the Indian boy, I could have a go at getting a fur coat. Or a ring. We could sell a ring.'

Tim rubbed his face against her hands, making purring noises. 'Did you switch our blanket on?'

He had bought them an electric blanket for Christmas. 'When I took Lindsay to bed,' she said.

'Then why don't you take me to bed and tell me all about the times you've misbehaved yourself with Dr Livingstone?'

'Miss Urban,' said Francesca somewhat breathlessly.

'Mah honey chile should tak' shame talking like dat befo' her Uncle Tim, Lawd God!'

Francesca and Tim had been living together for three years. Tim had moved into the flat in Samphire Road, instead of just spending nights there, when Francesca found she was pregnant with Lindsay. They had never really considered getting married and couldn't have done anyway since Francesca was still married to Russell Brown. After Tim had met Martin Urban in the wood he had several times invited him to Samphire Road but Martin always refused, Tim hadn't known why.

He had been wounded by it, Francesca thought, though Tim never showed that he could feel pain. Then had come the Saturday in November when Tim checked his pools and found, as usual, that he had won nothing while the formula he had given Martin must have scooped the first dividend.

It had disturbed Francesca to see Tim waiting for Martin to phone. Her placid happy-go-lucky nature was ruffled by Tim's intense neurotic anxiety. The days had passed and there had been nothing. As taut as a bowstring, Tim had gone to that interview at Urban, Wedmore, Mackenzie and Company, but still Martin hadn't spoken. The worst thing for Tim had been Martin's refusing to come to the party. Getting a party organized at Samphire Road was no mean feat. They had cancelled it at the last minute because there was nothing much to celebrate and no point in opening the champagne.

'I fear,' Tim had said, camping it up, pretending, 'she's keeping it all the darkest because she doesn't want to have to give any to poor me. Though what I've done I never will know, save be friendly and helpful. Maybe I wasn't quite friendly enough, which some girls, you know, can resent.'

Francesca couldn't hazard an opinion on that but she knew Tim had hoped for something from Martin, even a loan to help them buy a place that would be a cut above Samphire Road. He walked up and down shouting that he would be revenged. He would get hold of some of that money by hook or by crook. After that it was a short step for Francesca to go round with the flowers and – hang on hard.

She was a good-tempered easy-going girl and nothing put her out for long. Tim had once told her that one of the things he liked about her was that she had no morals and no guilt. This made playing the part of Martin's Francesca, the moral and guilty Francesca, rather difficult at first, but Tim had instructed her and even set her a course of reading, Victorian and early twentieth-century fiction mainly, with suitable heroines. She had worked hard at moulding herself according to these models and sometimes after meetings with Martin she felt quite tired. She spent a lot of the time in his company silent and apparently raptly listening, while in fact she was concentrating on how to escape in a taxi and get out of being driven up to Finchley. Now she was faced with the additional problem of how to make Martin believe she loved him and wanted to live with him while refusing to submit to any plan for their living together he might make.

Accordingly, the next time he phoned, she said that she would hate to think of him selling his flat in order to buy a house. She knew how much he loved his flat.

'But I'll have to sell it one day, darling. When you're free and we can get married we'll need a house.'

'I'd much rather you waited till then, Martin.'

'Yes, but that doesn't solve the problem of how we're going to live *till* then, does it?'

That lunchtime, Francesca went across the Archway Road and sold the two cut-glass scent bottles for seventeen pounds fifty. All those taxis were making inroads into her resources and if Martin was taking her to dinner at the Mirabelle, as he had promised, on Wednesday she ought to have a new dress. She ought to try and rake up enough to buy the burgundy crêpe that Kate Ross, who owned the flower shop, had for weeks been trying to sell for twenty-five pounds.

Martin had got into the habit of ringing the shop every morning at ten. At two minutes to ten on Wednesday he phoned, sounding excited, and said he had had a wonderful idea which he would tell her about that night. Francesca went into the room at the back and tried on the burgundy crêpe which Kate had brought in with her and got Kate to agree to take twenty-three pounds fifty for it.

It started to snow at about five, great flakes like goose feathers. Kate always went home at half-past because she didn't have a day off or Saturday afternoon. Martin gasped at the sight of Francesca in the dark red dress with her hair piled up and a dark red and white speckled orchid tucked into a curl. He stared at her adoringly. These transports of his, though she knew they were sincere, always irritated Francesca. She preferred a lecherous reaction which was what she had had from

Russell Brown and those other men who had preceded Tim and which she had, in his own individual way, most satisfactorily from Tim. But she smiled and looked rather shy and said quietly:

'Do I look nice?'

'Francesca, you look so beautiful, I don't know what to say. I wish I was more articulate, I should like to write poems to you.'

'I just hope I'm going to be warm enough,' said Francesca, her mind on mink coats, but Martin assured her she would be exposed to the open air for no longer than it took to cross the pavement.

'So what's this wonderful idea?' she said when they were in the car. Martin said he wasn't going to tell her until they were eating their dinner.

Francesca had an enormous appetite and a hearty capacity for alcohol. She and Tim were both the sort of very thin people who can eat as much as they like without putting on weight. But she never ate and drank anywhere near as much as she wanted when with Martin, it didn't fit the image. Tonight, however, she was going to start off with *quenelles* of lobster, *quenelles* of anything being among her favourite food. To precede it, a brandy and soda would have gone down well. Francesca asked for a dry sherry.

Martin's shyness and awkwardness increased during the meal. He had become almost tongue-tied by the time Francesca started on her roast pheasant, and although this suited her well enough, she couldn't help speculating as to what it might be about the wonderful idea that was so inhibiting. Then, suddenly, like a man confessing a sin that has long been on his conscience, he began. Fascinated, she watched the slow process of the blush spreading across his face.

'I haven't told anyone this except my parents. In November I won a hundred and four thousand pounds on the football pools. No, don't say anything, let me finish. I decided I'd keep half and give half away. You can imagine my reasons for wanting to do that.'

Francesca couldn't at all but she said nothing. She felt a curious breathless excitement as if she were on the brink of enormous revelations. Yet he was only confirming what Tim had said all along.

'You see, I felt grateful to – well, to fate or God or something for having had such a fortunate sort of life. I made up my mind to help people who were having housing difficulties but I haven't got very far with that, it's much harder than you'd suppose to get people to accept money. All I've managed to do so far really is pay for a boy to have a heart operation.'

'That's not housing difficulties,' said Francesca.

'No, that was to be the one exception. Apart from that, I'm considering my cleaner's sister-in-law who's having a nervous breakdown because of noise in the place where she lives, and I've managed to get a young couple on very low wages to accept a loan.'

He was smiling tentatively at her, leaning forward, waiting for her approval. Francesca looked blankly at him. It occurred to her that he might actually be off his head. But, no, he was just innocent, he didn't know he was born . . . Suppose she were to throw herself on his mercy, tell him who she was and that Tim was her lover and Lindsay's father and that they were doomed to live in worse conditions than maybe any of those people he had talked about? She couldn't do it, it was impossible. He re-filled her wine glass and said:

'So now I've told you. I don't want to have any secrets from you.' As if he'd just confessed to some weird perversion, thought Francesca. 'But the point of telling – well, I've been a complete fool. I've been worrying about buying homes for other people and worrying about where you were going to live when you left Russell, but it never occurred to me till last night that I don't have to sell my flat or get a mortgage. Apart from what I'm going to give away, I've got fifty thousand of my own. I've got my own half-share of the win.'

'So what's the wonderful idea?' said Francesca carefully.

'To buy a flat for you and Lindsay to live in.' He paused but she said nothing. 'I mean, that solves everything, doesn't it?

Lindsay can have her own room, Russell can't possibly accuse you of corrupting her, and after two years when you've got your divorce we can sell both flats and buy a house. How does that suit you? I'm not going to make any conditions, Francesca . . .' Martin smiled and reached across the table for her hand, ' . . . only I hope I can come and stay sometimes and I'll be the happiest man on earth if you'll choose a flat that isn't far from mine.'

'So we're going house-hunting on Saturday. He's out on Cloud Nine already, planning colour schemes and fussing about something called cubic footage.'

'Miss Urban was always houseproud, she'll make some lucky chap a wonderful wife one of these days. What did you have to eat?'

'Lobster *quenelles*, roast pheasant and roast potatoes and calabresse and *sautéed* mushrooms *and* asparagus, and a sort of chartreuse soufflé with cream.'

'You should have asked for a paper bag and said you wanted to take some home for your aged relative.'

Francesca giggled. She sat on Tim's lap and took the cigarette out of his mouth and put it in her own. 'But, seriously, Tim, what's the future in letting him buy a flat for me to live in? I shan't live in it. But I can't think of any way of getting out of it, short of flatly saying I won't leave my husband.'

'Suppose I said give it just two weeks more? Just till Monday, the twelfth of Feb? If he's going to buy mah honey chile a love nest he's got to furnish it, hasn't he? In these scandalous times five grand is the least, but the leastest, he can expect to spend on furnishings.'

'He said I could have the cane chairs out of his living room.'

'What a miscreant he is!' said Tim. 'Still, you won't stand for that, will you? Not a girl of spirit like you. You'll ask for five thousand to splash about in Heal's.'

'Oh, dear,' said Francesca with an enormous yawn, 'I'll try, I'll do my best, but not a minute more after Feb the twelfth.'

14

Francesca didn't know whether to fix on the first flat they saw so that she could go home early, or pretend to find nothing to please her so that things would have progressed no further by the time her deadline came. In the event she did neither, for as soon as they were really doing something together, conducting practical business, Martin made clear his belief in man as the master. In this, as in all matters on a higher level than that of deciding what she would wear or perhaps what they should eat, he took it for granted he made the decisions, asking for her approval only as a matter of courtesy.

During the two days since their dinner at the Mirabelle he had been in touch with estate agents, had made himself familiar with the specifications of every flat for sale in the area of Highgate and Crouch End, and had already viewed several. This led to his making of a short list and from it a shorter list which by Saturday afternoon had fined down to one. The flat in question wasn't quite as near Cromwell Court as he would have liked but it was in other respects so suitable that he thought they must overlook that small defect.

Francesca hadn't expected to react with either enthusiasm or dislike to the prospect before her. She had expected to be bored. Her feelings on entering the flat surprised her very much. She had never lived anywhere very spacious or elegant or even ordinarily attractive. There had been her parents' mansion flat in Chiswick, big and cold and pervadingly dark brown, a furnished room in Pimlico and a furnished room in Shepherd's Bush, the little house she had shared with Russell, the basement squat she had shared with Russell's supplanter, her three rooms in Stroud Green. Home to Francesca had never been much more than a place to keep out the rain, where there was a table to eat meals off and a bed to go to with someone she liked. But this was another thing. The fourth floor, the penthouse, of Swan Place, Stanhope Avenue, Highgate, was a different matter altogether.

The living room was very large and you went into the dining part of it through an arch. One wall was all of glass. The heating made it too hot for even her thin coat, she could have gone naked. Looking out of the big plate-glass windows on to hilly streets and patches of green and snowy roofs, being led into the pastel blue kitchen and the pastel apricot bathroom, Francesca found herself thinking that she would like to live here, she would like it very much indeed. It was a crying shame that she couldn't, or that the price to pay for doing so was too high, because she would like it – oh, wouldn't she! And Lindsay would like it and probably Tim too, though you could never tell with him. It was just too awful that she could only have it by being stuffy old Martin's kept woman. She wondered how much it cost.

'What do you think?' said Martin in the car.

'It's lovely.'

'I'm glad you like it, darling, because although you'll think me very high-handed and a real male chauvinist pig, I've actually already told the agent I'll have it and I've put down a deposit.'

'What would you have done,' said Francesca curiously, 'if I'd hated it?'

'I knew you wouldn't, I think I know you pretty well by this time.'

'How much is it, Martin?'

'Forty-two thousand pounds.'

Francesca was silenced. She felt quite weak and swimmy in the head at the thought of so much money. Martin said it would be a good investment, house property was the best investment these days, and before they got married he would sell both flats and buy a house. The property market, he had been told, was due for another steep rise in the spring. With luck he ought to make a big profit on both flats.

They went back to Cromwell Court where Martin had got chocolate éclairs and a Battenberg cake in for tea. Francesca partook heartily of both. It was the most miserable shame she didn't find Martin in the least attractive. If only she fancied him she could have put up with the yawning dullness and the accountant's talk and the pomposity, for the sake of that lovely flat. But she didn't fancy him, not a scrap, which was odd really because, like Tim, he was tall and dark and though not so good-looking, he was younger and cleaner and he didn't permanently stink of Gauloises. Francesca pondered rather regretfully on the anomalies of sexual attraction while Martin lectured her gently on house property and the registration of land and stamp duty and the making of searches and the mysteries of conveyancing.

Francesca ate another chocolate éclair. Martin wasn't the sort of person who would even consider going to bed in the afternoon, he would think it perverse. She let him hold her hand across the spread of sofa cushions.

'I suppose it'll be months and months before you actually own it?' she said.

'Oh, no. I'm paying cash, you see. My friend, Norman Tremlett – you met him here – he'll do a survey for me on Monday. I've already talked to my solicitor, he's another friend, we were all at school together, and he says provided the survey's favourable there's no reason why the contract shouldn't be ready for my signature by February the twelfth, that's Monday week. Then I'd get completion as soon as possible, maybe three weeks, and you could move in.'

Francesca thought how when she and Russell had tried to buy a house, what difficulties and obstacles there had been! The first two they fixed on had been sold over their heads while the building society hesitated over giving Russell a mortgage. Securing the one they had finally lived in took months and months, nearly a year of their hopes being raised and dashed. But they, of course, had had no money and no old boy network.

It no longer mattered, it was history, ten years gone, swept away by oceans of water under the bridge. She smiled at Martin.

'What about furniture, darling?'

'I thought of making a separate deal with the owner for the carpets and curtains and the bedroom furniture and the fridge and cooker. He wants to sell. Of course, if there was anything special you wanted we could go shopping together next Saturday.'

Was there any point now in waiting till February 12? None except that she had given Tim an undertaking. Martin seemed to take it for granted that she would now be spending every evening with him. Francesca pointed out that while she was still with Russell she couldn't go out every night and leave him to look after Lindsay. Perhaps she might manage another day in the week as well as Monday . . .

'I want my parents to meet you,' said Martin.

She insisted on going home at six o'clock and he insisted on driving her. This time he didn't drop her a hundred yards away but set her down outside number 54 and there he waited to see her into the house. Francesca stood outside the white iron gate, waving impatiently at him, while he sat in the car, refusing to go till she did. After a few seconds she saw it was useless. She must either make it look as if she were going into that house or else give up the game.

There was a light on in the hall but nowhere else. She unlatched the white gate and walked quickly to the side entrance which was a wooden door set into a six-foot-high fence. It was rather more than dusk and not quite dark. Francesca boldly tried the handle on the wooden door, and when it worked pushed the door open and found herself on a concrete strip of back yard. It would be rather awful, she thought, but rather funny too if someone saw her lurking there and called the police. After a little while she heard Martin's car go, so she opened the wooden door again and got out as fast as she could, running away down the side street on to which the garden of 54 abutted.

It wasn't until her next meeting with him that she learned how Martin had come back to 'see if she was all right'. How, from a car in the street, he could have known whether she was or wasn't he didn't say. But while there, he said, he had seen Russell Brown come out of the house and walk away towards Coldfall Wood.

First of all he told her that he had felt so happy about the new flat and their future that on Sunday he had decided to rush in (as he put it) where angels fear to tread and had actually called on Miss Watson. There in her employer's house in Hurst Avenue he had explained what his letters perhaps hadn't explained and had convinced her of his good intentions. She had agreed, in tears and some bewilderment, to accept ten thousand pounds with which to buy a small terraced house in the Lincolnshire town where her married sister lived.

'So that's twenty-five thousand disposed of. Do you think it would be wrong of me if I only gave away another twenty? You see, I'm going to have rather more expense than I thought with your flat.'

Francesca said with perfect sincerity that she didn't think it would be wrong at all. Every time he talked of giving money away to these people she didn't know and didn't want to know, she had to turn her face away so that he couldn't see her expression of disgust and dismay. She turned her back on him, picking red tulips and blue irises out of the jars on the floor to make a bouquet for his mother.

'And I've got something else to tell you. I've seen Russell.'

She turned round slowly, holding the flowers. He smiled, looking triumphant.

'He only waited for you to come in to go out himself, didn't he? I must say, it gave me a strange feeling to see him. He looks older than he is, don't you think?'

'I don't know, Martin.'

'More than thirty-five, I thought. D'you like those coneyskin coats on men? They're very "in" this year, I could get one.'

'Was Russell wearing his coneyskin then?' said Francesca with care.

'When I saw him I remembered what he'd done to you and I longed to get out of the car and hit him. But of course I didn't, I thought of how upset you'd be. He went off up towards the wood or the North Circular or somewhere.'

'He's got friends in Coppetts Lane,' said Francesca.

They went out to the car with the flowers.

'I've told my parents a bit about you. I'm afraid I've had to stretch the truth a bit. It seemed politic.'

The truth had been stretched so far by now, thought Francesca, it seemed unlikely to snap tonight.

'I've given them to understand you're already living apart from your husband,' said Martin. 'I refer to you as my fiancée.'

'Then I ought to have a ring,' said Francesca.

'I'm afraid you wouldn't wear it any more than you wear Russell's wedding ring. But shall I get you one for when your divorce comes through, so you can wear it to the registrar's office?'

The Urbans were very much what Francesca had expected, except that Walter Urban was younger and better looking. She found him rather attractive and speculated as to what it would be like to go to bed with a man twice one's age. Margaret Urban sat making patchwork of the same sort as that with which the cushions were covered. It looked a tedious and intricate task, putting all those hexagons together evenly. Francesca wondered why she did it, for they seemed to have heaps of money, but she would have liked a skirt for herself made in that sort of patchwork. It was a shame really that she wasn't, whatever the Urbans might think, in the running to get one.

They were like the Three Bears, she thought. She had gone to sit down on the right-hand side of the log fire and been told *sotto voce* by Martin that that was his mother's chair. They drank sherry, oloroso for Mrs Urban, amontillado for Walter and Tio Pepe for Martin. She felt that, like Goldilocks, she should have tried a little bit of each but settled instead for the Tio Pepe too.

Inwardly, she was amused. How dismayed the two senior Urbans must be at the thought of their only son (a boy brought up with the utmost care) marrying a divorced woman with a child. She tried to read some hint of it in their faces and in Mrs Urban's tone when she looked up from her sewing to ask questions about Lindsay. But there was nothing. They were playing safe, humouring Martin, in the hope, no doubt, that if they didn't oppose him he might get over her before any irreversible step was taken. It was just the way she envisaged behaving herself if anything so awful was to happen as Lindsay bringing home an accountant or a solicitor and saying she wanted to marry him.

When they were on their second glasses of sherry, Martin told them about buying the flat in Swan Place.

'For Francesca and Lindsay,' he said.

Where did they suppose she was living now? Francesca wondered. She expected Martin's announcement to be greeted with grave disapproval. In her experience parents never like you spending money, even your own, but she had reckoned without the passion for wise investment which throbs in the heart of every good accountant. Francesca noticed too that Martin's mother took it very coolly. She had a sensitive awareness of women's reactions and she understood that Margaret Urban, mother of an only son, would now be able to convince herself that if her son and his fiancée lived under separate roofs before marriage, they wouldn't sleep together before marriage either.

'A very sound idea,' said Walter, 'buying the place before prices go up again. Of course you'll elect to describe it as your principal residence?'

'It won't be *his* residence at all, Walter,' said Mrs Urban.

Her husband took no notice of this interruption which had made Francesca discreetly smile. 'Because if Swan Place is your secondary residence you won't forget, will you, that you'll be liable for Capital Gains Tax when you sell it.'

'Do you know,' said Martin, 'I *had* forgotten. The tax payable would be a third of my profit, wouldn't it?'

'Thirty per cent,' said Walter.

They talked about tax and tax avoidance all through dinner. Mrs Urban watched them placidly from under her slate-blue fringe but Francesca was so bored she couldn't control her yawns.

On Saturday afternoon they paid another visit to Swan Place and saw the owner, a Mr Butler, and he and Martin went through what Martin called 'negotiating a price' for the carpets and curtains and bits of kitchen equipment and bedroom furniture. Afterwards he took Francesca out to tea at Louis' in Hampstead. He said that they would go and buy any other furniture she might want next weekend, and when she said she could do that on her own, he said he thought he would like to be there too. After all, it would one day be his furniture as well as hers. Francesca didn't much care, she had given up, the long drag was nearly over. She would see him on Monday and say she couldn't leave Russell or contrive to have a tremendous quarrel with him, and that would be that.

When Francesca had eaten as many cream slices and rum babas as she could manage – it was too late in the day to worry about sticking to a Victorian lady's appetite – Martin suggested they go across the road and see the Bunuel film at the Everyman. But Francesca wasn't having that. If Goldie upstairs would keep an ear open for Lindsay she wanted to go round the pub with Tim. So she said she had to get back to Lindsay because Russell was having dinner with his publisher and someone who might be interested in doing *The Iron Cocoon* for television. This was an excuse in which Tim had rehearsed her and she was glad to have an opportunity of using it. Martin, of course, drove her up to Fortis Green Lane. Once more she had to hide in the side entrance. After Monday, she thought, she would never set foot in Finchley again.

February 10, February 11 . . . It would soon be all over. Francesca tried to think of ways of breaking off with Martin that were not too brutal. It was no good discussing this with Tim who would have advised the bald truth, presented as savagely as possible.

Martin walked into the shop at a quarter to six on Monday, February 12. Last time, thought Francesca, last time. She gave him a vague kiss. She hadn't bothered with pink *panne* velvet or burgundy crêpe but was wearing *her* favourite collection of garments, a patchwork skirt, a Hungarian peasant top with a long cardigan over it, and her Olaf's Daughter's boots which were heaven to wear in the shop whatever Martin might think of them.

'I'm awfully sorry, darling, but before we have dinner I've got to go round to my solicitor's and see about this contract. You won't mind, will you?'

Francesca didn't particularly mind. She wouldn't have minded if they had spent the entire evening at his solicitor's. All that interested her was how to pave the way for disappearing permanently from Martin's life. Perhaps it would be best to stage a quarrel over dinner or make use of an idea which had come to her earlier in the day. This was to say that she was pregnant and that it was Russell's child, so she would have to stay with him, wouldn't she? Francesca thought she could really enter into the spirit of this. And it had the great merit of not humiliating or even much disillusioning Martin. Francesca was amoral and greedy but she wasn't entirely heartless. Martin sometimes reminded her of a big kind dog, a Newfoundland perhaps, that one might have to abandon at the Battersea Dogs' Home but which one wouldn't kick in the face. She would try to let him down as lightly as possible, for her sake, she admitted, as well as his. She hated scenes, recriminations, fuss.

Martin introduced her to Adrian Vowchurch as his fiancée. There was a Mrs Vowchurch somewhere, clattering about in the kitchen regions. Francesca sized Adrian up. She didn't like little hatchet-faced men with supercilious eyes and the sort of public school accent so affected as to be a joke. He shook hands with her and said, insincerely she thought, that it gave him really tremendous pleasure to meet her at last. While he and Martin talked more or less incomprehensibly, it was borne in on Francesca that they were there for the express purpose of signing the contract for the purchase of the Swan Place flat. She could see it, or what was probably it, lying on a blotter on a mahogany desk. Adrian saw her looking and said they hoped for completion within a couple of weeks, allowing for searches (whatever that might mean) and would Mrs Brown like to have a look at the contract? Francesca hesitated. It seemed too unkind to let Martin buy the flat when she hadn't the slightest intention of ever living in it. Somehow the purchase of the flat hadn't seemed real until she saw what, in black and white, it involved.

This agreement is made the Twelfth Day of February, Nineteen Hundred and Seventy——, between John Alexander Butler, of Flat 10, Swan Place, Stanhope Avenue, Highgate, in the County of London (Hereinafter called 'the Vendor'), and Mrs Francesca Brown. . . . Martin had given her address as 12 Cromwell Court. It was absurd on the strength of that one weekend, it was rather touching. She read the rest of the first page. He had presumably brought her here to witness his signature. And once that was done and this contract exchanged with Butler's it would be difficult, if not impossible, for him to get out of buying the flat. Even she knew that. What she ought to do was ask him to postpone signing it, and when they were alone tell him the truth.

She found she lacked the courage to do that. She looked up and met the cold, suspicious eyes of Adrian Vowchurch. He didn't like her. It was far more than that, he distrusted her and resented her presence. He gave an infinitesimal shrug and passed a fountain pen to her.

'Can we have your signature then, Mrs Brown – er, Francesca?'

She took the pen.

'Not there,' he said. 'Up here.'

Martin gave a soft indulgent laugh. She didn't quite understand but she signed where Adrian told her to and then Julie Vowchurch, who had come in and given her a tight smile, signed as witness. Francesca felt excited and puzzled and rather frightened. Martin refused the Vowchurches' offer of drinks and they drove up to Hampstead and had dinner at the Cellier du Midi.

'You don't know how relieved I am,' said Martin, 'that I told you about winning that money. We'll never have secrets from each other, shall we?'

'No,' said Francesca, trying furiously to think. She couldn't wait to be home with Tim.

'Now we've got your flat fixed up and the future settled I want to get the other thing settled too. I mean the philanthropy part or charity or whatever you like to call it. So I'm going to have another go at Mrs Cochrane and I really think the last ten thousand had better go to Mrs Finn. Have I told you about her? She used to be our cleaner and she's a bit crazy, poor old creature, and I'll have to reach her through her son. But I'm sure she's a deserving cause . . . Are you all right, darling? You look as if you're off somewhere in a dream.'

'I'm awfully tired. I won't come back with you, if you don't mind. I'll just get a taxi in Heath Street.' His face fell. 'But I could see you tomorrow, if you like.'

'Darling,' he said, 'if that's a promise I shan't mind letting you go.'

Tim was sitting at the kitchen table doing his reporter's expenses, the greatest work of fiction, he sometimes said, since *War and Peace*. He was smoking what smelt like his hundredth Gauloise of the day and drinking retsina out of a bottle. The oven was on and the wall heater and as usual the condensation was running down the walls.

'Oh, Tim,' said Francesca, 'I feel very peculiar, wait till I tell you. Can I have some wine, please, and a cigarette?'

'Have you had a heart-rending renunciation scene?'

'No, listen, Tim, we went to his solicitor and he had this contract thing for buying the flat and I read it and it said something about being between John Alexander Butler and Francesca Brown. And I nearly didn't sign it because it seemed a bit mean and rotten making him pay for something I wasn't going to live in, but you needn't look like that, I did sign it, and . . .'

'Thank Christ,' said Tim, and his sallow face had become even paler, the red mouth and the black brows standing out like paint. 'Think – you're sure it was made just between this Butler guy and you?' She nodded with eagerness. 'And you signed it on your own? Livingstone didn't sign it?'

'No.'

'When you went to see old Urban didn't he say something about Livingstone having to pay Capital Gains Tax on one of his properties if he sold them both?'

'Yes, he sort of reminded Martin about some law about that and he said if Martin owned two flats and sold them both he'd have to pay this tax on one of them. Thirty per cent of his profit, he said. What's he done, Tim? He didn't say anything to me, he didn't mention it after we'd left the solicitor's. And I didn't say anything and I didn't break things off either . . .'

'Break things off?' said Tim. 'You'll see that guy every night till completion if it kills you *and* me. Don't you see what he's doing? He's buying it in your name so that he can avoid giving the government two or three grand in tax. In other words, in a couple of weeks' time, barring acts of God, that forty-two thousand quid luxury apartment will become the exclusive, undisputed, unencumbered property of mah honey chile.'

'Oh, Tim, I really have done it, haven't I? This is better than a ring or a bit of furniture.'

'And revenge will be very sweet,' said Tim.

He put out his arms and she came into them and they hugged each other.

15

It was rare for any post to arrive for Finn or Lena. There would be the electricity and gas bills every quarter and the little pension from Finn's father's firm and at Christmas, a card from Brenda. That was all. Months could pass by without Finn's receiving a single item addressed to himself and it was therefore with the nearest he ever got to astonishment that he picked up the long white envelope from the doormat.

The direction was to T. Finn Esq. and it was typewritten. Finn was on his way to Modena Road where he was papering walls. When he was in the van he took out the letter and read it.

Dear Mr Finn,

I do not think we have ever met, though our mothers are old friends. Perhaps Mrs Finn has mentioned to you that they had tea together a few weeks ago. I expect you will be surprised to hear from me but the fact is that I have a business proposition to put to you and I wonder if we could meet and discuss this. Could you ring me at the above number in the next few days? I shall be there between 9.30 and 5.30.

Yours sincerely,

Martin W. Urban.

Finn started the van and drove off to Parliament Hill Fields. Martin Urban had been wrong in saying they had never met. Finn seldom forgot a thing like that. He remembered Martin clearly as a spotty adolescent when he himself was eleven or twelve. Lena had taken him with her to Copley Avenue because it was the school holidays and Queenie was ill with flu. He had opened a bedroom door and seen Martin sitting at a desk, using a protractor and a set square. The older boy had turned on him a look which Finn, at the time, had taken for outrage and disgust but which later he understood. That look had in fact only been astonishment that Finn had seemed to be attempting to bridge the huge social gulf between them.

What did the grown-up Martin want of him now? If it was true that Mrs Urban had admired the partitioning of Lena's room, it might be that she had talked about it to her son and he was looking for a builder to do a conversion job for him. Finn was more or less willing, provided the money was right and he wasn't hassled about time. The words 'business proposition' seemed to imply something like that. He let himself into the house in Modena Road and walked from room to room, assessing the stage he had reached. Once the paper was up in the ground-floor front room and the hall floor re-tiled, he could be finished and at leisure. But he would see how he got on before making that phone call.

Remembering that look of Martin's all those years ago in Copley Avenue, he was slightly surprised to read that bit about their mothers being old friends. 'A few weeks ago' wasn't exactly accurate either. A few months was more like it; it had been November 16, he recalled, his birthday. Just as well, he reflected, that the woman hadn't been back again during the terrible month, the weeks of Lena's sufferings. No wonder he hadn't yet finished the work for Kaiafas . . .

She had said there were maggots coming out of the walls. That had been at the beginning when she could still see colours and smell smells, the real and the imaginary. After that she could only see in black and white and grey, and had lain crying all night, all day. He had never left her. If she had gone to the hospital they would have put her in the locked ward. He hadn't dared sleep unless she was drugged and out, for she would spring upon him if she thought he was off guard. Twice she had tried to set the place on fire and when he prevented this she burned herself instead. There were still burn scars on both her wrists and in the hollows of her elbows.

But she had come out of it at last. She always did, though

Finn was afraid the time might come when she wouldn't. She could hear people's voices again and see colours again and remember who he was. On the day she held his hand and asked him if had worn her birthday present yet, he knew she was better and he brought the bird back from downstairs. Mrs Gogarty started coming in to give him a break and he got back to work. In the past week Lena had twice been up to Second Chance and this afternoon Mrs Gogarty was taking her to a street market – somewhere in Islington, he thought it was, miles away from Parliament Hill Fields.

Coming back to Lord Arthur Road at six, Finn found them occupied with the Tarot, not telling fortunes this time but studying the pictures on certain cards. Mrs Gogarty had just bought the pack off a stall for seventy-five pence. It appeared that the Hermit and Eight of Cups were missing. Lena gave a strong shiver as she picked up and looked at the Ten of Swords. It showed the body of a man, pinned to the ground by ten sharp blades down the length of his back and lying by the waters of a lake. Finn covered up the card with the pretty Queen of Pentacles and he thought how if ever he killed again, it must look like an accident, it must be taken for an accident, for Lena's sake.

She gave him a tremulous smile and began to produce from a bag for his inspection the things she had bought that day, a man's trilby hat, a pair of wooden elephant bookends, a green china quadruped with its tail missing, half a dozen copies of a magazine called *Slimming Naturally*.

Later on, Mr Beard who kept the fur and suede cleaner's shop in Brecknock Road and who had once tried, with some success, to raise up the spirit of Cornelius Agrippa, was coming round and bringing his Ouija board. Finn felt a quiet relief that things were getting back to normal. While they waited for Mr Beard, Mrs Gogarty set out the Tarot for Finn and foretold an unexpected accession of wealth.

Finn waited for a couple of days before phoning Martin Urban and then he did so from a phone box by Gospel Oak station at ten in the morning.

'You wanted me to ring you. The name's Finn.'

'Oh, yes, good morning. How do you do? Nice of you to phone. I expect you gathered from my letter that I've got a proposition to put to you that's rather to your advantage. It's not something I'd feel like discussing on the phone. Could we – er, meet and have a word, d'you think?'

'If you want,' said Finn.

'A pub? I'll suggest somewhere halfway between our respective homes, shall I? How about the Archway Tavern? If tonight would suit you, we could say eight tonight in the Archway Tavern.'

He rang off without asking Finn how he would recognize him or telling him what he himself looked like. Finn wasn't much bothered by that, he knew he would somehow smell out in the man the studious and superior adolescent of long ago. But for a little while he did wonder why, if Martin Urban only wanted him to divide a room into two or make two rooms into one, he hadn't felt like even hinting at it on the phone.

Mr Bradley was spending the evening as well as most of the day with Lena. His daughter-in-law was having an operation for gallstones and he couldn't get into the house till his son came back from the hospital at nine. It was a cold, misty evening with not much traffic about and a few people. Finn wore the yellow pullover and the black scarf with the coins on and Lena's birthday present. He walked into the Archway Tavern at two minutes past eight and stood still just inside the door, looking about him. As he had expected, he knew Martin Urban at once, a tallish, square-built man, becoming burly and looking older than his age. He was sitting at a table, reading the *Evening Standard*, and as Finn's pale piercing eyes fixed him, he lifted his own. Finn walked up to him and he got to his feet.

'Mr Finn?'

Finn nodded.

'How do you do? You're very punctual. It's good of you to come. I've been thinking about it, I didn't give you much notice, did I? I hope that's all right.' Finn didn't say anything. He sat down. 'What will you drink?'

'Pineapple juice,' said Finn.

'*Pineapple juice?* What, just by itself? You're sure that's all right?'

'Just pineapple juice,' said Finn. 'The Britvic.'

He expected Martin Urban to drink beer, he was the sort who always would in pubs, except perhaps for the last drink. But he bought himself a large whisky, at least a double measure, and a small bottle of soda water. Finn supposed he was nervous about something or someone, and that someone was very likely himself. He inspired trepidation in otherwise quite confident people but he didn't know how to put them at their ease and wouldn't have done even if he had known. He sat silent, pouring the thick yellow juice from the bottle into a small squat glass. They hadn't been alone at their table but now the other man who sat there finished his beer, picked up his coat and left.

'And how's your mother these days?'

'She's O K,' said Finn.

Martin Urban turned his chair away from the table and edged it a little nearer to Finn's. 'Cheers,' he said and he drank some of his whisky. 'My mother does see her sometimes, you know. She looks in when she gets a chance.' He waited for a rejoinder to this but none came. 'I think it was November when she last saw her. She thought – well, she was a bit worried about her.'

'Well, well,' said Finn.

'She was always very fond of her, you see. They'd known each other for a long time.' It was apparent to Finn that he was trying to avoid saying that Lena had been Mrs Urban's cleaner, a statement about which Finn wouldn't have cared at all. He swilled the juice round his mouth, savouring it. A particularly good batch, he thought. 'That stuff you're drinking, is it all right?'

Finn nodded. He watched Martin Urban's face flush to a dark brick red. 'I don't want you to think I'm criticizing, finding fault or anything like that. If you don't own your own home these days, or have a council place, it's pretty difficult to find anywhere to live, let alone anywhere decent. And to buy somewhere you don't just have to be earning good money, you need a bit of capital as well. What I'm trying to say is, when my mother told me the way Mrs Finn was living – through no fault of anybody's actually – I thought, well, maybe I could do something to change all that, to sort of benefit you both, because we're all old friends, after all, aren't we?'

Finn finished his drink. He said nothing. He was beginning to be aware that an offer was about to be made to him but for what and in exchange for what he couldn't tell. This man was as shy of approaching the point as Kaiafas was. Reminded of the Cypriot, he seemed to hear a voice saying in another pub, 'I give it to my friend Feen instead', and at that recollection, at certain apparent parallels, he raised his eyes and let them rest on the flushed, square, somewhat embarrassed, face in front of him.

'I hope I haven't offended you.'

Finn shook his head.

'Good. Then I'll come to the point.' Martin Urban looked round to see that they weren't overheard and said in a lower voice, 'I could manage to let you have ten thousand pounds. I'm afraid I can't make it more than that. You'd have to go outside London, of course.'

Finn's gaze fell and rose again. He was overwhelmed by the munificence of this offer. His fame had indeed spread before him, and it wasn't his fame as a plumber and decorator. Yet one to him were fame and shame, he was without vanity. He drank the remains of his pineapple juice and said, 'It's a lot of money.'

'You wouldn't do it for less.'

Finn did a rare thing for him. He smiled. He spoke one word. 'When?'

Martin Urban seemed slightly taken aback. 'When you like. As soon as possible. You're going to accept then?'

'Oh, yes. Why not?'

'Good. That's splendid. I'm very happy you don't feel you have to put up any show of refusal, that sort of thing. It wastes so much time. Let's drink to it, shall we?' He fetched another pineapple juice and a second whisky. Facing Finn again, he seemed to become doubtful and his expression took on its former shade of mystification. 'I have made myself plain? You have understood me?'

Rather impatiently Finn said, 'Sure. You can leave it to me.'

'That's fine. It's just that I thought you might not exactly have known what I meant. Would you like me to send you a cheque?'

'I haven't got a bank account. I'd like cash.'

'*Cash?* My dear chap, that'd make quite a parcel.'

Finn nodded. 'Pad it out a bit with newspaper. You can let me have half now and half later. That way you needn't let me have the rest till you know I've done what you want. Right?'

'I suppose so. Are you going to be able to do it on your own? You know how to go about it?'

'Find someone else then,' said Finn.

'I'm sorry, I didn't mean that. I *have* offended you. Anyway, it's no business of mine how you go about it. I want to think that once I've let you have the money you're on your own, you're free.' Martin Urban swallowed his whisky very rapidly. He wiped his mouth, he sighed. 'But you will – you will do it, won't you?'

'Haven't I said?'

He was far worse than Kaiafas, Finn thought. And now, as if it was any concern of his where Lena lived or what Lena did, he began talking once more about buying her a house, moving her out of Lord Arthur Road.

'You can still get small houses for less than ten thousand in the country towns. If you don't mind going a good distance, there are building firms putting up houses for that. I'd get her to decide where she'd like to live – near some relative maybe – and then you and she could have a Saturday out there, calling on the agents.'

Finn understood it. Martin Urban wanted him out of the way, a long way away, once the deed was done. He didn't understand how ludicrous it was recommending some country town for Lena, Lena would go mad, madder, maddest away from her precious tiny segmented home, the only home she could bear to live in, away too from her friends, from Mrs Gogarty and Mr Bradshaw and Mr Beard. Finn almost felt like telling Martin Urban to shut up, to *think*, to look at reality, but he didn't do this. He sat silent and impassive while the other talked on about surveyors' reports and freeholds and frontages and party walls. For he was understanding more and more. Martin Urban, like Kaiafas, believed that if he talked in this way of mundane, harmless and practical matters he wouldn't quite have to realize the enormity of the deed for which he was to pay those thousands of pounds.

At last he paused for breath and perhaps for some sign of appreciation. Finn got up, nodded to him and left without speaking again. He had been given no further instructions but he didn't doubt that such would be sent to him in due course.

Over the Archway concourse the snow was dancing down in millions of soft plumy flakes that whirled like fireflies in the light from the yellow lamps.

16

The parcel containing the first instalment of the money was brought to Finn by an express delivery service. A man in a green uniform handed it to him at the door. Finn took it upstairs. The house in Lord Arthur Road had its Saturday smell of baked beans and marijuana, as against its weekday smell of stale waste bins and marijuana. Finn had unwrapped the parcel and was counting the money when he heard Lena coming down the stairs. Her footsteps were almost jaunty. Mr Beard was taking her to a meeting of the Tufnell Theosophists. Lena didn't have many men friends so it was an exciting event for her. Finn opened his door.

'Will you be bringing him back with you?'

Smiling a little and bridling, she said she didn't know. She would like to, she would ask him. Her eyes shone. She was wearing the mauve dress with the fringe and over it a red cloak lined in fraying satin. If you half-closed your eyes and looked at her you might fancy you were seeing – not a young girl, never that, but perhaps the ghost of a young girl. She was like a moth from whose wings most of the dust has rubbed away, a faded fluttering moth or a skeleton leaf. She laid her hand on Finn's arm and looked up into his face as if he were the parent and she the child.

'Here,' he said, 'get something for your tea then.' He thrust a bundle of notes, forty, fifty pounds into her hands.

She smelt of camphor, the mistletoe-bough bride who has been resurrected after fifty years in the trunk. Over the banisters he watched her go down, stuffing notes into her dorothy bag, into her cloak pocket, miraculously spilling none. Rich now, young again, sane again, down the dirty pavements to her psychic swain. Finn returned to his room.

Putting the money away with the rest in the bag under his mattress, he reflected once more on Martin Urban's recommendations. At the thought of Lena alone in a small country town, of Lena alone anywhere, he smiled a narrow smile of contempt. For a moment he imagined her removed from Lord Arthur Road, the only place he could remember where she had found fragments of happiness and peace; removed from him and her dear friends and the second-hand shops and her little cosy segmented space. He thought of the terrified feral mania which would overcome her when she smelt the fresh air and felt the wind and had to hunt for sleep, always elusive, in the spacious bedroom of a bungalow.

But Martin Urban, of course, hadn't talked of transferring Lena to the country because he sincerely believed Finn should buy her a house with the money. His talk of prospective house-buying had been the precise equivalent of Kaiafas's references to his homeland and Anne Blake's expressed regret that he had ever left it. They couldn't bring themselves, these squeamish people, to put their desires into plain words. Finn wondered at it. He thought he could simply have said, fixing his water-bright eyes on his listener, 'Kill this woman, this man, for me,' always supposing he was ever in the unlikely situation of wanting anyone else to do anything for him.

Sitting cross-legged on the floor, he opened a large can of pineapple and ate it with some wholemeal bread and a piece of cheese. He was rather surprised that he hadn't yet been told who his victim was to be. He had expected Martin Urban to bring the money himself and in a note or by circumlocutory word of mouth to give him a name and a description. In the middle of the floor, between the mattress and the pineapple can and other remains of his meal, lay the wrappings from the parcel. They lay in a puddle of sunlight cast by the only sunbeam that had managed to insert itself through the Chinese puzzle of brick walls and penetrate the room. Finn had told Martin Urban to wrap the money up in newspaper, and now his eye was caught by the picture on the front page of the copy of the *North London Post* which had been around the notes and under the brown paper covering. He stretched out a long arm, picked up the newspaper and looked more closely at this picture.

He seldom so much as glanced at a newspaper. He had never seen this copy before but he recognized at once the scene of the photograph. It was the path between the railway bridge and the end of Nassington Road by Parliament Hill Fields. He recognized it because he had been there and because it was there that he had killed Anne Blake – and also because he had seen this photograph in another newspaper, that which Kaiafas had used to wrap *his* payment as a macabre joke.

So Martin Urban knew. Indeed, it must be because Martin Urban knew that he had picked him to do this particular, as yet unspecified, job for him. How did he know? Finn felt a prickling of the skin on his forehead and his upper lip as a little sweat broke. There was no telling how Martin Urban knew, but know he must or why else would he have sent Finn that newspaper with that photograph in it?

The unfamiliar sensation of fear subsided as Finn reflected that Martin Urban would hardly, considering what he was paying for and was about to have done for him, pass his information elsewhere. He shook the newspaper, expecting a note to fall out. He turned the pages slowly, looking for some hint or clue. And there, on page seven, it was.

A paragraph, ringed in red ball-point, with a street number inserted and a name underlined. Finn read the paragraph carefully, committing certain details to memory. Then he put on the yellow pullover and the PVC jacket. This was an occasion for covering his distinctively pale hair with a grey woolly hat and his memorable eyes with dark glasses. Both these items of disguise were acquisitions of Lena's. Finn locked his door and went down to the garage in Somerset Grove.

There he replaced his licence plates with a pair bearing the number TLE 315R. These he had, two years before, removed from a dark brown Lancia which had been left parked in Lord Arthur Road during a day and a night. He had known they would come in useful one day. Slightly disguised and in his slightly disguised van, Finn drove up to Fortis Green Lane and parked a little way down from number 54. It was just on three o'clock.

It was impossible to tell whether the house was at present empty or occupied. The day was chilly, the kind of day that is called raw, with a dirty-looking sky and a damp wind blowing. All the windows in 54 Fortis Green Lane were closed and at the larger of the upstairs windows the curtains were drawn. It was too early to put lights on.

The front garden was composed entirely of turf and concrete, but the concrete predominated. On the strip of it which ran round and was joined on to the walls of the house, was a dustbin with its lid on the ground beside it. The lid lay inverted with its hollow side uppermost and the wind kept it perpetually rocking with a repetitive faint clattering sound. Finn thought that if there was anyone in the house they would eventually come out to pick up the dustbin lid and stop the noise.

Quite a lot of people passed him, young couples, arm-in-arm or hand-in-hand, older people who had been shopping in Finchley High Road. Their faces looked pinched, they walked quickly because of the cold. Nobody took any notice of Finn, reading his newspaper in his plain grey van.

The dustbin lid continued to rock in exactly the same way until five, when a sharper gust of wind caught it and sent it skittering along the concrete to clatter off on to the grass. Still no one came out of the house. Finn gave it another half-hour and then, when he could tell by the continued darkness of the house that it must be empty, he drove home.

Lena was having tea with Mr Beard. There was a net curtain with scalloped edges spread as a cloth on the bamboo table and this was laden with all the things Lena had bought for tea, lattice pastry sausage rolls and anchovy pizza and Viennese whirls and arctic roll and Mr Kipling almond slices. Mr Beard was talking very interestingly about Dr Dee and the Enochian language in which he was instructed by his spirit teachers, so Finn sat down to have a cup of tea with them. Lena kept giving him fond proud smiles, she seemed entirely happy. He tried to listen to Mr Beard's account of Dee's angel but he found himself unable to concentrate. He kept thinking, turning over in his mind, how was he going to do it? How was he going to kill this stranger he hadn't yet seen and make it look like an accident?

The next day he went back to Fortis Green Lane in the morning. The dustbin and its lid had gone. Finn sat in the van, on the opposite side of the wide road this time, and watched people cleaning cars and pruning rose bushes. No one came out of or entered number 54 and the bedroom curtains were still drawn.

It wasn't until Monday evening, though he went back again on Sunday afternoon and Monday morning, that his watching was rewarded. First, at about a quarter to seven, a tallish man in early middle age appeared from the Finchley High Road direction, unlatched the white gate, walked up the path and let himself into the house. He was wearing a thigh-length coat of a sleek, light brown fur and dark trousers and a dark grey scarf. The appearance of this man rather puzzled Finn who had expected someone younger. He watched lights come on in the hall, then the downstairs front room, then behind the drawn bedroom curtains. The bedroom light went out but the others remained on. After a while Finn went off and had a pineapple juice at the Royal Oak in Sydney Road and then he walked about in Coldfall Wood, in the dark, under the old beech trees with their steely trunks and sighing, rustling boughs. Finn wasn't the kind of person one would much like to meet in a wood in the dark, but there was no one there to meet him.

The lights had gone out in the house when he returned. It was as well for Finn that he was never bored. He sat in the van, on the odd-numbered side of Fortis Green Lane and, putting himself into a trance, projected his astral body to an ashram in the foothills of the Himalayas where it had been before and sometimes conducted conversations with a monk. Such a feat he could now accomplish with ease. The transcending of space was relatively simple. Would he ever accomplish the transcending of time so that he could project himself back into history and forward into the future?

He slept a little after his astral body had come back and awoke angry with himself in case his quarry had passed by while his eyes were shut. But the house still remained dark. Finn thought he would wait there till midnight, the time now being ten to eleven.

While he had been there cars had passed continually, though the traffic had never been heavy. At just seven minutes to eleven, a white Triumph Toledo pulled up outside number 54 and after a little delay a woman got out. She was young and tall with a straight nose and lips curved like the blades of scimitars and hair like a bronze cape in the sulphur light. Finn lowered his window. He expected to see emerge from the car the man in the fur coat but instead he heard the voice of Martin Urban call softly:

'Good night, Francesca.'

That settled for Finn certain questions that had been perplexing him. This was the right place, after all, this was it. He had doubted. He raised his window and watched the woman stand by the gate, then open the gate and walk up one of the concrete strips to a door between the house wall and the boundary fence. She waved to Martin Urban, opened the door and let it close behind her. Finn felt relieved. He watched the white car slowly depart, then gather speed.

As it disappeared into a turning on the right-hand side, his eyes following it, there passed very close to the van's window on the nearside, almost brushing the glass, a brown furriness like the haunch of an animal. Finn turned to look. Russell Brown was crossing the road now, unlatching the white gate, walking up the path. Although the woman must now have been in there for at least a minute no lights had yet come on. Though, since she had entered by the back way, she might have put lights on only in the back regions. Russell Brown unlocked the front door and let himself into the house. Immediately the hall light came on.

Finn switched on his ignition and his sidelights and drove away.

17

It saddened Francesca to have to give in her notice. She had liked working for Kate Ross, being among flowers all day, arranging flowers in the window and in bouquets, delivering flowers and seeing on people's faces the dawning of delighted surprise. Tim had once said that there was something especially flower-like about her and that – he was presumably quoting – her hyacinth hair, her classic face, her naiad airs had brought him home from desperate seas. He had been rather drunk at the time. But there was no help for it, she had to leave. February 24 would be her last day at Floreal and Adrian Vowchurch had promised completion of the purchase of the Swan Place flat two days later.

'You'll be too grand, anyway, to work in a flower shop,' said Tim, and he put his mouth to the soft hollows above her collar bone. Francesca made purring noises. The air in the room was so cold that their breath plumed up from the bed like smoke. 'Why don't you ask Livingstone to buy you a garden centre?'

'That would be pushing it,' said Francesca primly. 'I think I've done marvels actually. I shan't be getting any more out of him because I shan't be seeing him. Not after he's paid for the flat and that Adrian person has done the what-do-you-call-it. He won't know where to find me when I've left Floreal.'

'He'll be able to find you in delectable Swan Place, though perhaps mah clever honey chile won't give him a key?'

From the electric blanket came up waves of heat that made them both sweat, but that morning Francesca had found ice on the inside of the windows. The atmosphere held a bitter and quite tangible dampness. Tim lit a Gauloise and smoked it in the darkness. The glowing tip of it was like a single star in a cold and smoky sky.

'I don't think I'm going to go there at the beginning. I did think of moving in like he expects me to and after I'd been there a few days stage a tremendous irrevocable sort of row with him and say I never wanted to see him again. But I don't think I could, I'm not good at rows. So what I think now is, I'll just stay at home here very quietly for two or three days and then I'll write him a letter. I'll tell him in that what I'd have told him in the row, that it's all over but that I know the flat's mine and I need it and I'm going to live in it. How's that? Shall we go and live in that lovely place, Tim, or shall we sell it and buy another lovely place?'

'That will be for you to say.'

'What's mine is yours, you know. I think of you as my common law husband. Can you have a common law husband if you've already got an uncommon law one?'

Tim laughed. 'I'm wondering what steps, if any, Miss Urban will take when she discovers your *coup*. You'd better not count on keeping the furniture.' He drew on his cigarette and the star glowed brightly. 'I must say I shan't be sorry when mah honey chile isn't deceiving me every night with another woman.'

'You must feel like a ponce,' said Francesca. 'Ponces never seem to mind, do they?'

'The minding, as you call it, fluctuates in direct proportion to the immoral earnings.' He stubbed his cigarette out and turned to her. 'It has nothing to do with the activities. Personally, I hope you're giving Livingstone a good run for his money.'

'Well, yes and no. Oh, Tim, you've got one warm hand and one icy cold one. It's rather nice – it's rather fantastic. . . .'

Francesca brought Martin a large specimen of *Xygocactus truncatus* from the shop. It had come late into flower and now, at the end of February, its flat scalloped stems each bore on its tip a bright pink chandelier-shaped blossom. Martin was childishly, disproportionately, pleased by this gift. He put it on the window sill in the middle of the window with the view over London. It was snowing again, though not settling, and the flakes made a gauzy net between the window and the shining, yellow and white city.

That was Wednesday and Martin let her go home in a cab, but on Thursday she spent the day and stayed the night in Cromwell Court. Martin took the day off and they bought bed linen and towels, a set of saucepans and a French cast-iron frying pan, two table lamps, a Japanese portable colour television and a dinner service in Denbyware. These items they took away with them. The three-piece suite covered in jade-green and ivory velvet, the brass and glass dining table and eight chairs would of course have to be sent. Francesca said she would be bringing her own cutlery and glass. She was bored with shopping for things she doubted she would be allowed to keep.

They had dinner at the Bullock Cart in Heath Street and Martin said he had heard from John Butler that he and his wife would move out of Swan Place first thing Monday morning. He would give the key to the estate agent or if Martin liked he could call in and fetch it himself during the weekend.

'We could collect it on Saturday,' said Francesca who could foresee the difficulties of any other course.

When Mr Cochrane rang the bell at eight-thirty in the morning Francesca opened the door to him. She was wearing the top half of Martin's pyjamas and a pair of blue tights. Martin had come out of the kitchen with the Worcester sauce apron on. His expression was aghast. Mr Cochrane came in without saying anything, his eyes perceiving the flowering cactus, his nostrils quivering at the scent of *Ma Griffe*. He closed the door behind him, said, 'Good morning, madam,' and walked into the kitchen where he put his valise down on the table.

'How's your sister-in-law?' said Martin.

'Home again,' said Mr Cochrane. He looked at Martin

through the bifocals, then carefully over the top of them. Then he said, 'Yes, home again, Martin, if you can call it home,' and, carrying a tin of spray polish and two dusters, he went into the living room where he scrutinized the cactus and, lifting up each item and examining it, the sheets and towels and saucepans and lamps they had bought on the previous day. At last he turned to Francesca, his death's head face convulsed into a smile.

'What a blessing to see him leading a normal life, madam. I like a man to *be* a man, if you know what I mean.'

'I know what you mean all right,' said Francesca, giggling.

'Is there anything special you'd like me to do, madam, or shall I carry on as usual?'

'Oh, you carry on as usual,' said Francesca, 'I always do,' and she gave him her best and most radiant smile.

It was her last day at the shop since Kate had said she needn't come in on Saturday morning. Next week, when she had disappeared, would Martin come to the shop and ask Kate about her? It wouldn't really matter what Martin did after Monday, after the deal was completed and the money handed over. Perhaps she should screw up her courage and really move in on Monday afternoon, as Martin thought she was going to, move in, invite him that evening – and tell him the truth, that legally the flat was hers and she intended to live in it without ever seeing him again. She would never summon up that courage. The only way was to do as she had told Tim she would do, disappear, write to him, when he made a fuss let Tim explain to him, finally take possession when it had all blown over. The flat is *yours*, hang on to that, she told herself, it's yours in the law and nothing can shake that.

Martin called for her at ten to six and they went back to Cromwell Court where he cooked the dinner. At about eleven he drove her up to Fortis Green Lane and Francesca was again obliged to take refuge in the back garden of number 54. Tonight the house was in darkness. She stood against the stuccoed wall, listening for the car to go. As it happened, she came out too soon. It hadn't been Martin's car but a small grey van pulling away. Martin was still there, still watching the house – watching for lights to come on?

She told him she had left her key in the house and would have to wake Russell to let her in.

'Please go, darling. I'll be all right.'

Reluctantly, Martin did go. Francesca was actually trembling. She had to sit down on the low wall for a moment. When she got up and turned round to look warily at the house she half-expected to see its occupant glaring at her from an upper window. But there was no one. It was colder tonight than it had been for a week, the sky a dense unclouded purple and the air very clear. She really needed something warmer on than the red and blue striped coat over her corded velvet smock. Each time Martin landed her up here she tried walking in fresh directions to find a taxi, but now she had exhausted them all. So was it to be down to Muswell Hill or across the Finchley High Road? Martin had headed for Muswell Hill...Francesca, who wasn't usually very apprehensive or given to improbable fantasies, found herself thinking, suppose his car broke down and I walked past it and he saw me...? Now that her task was so nearly accomplished, she was growing hourly more and more frightened in case anything should happen at the eleventh hour to stop her getting the flat. People said it was virtually impossible to withdraw from such a deal once the contracts were exchanged. He wouldn't have to withdraw, though, he would only have to have a new contract made with his name on it instead of hers.

Nothing must happen. She only had Saturday to get through now. They had agreed not to meet on Sunday, she would be too busy packing. She pulled up the hood of her coat and set off along wide, cold, empty Fortis Green Lane for Finchley High Road. A taxi picked her up just before she reached it.

'I don't usually ever feel nervous about anything, you know,' she said to Tim. 'I suppose anyone can get nervous if there's enough at stake. While I was sort of lurking in that garden I kept thinking how awful it would be if that man came out of his house. I mean, he might have chased me and Martin might have hit him, thinking he was my husband, I imagined the most fearful things.'

Tim laughed. 'The most fearful thing about that would have been the outcome, the loss of our future home. Otherwise I can't imagine anything funnier that Livingstone having a punch-up with a complete stranger in the middle of the night in darkest Finchley.'

Francesca thought about it. Then she laughed too and helped herself to one of Tim's cigarettes. 'What made you pick on that funny house, anyway? What made you pick on that man?'

'Me? I didn't pick on him. I didn't pick on the house. That was your fiancée. Remember? I didn't even know there was anyone called Brown living in Fortis Green Lane. The idea of writing that par for the *Post* was solely to give verisimilitude to your story. People say newspapers are full of lies but they believe everything they read in newspapers just the same. Fortis Green Lane is a long road and Brown is a common name. There may be half a dozen Browns living there for all I know. Livingstone happened to find this one in the phone book.'

With a giggle Francesca said, 'It would be most awfully unfair then if Martin had hit him.'

'You'll have to take good care he doesn't. He truly is that mysterious individual, the innocent bystander.'

There was a heavy frost that night and the roof tops were nearly as white as when they had been covered with snow. Francesca and Tim lay late in bed and Francesca brought Lindsay in with them. They talked about the flat in Swan Place while Lindsay sat on the pillow and braided Francesca's hair into Afro-plaits. Tim said they would probably have to sell the flat and buy one that wasn't in Highgate, it would be so awkward if they ever ran into Martin. That would be all right, Francesca said, she would quite like to live up near the Green Belt or out towards Epping Forest, she wasn't wedded to London. Nor to the distinguished author of *The Iron Cocoon*, said Tim, and they both laughed so much that Lindsay pinched their lips together.

Tim drove her as near as he dared to Cromwell Court. Martin wanted to know what arrangements she had made for Monday. Had she booked a car? Was Lindsay going to the nursery that day or not? Could she manage all her clothes at one journey? And what about Russell? Had she told him there should be a fair division of their property and had he agreed? Francesca answered these questions as best she could while they were on their way to Swan Place to pick up the key from Mr Butler. She felt elated when the key was in her possession. A key gives such a secure feeling of rights and privacy and ownership. Mrs Butler took her round the flat once more and Francesca could hardly contain her excitement. How different it was to view all this, to tread those soft, subtle-shaded carpets, finger stiff silky curtains, feel the warmth, turn on a tap, press a switch, in the knowledge it was going to be all her own!

'Will you ask me to supper on Monday evening?' Martin said.

'Tuesday. Give me just one day to settle in. Lindsay's bound to be difficult, you know.'

'Yes, I suppose so. Tuesday then.' His face wore the hurt look that blurred his features and made it dog-like. 'Adrian hopes to complete by midday on Monday so you can come any time after. I expect the Butlers will still be moving out.'

Francesca didn't see much point in talking about it when she wasn't going to move in at all. She wished she had the nerve to ask Martin what was to be done with the deeds or lease or whatever it was. Deposited in his bank maybe. Not for long, she thought, not for long. Tim would deal with that, she had done her part, she had almost done it. She held Martin's hand in the car, held it on her knee and said, Let's not go out to dine, let's have a quiet evening at home on our own.

18

Most of the time there was nobody in the house but the man was there more often than the woman. This was a reversal, Finn thought, of the usual order of things. He had never seen them together, though he had been to Fortis Green Lane on five evenings now, each time parking in a different place. He had seen the woman twice and the man three times and once he had seen the man with another woman. This didn't trouble him, nor was he perplexed about the relations of these people to each other or that of Martin Urban to them. Emotions, passion, jealousy, desire, even hatred, were beyond or outside his understanding. They bored him, he preferred magic. He longed now to be able to wield practical magic, to conjure his victim out of the house and into his trap.

But he had lost that power even before the death of Queenie. Sitting in the van, watching, he thought of how, in Jack Straw's, he had concentrated on that reporter and made him get out and light a cigarette. Or had he? Such doubt is the enemy of faith and it is faith which moves the mountains.

Come out of the house, he said in his mind to the darkened windows, the closed front door, the indestructible stucco. He said it over and over again like the mantras he repeated for his meditation. He had no idea, and no means of knowing, if the house was empty or not. There might be a light on in the downstairs back room or in the kitchen. He had been there since five, since before the dark came down, but there had been no sign of life from the house and no flicker of light.

It was a cold evening, the air already laying frost in a very thin silvery glitter on the tops of fences and the cross-pieces of gates, on twigs and laurel leaves and on the oblique rear windows of parked cars. The sulphur light showed tiny early spring flowers in some gardens, pale or white or no-colour buds and bells. Finn didn't know the names of flowers. The frost wasn't heavy enough to whiten the grass much. Inside the van it was cold. Finn wore the yellow pullover and the grey woollen cap and the leather coat and sat reading Crowley's *Confessions*. Back in Lord Arthur Road he had left Lena and Mrs Gogarty indignant because Mr Beard, proposing to raise up for their edification, Abremelin the Mage, meant to do so by indefensible methods. In fact, by the sacrifice of a pigeon, the emanation from whose blood would provide the material for the seer to build a body out of. Pigeons were commoner than flies in Brecknock Road, Mr Beard had said. Lena and Mrs Gogarty shuddered and twittered and sent Mr Beard to Coventry. Finn wished he was back there with them and the innocent pleasures of planchette to which they had retreated, scared by Mr Beard's sophistication.

A light had come on in 54 Fortis Green Lane, a not very strong light as from a sixty-watt bulb, in the hall. It showed through the slit of a window on the right-hand side of the door and through the small diamond-shaped pane of glass in the door itself. No one came out, no one went in. It was ten o'clock. Finn didn't think anything was going to happen tonight. Again it would have to be postponed. That he had taken Martin Urban's money and as yet done nothing to earn it, vaguely oppressed him. But because it was a waste of time sitting there any longer, he drove down to Muswell Hill, to the Green Man, and drank two bottles of Britvic pineapple juice.

Sitting alone at a table, he fixed his thought on a fat man in a checked sports jacket, willing him to get up and go outside to the gents'. After about five minutes of this the fat man did get up and go outside, but a smaller thinner man sitting with him had gone out a moment or so before. Finn didn't know what to think. As he came out into the street he was visited by a premonition so intense as almost to blind him. He felt it like a pain in his head.

Tonight *was* the time for it. If he would only seize his opportunity and go back to Fortis Green Lane now all would be well. In his mind's eye, as on a screen, he saw the house quite clearly, the light shining through and alongside the front door, the front garden with its alternating turf and concrete. He stared into this vision and silently commanded Martin Urban's enemy to appear. At once this happened and Finn seemed to be staring into a pair of puzzled and dismayed eyes. He got into the van and drove back to Fortis Green Lane as fast as he could go.

There was no need to watch and wait. As in his vision, Martin Urban's enemy was in the front garden, unlatching the white iron gate. But this time there was no meeting of eyes.

Finn hadn't even switched off the engine. He watched the figure in the fur coat close the gate and turn immediately left into the side street. For what purpose would anyone go out alone at this time on a Saturday night? Finn knew it was no good judging by himself. He might go out to commune with the powers of darkness but others lacked that wisdom. They would be more likely to visit some friend, a nocturnal person who had no objection to late callers.

He allowed his quarry two minutes' start and then he followed. Martin Urban's enemy was nowhere to be seen. The street was deserted. Coldfall Wood, grey and still under the indigo sky, lay ahead of him. He turned right along the edge of the wood and then he saw the figure in the fur coat ahead of him, a long way ahead, casting an attenuated black shadow as it passed under a lamp. There was scarcely any other traffic, parked cars everywhere but only one that moved, a sports car that passed him, going towards Finchley.

Finn lagged behind, stopped for a while. When he started again, driving slowly, it wasn't long before he came to a sign that indicated the nearness of the North Circular Road. The houses had stopped. Soon the parked cars had stopped. On either side of the road he had turned into, stretched open land. Not woods, though, or heath or anything that remotely approximated to real countryside except that grass grew on it. It was a vast acreage of tips, of heaps of rubble, dismantled cars, rusty iron, stacks of wood that looked like collapsed huts, the overgrown remains of abandoned allotments. The whole of this wilderness was weirdly but brilliantly lit by lamps on tall stems which coated the sky with a shimmering brownish fog and gave to the ground a look of total desolation.

There was no dwelling of any kind in sight. Finn knew that most new approach roads to motorways or trunk roads look like this, that the land only had this appearance of nightmare violation because heavy construction work had not long since taken place on it. Yet knowing this, he still had the feeling of having entered a different and uncanny world, a place where the ordinary usages of life were suspended and the occult reigned. In it he felt alone, he and the bobbing shadow in the distance ahead. He felt too that he might even be invisible, had perhaps discovered unwittingly the secret of invisibility which since the beginning of time magicians had sought for.

A thrill of power ran through him. The clear brown sky seemed to be meshed all over with a dazzling veil of gold. But for a distant throb there was silence. Finn made the van glide slowly along. On the left-hand side, ahead of the moving figure, the pavement petered out. It would be necessary, inevitable, soon to cross that wide curving roadway, white and gold and glittering at close on midnight.

The head above the fur collar turned to the right, to the left, to the right again. The black shadow dipped into the road. Finn was in second gear. He rammed his foot hard down on the accelerator, changed in one movement up into fourth, and shot towards the shining, moving pillar of fur. Now, at last, he saw the eyes, round, shining, dark with terror. He had to swerve in pursuit, to make sure. A shattering scream rang through the glittering empty air, arms were flung up in a desperate useless defence, and then, when it seemed as if the suddenly huge, screaming animal-like shape must flatten and paste itself against his windscreen, he felt it under the van, the wheels crunching flesh and bone.

Finn reversed over the thing he had crushed and then drove

over it once more in bottom gear. There was a lot of blood, dark and colourless as Anne Blake's had been, splashed blots of it on the white road. He made a U-turn and drove back the way he had come up. For a yard or so his tyres left their imprints in blood. He would clean those tyres when he changed the licence plates, before he went home to Lena.

19

As yet the wood showed no signs of greening but it had grown sparkling brown and the beech trunks silver. Their myriad delicate fronds, for twigs was too solid a word, fanned against a mother-of-pearl sky. Martin was inescapably reminded of Tim. He had a feeling, utterly absurd and one to which he wouldn't have dreamt of yielding, that he should park the car here on the winding bit up to Highgate, and go on a pilgrimage through the wood to find the spot where he had met Tim. The dying day – not so different from a day just born – and the coming spring recalled to him the warmth of that encounter and that other curious feeling which he had felt for no one, not even for Francesca, either before or since.

He drove on. The sky was deepening to lavender and the sunset had brushed it with pink and golden strokes. What had Tim been doing in the wood that morning? Strange that he had never asked himself that question before. While he had come in from Priory Gardens and was walking north, Tim seemed to have entered from the Muswell Hill Road as if he had come from the junction where the Woodman was. Martin was approaching this junction now and it occurred to him that he might go into Bloomers and buy Francesca some spring flowers. Of course he had promised not to see her today but he would phone her when he got home and if she really didn't want to see him tonight he would take the flowers to her on his way to work in the morning.

Bloomers, however, was closed and its lights off, though the time was only twenty to six. Martin drove up Southwood Lane and down the High Street to Cromwell Court. No letters had come by the second post. He had written again to Mrs Cochrane on Friday but perhaps it was too soon yet to expect a reply. In the living room, part on a chair and part on the floor, were still stacked the saucepans, the frying pan, the apricot and brown and cream patterned towels, the brown and white sheets and pillowcases, and the Denbyware dinner service. Francesca might be in need of those things.

In the flat on Saturday afternoon he had noted the Butlers' phone number. He dialled it now and got the unobtainable signal. The Post Office presumably hadn't let her keep the old number when they came in today to re-connect the phone. Perhaps you always had to have a new number. Should he now phone Tim? It was three months, more than that, since he had last spoken to Tim. There was nothing really that he would like more tonight since he couldn't be with Francesca, than to spend a couple of hours with Tim. They hadn't even quarrelled. They had parted because of his own absurd guilt over nothing, he had broken their friendship over that money. And it was nearly all gone now, would all be gone when he had settled with Mrs Finn and Mrs Cochrane.

Tim wouldn't be home yet. Martin phoned Adrian Vow-church and thanked him for getting completion so promptly.

'Francesca move in all right, did she?'

'Oh, yes,' said Martin.

'By the by, I had a message, heaven knows why, that there are two more keys with the agents. OK?'

Martin said it was OK and that he had wondered why there had only been one key. He kept Adrian talking for a while in the hope that he might invite him and Francesca round one evening but Adrian didn't. He said he must fly because he and Julie were going out to dinner with the senior partner and his wife. Martin thought it likely that Francesca would phone once she had got Lindsay to bed and off to sleep. He drank some whisky, he made himself an omelette with four eggs and two rashers of bacon and a lot of mushrooms, and when he had eaten it and washed up it was half-past eight.

The phone rang at nine. It was Norman Tremlett. Norman

lived at home with his parents and he wanted to know if Martin would bring Francesca to dinner on the evening of Saturday week. Martin didn't much want to dine with the Tremletts but he felt excited at the idea of having the right to accept for himself and Francesca just as if they were already a married couple, so he said yes, they'd like to.

Just as it had previously been too early, it now seemed too late to phone Tim, too late anyway for them to arrange to meet and go out anywhere that night. He would phone Tim tomorrow or the next day. For the first time since the autumn Martin unlocked the glass door and went out on to the balcony. The night was cool but the sky so unusually clear that you could see the stars, though so tiny and faint that it was as if the gloomy pall of London had pushed them even greater distances into space. Francesca wasn't going to phone tonight. He realized it with resignation but it was silly to feel such intense disappointment. She would be tired after her long day which had started perhaps with a final quarrel with Russell and ended with Lindsay's tantrums, by now she might well be asleep.

The post brought a letter, not from Mrs Cochrane, but from her brother-in-law. The tone was that of Mr Cochrane's notes, clipped and censorious. It began 'Dear Martin' and the gist of it was that he and Mrs Cochrane would come to Cromwell Court that evening, eight o'clock if this was convenient. Martin looked in the phone book to see if Mr Cochrane was on the phone and found, to his surprise, that he was. But when he dialled the number there was no answer. He would have to try again later. This evening he was to dine with Francesca in Swan Place, so of course he couldn't see Mr and Mrs Cochrane.

He drove to work via Shepherd's Hill, thus passing close by Stanhope Avenue but Francesca's windows weren't visible. It was a nuisance having no phone number for her. He had an appointment with a client at eleven which eventually lengthened over lunchtime and it was half-past two before he got back.

Francesca hadn't phoned.

'Are you positive there haven't been any calls for me?'

Caroline, with black-varnished fingernails today and red

hair cropped to a crew cut, said that of course she was positive, he ought to know she didn't make mistakes like that.

'OK, well, would you like to get hold of directory enquiries and find if they've got a number for Brown of Flat 10 Swan Place, Stanhope Avenue, Highgate?'

She came back after about five minutes. 'No, they haven't, Martin, and I'm quite *positive*. He was a very nice man at directory enquiries, got a voice just like Terence Stamp.'

So the Post Office hadn't yet got around to fixing Francesca's phone. She was probably waiting in for them which could be why she hadn't phoned him from a call-box. It didn't matter particularly, he would just go straight there on his way from work.

He left at five-thirty sharp. Swan Place was, if anything, more attractive than Cromwell Court. The block was newer and there were lifts and carpet on the stairs. Martin smiled to himself to think he had spent more on Francesca's home than he had on his own. He went up in the lift and rang the bell of number 10.

No one came. He rang again. She was out. What on earth was she doing out now? Wasn't she expecting him? He wondered where she could have gone at this hour when nearly all the shops were closed. Perhaps to tea with some friend who had a child of Lindsay's age? Martin had never heard of any friend of Francesca's apart from Annabel. He hung about outside the door, wishing he had thought of calling in at the estate agent's to collect those other keys. They would be shut now.

He waited nearly half an hour for her. Then he wrote a note on the back of an envelope he found in his pocket and put it through the letter box. The note said to phone him as soon as she got in.

It began to worry him, thinking something might have happened to her. Suppose Russell had asked her to go back and have a talk with him and was preventing her from leaving again? He drank some whisky, not too much because he was sure to have to drive again that evening. There was nothing to eat in the flat apart from bread and cheese and things in tins.

The phone didn't ring but at just before eight the doorbell did. Martin was sure it was Francesca who had thought that if she had to go out into the street to find a call-box she might as well get in a taxi and come straight to him. On the doorstep stood Mr Cochrane and a very small woman in a scarlet coat and black fur pixie hood. He had forgotten all about them.

"Evening, Martin. This is Mrs Cochrane, Martin. Rita, this is Martin.'

Mr Cochrane was in casual gear, denim jeans, a Fair Isle pullover and a kind of anorak with fur trimmings. Martin felt bereft of ideas and almost of speech by the sight of them. But there was no help for it. Mr Cochrane hadn't waited to be invited in or asked to sit down. He had gone in, taken his sister-in-law's coat and hat, seated her on the sofa, hung up her coat and his own in the hall cupboard, and was now alternately rubbing his hands and warming them on a radiator.

'Would you like a drink?' Martin said.

'Whisky for me, Martin, and Mrs Cochrane will have a lemonade with a drop of port in it.'

Martin had neither port nor lemonade. Every bottle had to be removed from the drinks cupboard before Mr Cochrane could decide on a substitute. His sister-in-law hadn't opened her mouth. When she was at last given a wine glass containing a mixture of sweet red vermouth and soda she nodded her head very fast and on and on as if she had a spring where her neck should be. Her mouth had set into a pinched, tight and intensely nervous smile.

Mr Cochrane, now sitting on the radiator, launched into a speech. His attitude was one which Martin hadn't met before in his dealings with the objects of his charity. His sister-in-law was prepared to accept Martin's offer – here Mrs Cochrane, who hadn't ceased to smile, began nodding again – provided she was allowed absolute freedom of choice as to where she lived and what kind of dwelling she lived in. Also Martin must understand that one must move with the times, things had changed out of all knowledge in the past few years and you couldn't buy anything worth considering in the London area for less than fifteen thousand pounds. At this point the phone rang and Martin leapt for it. It was a wrong number. Mr Cochrane said that he supposed it was all right to help himself to more scotch, did so, and terminated his speech with words to the effect that now they understood each other and had cleared the air he would start house-hunting in the morning.

Martin felt he only wanted to get rid of them. If it cost him his last five thousand did it so much matter? He realized that that was what it would do, it would all be gone. Deliberately and methodically he half-filled his glass with whisky and drank it at a gulp.

'I'm glad to be of help,' he said. 'It's good we've been able to arrange things so easily.'

The phone rang. It was Norman Tremlett to ask if Martin and Francesca could make it Saturday fortnight instead of Saturday week. Martin said yes and he would call Norman back. Mr Cochrane had got himself into his anorak and his sister-in-law into her coat and pixie hood and was staring piercingly at the stack of saucepans and china and towels and bed linen.

'If I don't see madam on Friday, Martin, you can tell her I mean to commence the spring cleaning. Subject to her approval of course.'

Martin didn't know what to say to this.

'Come along, Rita.'

Martin closed the door on them and finished his whisky. There was only about an inch left in the bottle so he had that too. After the phone had rung the second time he had made up his mind to drive round to Swan Place as soon as the Cochranes had gone. But he couldn't go now, he had drunk too much. He slept heavily and dreamlessly that night, awakening early with a headache.

By a quarter to nine he was ringing Francesca's doorbell. He continued to ring it long after there was no point. Then it occurred to him that she might still be taking Lindsay to the nursery and he wrote her another note, on the back of the bill for the sheets and towels this time, asking her to phone him before lunch.

When it got to twelve, to half-past, and she hadn't phoned he began to feel real anxiety for the first time. He excused himself to Gordon Tytherton with whom he had said he would have lunch, and went back to Swan Place. Francesca was still out. He simply didn't know what to do, and then he remembered the two spare keys. He drove up to Highgate Village and was given the keys without demur by the estate agent's receptionist.

His notes were still on the doormat. That was the first thing he absorbed. The second – though this took some time fully to register – was that no one had occupied the place since the departure of the Butlers. There were the carpets on the floors and the curtains at the windows, the chairs and tables, the fridge and the cooker and an electric kettle, but there was no food in the kitchen, the fridge door still stood open after Mrs Butler's final defrosting, and in the bathroom there was no soap, no toothbrush. Martin went into both bedrooms to find that the beds hadn't been made up. The cupboard in the main bedroom was empty but for five wire coathangers.

For a while he was nonplussed. He sat down in the penthouse living room by the window that was even bigger than his own in Cromwell Court. But almost immediately he jumped up again. The first thing he must do, obviously, was phone her at home in Fortis Green Lane. For some reason, because she was ill or Lindsay was ill or Russell had intervened and used force, she had been prevented from leaving home on Monday.

Rejecting the idea of phone boxes, which he had hardly ever in his life had occasion to use, he drove home to Cromwell Court. There, for the first time, he dialled the number the directory gave for H. R. Brown of 54 Fortis Green Lane, N10. The bell rang unanswered. She couldn't be at home ill. He felt rather sick, with hangover perhaps or hunger. He made himself a cheese sandwich but he couldn't eat it. The idea of taking the afternoon off to look for Francesca didn't cross his mind. He tried the phone again and then he went back to work, remembering a fear that had come to him during the first days of their acquaintance when she had told him nothing of her circumstances or history and had withheld from him her address. He had wondered what he would do if she left her job, for the flower shop had been the only place where he could be sure of finding her.

Floreal was again closed and unlit when he drove past it just before six. He went home and poured himself a stiff brandy because all the whisky was gone. He thought inconsequentially how a week ago he could have afforded cases of whisky without thinking about it, but not now. He had no more money now than on the last occasion he sent in Tim's pools perm.

No one was answering the phone at 54 Fortis Green Lane. He tried it four times between six and seven. Immediately after he put the phone back for the fourth time it rang. Norman Tremlett. Why hadn't he rung back last night as he had promised? Martin dealt with Norman as best he could, trying not to lose his temper at facetious questions about his 'lovely betrothed' and when the 'happy day' was to be. As soon as he could terminate the conversation he did. He grilled the steak he had brought in with him and ate it without enjoyment. The brandy bottle beckoned him, but he knew that if he drank any more he wouldn't dare drive up to Finchley.

He could tell the house was empty before he even got out of the car. What now? Enquire of the neighbours as he had enquired for Annabel? After sitting in the car for an aeon of minutes, after some painful soul-searching, he tried number 52.

A girl of about fifteen came to the door. He might have been speaking to her in Hausa or Aramaic for all her comprehension.

At last she said, 'You what?'

He realized he had asked questions which, in these lawless times, gave rise to deep suspicion. The girl went away to fetch her mother. Martin rehearsed in his mind better ways of eliciting information but they weren't much better. The woman appeared, drying her hands on a tea towel.

'I'm sorry,' Martin began, 'I know you must think this very

odd, but I only want to know if Mr and Mrs Brown next door are away. I'm . . .' It wasn't exactly true but what else could he say? '. . . a friend of theirs.'

It was as if he had demanded payment for goods she hadn't bought or even wanted. She gave a humourless, cynical laugh.

'That's not true for a start. There is no Mrs Brown. He's a widower. He's been a widower for all of five years.'

Martin couldn't speak.

Perhaps she sensed that he had had a shock. Her manner softened. 'Look, you could be anybody, couldn't you, for all I know? Such a lot of funny things go on these days. He's not in, you can see that. I haven't seen him since Saturday but that doesn't mean a thing. He keeps himself to himself.'

She had closed the door before Martin was halfway down the path. His hands shook when he got hold of the steering wheel. He flexed them and took deep breaths and tried to blank out his mind. When he tried again his hands were steady. It wasn't more than a couple of miles down to Highgate, though he was slowed up by the rain which had suddenly begun and now was lashing down.

The phone was ringing as he walked into the flat. He thought that if it was Francesca he wouldn't know what to say, he would be able to find no words in which to speak to her, to ask, even to begin. What she had done to him he didn't know, only that it was terrible.

He picked up the phone. There were pips, six of them.

A voice said, 'This is Finn speaking.'

20

'Yes,' Martin said, 'yes?' He had forgotten who Finn was and the flat low voice meant nothing to him.

'I thought I'd have heard from you by now.'

Heard from him . . . Oh, yes. Finn was Mrs Finn's son and Mrs Finn was . . . He was surprised to hear his own voice sounding so normal, so characteristic even. 'You've been successful, have you?'

A short toneless 'Yes'.

Martin was getting used to ingratitude. He no longer cared. 'I'll send the rest round like I did the first lot, OK?'

'In cash again,' said Finn and put the phone down.

It was still only nine o'clock. Martin poured himself some more brandy but he couldn't drink it, the smell of it made him feel sick. Was it possible that the woman in the house next door had been lying? Why should she, except from madness or motiveless malevolence? Francesca didn't live there, had never lived there. But he had seen her go into the house. . . . No, he had never quite seen that. He remembered little things, that insistence on taxis, her refusal ever to invite him into the house. Where was she now?

She must have a home somewhere. She hadn't come to him like some fairy woman out of the sea or from another world. Surely she had loved him . . .? There must be some motive for the lies she had told him but that motive might not in itself be evil. He tried to think of reasons for it, sitting there in the chair by the window long into the night. At last he drank up the brandy and went to bed. London went on glittering down there as if nothing had happened.

Next day the world had become a different place. The day was cold and wet, a high wind blowing. He awoke to some sense of indefinable misery. A moment later it was no longer indefinable but had settled into the knowledge that Francesca had deceived him.

The wind was blustery and sharp. He saw it blow someone's umbrella inside out as he crossed the Archway Road. The lights weren't on in Floreal but it wasn't yet nine-thirty. Stuck up on the door, on the inside of the glass, was a notice that hadn't been there last week. *Closed till Monday, March 5.* He turned away. Kate Ross could be ill or just taking a holiday. He went back to his car and drove to work.

Kate would be bound to have Francesca's true address. There were a dozen or so people in the phone book called K. Ross but none in Highgate where Kate lived. Or where Francesca had said she lived. Could he believe anything Francesca had told him?

Her parents lived in Chiswick. Her maiden name had been Blanch. But was that true? There was an E. Blanch in a place called Petrarch Court, Barrowgate Gardens, Chiswick. She had said they lived in a flat, an old mansion block. She had said, she had said . . . He dialled the number, tried to resign himself to hearing a voice say she had no daughter, had never even married.

A man answered. He sounded elderly, as if he might be retired.

'I'm trying to get in touch with your daughter, Francesca Brown.'

There was a dense silence. Then, 'I might say I don't have a daughter.'

Martin didn't know what to say. He nearly put the receiver down. But the old voice, very dry now, said, 'I haven't seen Francesca for five years.' There came a crackling chuckle. 'She was never very filial. A cold-hearted girl. I can give you her husband's phone number, though God knows when she left him. She leaves everybody.'

Martin said he would have the number. He wrote it down.

'That's right,' said Mr Blanch. 'Russell Brown's his name but he'll be out now. At work. She hasn't by any chance left *you*, has she?'

The exchange was an East London one, Ilford or Stratford. Had Francesca given him the Fortis Green Lane address because she was ashamed of her real one? He seemed to hear the dry rasping voice again, 'God knows when she left him. She leaves everybody.' There had been a bitter cynical amusement underlying Mr Blanch's words. For the first time Martin felt the absurdity of his position, the humiliation. How was he going to explain to his parents, to Norman and Adrian, that he had bought Francesca a flat and she had left him without even living in it. 'She leaves everybody . . .'

He couldn't think of an excuse for getting out of dinner with his parents. His mother, drinking oloroso, said she had half expected Francesca too, though she supposed that would have meant a baby-sitter for the little girl. Mr Urban leant against the mantlepiece with his amontillado. Martin had three glasses of Tio Pepe, wondering where Francesca was now and who Lindsay's father was and why she had lied to him so that it seemed almost everything she had said was a lie.

'Do you think Francesca would like me to make her a patch-work skirt?' said Mrs Urban.

Martin said he didn't know, which was the answer he would have been obliged to make to any question put to him about Francesca.

'I don't care for them myself,' said his mother, 'but she looks the type to wear them.'

Martin left early, having taken from the bathroom cabinet one of the sleeping pills his mother had for when she went on holiday. He was home by half-past nine. What did he hope to learn, anyway, by phoning Russell Brown? According to her father, 'God knows when' Francesca had left him, years ago, perhaps, he couldn't be Lindsay's father. At last he did try the number that Mr Blanch had given him, but there was no answer. He took the Mogadon tablet and washed it down with brandy and went to bed.

Mr Cochrane, arriving at eight-thirty in the morning, made no reference to the events of Tuesday evening. He had brought Martin's letters up with him, having encountered the postman on the way in. Martin didn't open them, didn't so much as glance at them. He was in no mood for bills or for querulousness from Miss Watson or the Gibsons which he felt those envelopes might contain.

He carried the saucepans and the frying pan, the dinner service, the two lamps, the bed linen and towels into his bedroom and stuffed them into the bottom of the clothes cupboard. They would come in useful one day, he thought with dry anger, for other people's wedding presents.

Mr Cochrane, in his ironmonger's coat, was emptying cupboards and shelves on to the kitchen floor, the first stage of his spring cleaning. On the table were the two piles of newspapers, the broadsheets and the tabloids.

'Beats me what you want all this muck for, Martin,' said Mr Cochrane. 'Hoarding up rubbish like an old woman.'

Martin took no notice. He was looking through the *Posts* for the copy of December 8, the one that had contained the paragraph about Russell Brown. Surely it had been on the top because it was the last one he had ever received, after that he had stopped taking the *Post*. Then he remembered. He must have used it to wrap up Mrs Finn's money. Naturally he had used the paper that was on top of the pile. Mrs Finn. Some time today, he thought, he had better go to the bank and draw out the other five thousand, phone them first, maybe, as he had done last time . . .

He had been at work ten minutes when Adrian Vowchurch phoned. He said it was rather embarrassing (he didn't sound embarrassed) but he simply had to know whether his account for the conveyance was to go to Francesca or to Martin.

Martin hadn't expected an account at all. It was true that Adrian had charged him for the conveyance of his own flat but since then he, Martin, had put in a whole lot of hours sorting out some family trust muddle for Julie and he wouldn't have dreamt of expecting payment for that. He said shortly:

'To me, of course. Who else?'

'My dear old chap, I only asked. Ladies get very uptight these days if their equality isn't respected. Francesca is a property owner now and a ratepayer. It can go to their heads, you know, and you do rather . . .'

'Adrian . . .' he interrupted but he couldn't finish.

'What? I was merely going to say – if merely is the word – that you do rather talk as if her flat was sort of yours. You can't have it both ways, avoid your tax *and* keep a foot in the door.'

The flat was hers. Did she know that? He had never exactly explained this to her but she must know it, she was no fool. If she knew it was hers surely she would come to it. He put his head round his father's door to say he was going out for an hour. Walter Urban was preoccupied with a client's letter. He looked up, irritability making him more than usually dog-faced.

'Extraordinary chap,' he said, tapping the letter. 'Calls himself the chairman of a financial P R company and he doesn't know the first thing about finance. Here he is telling me he's given away – *given*, if you please – ten thousand pounds to his sister to start some sort of business and can he get tax relief on it? He won't find the government giving anything to him, he'll be giving it to them. Hasn't he ever heard of C T T?'

'C T T?' repeated Martin, although he knew perfectly well what those initials stood for.

'Capital Transfer Tax. Wake up, Martin. His sister's not a charity. Why didn't he consult me before he started throwing his money about?'

Martin asked himself why he too hadn't consulted Walter or even consulted his own knowledge. Was it because he hadn't wanted to know and have his noble-hearted schemes spoiled? Just as he hadn't wanted to know of the true relations between Francesca and her husband? Now, in both cases, he was going to have to pay for wilfully shutting his eyes. Almost all his money was gone and he was presumably going to have to pay tax, at least on what he had given Miss Watson and Mrs Cochrane, though perhaps not Mrs Finn since that was cash . . . Was he planning on being dishonest about it as well? He pushed all thought of money out of his mind – did he really care about it at this juncture? – and drove to Swan Place. The flat was just as it had been on Wednesday, empty, waiting, the fridge door open, the carpet marked with circular depressions where furniture legs had stood.

He had wanted to tell Adrian about it but he hadn't been able to. Adrian's voice had been too cool, too mocking and urbane. He thought of those friends of his whose advice he could ask, Norman, the Tythertons . . . They couldn't help him any more than he could help himself, and behind his back, because they were deeply conservative and unshakeably conventional, they would laugh nervously.

Back in the office, he reverted to that paragraph in the *Post*. He could remember perfectly what it had said. Russell Brown was thirty-five, was a teacher in a technical college who had written a book about the fourteenth century and the Black Death, wife Francesca, daughter Lindsay. Martin sighed and dialled the Ilford number Mr Blanch had given him. There was no answer.

Could the *Post* have got it wrong? Could it have been Fortis Green Road or Fortis Green Avenue instead? That wouldn't explain how Francesca had seemed to live, had repeatedly said she lived, in Fortis Green Lane. The *Post* must have some sort of clue to all this and he knew someone who worked on the *Post* . . .

Tim Sage.

Tim might not know the answer but Tim would be able to help him. Journalists always knew how to go about finding elusive addresses and phone numbers, and elusive people, come to that. And it was foolish to think of himself and Tim as enemies. Why did he do that? There had been no quarrel except in his own mind and in his dreams.

He dialled the *Post's* head office in Wood Green. No, Mr Sage wasn't there but he could try their Child's Hill office. Martin tried Child's Hill and was told Mr Sage hadn't been in all day. It was always hard to get hold of Tim. In the old days – he thought of pre-November as the old days – it was nearly always Tim who had phoned him. A feeling of desolation crept over him. He sat at his desk, unable to work for the first time in as long as he could remember.

It was about an hour later that Caroline came in to say that an Indian family had arrived and were asking for Mr Urban.

'A man and a woman and a little boy and an old man and an old woman who looks just like Mrs Gandhi.'

He stared at her.

'What do they want?'

'You,' said Caroline. 'They've just got back from India today, or some of them have, and they've been in Australia first and they want to see you and thank you for something. That's what they said.'

The Bhavnanis.

For months he had hoped to see them, had longed, though never quite admitting it to himself, for some crumb of gratitude from someone. And now they had come he knew he couldn't face them.

'Take them in to my father,' he said. 'He's called Mr Urban too.' Although it was only four he walked out of the office and drove back to Swan Place where he sat by the window, waiting for Francesca to come, although he knew she wouldn't come.

Samphire Road. Martin found it in the *London Atlas* he kept in the glove compartment of his car. It was Finsbury Park really, North Four. He didn't think he had ever been there or known anyone else who lived there.

If Tim was out he would sit in the car and wait for him. He would wait till midnight if necessary, he had nothing else to do. But he probably wouldn't have to wait like that because the man Tim lived with would be there. Why had he ever worried about having to meet this man, about seeing him and Tim together? He couldn't have cared less now.

It was getting on for six when Martin left Swan Place. If Tim had had an afternoon job he would be home by now, and if he had an evening job it was unlikely he would go out before seven. He and his friend might be eating their evening meal. Martin recalled the big red sofa he had dreamed about, red velvet, sponge-like yet dusty. It embarrassed him even to think of it.

He drove up Crouch End Hill and down Hornsey Rise. The sky was like a thick grey veil which the sunset had torn open to show through the rents radiant flesh colours. He would tell Tim everything, he thought, and the prospect of being able to be open and candid with Tim at last filled him with a joy so intense that his hands actually trembled on the wheel. For a moment he forgot the loss of Francesca and the bitter, growing disillusionment. The secret he had kept from Tim for three months had weighed upon him – how heavily he was only now realizing – and at last, within a few minutes perhaps, he was about to unburden himself. That his purpose in coming here was to question Tim about the paragraph in the *Post* had receded and dimmed in the fierce light of the confession, the money and its source, Francesca, his long silence and coldness, he was going to make. He longed for it as the devout sinner longs for the confessional and the exhausted tormented prisoner for a chance to admit his guilt.

He had entered a desolate wilderness where streets, walled-in wooden barricades, traversed a grassless, treeless, and almost building-less waste. A few new houses, in strange colours of brick, lemon, pasty white, charcoal, rose here and there in straggling lines. The old streets of old brown houses clung to the perimeter like low cliffs surrounding a crater in a desert. Martin found Samphire Road quite easily, even though his map no longer gave a very clear idea of the layout. It was a gorge in the brown cliff with shabby houses which made Martin think of the living quarters in some aged and perhaps abandoned garrison. Compared to it, Fortis Green Lane was paradise.

He walked up broken concrete steps to the liver-coloured front door and pressed the bell marked Sage. Nothing happened for a moment and then a light came on behind the green and yellow glass transom over the door. He was aware now that he could smell Gauloise smoke, as if Tim hadn't long come in.

The door opened and Tim stood there. He wore jeans and an old grey, heavy, stringy sweater that made him look thinner than ever, gaunt almost. His face was very pale, his mouth as red as fresh blood. Had he always been so pale? He took the cigarette out of his mouth and said:

'I thought you'd turn up. It was only a matter of time before you cottoned on.'

Martin stared at him. He didn't know what he meant. Then something so strange happened, so amazing really, that temporarily he forgot all about Tim. The door at the end of the passage opened and a child came running out and towards them. The child was, must be, but couldn't be, Lindsay.

She came to an abrupt halt and looked at Martin. Her look was full of anger and dislike. She threw herself against Tim's legs, holding up her arms. Tim lifted her up and held her against his shoulder, black hair against black hair, sallow velvet skin touching sallow waxen skin. Four blue eyes looked at Martin. He felt the earth move under his feet, the walls tilt, the dark, frowsty, uncarpeted passage rock back and forth and steady itself.

'You'd better come in,' said Tim.

Martin came in and felt the door closed behind him. He was unable to speak. He took a few steps down the passage, then turned, shaking, to contemplate again Lindsay and her undoubted father. But Francesca was her undoubted mother . . .

'I don't understand,' he began. 'You and Francesca . . . Where's Francesca?'

Tim put the child down. He leant against the door, his arms folded. 'She's dead. You didn't know? No, I reckon – well, how could you? She was killed last Saturday night, run over, the car didn't stop.'

Lindsay, clinging to his legs, began suddenly to cry.

21

Lindsay's screams seemed to express the grief of both men, Tim's sorrow, Martin's stunned, incredulous dismay. They were both silent, oblivious of the sobs and howls, the stamping feet, the fists beating at Tim's legs. They stared at each other but Martin was the first to let his gaze drop and to turn away. Slowly Tim reached down and picked Lindsay up. She stopped screaming but continued to sob, her arms and legs clamped against him like a starfish.

A door opened upstairs and a woman's voice called:

'Everything OK, Tim? God, she was making a racket.'

Tim went to the foot of the stairs with Lindsay in his arms. 'Could you have her for half an hour, Goldie?'

'Sure, if you want. She'll have to watch telly, though, it's my serial on.'

'Lindsay wants Goldie!' The child scrambled down her father's body and up the stairs on all fours.

'You'd better come in here and have a drink,' said Tim. 'We could both use a drink.'

He led Martin down the passage into the room from which Lindsay had emerged. It was a kitchen, modernized in skimpy patches round the sink area and a unit of cupboards but otherwise dismally old-fashioned with a defunct boiler in one corner and, in the wall facing them, a fireplace whose flue was blocked up with red crêpe paper. The oven was on and so was a wall heater. On the table, which was littered with newspapers and Gauloise packets, were the remains of a meal and a half-empty bottle of Dominic's military gin.

Martin moved as if in a daze. Tim motioned him to one of

the small shabby fireside chairs that flanked the wall heater but Martin sat, or sank, into a bentwood chair at the table and put his head in his hands.

'D'you want it neat or with water?'

'Doesn't matter.'

Martin had never before drunk gin without tonic or martini or some other fancy mixer. He had never drunk it warm which this was. It tasted so disgusting that he gave a strong shudder, but the fiery stuff bolstered him. He turned to look at Tim with haggard eyes. Tim was watching him with something that might have been despair or just indifference. When he spoke it was in a cool detached voice, such as a sociologist might use, reporting on failure, misery, defeat.

'I'll tell you what the police told me and fill in the gaps from my own knowledge. After you'd dropped her at that place in Finchley, she went to look for a taxi to take her home. It wasn't the first time, it's not easy to find taxis up there. She walked a long way, nearly up to the North Circular.' Tim paused, resuming in the same flat voice. 'You can't see how anyone could have failed to see her crossing the road, it's so brightly lit. Maybe the guy was drunk or just not looking. Another motorist found her ten minutes afterwards – or that's what they think. She wasn't dead. She died in hospital on Sunday evening.'

Martin said softly, 'She lived all that time . . .?'

'She wasn't conscious. Have some more gin?'

Tim re-filled their glasses. He lit another cigarette. The only sign of emotion he gave was the way he drew on that cigarette with nervous, greedy gasps.

'Right,' he said. 'Question time.'

The gin was making Martin hot and dizzy and brave. 'Were you *married* to Francesca?'

Tim laughed, a sound that had nothing to do with amusement. 'You know better than that, you're my accountant. Wouldn't I have had to tell you if I'd been married? Francesca was still married to a guy in Ilford. He's called Russell Brown, *he* really is."

'But that piece in your paper . . .'

'Pieces in the paper are of human origin. They're not messages from some infallible source of truth.' Tim shrugged. 'I made it up, bar the names. You found the house yourself. I didn't tell you she lived at 54 Fortis Green Lane and, incidentally, neither did she. You fabricated it. You made conjecture into truth just as you did when you saw those bruises on Francesca and thought Russell had put them there. In fact, she'd fallen over on the ice like several thousand other people did that day.'

Martin was silent. Then he said slowly, 'Do you mean that it was all a conspiracy between you and Francesca? All of it?' The enormity of what had been done to him was now breaking over Martin in waves. He could feel a pulse drumming in his head. 'You both of you set out to con me, to get . . .' He understood now, '. . . a flat out of me? You were two – criminals who did that?'

'At the beginning,' said Tim, 'Francesca set out only to get money or a piece of jewellery. I knew about your pools win, of course, I've known from the first. You must have forgotten that though I'm not much of a success at things I've got a spectacularly good memory.' He took a gulp of gin and it made him shudder. 'You aren't the soul of generosity, are you? I got nothing and she got nothing until you hit on your bright idea of a tax dodge. By that time, as you accountants might say, she was in for a penny, in for a pound.'

Martin had got to his feet. He swayed and steadied himself. There was one thing still, one last thing. If she had been unfaithful to Russell Brown with Tim, she had been unfaithful to Tim with him. He looked into Tim's eyes and the voice which he meant to be defiant, spitting revelations, came out falteringly.

'She slept with me! Did she ever tell you that?'

Tim had half-risen, his mouth smiling, his eyes dead. He shrugged. 'So? It was hard work. There was no question of mixing pleasure with business.'

Without thought or preparation, Martin hit him. He doubled his fist and swung and struck Tim on the jaw. Tim let out a grunt and fell back into the chair, but he was up again straightaway, leaping on Martin with both hands raised. Martin ducked and struck out again and fell across the table, knocking over the lamp which rolled on to the floor and went out.

The room was dark but for the fierce red glow from the wall heater, so that redness lay on the air and on the furniture and on Tim, backed against the door, a demon, a fallen angel, painted with red light. He came at Martin again, punching to his face, but this time Martin seized him by the shoulders, by his thin hard rib cage. For a moment they remained upright, locked together, struggling, then they tumbled to the floor and rolled, clutching each other, into the deep dark shadows of the floor and across the thick, old, rumpled rug.

Tim was trying to grab his shoulders so as to beat his head against the ground. Martin was stronger. He was bigger and heavier than Tim, and more powerful. He got hold of Tim's wrists and held them behind his back, wrapping him in his arms.

With this success, this subduing of Tim, a tremendous excitement seized him. He was wrestling with Tim, he was doing what he had longed to do in those dreams. And in the pressure of Tim's hard flesh, the friction of his body writhing and turning so that they rolled this way and that, embraced so tightly that each body seemed to penetrate the other and fuse with it, he felt himself charged and stiff with desire. He felt a passion which made his relations with Francesca seem thin and cold.

Whether Tim realized or not he didn't care. He was lost to all caution and all inhibiting restraint. He spoke Tim's name in a hoarse whisper and the struggling slackened. There was a moment in which Martin hardly seemed to breathe and then, because he couldn't help himself, he put his mouth over Tim's and gave him a long, enduring kiss. The release that came with that kiss seemed to take with it the repressive burdens of a lifetime. He rolled away from Tim and lay on his face.

Tim got up first. He did what he would do on the gallows or at an H-bomb early warning. He lit a Gauloise. His mouth quirked up on one side at Martin and he gave a sort of half-wink. Martin was flooded with shame, the burdens of a lifetime were still there. He got to his feet and sat, hunched, in one of the fireside chairs.

'Don't put the light on.'

'OK, not if you don't want.'

'I'm sorry about that. Just now, I mean.' Martin tried not to mumble. He tried to look at Tim through the red gloom, to meet his eyes and speak lucidly. It was nearly impossible. 'I don't know why I did that.'

'It was the military gin. The fact is, it's meant for guardsmen and you know what guardsmen are.'

'I'm not queer, gay, whatever you call it.'

'It was the gin, love,' said Tim.

He had perched himself on the edge of the table. Martin managed to focus on him now, and if he was flushed it didn't show in that light. 'Perhaps I am, though,' he said in a low voice. 'Perhaps I am really and I never knew it. Why have there been so many things I didn't know and couldn't see, Tim?'

'"Humanity treads ever on a thin crust over terrific abysses". I remember I said that to you before all this started. We've both fallen in with a crash, haven't we?'

Martin nodded. He was embarrassed still and ashamed still but a warmth that had nothing to do with the heater was slowly engulfing him. He loved Tim, he knew it now. Nothing that Tim had done to him mattered any more. He said:

'That flat, the one Francesca was going to move into, you can have it, I want you to have it.'

'Is it yours to give, my dear?'

'Well, I . . .' Technically, legally, it wasn't. It was the technical, the legal, aspect which mattered, though.

'It'll be shared between four people, I should think. Francesca had a husband and a child and parents. Lindsay will get some of it and I suppose Russell Brown will get most of it.'

'Tim, I'll give you . . .' What? He had nothing left to give. 'I want to do something. We've both lost Francesca, that ought to bring us together, it ought to . . . What are you smiling at?'

'Your naïvety.'

'I can't see that it's naïve to want to help someone because you feel you owe it to them. Look, I could sell my flat and buy a small house somewhere – well, not so nice, and you could bring Lindsay and come and live there with me and . . . We have to be friends, Tim.'

'Do we, my dear? I've injured you and we dislike those we've injured.' Tim walked across the room and switched on the central light. It was bright, glaring, uncompromising. 'I'm sorry for what I did now, I bitterly regret it, but being sorry doesn't make me like you any more. I wouldn't dream of sharing a house with you and if you offered me money I should refuse it.' He stubbed out his cigarette, coughing a little. 'It's time you went home now. I have to fetch Lindsay and put her to bed.'

Martin got up. He felt as if he had been hit in the face with something cold and wet, a wet glove perhaps.

'Is that all?' he stammered. 'Have we said it all?'

Tim didn't answer. They were out in the icy dank hallway now and from upstairs, distantly, came a wail, 'Lindsay wants Daddy.'

Tim opened the front door. 'The inquest was today. Accidental death. Cremation Monday, three o'clock, Golders Green. A hearty welcome will be extended to all husbands, real, imaginary, future and common law.'

Martin walked down the steps and into the street without looking back. He heard the door close. His head was banging from bewilderment and incredulity and gin.

It was a quarter past seven. He had been with Tim for less than an hour. In those forty-five or fifty minutes his whole life, the past as well as the present and the future, had been changed. It was as if the world had tilted and he been thrown sliding down the slope of it to hang there, breathless, by his hands. Or as if, as Tim said, the thin crust had given way.

His head was hurting him now. He had drunk a lot of that

gin, probably a tumblerful. But he didn't feel drunk, only sick and headachey and drained. He was tired as well but he didn't think he would sleep, he felt as if he would never sleep again.

For a long time he sat in the car in Samphire Road. He only drove away because he was afraid Tim might come out and find him still there, and even then he parked again almost immediately, in one of the streets that had been turned into a cul-de-sac by the crater of devastated land.

It was quite dark now and the rubble-covered waste was totally unlighted. The edges of it only were visible, a horizon of black jagged roofs, punctured with points of light, against the crimson-suffused sky. Francesca had lived here, come from here every morning, returned here each night. It seemed to him infinitely strange, something he would never fully understand. She was dead and had been dead for nearly a week now. In her dying she had somehow come back to him, there had been no terrible betrayal. How could Tim know how she had felt? How could Tim tell that for all her early motives she hadn't, at the end, come to prefer the new man to the old?

From taking a vicious pleasure in the fact of her death – he had felt like that when he first began to understand – he found he could now think of her with a pitying tenderness. They would never have been happy together, or not for long, he could see that. He was getting to know himself at last, he thought.

His head wasn't going to get any better just sitting here. If the place had been more attractive – less downright sinister, in fact – he would have gone for a walk, walked to clear his head, for it was a mild evening with that indefinable smell and charge in the air that heralds spring. But he couldn't walk here. He started the car and drove away into Hornsey Rise.

Someone walked across a pedestrian crossing ahead of him. He braked and waited rather longer than usual. He thought of the manner of Francesca's death. Who could do such a thing? Knock someone down and drive away to leave her dying? She had taken a night and a day to die. He shivered uncontrollably. Whoever it was, the police would find him, the police would be relentless . . . Martin reflected that he shouldn't be driving at all, he had had far too much to drink, a lot over the permitted limit. Perhaps Francesca's killer had also been drinking, had sobered up in terror when he saw what he had done, and terror had made him flee. Martin drove home over the Archway, the road in its deep concrete gorge flowing northwards beneath him.

He put the car on the hard-top parking in front of Cromwell Court, parking it between an orange-coloured Volvo and a small grey van. The Volvo belonged to a doctor at the Royal Free who lived on the ground floor. The grey van was probably some tradesman's, though Martin felt obscurely that he had seen it somewhere before, and recently, and in a context he couldn't at the moment recall. It couldn't be of the slightest importance. He walked across the asphalt to the entrance of the block, aware that someone had got out of the van and was also coming in.

But he didn't hold the door open. He let it swing shut and made for the stairs, wishing, not for the first time, that there was a lift here as there was in Swan Place. Should he get Adrian to fight for Swan Place against that family of Francesca's? Was there any chance of success? At least, he thought as he climbed the third flight, he could now tell Adrian and Norman and his parents the melancholy truth, that Francesca was dead.

The soft but regular footsteps which, lower down, he had heard coming behind him he could now hear again. They were coming up to the top. The driver of the grey van must be calling at one of the other three flats on this floor. Martin got to the top and crossed the corridor to his own front door. There, standing on the threshold of his home, he was suddenly and sharply reminded by the memory of himself and Tim embraced in Tim's red-lit kitchen, and of kissing Tim and holding him in his arms. What would become of him if this was what he wanted? What must he look forward to? He released his pent-up breath and put his key into the lock.

As he did so he heard a low cough behind him. It made Martin jump and he wheeled round. Standing about a yard from him, in grey woolly hat, yellow pullover, black velvet waistcoat and a black scarf with coins sewn round it, was Finn. Martin hadn't really noticed before what extraordinary eyes the man had. They were almost silver. The man with the silver eyes . . .

'Well, well,' said Finn. 'I've been waiting long enough.'

He pushed past Martin and into the flat.

22

The flat was warm and very stuffy. For most of the day the sun must have been shining on that big window. It was rare for Finn to be a guest in anyone's home. He could count on the fingers of his large, splayed hands the number of times it had happened: twice at Mr Beard's, once at Mrs Gogarty's, three or four times in girls' rooms.

He stood looking about him. At the structure and the paintwork mainly, he had a business interest in things like that. He took off his woolly hat but kept his gloves on.

Martin Urban was getting a brandy bottle out of a drinks cabinet. You would think he had had enough, he stank of gin. Finn could tell that something had frightened or upset him. His hands trembled and made the bottle chatter against the glass.

'Brandy? There's no whisky but there's vodka and martini and sherry.'

'I don't drink,' said Finn.

The voice sounded both weary and awkward. 'Look, I'm sorry about the money. I've had a lot on my plate and I'm afraid I forgot all about you. I could give you a cheque here and now, only you will insist on cash.'

Finn didn't say anything.

'Sit down, won't you? I'm sorry you've come all the way here for nothing, you should have phoned.' He sat down and drank his brandy at a gulp as if it were medicine. Finn watched him curiously, watched a flush mottle his skin. He wasn't going to sit down. What would be the point?

'I haven't come here for nothing,' he said.

'Well . . ' Into the glass slopped more brandy. 'Not in the sense that you've reminded me. I can get it for you sometime next week. Cash is difficult, you know, that sort of cash. I'll have to phone my bank first, I'll have to . . .'

Finn took a step forward from the position he had taken up by the balcony door. 'You can get it for me Monday morning,' he said. 'And I don't want it sent, not this time. Put it in your car on the front passenger seat and leave the car in the car park outside the palace.'

'The palace?' repeated Martin Urban, staring at him.

'Alexandra Palace.' Finn was getting impatient. 'Have you got that? Put the money in a carrier on the front seat of your car and leave it there between one and two Monday, O K?'

Martin Urban had flushed a dark crimson. His eyes had become very bright, his features blurred and thickened. He set down his glass and stood up. Very deliberately he said, 'No, it is not O K. It is very much not O K.' He passed a hand over his forehead, and when he took it down Finn saw that his face was working with fury. 'Just who the hell d'you think you are, coming here, barging in here, telling me what I should do with my own money? You haven't got some sort of right to it, you know. You people, you're all the same, you think anyone with a bit more than you've got owes you a living. It's purely out of the kindness of my heart I'm making it possible for your mother to have a decent place to live in. But I'm damned if I'm going to break an important appointment on Monday morning to go to the bank for you or do without my car for an hour. Why should I? Why the hell should I?'

Finn thought the man was going to fall. He watched him get hold of the back of a chair and hang on to it and draw a long breath and seem to get a grip on himself. Enough control, at any rate, to say coldly now, 'You'd better go,' and then, pushing past Finn to unlock the balcony door, 'Excuse me, I must have some air.'

Martin Urban went out on to the balcony. Finn watched him standing there, looking down on London and then up at the clear, faintly starry, purplish sky. After a moment or two he came in again, appearing partially recovered, and stood staring with a curiously pained expression, like a hurt dog, at the big cactus which stood on the window sill, at its pink, waxen flowers. Without turning to Finn, he said:

'I thought I told you to go.'

Finn didn't reply to this rhetorical question. He said, 'I don't want the money sent. Is that understood? I don't want those delivery people knowing.'

'Knowing what, for God's sake?' Martin Urban turned round and said sharply, 'I'm sick of this. I'm tired, I've had a bad day. If it wasn't that I promised and I don't like to break my word I'd tell you you can forget the money. Right, so you can have a cheque or nothing.'

'Well, well,' said Finn. 'Now we know.'

'Indeed we do. And when that's over I think I'll have done quite a favour to you and your mother.' He went to the writing desk, though none too steadily, and fumbled about inside it for a cheque book.

'Haven't I ever done anything for you?' said Finn.

Without looking at him, Martin Urban said, 'Like what? Like making a damned nuisance of yourself. What have you ever done for me?' He began to write the cheque. Finn went up to him, laid a heavy hand on his arm and took the pen away. Martin Urban jumped to his feet, shouted, 'Take your hands off me!'

Finn held him by the upper arms and looked searchingly into his face. The square, flushed, puffy face was resentful and indignant – and utterly bewildered. Finn could read faces – and minds too sometimes.

'You don't know about it,' he said flatly. 'It wasn't in the papers. Well, it's done. Last Saturday.'

Martin Urban struggled to free himself and Finn let him go. 'How dare you touch me! And what the hell are you talking about?'

It was a strange thing but now that he had to do it Finn found it as hard to put the act into words as his clients had done. He looked around him, he cleared his throat.

'Last Saturday,' he said gruffly. 'I did for the girl. Like you wanted.'

Martin Urban stood quite still.

'*What did you say?*'

'You heard.'

'Last Saturday you . . .'

'I did for that girl, like you're paying me for. I've done it and now I want my money.'

The sound he made was a kind of ghastly groan, the like of which Finn had only previously heard from Lena, and he fell back on the sofa, covering his face with his hands. Finn regarded him as he rocked backwards and forwards, pushing his fists into his eyes, beating them against his temples. Finn stepped away and sat down on an upright chair, understanding now that he had made a mistake. Things, details, fell gently into place like the silver balls in Lena's Chinese puzzle dropping into their slots.

'Give me some more of that brandy.'

Finn poured some brandy and pushed the glass at Martin Urban's mouth. The brandy was drained and there was a shuddering and a kind of sob and the thick broken voice said:

'You were – in the car – that – didn't – stop?'

'I've said so.'

'What am I to do? My God, what am I going to do? You thought I'd paid you to do that? What sort of a monster *are* you?' He got up shakily and stood with his hands pressed to his head. 'I loved her,' he said. 'She loved me. We were going to be married. And you . . .'

He turned towards modern man's succour, lifeline, first aid – the phone. He took an uncertain step towards it. Finn calculated how to get there first, take him by surprise, wrench the wires out of the wall. And then? There was only one way to make certain no one was ever told what Martin Urban knew.

Swaying, holding his head, he stood staring hypnotically at Finn. Finn began to get up. Sweat beads had started to prickle his face. Somehow he must get Martin Urban out of here, into a car, away from this place into some lonely place. In order to

silence him he must put on an act, make promises, play along.
. . . He didn't know how to do these things, he was powerless,
bereft of energy, as if a fuse had blown in him and there was no
current to power his limbs.

Martin Urban took down his hands and turned away from
the phone. The attack he made on Finn was entirely unexpected.
One moment he was standing there in the middle of the room,
his fists clenched, his arms gradually falling to his sides, the
next he had sprung upon Finn, flailing out, using his hands like
hammers. Finn toppled backwards. It was the first time in his
life he had ever been knocked down by another.

He rolled over on to his front, pressed himself up with a
violence that sent the other man staggering back, and leapt like
a panther. Martin Urban ducked and stumbled out on to the
balcony. London glittered out there like the window of a
tourist souvenir shop. Finn stood poised in the doorway, his
arms spread, his body quivering. And the man who had given
him five thousand pounds from some quixotic altruism Finn
couldn't even begin to understand, stood against the low
parapet, convulsed, it seemed, with some kind of passionate
need for revenge. He leapt forward again, deceived perhaps by
Finn's white thinness.

But Finn was there a split second before him, to smash with
his right arm harder than he had ever smashed before. And a
strange thing happened. Martin Urban raised his arms hugely
above his head in some exaggerated defensive gesture. He
staggered backwards in an almost comic, tip-toe slow motion,
bathed in the shining night air, against the spangled backdrop,
staggered, teetered, until the parapet wall that reached lower
than the tops of his thighs, was just behind him. Finn could see
what would happen and he jumped to catch the man before he
fell. He jumped just too late. Martin Urban made contact with
the wall, doubled over backwards, and with a low cry, fell.

Forty feet into a pit of blackness. There was a concrete well
down there, an area that perhaps gave access to a porter's
basement. Finn stood, looking down. No other windows
opened, no one appeared, no one had been alerted by the

groaning sound the man had made as he starfished to earth. Finn went in and closed and locked the balcony door. He turned off the lights and stood listening for movement in the corridor outside, for doors opening and footsteps. There was nothing.

He had been a fool to lock that door. It must look like suicide. It must look as if Martin Urban had killed himself over the death of the woman he was to have married. Finn unlocked the door again. He didn't touch the brandy glass. A man might well drink brandy before he committed suicide. The irony of it struck Finn, though, as he moved towards the front door of the flat, the irony that now, at this moment, in this place, he was at greater risk through this man's accidental death than he had ever been when he had done murder.

When he was satisfied that all was quiet and still he passed stealthily out of the flat and pulled the front door softly shut behind him. He went downstairs very fast, passing no one, hearing nothing. The van was waiting for him in a deserted car park. And deserted, too, Cromwell Court and its environs would have seemed but for the lights which shone with tranquillity in most of its broad rectangular windows.

Still, it was only a matter of time, of short time, before that body would be found. He must get away, not linger, not yield to the temptation to steal softly around to the other side of the block and peer into that dark well, check what light must go on or which door open to reveal its occupant . . .

He resisted. As he was driving down Dartmouth Park Hill, coming up to the traffic lights at Tufnell Park station, he heard the wail of a siren. But there was nothing to say it was an ambulance summoned for Martin Urban, it could just as well have been a fire engine or a police car. He put the van away in the garage at the corner of Somerset Grove and walked home along the street where the sulphurous light laid a pinchbeck gleam.

The house smelt of cannabis and waste bins. Finn went on up to the top, taking two stairs at a time with his great loping stride. He felt a surge of confidence and contentment. This time it really had been an accident, he could face Lena without dread. And there was no possibility now of anyone suspecting

Martin Urban might not have been alone in the flat, not a soul who knew of any connection between himself and Martin Urban. He was sure no one had seen him or would know him if they had. Yet Martin Urban was out of harm's way, silenced, taking the secret of Finn's mistake with him into the dark spaces or losing it in oblivion as he began on a new cycle of life.

The green bird began a shrill twittering when he came into the room. Mrs Gogarty, who had been making forecasts with the aid of the Tarot, got up and threw the shawl over its cage.

'Well, well,' said Finn, 'we *are* cosy.'

He pulled off his gloves and put them in his pocket and took Lena's hand. She was as transparent as an insect tonight and dusty like a moth. Her dull leaden eyes met his silver eyes and she smiled.

'The picture of devotion!' said Mrs Gogarty with admiring sighs. She studied the cards, laid out now for Finn. 'There's a lot of death here . . .' she began.

Over Lena's head Finn gave her a warning look.

'Ah!' She slid the cards together and the Death Card, Scorpio's death card, death cloaked and riding a pale horse, came out on top. She covered it with the Queen of Wands. In her mechanical gypsy voice she said, 'There's money here, my darling, a lot of money. But wait. . . . No, it's not coming your way, you'll have a disappointment.'

The hand that held Lena's grew cold and limp. He bent down, he looked unseeing into the soothsayer's face.

'What? What did you say?'

'A disappointment over money. . . . Why are you looking at me like that?'

Finn saw, not the cards which Mrs Gogarty's hands now covered in fear, not Lena's face, apprehensive, growing stricken, but a cheque that lay on a writing desk, locked up in Martin Urban's flat. The date had been written – had his name?

The women's eyes fearfully upon him, he stood upright yet trembling in that tiny room, listening to the distant sound of a siren crying through the dark, a herald of the one that must cry for him.

THE VEILED ONE

For Simon

1

THE woman was lying dead on the floor when he came in. She was already dead and covered up from head to toe but Wexford only knew that afterwards, not at the time. He looked back and realized the chances he had missed but it was useless doing that – he hadn't known and that was all. He had been preoccupied, thinking of an assortment of things: his wife's birthday present that was in the bag he carried, modern architecture, yesterday's gale which had blown down his garden fence, this car park that he was entering from the descending lift.

Even the lift was not as other lifts elsewhere, being of rattling grey metal undecorated except by graffiti. Irregular printing from whose letters the red paint had dripped like trails of blood, informed him that someone called Steph was 'a diesel dyke'. He wondered what that meant, wondered too where he could look it up. The lift was going down. Into the bowels of the earth, he thought, and there was something intestine-like about this place with its winding passages and its strictly one-way direction. Perhaps, though, it was better to excavate for this purpose than to erect above the ground, especially as any extraneous building would inevitably have been in the style of the shopping centre itself – ramparts, perhaps, or the walls of a city, some quaint attempt at a reconstruction of the Middle Ages.

He had just come from the Barringdean Centre, the new shopping complex built to look like a castle. That was the style modern planners thought suitable on the outskirts of an ancient Sussex town where nothing genuinely medieval remained. Perhaps that was why. Anyway the centre looked less like a real castle than a toy one, the kind you have to assemble from a hundred plastic bits and pieces.

Shaped like a capital 'I', it had four towers on the ends and a row of little turrets along its length. Looking back at it, he half-expected bowmen to appear at the Gothic windows and arrows to fly.

But inside all was of the late twentieth century, only. to be expressed in eighties words — amenities, facilities, enclaves and approaches. A great fountain played in the central concourse, its waterspouts almost reaching but not quite touching the pendent chandelier of shards of frosted glass. Wexford had entered at this point by the automatic doors and approach from the glass covered way. He had gone up the escalator where a breath of spray stung his fingers on the hand-rail, realized at the top that the shop he sought must be downstairs after all — was not Suzanne the hairdresser who also sold wigs and leotards, or Linen That Shows or Laceworks — and went down again by the escalator to the Mandala. This was a set-piece in the area at the other end with potted plants in concentric circles — brown chrysanthemums, yellow chrysanthemums, white poinsettias and those plants with cherry-like orange fruit that are really a kind of potato. The crowds were thinning out; it was getting on for six when the centre closed up. Shop assistants were weary and growing impatient and even the flowers looked tired.

A Tesco superstore filled the whole crosspiece of the 'I' on both floors at this end, British Home Stores the other. Between them was Boots the Chemist with W. H. Smith facing it, the Mandala in between. Down a side passage that led from the main above-ground car park, children still played on a fat zebra made of black and white leather, a hi-tech climbing frame, a dragon on wheels. Wexford found the shop where Dora, a week ago, had pointed out to him in the window a sweater she liked. Addresses it was called, with the chocolate shop next to it and a wool and crafts place Knits 'n' Kits on the other side. Wexford was not a man to hesitate or deliberate over a matter like this. Besides, Demeter the health-food shop opposite was already closing and the jewellers next to it were lowering the fancy gilt latticework bars inside the window. He went into Addresses and bought the sweater, the transaction taking four minutes.

By now shoppers were being hustled out, even Grub 'n' Grains the café having someone suspiciously like a bouncer on its door. And the lights were dimming, the leaping spouts of the fountain slowing . . . subsiding, until the ruffled surface of the pool into which it played became glasslike. Wexford sat down on one of the wrought-iron benches that were ranged along the aisle. He let the crowd make its way out through the various arteries that led from this central column and then he too left by the automatic doors into the covered way.

A great exodus of cars from the above-ground car parks was under way. At the far end he looked back. Flags flew from all the turrets along the centre's spine, red and yellow triangular pennants which had fluttered all day in the tail-end of the gale but drooped now in the stillness of a dark, misty evening. Slits of light still showed in the narrow pointed-topped Gothic windows. Wexford found himself alone here at the entrance to the underground car park, the only evidence of those hordes of shoppers being their abandoned trolleys. Hundreds of these jostled each other in higgledy-piggledy fashion, and would no doubt remain here till morning. A notice informed their users that the police took a serious view of those who allowed a shopping trolley to obstruct the roadway. Not for the first time, Wexford reflected that the police had more important things to do – though how much more important he was only to realize later.

The planners had decreed that this car park must be subterranean. He came into the lift and the stairs by way of a metal door whose clanging reverberations could still be heard as the lift descended. Wexford heard its echoes and at the same time feet pounding up the stairs, the feet of someone running hard; that was something else he remembered later. Down here it was always cold, always imbued with an acrid chemical smell as of metal filings awash in oil. Wexford stepped out of the lift at the second of four levels and came into the wide aisle between the avenue of pillars. Most of the cars were gone by now and in their absence the place seemed more desolate, uglier, more of a denial. Of course it was foolish and fanciful to think like this – a denial of what, for instance? The car park merely served a purpose, filled a need in the most practical utilitarian way. What would he have had instead? White paint? Murals? Tiles on the wall depicting some episode of local history? That would have been almost worse. It was irrational that the place reminded him of a picture it did not in the least resemble – John Martin's illustration of 'Pandemonium' for *Paradise Lost*.

His car was parked at this end. He didn't have to walk the length of the place – under the low concrete ceiling, between the squat uprights, into the wells of shadow – but merely cross over to the bays along the left-hand wall. There was an echo down here and the sound of his footsteps rang back at him. If his powers of observation, in general so sharp, were less acute than usual, at least he noticed the number of cars that remained and their makes and colours. He saw the three between him and the middle of the car park where one ramp came up and another went down: one on the left, a red Metro, and diagonally opposite it on the right, parked side by side, a silver Escort and a dark blue Lancia. The woman's body lay between these two, closer to the Escort, concealed by a shroud of dirty brown velvet which made it look like a heap of rags.

Or so they told him afterwards. At the time he saw only the cars, the colours of their bodywork not entirely drained by the cold strip lights but muted, made pale. He lifted the boot-lid and put inside it the dark blue bag with 'Addresses' stamped on it in gold. As he closed it a car went by him, a red car going rather too fast. There were more red cars than any other colour, he had read somewhere. Motorists are aggressive and red is the colour of aggression. He got into the car, started it and looked at the clock. This was something he always did quite naturally, looked at the clock when he started the ignition. Seven minutes past six. He put the automatic shift into drive and began the climb out of the earth's bowels.

4

On each level the way out wound round half the floor-space at the opposite end from where the lift and stairs were, wound round anticlockwise and turned right up the ramp to the next level. He passed the three cars – the two on the left first, then the red Metro. Of course he didn't look to the right where the woman's body was. Why should he? His exit route took him round the loop, on to the straight on the other side. Not a car remained here; the bays were empty. He climbed up to the first level, looped round and out into the night. There might have been cars remaining on that level, but he hadn't noticed and he could only remember the red Vauxhall Cavalier with a girl in the driving-seat facing him as he came up the ramp. She pulled out and followed him, impatient to be off and exceed the speed limit. Teenage girls at the wheels of cars were worse than the boys these days, Burden said. Wexford emerged into the open air, up the ramp. Most of the shoppers were gone; it was ten past six, they closed the centre at six and only the last stragglers remained, moving towards cars in the above-ground parking areas. The girl overtook him as soon as she could.

Wexford had pulled in and slowed to allow her to do so and it was then that he saw the woman emerge from the glass-covered way. He observed her because she was the only person to approach the car park and because she wasn't hurrying but walking in a controlled, measured fashion threading her way between the trolleys, fending off with her foot one that rattled into her path. She was a small, slender, upright woman in coat and hat carrying two bags of shopping, both red Tesco carriers. The metal door clanged behind her and he drove on across the wide nearly empty car-less space where the mist hung as a glaucous clouding of the air, out of the exit gates and half a mile on into Castle Street and the town. The traffic lights in the High Street outside the Olive and Dove turned red as he approached. The handbrake on, he looked down at the evening paper he had bought before he drove to the centre but so far had not even glanced at. His own daughter's famous face looked back at him, affording him only a mild jolt. Pictures of Sheila in the papers weren't unusual. Seldom, however, were they accompanied by revelations of this sort. There was another photograph beside the portrait; Wexford looked at that one too and with lips pursed drew in a long breath. The lights slipped through amber into green.

The Barringdean Shopping Centre was on the outskirts of Kingsmarkham but nevertheless within the town. It had been built on the site of the old bus station when the new bus station was put up on the site of the old maltings. Everyone went shopping there and the retailers in the High Street suffered. By day it was a hive of bees buzzing in and swarming out, but at night the centre was left to its fate — two break-ins during its first year of life. Apart from the security men and store detectives within the centre itself, there was a caretaker who called himself the supervisor and who patrolled the grounds or, more usually, sat in a small concrete office next door to the car-park lift-shaft, reading the *Star* and listening to tapes of *Les Misérables* and *Edwin Drood*. At six-fifteen each evening David Sedgeman performed his last duty of the day as Barringdean Shopping Centre supervisor. He put the trolleys into some sort of order, slotting one inside another to form long articulated carriages, and closed the gates of the pedestrian entrance in Pomeroy Road, fastened the bolts and attached the padlock. These gates were of steel mesh in steel frames and the fence was eight feet high. Then Sedgeman went off home. If anyone remained about the grounds, they had to leave by the traffic exit.

The residents of Pomeroy Road had benefited from the removal of the bus station. It was quieter now that no buses turned in and departed from six in the morning until midnight. Instead there were all the shoppers coming and going, but soon after six they had all left. On the opposite side of the street short terraces of Victorian houses alternated with small blocks of flats. Directly facing the gates, in one of these houses, Archie Greaves lived with his daughter and son-in-law. He spent a large part of his days sitting in the downstairs bay window watching the people; it was far more entertaining for him now than in the bus station era. He watched the people go into the phone box just outside the gates on the right-hand side and some of them must have seen him watching them, for more than once he had been approached, accosted by a tap on the window and asked for change for the phone. He watched the shoppers arrive and the shoppers leave; it amused him to make a mental note of arrivals and check on their departure. He recognized certain regulars and because he was a lonely man – his daughter and her husband out all day – thought of them almost as his friends.

This evening was misty. It had got dark very early and by six was black as midnight, the mist very apparent where lights caught it and made a greenish shimmer. The gutters of Pomeroy Road were clogged with fallen leaves, the plane trees almost bare. Beyond the open gates lamps lit the car parks that were fast emptying and in the shopping centre building itself, where the turrets were silhouetted black like the teeth of a saw against the streaked cloudy purple of the sky, the lights were beginning to dim. Before many more minutes had passed by, they would all have gone out.

Pedestrians had been coming out sporadically ever since Archie first went to sit there at four o'clock. His breath clouded the glass and he rubbed it with his jacket sleeve, taking his arm away in time to see someone running out of the gates. A young man it was – a boy to him – empty handed, going as if all the devils in hell were after him. Or store detectives, Archie thought doubtfully. Once he had seen a woman running with people pursuing her and he guessed she had been shoplifting. This boy he had never seen before; he was a stranger to him and he passed out of sight under the plane trees into the misty dark.

Archie hadn't put a light on because he could see better sitting in darkness. An old-fashioned electric fire made a

7

glow in the room behind him. No one was pursuing the boy – perhaps he had only been in a hurry. The people who were leaving at a more leisurely pace had looked at him without much curiosity and, like Archie, expected to see retribution coming. But the darkness absorbed them as well. He saw a car come up out of the mouth of the underground park and then another. The lights that illuminated the shopping centre turrets went out. Then Archie saw David Sedgeman appear from behind the angle of the concrete wall with the padlock keys in his hand. Because of the mist and because Archie hadn't put his light on, Sedgeman had to peer to see the pale blur of the old man's face and then he nodded and raised his hand. Archie gave him a salute. Sedgeman closed the gates, looped the chain through the steel mesh, fastened and locked the padlock. Then he shot both bolts, one at the bottom and another a foot above his head. Before he went back, he gave Archie another wave.

This was the signal for Archie to get moving. He got up and went to the kitchen where he made himself a mug of tea with a tea-bag and took two chocolate chip cookies out of the biscuit tin. No potatoes to peel tonight because his daughter and her husband would be out at a friend's son's engagement party. There would be no cooked supper for Archie, but at his age he preferred little snacks of tea and biscuits and bits of chocolate anyway. Back in the front room he put the television on, though he had missed most of the six o'clock news and the bit he got was all about the trial of terrorists and some actress damaging Ministry of Defence property. He didn't turn it off but just turned down the sound and switched on the central light. Archie had read somewhere that watching television in the dark turns you blind eventually.

The light was also on in the phone box now. It came on at six-thirty when the box hadn't been vandalized and the lamp smashed as sometimes happened. Archie sat on the window once more, one eye watching the street and another the screen, hoping something more cheerful would come on soon. By now the shopping centre was in darkness, though two lamps were still alight in the open-air car parks. A middle-aged man, one of the neighbours, came along with his dog which lifted its leg against the red metal door of the call box. Archie felt like banging on the window but knew it would do no good. Dog and owner went off into the mist while Archie drank his tea, ate the second biscuit and wondered whether he should get himself a third or wait an hour. Weather forecast now; he couldn't hear it, but he could see by all those little clouds and whirly lines that it was going to be the mixture as before.

Outside was silence, darkness, mist which moved and cleared and rolled sluggishly back, which the lights – half-obscured by plane-tree branches – turned to a watery, acid-green phosphorescence. The darkness was deep in the tarmac desert, nothing visible but two islanded spots of light and now these also went out ... one, two ... leaving blackness that met a dark grey but luminous sky. Only the lamps of Pomeroy Street and a ray or so from the mouth of the underground car park faintly lit the area behind the gates. And into this a little woman walked from behind the concrete wall, having perhaps come from the car-park lift, Archie thought. She walked a few yards in one direction to stare into the blackness, then she turned and gazed towards the gates and him. She seemed to be looking to see if there was anyone about, or looking for someone or something. There was anger, repressed and contained, revealed in the slow deliberate way she moved – he could tell that even in the dark.

She might have a car in there and be unable to get it started. There was nothing he could do and now she had gone again, the wall cutting her off from his view. Archie switched off the television, for he could stand no more of what had appeared silently on the screen – starving Africans with pot-bellied dying babies, more of those people that he in his impotence and penury could not aid. He looked back at the empty stillness outside. Fetching the third biscuit might be postponed for an hour or so. He had to find ways to fill up his evening, for he couldn't very well go to bed until nine which was more than two hours away. The chances were that nothing more would happen out there until eight next morning when the shopping centre opened, nothing at all except cars passing and maybe a couple of people coming to use the phone box. He was thinking this, reflecting on it, when the woman appeared again, walking now in the stalking single-minded fashion of a cat homing on its prey.

When she came up to the gates, she got hold of them as if expecting they would open, as if the padlock would fall apart and the bolts slide back. Archie got to his feet and leaned forward on the window sill. The woman was much too short to reach the top bolt; she seemed now to have realized that the padlock was fastened and the key gone, and she began to rattle the gates. Her eyes were not on him but on the phone box, which was only a few yards from her but tantalisingly outside those gates.

She shook the gates more and more violently and they clanged and rattled. Anyone could see it was useless doing that because of the bolts and the padlock, and Archie began to wonder, because of the sudden and violent change in her demeanour, if she wasn't quite all there, if she were a bit mad . . . crazy. His reaction to anything like that would usually be to ignore it, to shut his eyes or go away. But it was the phone box she wanted; all this frenzy was on account of not being able to reach the phone box. There were always the neighbours – let someone else attend to it, someone younger and stronger. Only no one ever did. Archie sometimes thought a person could be murdered in Pomeroy Street in full view, in broad daylight, and no one would do anything. The woman was shouting now – well, screaming. She was stamping her feet and shaking the gates and roaring at the top of her voice, yelling things Archie couldn't make out but which he heard all right when he had put his cap on and his raincoat round his shoulders and was making his way out on to the pavement.

'The police! The police! I've got to get the police! I've got to phone. I've got to get the police!'

Archie crossed the road. He said, 'Making all that fuss won't help. You calm down now. What's the matter with you?'

'I've got to phone the police! There's someone dead in there. I've got to phone the police – there's a woman and they've tried to cut her head off!'

Archie went cold all over; his throat came up and he tasted tea and chocolate. He thought, my heart, I'm too old for this. He said feebly, 'Stop shaking those gates. Now, come on, you stop it! I can't let you out.'

'I want the police,' she shrieked and fell to lean heavily against the gates, hanging there with her fingers pushed through the wire mesh. The final clang reverberated and died away, as she sobbed harshly against the cold metal.

'I can go and phone them,' Archie said and he went back indoors, leaving her sagged there, still, her hands hooked on the wire like someone shot while trying to escape.

THE phone rang while he was in the middle of going through it all with Dora. Supper had been eaten without enthusiasm and the bag containing Dora's birthday sweater lay unregarded on the seat of a chair. He had turned the evening paper front-page downwards but – unable to resist the horrid fascination of it – picked it up again.

'Mind you, I knew things weren't going well with her and Andrew,' Dora said.

'Knowing one's daughter's marriage is going through a bad patch is a far cry from reading in the paper that she's getting a divorce.'

'I think you mind about that more than about her coming up in court.'

Wexford made himself look coolly at the newspaper. The lead story was the trial of three men who had tried to blow up the Israeli Embassy and there was something too about a by-election, but the page was Sheila's. There were two photographs. The top picture showed a wire fence – not unlike the fence that surrounded the shopping complex he had recently left, only this one was topped with coils of razor wire. The modern world, he sometimes thought, was full of wire fences. The one in the picture had been mutilated and a flap hung loose from the centre of it, leaving a gaping hole through which a waste of mud could be seen with a hangar-like edifice in the middle of it. From the darkish background in the other photograph his daughter's lovely face looked out, wide-eyed, apprehensive, to a father's eye, aghast at the headlong rush of events. Wisps of pale curly hair escaped from under her woolly cap. The headline said only: 'Sheila Cuts the Wire'; the story beneath told the rest of it, giving among all the painful details of arrest and magistrates' court appearance the surely gratuitous information that the actress currently appearing in the television serialization of *Lady Audley's Secret* was seeking a divorce from her husband, businessman Andrew Thorverton.

'I would have liked to be told, I suppose,' Wexford said. 'About the divorce, I mean. I wouldn't expect her to tell us she was going to chop up the fence round a nuclear bomber base. We'd have tried to stop her.'

'We'd have tried to stop her getting a divorce.'

It was then that the phone rang. Since Sheila had been released on bail, pending a later court appearance, Wexford thought it must be her at the other end. He was already hearing her voice in his head, the breathy self-reproach as she tried to persuade her parents she didn't know how the paper had got that report about her divorce ... she was overcome ... she was flabbergasted ... it was all beyond her. And as for the wire-cutting ...

Not Sheila though. Inspector Michael Burden.

'Mike?'

The voice was cool and a bit curt, anxiety underlying it, but he nearly always sounded like that. 'There's a dead woman in the shopping centre car park, the underground one. I haven't seen her yet, but there's no chance it's anything but murder.'

'I was there myself,' Wexford said wonderingly. 'I only left a couple of hours ago.'

'That's OK. Nobody thinks you did it.'

Burden had got a lot sharper since his second marriage. Time was when such a rejoinder would never have entered his head.

'I'll come over. Who's there now?'

'Me — or I will be in five minutes. Archbold. Prentiss.' Prentiss was the Scene-of-Crimes man, Archbold a young DC. 'Sumner-Quist. Sir Hilary's away on his hols.'

In November? Well, people went away at any old time these days. Wexford rather liked the eminent and occasionally outrageous pathologist, Sir Hilary Tremlett, finding Dr Basil Sumner-Quist less congenial.

'There's no identification problem,' said Burden. 'We

know who she is. Her name's Gwen Robson, Mrs. Late fifties. Address up at Highlands. A woman called Sanders found her and got hold of someone in Pomeroy Street who phoned us.'

It was five-past eight. 'I may be a long time,' Wexford said to Dora. 'At any rate I won't be back soon.'

'I'm wondering if I ought to phone Sheila.'

'Let her phone us,' said Sheila's father, hardening his heart. He picked up the bag with Dora's present in it and hid it at the back of the hall cupboard. The birthday wasn't until tomorrow anyway.

The car-park entrance was blocked with police cars. Lights had appeared from somewhere, the place blazed with light. Someone had shot the linked shopping trolleys across the parking area to clear a space and trolleys stood about everywhere but at a distance, like a watching crowd of robots. The gates in the fence at the pedestrian entrance in Pomeroy Road stood wide open. Wexford pushed trolleys aside, spinning them out of his way, squeezed between the cars, opened the lift door and tried to summon the lift. It didn't come, so he walked down the two levels. The three cars were still there – the red Metro, silver Escort and dark blue Lancia – but the blue one had been backed out of its parking slot up against the wall and reversed into the middle of the aisle, no doubt to allow room for pathologist, Scene-of-Crimes officer and photographer to scrutinize the body that lay close up against the offside of the silver Escort. Wexford hesitated a moment, then walked towards the group of people and the thing on the concrete floor.

Burden got to his feet as Wexford approached and Archbold, who had old-fashioned manners, nodded and said, 'Sir!' Sumner-Quist didn't bother to look round. The fact that he happened at that moment to move his shoulder so that the dead woman's face and neck were revealed was, Wexford thought, purely fortuitous. The face bore the unmistakable signs of someone who has met her death by strangulation. It was bluish, bloated, horrified, and the mark on her neck of whatever was responsible for her asphyxiation was so deep that it had more the appearance of a circular cut, as if the blade of a knife had been run round throat and nape. Blazing lights in a place usually feebly lit showed up all the horror of her and of her surroundings – stained and discoloured concrete, dirty metal, litter sprawling across the floor.

The dead woman wore a brown tweed coat with fur collar and her hat of brown and fawn checked tweed with narrow brim was still on her grey curly hair. Apparently small and slight, she had stick-like legs in brown lacy tights or stockings and on her feet brown lace-up low-heeled walking shoes. Wedding and engagement rings were on her left hand.

'The Escort's her car,' Burden said. 'She had the keys to it in her hand when she was killed. Or that's the way it looks, the keys were under the body. There are two bags of groceries in the boot. It looks as if she put the bags in the boot, closed the boot-lid, came round to unlock the driver's door and then someone attacked her from behind.'

'Attacked her with what?'

'A thin length of cord, maybe. Like in thuggee.' Burden's general knowledge as well as sharpness of intellect had been enhanced by marriage. But it was the birth of his son, twenty years after his first family, that had made him abandon the smart suits he had formerly favoured for wear even on occasions like this one. Jeans were what the inspector had on this evening, though jeans which rather oddly bore knife creases and contrasted not altogether happily with his camel-hair jacket.

'More like wire than a cord,' Wexford said.

The remark had an electric effect on Dr Sumner-Quist who jumped up and spoke to Wexford as if they were in a drawing room, not a car park, as if there were no body on the floor and this were a social occasion, a cocktail party maybe: 'Talking of wire, isn't that frightfully pretty TV girl who's all over the paper this evening your daughter?'

Wexford didn't like to imagine what effect the epithet 'TV girl' would have had on Sheila. He nodded.

'I thought so. I said to my wife it was so, unlikely as it seemed. OK, I've done all I can here. If the man with the camera's done his stuff, you can move her as far as I'm concerned. Myself, I think it's a pity these people don't go cutting the wire in Russia.'

Wexford made no reply to this. 'How long has she been dead?'

'You want miracles, don't you? You think I can tell you that after five minutes' dekko? Well, she was a goner by six, I reckon. That do you?'

And he had been here at seven minutes past . . . He lifted up the grubby brown velvet curtain that lay in a heap a few inches from the dead woman's feet. 'What's this?'

'It was covering the body, sir,' Archbold said.

'Covering it as might be a blanket, do you mean? Or right over the head and feet?'

'One foot was sticking out and the woman who found her pulled it back a bit to see the face.'

'Yes – who was it found her?'

'A Mrs Dorothy Sanders. That's her car over there, the red one. She found the body, but it was a man called Greaves in Pomeroy Street phoned us. Davidson's talking to him now. He found Mrs Sanders screaming and shaking the gates fit to break them down. She went raving mad because the phone box is outside the gates and she couldn't get out. Diana Pettit took a statement from her and drove her home.'

Still holding the curtain, Wexford tried the boot-lid of the red Metro. There was shopping inside that too, food in two red Tesco carriers and a clear plastic bag full of hanks of grey knitting-wool done up with string like a parcel. He looked up at the sound of the lift, an echo from it or reverberation or something; you could always hear it. The door to the lift had opened and a man appeared. He was walking very diffidently and hesitantly towards them and when his eyes met Wexford's he stopped altogether. Archbold went up to him and said something. He was a young man with a pale heavy face and dark

16

moustache and he was dressed in a way which while quite suitable for a man of Wexford's own age, looked incongruous on someone of – what? Twenty-one? Twenty-two? The V-necked grey pullover, striped tie and grey flannel trousers reminded Wexford of a school uniform.

'I've come for the car,' he said.

'One of these cars is yours?'

'The red one, the Metro. It's my mother's. My mother said to come over and bring it back.'

His eyes went fearfully to where the body lay, the body that was now entirely covered by a sheet. It lay unattended – pathologist, photographer and policeman having all moved away towards the central aisle or the exits. Wexford noted that awe-stricken glance, the quick withdrawing of the eyes and jerk of the head. He said, 'Can I have your name, sir?'

'Sanders, Clifford Sanders.'

Burden asked, 'Are you some relation of Mrs Dorothy Sanders?'

'Her son.'

'I'll come back with you,' Wexford said. 'I'll follow you; I'd like to talk to your mother.' He let Clifford Sanders, walking edgily, pass out of earshot and then said to Burden, 'Mrs Robson's next-of-kin . . .?'

'There's a husband, but he hasn't been told. He'll have to make a formal identification. I thought of going over there now.'

'Do we know who that blue Lancia belongs to?'

Burden shook his head. 'It's a bit odd, that. Only shoppers use the car park – I mean, who else would want to? And the centre's been closed over two hours. If it belongs to the killer, why didn't he or she drive it away? When I first saw it I thought maybe it wouldn't start, but we had to move it and it started first time.'

'Better have the owner traced,' said Wexford. 'My God, Mike, I was in here, I saw the three cars, I drove past her.'

'Did you see anyone else?'

17

'I don't know, I'll have to think.'

Going down in the lift, he thought. He remembered the pounding footsteps descending, the girl in the red Vauxhall following him, the half-dozen people in the above-ground parking areas, the mist that was visible and obscuring but really hid nothing. He remembered the woman carrying the two bags coming from the covered way, strolling, languidly kicking the trolley aside. But that was at ten-past six and the murder had already taken place by then . . . He got into the car beside Archbold. Clifford Sanders in the red Metro was waiting a few yards along the roadway while a uniformed officer – someone new that Wexford didn't recognize – trundled the scattered trolleys out of their path.

The little red car led them along the High Street in the Stowerton direction and turned into the Forby Road. Archbold seemed to know where Sanders lived, in a remote spot down a lane that turned off about half a mile beyond the house and parkland called 'Sundays'. In fact it was less than three miles outside Kingsmarkham, but the lane was narrow and very dark and Clifford Sanders drove even more slowly than the winding obscurity warranted. Thick, dark, leafless hedges rose high on either side. Occasionally a pulling-in place revealed itself, showing at least that passing would be possible if they met another vehicle. Wexford couldn't remember ever having been down there before, he doubted if it led anywhere except perhaps finally to the gates of a farm.

The sky was quite black, moonless, starless. The lane seemed to wind in a series of unneccessary loops. There were no hills for it to circumvent and the river to flow in the opposite direction. No longer were any pinpoints of light visible in the surrounding countryside. All was darkness but for the area immediately ahead, illuminated by their own headlights, and the twin bright points glowing red on the rear of the Metro.

But now Clifford Sanders' left-hand indicator was winking. Plainly, he was the kind of driver who would signal his intention to turn a hundred yards before the turning.

A few seconds elapsed. There were no lights ahead, only a break in the hedge. Then the Metro turned in and Archbold followed, guided by the red tail-lights. With a kind of amused impatience Wexford thought how they might be in some Hitchcock movie, for he could just make out the house -- a house which probably looked a lot less disagreeable by daylight but was now almost ridiculously grim and forbidding. Behind two windows only a pallid light showed. There was no other light either by the front door or about the garden. Wexford's eyes grew accustomed to the darkness and he saw that the house was biggish, on three floors, with eight windows here in the front and a slab of a front door. A low flight of steps without rails led up to it and there was neither porch nor canopy. But the whole façade was hung, covered, clothed in ivy. As far as he could see it was ivy, at any rate it was evergreen leaves, a dense blanket of them, through which the two pale windows peered like eyes in an animal's shaggy face.

A garden surrounded the house – grass and wilted foliage at any rate, extending at the back to a wooden fence. Beyond that only darkness, fields and woods, and over the low hill the invisible town which might as well have been a hundred miles away.

Clifford Sanders went up to the front door. The bell was the very old-fashioned kind which you ring by turning a handle back and forth, but he had a key and unlocked this door, though when Wexford started to follow him he said in his flat chilly tone, 'Just a minute, please.'

Mother, evidently, had to be warned; he disappeared and after a moment or two she came out to them. Wexford's first thought was how small she was, tiny and thin; his second that this was the woman he had seen entering the underground car park as he had left it. Within moments then she had found the body that he had missed. Her face was very pale, as near a white face as you could find, very lined and powdered even whiter, a young girl's scarlet lipstick unbecomingly coating her mouth. She was dressed in a brown tweed skirt, beige jumper, bedroom

19

slippers. Did her recent discovery account for the curious smell of her? She smelt of disinfectant, the apparent combination of lime and thymol which hospitals reek of.

'You can come in,' she said, 'I've been expecting you.'

Inside, the place was bleak and carvernous; carpets and central heating were not luxuries that Mrs Sanders went in for. The hall floor was quarry-tiled, in the living room they walked on wood-grain linoleum and a couple of sparse rugs. There was scarcely an ornament to be seen – no pictures, only a large mirror in a heavy mahogany frame. Clifford Sanders had seated himself on a very old, shabby horsehair sofa in front of a fire of logs. He now wore on his feet only grey socks; his shoes were set in the hearth on a folded sheet of newspaper. Mrs Sanders pointed out – actually pointed with an extended finger – precisely where they were to sit: that armchair for Wexford, the other section of the sofa for Archbold. She seemed to have some notion of rank and what was due to it.

'I'd like you to tell me about your experience in the Barringdean Centre car park this evening, Mrs Sanders,' Wexford began. He forced himself to shift his eyes from the newspaper on which his daughter's face looked out at him from between the pair of black lace-up brogues. 'Tell me what happened from the time you came into the car park.'

Her voice was slow and flat like her son's, but there was something metallic about it too, almost as if throat and palate were composed of some inorganic hard material. 'There isn't anything to tell. I came up with my shopping to get my car. I saw something lying on the ground and went over to look and it was . . . I expect you know what it was.'

'Did you touch it?'

'I pulled back the bit of rag that was over it, yes.'

Clifford Sanders was watching his mother, his eyes still and blank. He seemed not so much relaxed as sagging from despair, his hands hanging down between his parted legs.

'What time was this, Mrs Sanders?' Wexford had noted the digital watch she wore.

'Exactly twelve minutes past six.' To account for her leaving the shopping precinct so late, she gave an account of a contretemps with a fishmonger, speaking in a measured level way – too measured. Wexford, who had been wondering what her tone reminded him of, now recalled electronic voices issuing from machines. 'I came up there at twelve minutes past six – and if you want to know how I can be sure of the time, the answer is I'm *always* sure of the time.'

He nodded. Digital watches were designed for people like her who, prior to their arrival on the scene, had to make approximate guesses as to what time was doing between ten-past six and six-fifteen. Yet most of them were speedy people, always in a hurry, restless, unrelaxed. This woman seemed one of those rare creatures who are constantly aware of time without being tempted to race against it.

She spoke softly to her son. 'Did you lock the garage doors?'

He nodded. 'I always do.'

'Nobody always does anything. Anybody can forget.'

'I didn't forget.' He got up. 'I'm going into the other room to watch TV.'

She was a pointer, Wexford saw, a finger-post. Now the finger pointed into the hearth. 'Don't forget your shoes.'

Clifford Sanders padded away with his shoes in his hand and Wexford said to Dorothy Sanders, 'What were you doing between twelve minutes past six and six forty-five when you managed to attract the attention of Mr Greaves in Queen Street?' He had registered very precisely the time of the phone call Greaves made to Kingsmarkham police station: fourteen minutes to seven. 'That's half an hour between the time you found the body and the time you got down to the gate and . . . called out.'

She wasn't disconcerted. 'It was a shock. I had my shock

21

to get over and then when I got down there I couldn't make anyone hear.'

He recalled Archbold's account, albeit at third hand. She had been screaming and raving inside those gates, shaking them 'fit to break them down' because the phone box was on the other side. Now the woman looked at him coldly and calmly. One would have said no emotion ever disturbed her equilibrium or altered the tone of the mechanical voice.

'How many cars did you see parked at that time on the second level?'

Without hesitation she said, 'Three, including mine.'

She wasn't lying; perhaps she hadn't been lying at all. He recalled how when he had passed through the second level there had been four cars parked there. One had pulled out, the one driven by the impatient young girl, and followed him fretfully. That had been at eight or nine minutes past six . . .

'Did you see anyone? Anyone at all?'

'Not a soul.'

She would be a widow, Wexford thought, nearly pensionable, without any sort of job, dependent in many ways and certainly financially dependent on this son who no doubt lived not far away. Later on, he reflected that he couldn't have been more wrong.

A wave of disinfectant smell hit him and she must have seen him sniffing.

'Coming in contact with that corpse,' she said, looking at him with steady, unblinking eyes, 'I had to scrub my hands with antiseptic.'

It was years since he had heard anyone use the word corpse. As he got up to go, she crossed to the window and began to draw the curtains. The place smelt like an operating theatre. The better to observe Clifford's arrival with the car, Wexford supposed, the curtains – of brown rep, not velvet – had been left drawn back. He watched her pull them together, giving each an impatient tug. Attached to the top of the door into the room was one of those extendable brass rails made to accommodate a

22

draught-excluding curtain. No curtain, however, hung from it.

Wexford decided the time was not ripe to ask the question that came to his lips.

It had fallen many times to Michael Burden's lot to be the bearer of bad tidings of a particular kind, to break the news of a spouse's death. He, whose own first wife had died prematurely, flinched from this task. And it was one thing to have to tell someone, for instance, that his wife had died in a road accident; quite another that her murdered body had been found. No one knew better than Burden that the majority of those who are murdered have been done to death by a near relative. The chances are that a murdered wife has been murdered by her husband.

It was only a few moments before Wexford's arrival that he had looked inside the dead woman's handbag. After the first photographs had been taken and the dirty brown velvet curtain lifted from the body, her handbag had been revealed lying under her, half concealed by her thigh. More photographs were taken, Sumner-Quist came and at last he was able to free the bag from where it lay and, holding it in gloved hands, undo the clasp and look inside. It was a standard cache of documents: driving licence, credit cards, dry-cleaning bill, two letters still in their envelopes. Her name and address presented themselves to him before he had even noted the other contents of the bag – chequebook, purse, pressed powder, packet of tissues, ballpoint pen and two safety-pins. Gwen P. Robson, 23 Hastings Road, Highlands, Kingsmarkham KM10 2NW. One of the envelopes was addressed to her as Mrs G. P. Robson, the other to Mr and Mrs R. Robson.

It might not be a shock to Robson; part of Burden's job was to observe whether it was a shock or not. He silently framed the words he would use as the car climbed the long hill that led up to the Highlands estate. All this had been countryside when Burden first came to Kingsmarkham, heathy hillsides crowned with woods, and from the top of this incline by day you had been able to see the ancient landmark called Barringdean Ring. It was very dark tonight, the horizon defined only by an occasional point of light, and the circle of oaks was invisible. Nearer at hand Highlands was cosily lit. This was the way Gwen Robson had no doubt intended to come home, driving the silver Escort, entering Eastbourne Avenue and soon turning left into Hastings Road.

Burden had been here only once before, though the estate had been put up by the local authority some seven years ago. Street trees and garden trees had grown up and matured: the first newness of the houses had worn off and they looked less as if built from playbox bricks by a giant's child. Smallish blocks of flats no more than three storeys high alternated with terraced or semi-detached houses, and opposite the block in which No. 23 was located stood a row of tiny bungalows designed as housing for the elderly. Not too far a cry from the old almshouses, thought Burden, whose wife had made him a lot more socially conscious than he used to be. On the doorstep of the Robsons' house stood a rack made for holding milk-bottles; it was of red plastic-covered wire, surmounted by a plastic doll in a white coat with 'Thank you, Mr Milk-man' in red letters under it and a clip to hold a note in its outstretched hand. This absurd object made Burden feel worse, indicative as it was of domestic cheerfulness. He looked at DC Davidson and Davidson looked at him and then he rang the bell.

The door was answered very quickly. Anxious people fly to doors, to phones. Their anxiety, of course, may not be brought about by the obvious cause.

'Mr Robson?'

'Yes. Who are you?'

'Police officers, Mr Robson.' Burden showed his warrant card. How to soften this? How to ease it? He could hardly say there was nothing to be alarmed about. 'I am afraid we have very serious news. May we come in?'

He was a smallish, owl-faced man, rather overweight;

24

Burden noticed that he used a stick even to bring him this short distance. 'Not my wife?' he said.

Burden nodded. He nodded firmly, his eyes on Robson. 'Let's go in.'

But Robson, though they were in the hall now, stood his ground. He leant on his stick. 'The car? A car accident?'

'No, Mr Robson, it wasn't a car accident.' The bad part was that this could all be fake, all acting. He might have been rehearsing it for the past hour. 'If we could go into your . . .'

'Is she – is she gone?'

The old euphemism. Burden repeated it. 'Yes, she's gone.' and he added, 'She's dead, Mr Robson.'

Burden turned and walked through the open doorway into the well-lit, warm, over-furnished living room. A fire of gas flames licking beautifully simulated smokeless fuel looked more real than the real thing. The television was on, but more indicative of Robson's recent tension was the clock patience game laid out on a small appropriately round marquetry table in front of the armchair with its indented seat and crumpled pink silk cushions. Only a murderer who was also a genius would have dreamt up that one, Burden thought.

Robson had turned very pale. His thin-lipped mouth trembled. Still upright but leaning heavily on the stick, he was shaking his head in a vague, uncomprehending way. 'Dead? Gwen?'

'Sit down, Mr Robson. Take it easy.'

'Would you like a drink, sir?' DC Davidson asked.

'We don't drink in this house.'

'I meant water.' Davidson went off and came back with water in a glass.

'Tell me what happened.' Robson was seated now, no longer looking at Burden, his eyes on the circle of playing cards. Absently he took a minute sip of the water.

'You must prepare yourself for a shock, Mr Robson.'

'I've had a shock.'

'Yes, I know.' Burden shifted his gaze and found himself looking at the framed photograph on the mantel-shelf of a very good-looking girl who rather resembled Sheila Wexford. A daughter? 'Your wife was killed, Mr Robson. There is no way I can make this easier to hear. She was murdered and her body was found in the Barringdean Shopping Centre car park.'

Burden wouldn't have been surprised if he had screamed, if he had howled like a dog. They came upon all sorts in their job. But Robson didn't scream; he merely stared with frozen face. A long time passed, a relatively long time, perhaps nearly a minute. He stared and passed his tongue over the thin lips, then he began mumbling very rapidly.

'We were married very young; we'd been married forty years. No children, we never had chick nor child, but that brings you closer; you're closer to each other without them. She was the most devoted wife a man ever had; she'd have done anything for me, she'd have laid down her life for me.' Great tears welled out of his eyes and flowed down his face. He sobbed and wept without covering his face, sitting upright and holding the stick with both hands, crying as most men only cried when they were very young children.

3

'IT looks as if she was garroted.'

Sumner-Quist's voice sounded pleasurably excited as if he had rung up to impart a piece of gossip: that the Chief Constable had run off with someone else's wife, for instance.

'Did you hear me? I said she was garroted.'

'Yes, I heard,' Wexford said. 'Good of you to tell me.'

'I thought you might go for a tasty little titbit like that before I let you have the full report.'

Extraordinary ideas some people have about one's tastes, Wexford thought. He tried to assemble in his mind what he knew about garroting. 'What was it done with?'

'A garrote,' Sumner-Quist chuckled cheerfully. 'Search me what kind. Home-made, no doubt. That's your problem.' Still laughing, he told Wexford that Mrs Robson had met her death after five-thirty and before six and had not been sexually assaulted. 'Merely garroted,' he said.

'It used to be a method of execution,' Wexford said when Burden came into the office. 'An iron collar was attached to a post and the victim's neck placed inside. The mind boggles a bit when you start thinking how they *got* the victim's neck inside. Then the collar was tightened until asphyxiation occurred. Did you know this method of capital punishment was still in use in Spain as late as the 1960s?'

'And we thought it was only bull-fighting they went in for.'

'There was also a more primitive implement consisting of a length of wire with wooden handles.'

Burden sat on the edge of Wexford's rosewood desk. 'Haven't I read somewhere that if you were up for burning by the Inquisition the executioner would garrote you for a small fee before the flames got under way?'

'I expect that was where the wire-with-wooden-handles type came into its own.'

He wondered digressively if Burden's jeans were the kind called 'designer'. They were rather narrow at the ankle and matched the inspector's socks that were probably of a 'denim blue' shade. Unconscious of this rather puzzled scrutiny, Burden said, 'Is Sumner-Quist saying that's what was used on Gwen Robson?'

'He doesn't know, he just says "a garrote". But it has to have been something of that kind. And the murderer has to have had it with him or her, ready-made, all prepared – which when you come to think of it, Mike, is pretty strange. It argues unquestionably premeditated murder, yet in a situation where no one could have forecast the prevailing conditions. The car park might have been full of people, for instance. Unless our perpetrator carries a garrote about with him as you or I might carry a pen . . . I don't think we can say much more about that until we get the full forensic report. In the meantime, what's the sum total of our knowledge of Gwen Robson?'

She was fifty-eight years old, childless, a former home help in the employment of Kingsmarkham Borough Council but now retired. Her husband was Ralph Robson, also a former Borough Council employee, retired two years before from the Housing Department. Mrs Robson had been married at eighteen and she and her husband had lived first with his parents at their home in Stowerton, later on in a rented flat and then a rented cottage. Their names high on the borough housing list, they had been allocated one of the new houses at Highlands as soon as they were built. Neither was yet eligible for the state retirement pension, but Robson derived a pension from the local authority on which they had contrived to live in reasonable comfort. For instance, they had managed to run the two-year-old Escort. As a general rule they took an annual holiday in Spain and had been prevented from doing so this year only by Ralph Robson's arthritis, which was seriously affecting his right hip.

All this had been learned both from Ralph Robson

himself and from his niece Lesley Arbel, the original of the photograph that had so much reminded Burden of Sheila Wexford.

'This niece – she doesn't live with them, does she?'

'She lives in London,' Burden said, 'but she spent a lot of time down here with them. More like a daughter than a niece, I gather, and an unusually devoted daughter at that. Or that's how it appears. She's staying with Robson now – came as soon as he told her what had happened to his wife.'

According to Robson, his wife had been in the habit of doing their weekly shopping every Thursday afternoon. Up until six months ago he had always gone with her, but his arthritis had made this impossible. On the previous Thursday, two days before, she had gone out in their car just before four-thirty. He had never seen her again. And where had he been himself between four-thirty and seven? At home alone in Hastings Road, watching television, making himself tea. Much the same as Archie Greaves, Wexford thought, whom he had been to see earlier that morning.

A policeman's dream of a witness, the old man was. The narrowness of his life, the confined span of his interests made him into a camera and tape device for the perfect recording of incidents in his little world. Unfortunately, there had not been much for him to observe: the shoppers leaving, the lights dwindling and going out, Sedgeman closing and locking the gates.

'There was this young chap running,' he said to Wexford. 'It was just on six, a minute or two after. There were a lot of people leaving, mostly ladies with their shopping, and he came running from round the back of that wall.'

Wexford followed his gaze out of the window. The wall in question was the side of the underground car-park entrance beside which stood a small crowd of ghoulish onlookers. There was nothing to see, but they waited in hope. The gates stood open, an empty food package rolled about the tarmac propelled by gusts of wind. The pennants on the turrets streamed in the wind, taut and fluttering. I was there, Wexford thought, almost with a groan, I came out of there at ten-past six and saw – nothing. Well, nothing but the Sanders woman.

'I reckoned he was in trouble,' Archie Greaves said. 'I reckoned he'd done something he shouldn't and been spotted and they was after him.' The man was so old that his face as well as the skin of his hands was discoloured with the liver spots that are called 'grave marks'. He was thin with age, his knitted cardigan and flannel trousers baggy on a bony, tremulous body. But the pale blue eyes, pink-rimmed, could see like those of someone half his age. 'He was just a boy with one of them woolly hats on his head and a zip-up jacket and he was running like a bat out of hell.'

'But there was in fact no one after him?'

'Not as I could see. Maybe they got fed up and turned back, knowing as they wouldn't catch him.'

And then he had seen Dorothy Sanders who was later to scream and rattle the gates, walking up and down searching the car parks for something or someone, her anger contained but her affronted indignation vibrating as later a demented terror was to stream from her, making Archie Greaves shiver and shake and fear for his heart.

An incident room had been set up in Kingsmarkham Police Station on Thursday night to receive calls from anyone who might have been in the Barringdean Shopping Centre underground car park between five and six-thirty. The local television station had broadcast an immediate appeal for possible witnesses to come forward and Wexford had managed to get a nationwide appeal on that night's ten o'clock news going out on the network. Calls started coming in at once – before the number to call had even disappeared from the screen, Sergeant Martin said – but of these the great majority were well-meant but misleading or ill-meant and misleading, or were deliberate attempts to deceive. A call came from a young woman called Sarah Cussons who identified herself as the driver of the Vauxhall Cavalier which had followed Wexford's out of the car park, and another from a man beside whose car Gwen Robson had parked her silver Escort. He had seen her drive in and was able to give her time of arrival at the centre as about twenty to five.

Throughout Thursday night the calls continued to come in, many of them from drivers of cars parked on all the levels who had seen nothing untoward. They were interviewed just the same. Early on Friday morning came a call on behalf of the owner of the blue Lancia. Mrs Helen Brook, nine months pregnant, had gone into labour while in the health-food shop in the shopping centre at about five on the previous evening. An ambulance had been called and she had been taken to the maternity wing of Stowerton Royal Infirmary.

None of the obviously genuine and well-intentioned callers was able to describe anyone else they had seen while parking or fetching their cars, though plenty of fantastic descriptions came in from those jokers who enjoy teasing the police. Two assistants from the Barringdean Centre shops phoned in to say they had served Gwen Robson, one just before five and the other, Linda Naseem – a checkout assistant at the Tesco supermarket – half an hour later. But by that time two of Wexford's officers were at the shopping centre questioning all the shop-workers, and Archbold had interviewed the man in charge of the fish counter in the Tesco superstore who confirmed he had had a row with a woman answering Dorothy Sanders' description 'at around six when they were closing up'. All that did was confirm her time of coming into the car park which Wexford could confirm himself.

That same morning Ralph Robson made a formal identification of his wife's body; the neck had been discreetly covered during this ordeal. He hobbled in on his stick, looked at the horror-stricken face from which some of the blue colour had faded, nodded, said, 'Yes,' but didn't cry this time. Wexford had not seen him on that occasion, hadn't yet seen him. He had interviewed David Sedgeman, the car park supervisor, himself. The man should have been a valuable witness, yet he seemed to have seen nothing or to have registered nothing he had seen. He could recall waving to Archie Greaves because he did this every evening, and for the same reason could recall locking the gates. But his memory offered him no worried woman or running man, no fast-driven car or suspicious escaper. Everything had been normal, he said in his dull way. He had locked the gates and gone home just as he always did, collecting his own car from where he always left it in a bay in one of the open-air parking areas.

The November air felt raw and the sky was a leaden grey. A reddish sun hung over the roof-tops, not very high in the sky but as high as it would get. Burden had on a padded jacket, a pale grey Killy, warm as toast and turning him from a thin man into a stout one. His wife was away, staying with her mother who was convalescent after an operation, and that disturbed Burden, making him jumpy and insecure. He would spend tonight with her and their little son in his mother-in-law's house outside Myringham, but what he really wanted was his own family back home with him in his own house. His face took on a look both irritable and cynical as Wexford spoke.

'Did Robson strike you,' Wexford said in the car, 'as the sort of man who would sit himself down and with deliberation fashion a wire implement with a handle at each end for the express purpose of garroting his wife?'

'Now you're asking. I don't know what sort of a man that would be. He had no car, remember, his wife had the car. The centre's a mile away from Highlands . . .'

'I know. Is the arthritic hip genuine?'

'Even if it isn't, he had no car. He could have walked, or there's the bus. But if he wanted to murder his wife, why not do it at home like most of them do?'

Wexford couldn't keep from laughing at this insouciant acceptance of domestic homicide. 'Maybe he did, we don't know yet. We don't know if she died in that car park or the body was only dumped there. We don't even know if she drove the car.'

'You mean Robson himself may have?'

'Let's see,' said Wexford.

They had arrived at Highlands and Lesley Arbel opened the front door to them. She didn't remind Wexford of his own daughter; to him she bore no resemblance to Sheila. He saw only a pretty girl who struck him at once as being exceptionally well-dressed, indeed almost absurdly well-dressed for a weekend of mourning in the country with one's recently bereaved uncle. She introduced herself, explained that she had not waited until the prearranged time for her visit but had come on Friday morning.

'My uncle's upstairs,' she said. 'He's lying down. The doctor came and said he was to get as much rest as he could.'

'That's all right, Miss Arbel. We'd like to talk to you too.'

'Me? But I don't know anything about it. I was in London.'

'You know about your aunt. You can tell us something of what sort of a person she was, better than your uncle can.'

She said in a rather pernickety way. 'That's right, he's my real uncle. I mean, my mother was his sister; she was my aunt because she married him.'

Wexford nodded, aware that his impatience showed. Mentally he cautioned himself against deciding too soon that a witness was irredeemably stupid. She took them into the Robsons' brightly furnished living room where a conflict of textile patterns dazzled Wexford – flowers on the carpet, flowers of a more formal design on the curtains, trees and fruits on the wallpaper, a rug with a sunburst pattern. The flames of a gas fire licked indestructible coals. The girl sat down and her own face smiled over her shoulder out of a silver frame. His question astonished her.

'These curtains, are they new?'

'Pardon?'

'Let me rephrase it. Were there ever different curtains at these windows?'

'I think Auntie Gwen once had red curtains, yes. Why do you want to know?'

Wexford made no answer but watched her while Burden asked about the telephone call her uncle had made to her on Thursday evening. Her clothes were remarkable, somehow evoking the unreal elegance of actresses in Hollywood comedies of the thirties, as sleek and as unsuitable for the wear and tear of living. A bunch of gold chains that looked too heavy for comfort hung against her cream silk shirt between the lapels of the coffee-coloured silk jacket. Crimson-nailed hands lay in her lap and she lifted one to her face, touching her cheek as she replied to his questions.

'You intended coming down for the weekend on Saturday as you often did?'

She nodded.

'But your uncle phoned you himself on Thursday evening and told you what had happened?'

'He phoned me on Thursday, on Thursday night. I wanted to come then, but he wouldn't have that. He had one of the neighbours, a Mrs Whitton, with him so I thought he'd be all right.' She looked from one to the other of them. 'You said you wanted me to talk about Auntie Gwen.'

'In a moment, Miss Arbel,' Burden said. 'Would you mind telling me what you were doing yourself on Thursday afternoon?'

'What do you want to know for?' She was more than astounded; her manner was affronted as if she had encountered insolence. Her long elegant legs, the feet encased in high-heeled cream leather pumps, drew close together, were pressed together. 'Why ever do you want to know that?'

Perhaps it was pure innocence.

Burden said blandly, 'Routine questions, Miss Arbel. In a murder enquiry, it's necessary to know people's

34

whereabouts.' He attempted to help her along. 'I expect you were at work, weren't you?'

'I went home early on Thursday, I wasn't very well. Don't you want me to tell you about Auntie Gwen?'

'In a moment. You went home early because you weren't well. You had a cold, did you?'

A vacuous stare was turned on Burden, but perhaps not entirely vacuous for it seemed to contain an element of earnestness. 'It was my PMT, wasn't it?' she said as if she were famous for this disorder, as if all the world was aware of it. Wexford doubted if Burden even knew what those initials stood for, and now the girl seemed equally dubious. Frowning, she leaned towards Burden. 'I always have PMT and there's not a thing they can do about it.'

At this point the door opened and Ralph Robson came in, leaning on his stick. He had a dressing gown on, but with a shirt and pair of slacks underneath it. 'I heard voices.' His flat but beaky face was turned on Wexford with a puzzled look.

'Chief Inspector Wexford, Kingsmarkham CID.'

'Pleased to meet you,' Robson said, sounding anything but pleased. 'You coming here has saved me a phone call. Maybe one of you can tell me what's become of the shopping?'

'The shopping, Mr Robson?'

'The shopping Gwen got on Thursday, as was in the boot of the blessed car presumably. I can see I can't have the car back yet awhile, but the shopping's a different story. There's meat in those bags, there's a loaf and butter and I don't know what else. I don't say I'm poor, but I'm not so rolling in money as I can just let that lot go, right?'

Self-preservation or a tenacity for life overcame grief. Wexford knew this, but it never ceased mildly to surprise him just the same. It might be that this man felt no grief; it might be that he was responsible for his wife's death, but it might only be that he had ceased to feel much emotion for anyone or anything. That sometimes happened to people as they aged and Wexford had noticed it dispassionately but with an inner shiver. Yet Burden said he had wept when first told.

'We'll get it back to you later today,' was all Wexford said.

He had carefully gone over the contents of the shopping bag himself before having the perishable items placed in one of the police canteen fridges. There had been nothing among them to excite much interest: mostly food, but things from the chemist as well – toothpaste and talcum powder – and from the British Home Stores four light-bulbs; all of these contained in a BHS bag, indicating perhaps that she had stopped there first. Mrs Robson's handbag, which would also soon be returned and which Burden had first looked into in the car park, contained her purse with twenty-two pounds in it, plus some small change and a chequebook from the Trustee Savings Bank. The credit cards were a Visa and the card which the Barringdean Shopping Centre supplied for its patrons. Her handkerchief and the two folded tissues were unused. The letters which had provided the police with her identity and address were from a sister in Leeds and the other – scarcely a letter in any sense – an invitation to a Christmas fashion show at the shop where Wexford had bought Dora's sweater.

'Are you missing a brown velvet curtain, Mr Robson?'

'Me? No. What do you mean?'

'A curtain which might have been kept in the boot of your car for the purpose, say, of covering up the wind-screen in frosty weather?'

'I use newspaper for that.'

Lesley Arbel said suddenly, 'Could you eat a bit of lunch, Uncle? A little something light?'

He had sat down and was leaning forward in the chair, pressing one hand on his thigh in what seemed genuine pain, his face twisted with it. 'There's nothing I fancy, dear.'

'But you're not still having those pills, are you? The ones that upset your tummy?'

36

'Doctor took me off the blessed things. There's some they don't suit, he said; they can give you ulcers.'

'You've got arthritis, have you, Mr Robson?'

He nodded. 'You listen,' he said, 'and you can hear the hip joint grind.' To Robson's evident agony there came a shift of bone in socket and Wexford did hear it, heard with dismay an unhuman ratchet-like sound. 'It's a bit of bad luck for me that I'm allergic to the painkillers. Got to grin and bear it. I'm in line for one of those replacement ops, but there's a waiting list round here of up to three years. God knows what sort of a state I'll be in in three years. It'd be a different story if I could have it done private.'

This was no news to Wexford, that hip replacements could be carried out almost at once if the patient were prepared to pay but that the waiting time for National Health Service surgery might be very protracted. The unfairness of this was not lost on him, but he was more intent on trying to assess the genuineness of Robson's disability. He turned his eyes towards the girl and she looked at him artlessly, her face a beautiful blank.

'Where do you work, Miss Arbel?'

'*Kim* magazine.'

'Could you give me the address, please, and your own address in London too? Do you live alone or share?'

'I share with two other girls.' She sounded peevish, muttering the north-west London address. '*Kim*'s office is at Orangetree House in the Waterloo Road.'

Wexford had only once seen the magazine when Dora had bought it for the sake of some mail-order bargain it featured. A semi-glossy weekly, it had seemed aimed at a not very youthful market but at the same time making little provision for women past forty or so. The issue Wexford had seen had carried articles he thought dreary but which the magazine itself vaunted as controversial and lively, under such headings as: 'Is it OK to be a Lesbian?' and 'Your Daughter Your Own Clone?'

'Could you eat some scrambled egg, Uncle, and a little thin bread and butter?'

37

Robson shrugged, then nodded. Burden began speaking to him of Mrs Whitton, the neighbour who had come to sit with him before Lesley Arbel arrived. Had he seen anyone, spoken on the phone to anyone, while his wife was out?

Lesley got up, said, 'Well, if you'll just excuse me . . .'

While Robson told Burden about the Hastings Road neighbours, speaking in a wretched halting monotone and separating virtually every sentence from the next with a phrase to the effect that Gwen had known them all better than he did, Wexford left the room. He found Lesley Arbel standing in front of an electric stove, a printed tea-towel rather than an apron tied round her waist to protect the coffee silk skirt. Two eggs reposed in a bowl, a beater beside them, but instead of preparing her uncle's lunch she was examining her face in a handbag mirror and painting something on to it with a small, fat brush.

As soon as she saw Wexford she put brush and mirror away with extreme haste, as if this rapid manoeuvre would somehow render the prior activity invisible. She broke open the eggs, not very skilfully, got a piece of shell into the bowl and had to pick it out with a long red nail.

'Why would anyone want to murder your aunt, Miss Arbel?'

She didn't answer him for a moment, but reached up into a cabinet for a plate and put a cruet on to the tray she had laid with a cloth. Her voice when it came was nervous and irritable. 'It was some crazy person, wasn't it? There's never any reason for murders, not these days. The ones you read about in the papers, they're all people who say they don't know why they did it or they've forgotten or had a blackout or whatever. The one who killed her will have been like that. I mean, who would have wanted to kill her for a reason? There wasn't any reason.' She turned away from him and started beating the eggs.

'Everybody liked her?' he said. 'She wouldn't have had enemies?'

In her left hand she held the pan in which butter was

38

smoking too strongly, in her other the bowl with the egg mixture. But instead of pouring one into the other, she stood with the two vessels poised. 'It's a laugh really, hearing you talk like that. Or it would be if it wasn't such a tragedy. She was a wonderful, lovely lady – don't you understand that? Hasn't anyone told you? Look at Uncle Ralph, he's heartbroken, isn't he? He worshipped her and she worshipped him. They were just a lovely couple, like young lovers right up to when this happened. And this'll be the death of him, I can promise you that – this'll be the end of him. He's aged about twenty years since yesterday.'

She swung round, tipped the eggs into the pan and began rapidly cooking them. Wexford had the curious feeling that for all the apparent sincerity of her words what she was really trying to do was impress him with a kind of caring competent maturity – an ambition that went wrong when she seemed to realize that though the eggs were cooked she had forgotten about the bread and butter. Rather harassed by now, she cut doorsteps of bread and covered them with wedges of butter chipped from the refrigerated block. He opened doors for her, feeling something very near pity without exactly knowing what he pitied her *for*. The apron improvised from a tea towel fell off as she teetered into the living room on her stilt heels. But even so, as she passed the small wall mirror which hung between kitchen and living-room doorways, she was unable to resist a glance into it. Balanced on her pointed toes, holding the tray, flustered, she nevertheless took the opportunity of a narcissistic peep at her own face . . .

Robson was lying back in his armchair and had to be jolted out of his half-doze. This his niece did not only by propping him up with a cushion behind him and plumping the tray down on his lap, but also with the rough and somehow shocking, 'He asked me if Gwen had enemies! Can you credit it?'

Dull, bewildered eyes were lifted. Incredibly came the mumble, 'He's only doing his job, dear.'

'Gwen,' she said, and sentimentally, 'Gwen that was like a mother to me.' Suddenly her manner sharpened. 'Mind you, she wasn't soft. She had principles, very high principles, didn't she, Uncle? And she knew how to speak her mind. She didn't like that couple living together, the ones next-door-but-one, whatever they're called, the people that run a business from home. I said times had changed from when she got married, but it didn't make any difference. I mean, everyone does that now, I said. But she wouldn't have it, would she, Uncle?'

They were all looking at her, Robson as well. She seemed to realize how animated her manner had been for one so recently bereaved and she flushed. Not much real love there, Burden thought, and said, 'Now we'd like to take a look round the house. Is that OK?'

She would have argued but Robson, having eaten almost nothing, pushing away his plate, nodded and waved one hand in an odd gesture of assent. Wexford wouldn't have bothered with the house; there was nothing relevant to Mrs Robson's life or death he expected to find. He was already half-adhering to the girl's view, that some badly disturbed person had killed Gwen Robson for no better reason than that she was there and a woman, unprepared and frail enough. However, he made his way into the bedroom she had shared with Robson and saw everywhere signs of domestic harmony. The bed was unmade. On an impulse aimed at no particular enlightening discovery, Wexford lifted up the flatter and less rumpled of the pillows and found underneath it Mrs Robson's nightdress just as it must have been folded and tucked away by her on Thursday morning . . .

A framed photograph showed her as she had once been, her hair dark and plentiful, mouth widely smiling, plumper than now. She was seated and her husband was looking over her shoulder, perhaps to give an illusion of the greater height he had not possessed. The books on her bedside cabinet were two novels of Catherine Cookson, on his the latest Robert Ludlum. On the dressing table a small container of Yardley 'Chique' perfume stood between his hairbrush and a pincushion in which were pinned three brooches. A surprising number of pictures covered the walls: more framed photographs of the two of them, a framed collage of postcards, sentimental mementoes of their own holidays, cat and dog pictures perhaps cut from calendars, a cottage in a flowery garden embroidered by someone – perhaps Gwen Robson herself.

The curtains in the room were as floral as this picture. In spite of her sober style of dressing, she had liked bright colours – pinks and blues and yellows. She might have worn brown, but she would not have furnished her house with it. A neatly stacked pile of *Kim* magazines occupied half the top of a long stool and on top of these lay last night's evening paper. Did that mean that the night after his wife had been murdered Robson had taken the evening paper up with him for his bedtime reading? Well, why not? Life must go on. And no doubt he had been given sleeping pills, had needed something to read while waiting for the drug to take effect. Wexford just glanced at the lead story and the photograph of the barrister Edmund Hope, as handsome and striking-looking as any of the Arab bombers he was prosecuting, then he turned away to study the view.

Beyond the window the Highlands estate presented a panorama of itself she must often have seen while standing here: Hastings Road where the house was, Eastbourne Road leading down to the town, Battle Hill mounting to the crown of the estate, pantiled roofs deliberately placed at odd angles to one another to give the illusion of some little hillside town in Spain or Portugal – coniferous trees bluish, dark green and golden-green because conifers are cheap and grow swiftly, winding gravel paths and concrete paths, windows dressed in Austrian blinds, looped-up festoons and frills, one solitary resident only to be seen: an elderly, very stout woman in long skirt and multi-coloured jacket who was breaking into pieces the end of a loaf of bread and putting them on to a bird-table in a garden diagonally opposite. The house she returned to was the first of those past the row of old people's sheltered housing.

She looked back once at where Mrs Robson had lived, as anyone must look who lived here or came into this street. That was human nature. Her eyes met Wexford's and she immediately looked away. It was rather as Lesley Arbel had quickly put away her mirror and brush, as if this would negate the past act.

Wexford said, 'We may as well go. We'll give Mrs Sanders a ring and get her down to the station.'

'You wouldn't prefer to go to her?'

'No, I'd prefer to give her a bit of trouble,' said Wexford.

4

IT was spread out on the table in the interview room —
a curtain that had once been handsome, of a rich
thick-piled tobacco-brown velvet, lined and weighted
at the two corners of its lower hem. But splashed across
the centre of it was a large dark stain, a stain which
might have been blood but which Wexford had already
ascertained was not. Other stains had since been super-
added; there was certainly an impression that the original
splashings had ruined the curtain as a curtain, and that
since the occurrence which had led to them any further
damage to the velvet had been of no account.

Dorothy Sanders looked at it. Her eyes flicked and as
she looked back at Wexford he noticed for the first time
that they were of a curious pale fawn colour.

'That's the curtain that used to hang up on my door.'
And then, after a long blank stare at Wexford had elicited
no particular reaction, 'It's still got the hooks in it.'

He continued to stand and watch her, his face expressing
nothing, but now he gave a small reflective nod. Burden
was frowning.

'Where did you get it?' she said. 'What's it doing here?'

'It was covering Mrs Robson's body,' Burden said.
'Don't you remember?'

The change in her was electric. She jumped back, retract-
ing arms and hands as if it were offal or slime her fingers
had touched. Her face flushed darkly, her lips sucked in.
She put a hand to her mouth – a characteristic gesture, he
thought – and then flung the hand away, aware of what
it had been in contact with. He had a glimpse then of how
this slow, deliberate woman could become a screaming
demented creature, and for the first time he understood
that the old man called Archie Greaves might not have
been exaggerating.

'You've touched it before, Mrs Sanders,' he said. 'You pulled it back to look at her face.'

She shuddered, her arms stretched out and shaking as if she could shake off her hands and so get rid of them.

'Come and sit down, Mrs Sanders.'

'I want to wash my hands. Where can I go and wash my hands?'

Wexford didn't want her to run away, but as he picked up the phone DC Marian Bayliss tapped on the door and came in. She began on a routine question and he nodded assent and said, 'Would you take Mrs Sanders to the ladies' loo, please?'

Dorothy Sanders was brought back after about five minutes, calm again, stony-faced and with more red lipstick on her mouth. He could smell the police station liquid soap ten feet away.

'Have you any suggestions, Mrs Sanders, as to how your curtain came to be covering Mrs Robson's body?'

'I didn't put it there. The last time I saw it was in a . . .' she hesitated, went on more carefully, '. . . a room in my house. Folded up. In an attic, they call them attics. My son may have gone up there; he may have wanted it for something, though he'd no business . . . without me saying he could.' A grim look cramped her features.

This hadn't occurred to Wexford as a possibility before, but it did now. 'Does your son live with you, Mrs Sanders?'

'Of course he lives with me.' She spoke as if, though it were possible there were some very few grown-up children who through general viciousness or perhaps being orphans lived apart from their parents, such situations were rare enough to provoke incredulity and even disgust. She spoke as if Wexford were a depraved ignoramus to suppose otherwise. 'Of course he lives with me. Where did you think he lived?'

'Are you sure this curtain was in a room in your house? It couldn't have been in the boot of your car?'

She was no fool. At least, she was sharp enough.

'Not unless he put it there.' The identity of 'he' was evident enough. She thought, reasoned, nodded her head.

This was not one of those women, Wexford thought with a kind of grim amusement, who even at the cost of their own lives would protect a child, criminal or otherwise — the kind who hid a wanted son or lied when questioned as to his whereabouts, who regarded a son not so much as an extension of herself but as a precious superior. 'I expect he did put it there,' she now said. 'I'd sent through my catalogue for a proper nylon cover for the car. Nylon or fibreglass or one of those things.' Mail order she meant, Wexford decided. 'I'd sent for it a good two months ago, but they take their time, these people. I expect he couldn't wait.'

She looked up at him, making him perform one of those about-turns in his assessment of human nature. For a moment he felt he knew nothing; people and their ways were as much a mystery as ever they had been. She looked human at least, she spoke in a human way. 'He's not like me, he hasn't got much patience. He can't help it. I expect he thought he'd just take that curtain and use it when we had the cold spell. You can't be kept waiting about for ever, can you?' She looked down at her watch, drawn to this recorder of time's passage by her references to its delays. Her wrist was like a bundle of wires, thinly insulated.

Burden had been pacing up and down. He said, 'It's your car but your son uses it?'

'It's my car,' she said. 'I bought it and paid for it and I'm the registered owner. But he has to go to work, doesn't he? I let him use it to go to work and then if I want to go shopping, he can take me and pick me up. He's got to have transport.'

'What does your son do, Mrs Sanders?'

She was one of those who expect their private arrangements to be intimately known by others, to need no elucidation, yet who show affront when those others reveal a knowledge gained by sensitivity or intuition. 'He's a teacher, isn't he?'

'You tell me,' Burden said.

She curled her nostrils in disgust. 'He teaches in a school

45

for children who can't pass their exams without extra coaching.'

A crammer's, Wexford thought. Probably Munster's in Kingsmarkham High Street. It surprised him a little and yet — why not? Clifford Sanders, he thought in the light of his new knowledge, would be one of those who lived at home while they attended university, going to and fro by bus. It would be interesting to find out if he was right there.

'Part-time,' she said, and astonished them both by saying in the same level, indifferent tone, 'He's inadequate in some ways.'

'What's wrong with him? Is he ill?'

Her old harshly censorious manner was back. 'They call it ill nowadays. When I was young, they called it lacking character.' A dark flush moved into her cheeks, mottling them. She was dressed in green today, a dark dull green, though her shoes and gloves were black. When the blush faded, the dull seaweed green seemed to show up the pallor of her skin. 'That's where he was, wasn't he, when he was supposed to be coming for me in the car park? He'd been to this psychiatrist. They call them psychotherapists; they don't have any qualifications.'

'Mrs Sanders, are you telling me that your son was in the Barringdean Centre car park when you were?'

Emotions warred behind the blush, the succeeding pallor, the muffling screen of green and black. She had not meant to let that out. Protecting her son was not as unknown to her as Wexford had at first believed: he could even see that in an intense, self-disgusted, incredulous way she loved her son, but perhaps she had not been able to resist that dig at a profession she disapproved of. She spoke with extreme care now, the pace of the voice electronically slowed to make understanding easier.

'He should have been there but he was not. He had come in, the car was there, but he . . .' she paused, breathing deeply, '. . . was not.'

46

An abrupt halting explanation followed. At first, when she saw the car and a body, she had thought it was Clifford lying there dead. She couldn't see the body because it was covered up and believing it to be Clifford, she pulled back the brown velvet covering. It wasn't Clifford, but it had been a great shock just the same. She had had to sit in her car and rest, recover herself. Clifford had been going to pick her up as he always did on Thursdays, always. It was an unvarying arrangement, though the school time might vary. She looked at her watch as she said this. Clifford brought her to the shopping centre, went to his session with the psychotherapist, returned to pick her up. She didn't drive. This Thursday they had arranged for him to be in the car park on the second level by six-fifteen. On her arrival she had had her hair done at Suzanne's on the upper floor of the centre – another inflexible arrangement – shopped, come back to the car park at twelve minutes past six.

After the shock of finding the body, after she had recovered somewhat – Wexford found this frailty of hers rather hard to believe in – she had gone up to look for Clifford. She had walked about looking for him, a statement that was confirmed by Archie Greaves. At last she had gone to the pedestrian gates . . .

'I broke down,' she said, giving each work equal monotonous weight.

'Where was your son, then? No, you needn't answer that, Mrs Sanders. You tell him we're interested and we'll have a talk with him later. We'll all take a break and he can do some thinking. How's that?'

She moved towards the door. Someone would drive her home. Her manner had in it something of the sleepwalker, or as if almost everything she thought and felt – perhaps momentous or amazing things – she kept veiled. She was so thin and wiry you would expect her to be a brisk woman, Wexford thought, but she was as languid as some slippery, rotund sea creature. Burden said as soon as she had gone, 'Is she saying he's potty?'

'I should think that depends on how strict you are

and —' Wexford looked up at Burden with a half-smile, 'how out of date. Apparently he can hold down a job and drive a car and carry on a normal conversation. Is that what you mean?'

'You know it isn't. He sounds very much like a candidate for Lesley Arbel's psychopath role to me.'

' "The outstanding feature is emotional immaturity in its broadest and most comprehensive sense. These people are impulsive, feckless, unwilling to accept the results of experience and unable to profit by them . . ." ' Wexford faltered for a moment, then went on, ' ". . . sometimes prodigal of effort but utterly lacking in persistence, plausible but insincere, demanding but indifferent to appeals, dependable only in their constant unreliability, faithful only to infidelity, rootless, unstable, rebellious and unhappy." '

Burden gaped a bit. 'Did you make that up?'

'Of course I didn't. It's David Stafford-Clark's definition of a psychopath — or part of it. I learned it by heart because I thought it might come in useful, but I can't say it ever has.' Wexford grinned. 'I liked the prose too.'

The expression on Burden's face rather indicated that he didn't know what prose was. 'I think it's very useful. It's good. I like that bit about dependable in their constant unreliability.'

'Oxymoron.'

'Is that another mental disease?' When Wexford only shook his head, Burden said, 'That bit you quoted — is it in a book? Can I get it?'

'I'll lend you my copy. I expect it's out of print; it must be twenty years since I read it. But you can't apply that to Clifford Sanders, you know. You've hardly talked to him.'

'That can be remedied,' said Burden grimly.

It was dark as Wexford drove along the street where he lived and approached his own house. A car was parked on his garage drive, Sheila's Porsche. He felt a tiny dip of the heart and immediately reproached himself. He loved his daughters dearly and Sheila was his favourite, but for once he wouldn't be elated to see her. A quiet evening was what he had looked forward to; it might be the last for a long time, for he had no faith in Burden's forecast of the straightforwardness of this case. And now it would be given over not only to talk, but talk on serious matters.

Irritation of a different kind succeeded this initial flash of dismay. She had parked her car on the garage drive because she supposed him to be home already, even supposed this to be his day off as it should have been, and expected his car to be inside the garage. Now he would have to leave it out in the street. Unburdening her heart to her mother would have taken priority over everything. He could imagine her saying every ten minutes or so how she must rush out and move the car before darling Pop got home . . .

Thinking like that cheered him, made him smile to himself, hearing with his mind's ear her enchanting, slightly breathless voice. He would say nothing, he resolved, of the wire-cutting, the reports of her coming divorce; he would utter no word of reproach, certainly no intimation of disappointment or upset, would cast on her no grave looks. He touched the Porsche lightly on its long, gleaming, nearly horizontal rear window as he passed it. Did she go to demonstrations in that? Well, it was only a small Porsche and black at that . . . Would she come and kiss his cheek or would she hang back? There was no knowing. He went in the back way, into the hall from the kitchen, hung up his coat, hearing her voice from the living room – hearing the voice of Beatrice Cenci, Antigone, Nora Helmer and now Lady Audley – falter and fall silent. He went into the room and immediately she was rushing to him and in his arms.

Over her shoulder he saw the small satirical smile on Dora's face. He hugged Sheila and as she relaxed, distanced her with his arms stretched and said, 'Are you OK?'

'Well, I don't know.' she giggled. 'Not really. I'm not

really OK. I'm in an awful mess. And Mother's being very sniffy. Mother's being horrible, actually.'

Her rueful smile showed him this was only half-meant. Foolish this was, he knew it every time, but when he looked at her like this he could never help admiring afresh the beautiful, fair, sensitive face that would with luck defy time, the long, pale, soft hair, the eyes as clear as a child's and as blue, but not a child's. There was no wedding ring on her left hand, but often she wore no rings, just as she nearly always kept her fancy clothes for public or publicity appearances. The jeans she wore were shabby compared with Burden's. She had on a blue sweater of a similar shade and a string of wooden beads.

'Now you're home, darling,' said Dora. 'we can all have a drink. I'm sure I need it. In fact . . .' she looked from one to the other with a certain tact, with a knowledge that they might care for two minutes alone together, '. . . I'll get it.'

Sheila fell back into the chair she had jumped out of. 'Aren't you going to ask me why? Why, why, why everything?'

'No.'

'You have a blind faith in the rightness of everything I do?'

'You know I don't.' He was tempted to say of the husband she had left, 'I liked Andrew,' but he didn't say it. 'What are we talking about, anyway? Which of your sensational acts?'

'Oh, Pop, I had to cut the wire. It wasn't done hysterically or without thinking or for publicity or in defiance or anything. I *had* to do it. I've been psyching myself up to it for ever so long. People take notice of what I do, you see. I don't just mean *me*, I mean anyone in my position. They kind of say, "If Sheila Wexford does it there must be some meaning to it, there must be a point if a famous person like her does it."'

'What happened?' He was genuinely curious.

'I bought a pair of wire-cutters in a DIY place in Covent Garden. There were ten of us, all members of PANDA –

Players Anti-Nuclear Direct Action — only I was the only well-known one. We went to a place in Northamptonshire called Lossington and we went in three cars, mine and two others. It's an RAF station where they have obsolete bombers. The importance of the place doesn't matter, you see, it's the gesture . . .'

'Of course I see,' he said a little impatiently.

'There was this bleak plain with a couple of concrete huts and some hangars and grass all round and mud and a wire fence gone rusty — miles of it, and high enough not to lose tennis balls if you were playing inside. Well, we all stood up against the wire and each of us cut a bit and a great flap of wire came down, then we went to the nearest town and the police station and walked in and told them what we'd done and . . .'

Dora came in with their drinks on a tray — beer for Wexford, wine for herself and her daughter. Having heard the last words, she said, 'You might have given a little more thought to your father.'

'Oh, Pop, the first idea was for us to cut the wire at RAF Myringford, but I stood out against that because of you, because it was on your patch. I did think of you. But I had to do it, I *had* to — can't you understand?'

His temper for an instant got the better of him. 'You're not Antigone, however much you may have played her. You're not Bunyan. Don't keep saying you *had* to do it. Do you really believe your cutting the wire round an obsolete bomber station or whatever is going to lead to a total ban on nuclear arms? I don't like them, you know, I don't believe anyone likes them; I'm afraid of them. When you and Sylvia were little I used to be — oppressed with fear for you. And if they've kept the peace for forty-five years, that doesn't mean a thing; it certainly doesn't mean they'll keep it for ninety. But I know better than to suppose this kind of thing is going to affect government.'

'What else can we do?' she said simply. 'I often think I don't believe that either, but what else can we do? They all think that banning Cruise missiles solves everything, but they're getting rid of less than ten per cent of the

51

world's arsenal. The alternative is apathy, is pretending everything's solved.'

'You mean that "for evil to triumph",' Wexford said, '"it is only necessary for good men to do nothing"?'

But Dora followed sharply with, 'Or do you mean that between the early warning and the bomb going off you'll have ten minutes in which to congratulate yourself on not being an ostrich?'

Sheila sat up, was silent for a while. It was as if what her mother said had not touched her, had gone unheard. Then she said very quietly, 'If you're a human being, you have to be against nuclear weapons. It's a . . . a sort of definition. Like . . . like mammals suckle their young and insects have six legs. The definition of a human being is one who hates and fears and wants to be rid of nuclear weapons. Because they're the evil, they're the modern equivalent of the devil, of Antichrist – they are all we'll ever know of hell.'

After that, as he remarked to Dora while Sheila made a mysterious secret phone call, there didn't seem any more to be said. Or not for the present. Dora sighed. 'She says Andrew's right wing and only interested in capitalism and he doesn't have an inner life.'

'Presumably she knew that before she married him,' Wexford said.

'She isn't in love any more and that always makes a difference.'

'It's not so much a depraved society that we live in as an idealistic one. People expect to remain in love with their partners all their lives or else break up and start again. Are you still in love with me?'

'Oh, darling, you know I love you very much, I'm devoted to you, I'd be lost without you, I –'

'Exactly,' said her husband, laughing, and he went outside to get himself another beer.

Nothing had been said about Sheila staying the night. She had arrived at four and in the usual course of things would have started back for London at about nine. It was less than an hour's drive. But the phone call she had made changed her mind, or so it seemed. She came back into the room looking pleased, looking happier than she had since Wexford arrived home, and announced that if they didn't mind – this with the self-confidence of the always-beloved child to whom parents' 'minding' was unknown – she would stay until tomorrow, she might even stay until after lunch tomorrow.

'Mother's the only person I know who still cooks roast beef and Yorkshire pudding for Sunday lunch.'

Wexford thought that asking her where she was living now could hardly be construed as interference, but he resisted saying how much he had liked the house in Hampstead.

'I had to move out, didn't I? I couldn't go on living in Downshire Hill, in Andrew's house that he'd paid for, and turn him out. Someone told him it was worth two million.' She sat down on the floor, hugging her knees. 'I can't cope with that kind of money. I've got this flat in Bloomsbury, Coram Fields, and it's OK, it's really quite grand.' She flashed a smile at her father. 'You'll like it.'

Dora had the *Radio Times* on her lap. 'Nearly time for Lady Audley. I don't want to miss it, so if you don't like watching yourself I'll have to send you to bed.'

'Oh, Mother. Do you really imagine I haven't seen it? I don't mind watching it again with you, but of course I saw a preview. Look, I must rush outside though and move my car so that Pop can put his in. No, I'll move mine and put his in. It doesn't matter if I miss the beginning of –'

'I'll move the cars,' Wexford interposed. 'We've got five minutes. Keys, please, Sheila.'

She fished them out of her jeans pocket. His car was a little wide for the garage and he had made his offer less out of altruism than for fear of getting the new Montego scraped. Dora switched on the television. The wind had dropped and the night was dark and quiet, rather misty, each streetlamp a yellow blur. Between his garden and the empty site next door that had never been built on, the fence was sagging, in places laid flat on the flowerbed where the wind had felled it. The last few leaves on the cherry tree in his front lawn had been shrivelled by early frost and still clung to the nearly bare branches. Leaves lay everywhere, dark and wet, a blackened coating on path and pavement. Someone had found a child's Fair Isle glove on this mat of leaves and laid it on top of the low wall. The street was deserted. In a bay window opposite, between dark evergreen shrubs standing like sentries, between open curtains, he saw the blue glow of a screen suddenly flooded with colour and his daughter's face filling it in close-up.

Sheila hadn't locked the Porsche. Wexford opened the door and got into the driving-seat. It was an irony that his much cheaper and less prestigious car had automatic transmission, while this one had a manual gearbox. Presumably Sheila preferred it that way. The Montego had been his for only six months and it was the first automatic car he had ever possessed, but even so he was coming near to forgetting about letting in clutches and shifting handles. So much so that when he switched on the ignition he failed to notice she had left the car in bottom gear. It jumped — being a powerful sports car it bounded like a spirited horse — and stalled. Wexford grinned to himself. So much for his conviction that he was the more careful driver. Another two inches and the Porsche would have hit his garage doors.

He moved the gear lever into neutral and switched on the engine once more. His foot on the clutch pedal, he was moving the lever into reverse when he became aware of a feeling of unparalleled strangeness, an unaccountable sensation of being more than usually alert and alive. It was as if he were young again, a young man with the vigour and carefree nature of youth. Some strengthening elixir seemed to surge through his veins. On this damp, dark night when he was tired at the end of a long hard day, he was visited with a renewal of youth and power, a springiness in muscle and nerves like a young athlete's.

All this was momentary. It came in a flash that was also a piercing ray of enlightenment. Did he hear anything? The ticking mechanism as of a clock – or was that imagination, some vibration in his brain? The thrusting gear slid into the reverse position, made contact, and without knowing why, without a pause for reasoning, he flung open the car door and precipitated himself with all his force horizontally out as the roar came behind him, the earthquake, the loudest most violent explosion he had ever known.

It happened simultaneously, all of it – the bomb going off, the leap from the doomed car, the fierce blinding pain as he struck his head on something cold and upright and hard as iron . . .

5

AFTER Dorothy Sanders had been driven home, Burden meant to go to the Irelands' house at Myringford. But he would be too late now to see his son put to bed, too late to enjoy (as Wexford, quoting, had once expressed it) '. . . those attractions by no means unusual in children of two or three years old; an imperfect articulation, an earnest desire of having his own way, many cunning tricks and a great deal of noise.' His wife didn't expect him until later and the house would be full of visiting relatives.

Instead, after a lapse of ten minutes or so and without giving any warning of his intention, he followed Dorothy Sanders. Something in her son's appearance and manner told him this wasn't the kind of young man who went out on Saturday nights. And indeed it was Clifford himself who opened the door to him. His was a shut-in face, mask-like and inexpressive, with a pudginess about the features. He spoke lifelessly, showing no apparent surprise at another visit from a policeman. Burden was rather curiously reminded of a dog owned by a former neighbour of his. The owner had been inordinately proud of its submission, its total obedience, the subservience with which it had responded to his severe training. And one day, without warning, without any apparent prior change in its character, it had savaged a child.

Clifford, however, seemed to have the right idea and was leading Burden into that back room to which, on the inspector's previous visit with Wexford, he had retreated to watch television, when his mother opened the living-room door and said in her slow harsh voice to come in, as there could be nothing the policeman had to say to her son which she couldn't hear.

'I'll have a word with Mr Sanders on his own for the time being, if you don't mind,' Burden said.

'I do mind.' She was rude in a way that wasn't even defiant; it was uncompromising, straight rudeness, with a straight look into her interlocutor's eye. 'There's no reason why I shouldn't be there. This is my house and he'll need me to get his facts straight.'

Clifford neither blushed nor turned pale; he did not even wince. He simply stared ahead of him as if thinking of something deeply sad. Long, long ago Burden had learned that you do not let the public get the better of you. Lawyers, yes, inevitably sometimes, but not the untrained public.

'In that case, I'll ask you to accompany me to the police station, Mr Sanders.'

'He won't go. He's not well, he's got a cold.'

'That's unfortunate, but you leave me no choice. I've my car here, Mr Sanders. If you'd like to get your coat on? It's a nasty damp night.'

She yielded, going back into the room she had come from and slamming the door with calculation, not from temper. Burden resisted the hackneyed maxim that bullies give way if you stand up to them, but he had found nevertheless that it was usually true. Would Clifford profit by his example? Probably not. It had gone too far with him; he needed help of a more expert kind. And it was of this that Burden first asked him when they were seated in the bleak dining room, furnished only with table, hard upright chairs and television set. On one wall hung a mirror, on another a large dark and very bad painting in oils of a sailing vessel on a rough sea.

'Yes, I go to Serge Olson. It's a sort of Jungian therapy he does. Do you want his address?'

Burden nodded, noted it down. 'May I ask why you go to . . . Dr Olson, is it?'

Clifford, who showed no signs of the cold his mother claimed for him, was looking at the mirror but not into it. Burden would have sworn he was not seeing his own reflection. 'I need help,' he said.

Something about the rigidity of his figure, his stillness and the dullness of his eyes stopped Burden pursuing this. Instead he asked if Clifford had been to the psychotherapist on Thursday afternoon and what time he had left.

'It's an hour I go for, five till six. My mother told me you knew I was in the car park – I mean, that I put the car there.'

'Yes. Why didn't you tell us that at first?'

He shifted his eyes, not to Burden's face but to the middle of his chest. And when he answered Burden recognized the phraseology, the manner of speech, as that which people in therapy – no matter how inhibited, reserved, disturbed – inevitably pick up. He had heard it before. 'I felt threatened.'

'By what?'

'I'd like to talk to Serge now. If I'd had some sort of warning I'd have tried to make an appointment with him and talk it through with him.'

'I'm afraid you're going to have to make do with me, Mr Sanders.'

Burden was apprehensive for a moment that he was to be confronted with total silence against which even an experienced detective can do little. Sounds from Mrs Sanders could now be heard. She was in the kitchen, moving about, making an unnecessary noise by putting crockery down heavily and banging instead of closing cupboard doors. Whatever she was doing it seemed to be contrived to disturb. He winced at the sound of something breaking as it fell from her hands on to a stone floor. And then he heard another sound – he had got up to stand by the window – and this was far distant, the dull roar of an explosion. He stood quite still, his ear to the glass, listening to the reverberations die away. But he thought no more of it once Clifford began to speak.

'I'll try and tell you what happened. I should have told you before, but I felt threatened. I feel threatened now, but I'd be worse if I didn't tell you. I left Serge's place and I drove to the car park to pick up my mother. I saw there was a dead person lying there before I parked the car. I went to look at it – when I had parked the car, I mean – because I meant to call the police. You could see the person had been killed; that was the first thing you could see.'

'What time was this?'

He shrugged. 'Oh, evening. Early evening. My mother wanted me there at a quarter-past six. I think it was before that; it must have been, because she wasn't there and she's never late.'

'Why didn't you call the police, Mr Sanders?'

He looked at the picture on the wall, then at the dark shiny window. Burden saw his reflection in it, impassive, one would have said devoid of feeling.

'I thought it was my mother.'

Burden turned his eyes from the reflected image in the dark glass. 'You what?'

With patience, in a heavy, almost sorrowful way, Clifford repeated what he had said. 'I thought it was my mother.'

And she had thought it was her son. What was the matter with the pair of them that each expected to find the other dead? 'You thought Mrs Robson was your mother?' There was a slight resemblance between the two women, Burden thought wonderingly – that is, to a stranger there might be. Both were of an age, thin, grey-haired, dressed in the same kind of clothes of the same sort of colour . . . but to a son?

'I knew it wasn't really my mother. Well, after the first shock I knew. I can't explain what I felt. I could tell Serge, but I don't think you would understand. First I thought it was my mother, then I knew it wasn't and then I thought someone was doing it to . . . to mock me. I thought they had put it there to get at me. No, not quite that. I said I couldn't explain. I can only say it made me panic. I thought this was an awful trick they were persecuting me with, but I knew it couldn't be. I knew both things at the same time. I was very confused – you don't understand, do you?'

'I can't say I do, Mr Sanders. But go on.'

'I said I panicked. My "shadow" had taken me over completely. I had to get out of there, but I couldn't just leave it lying there like that. Other people would see it like I had.' Dark colour had come into his face now and he held his hands clasped tightly. 'I had an old curtain in the boot of the car I'd used to cover the windscreen in cold weather. I covered it up with that.' Suddenly he shut his eyes, screwing them up as if to drive away the sight, to blind himself. 'It wasn't covered, you understand, when I found it, not when I found it. I covered it up and then I went away, I ran away. I left the car and ran out of the car park. Someone was in the lift, so I ran up the stairs. I went home, I ran out into the street at the back and then home.'

'It didn't occur to you then that you'd meant to phone the police?'

The eyes opened and he expelled his breath. Burden repeated his question and Clifford said, with a tinge of exasperation now, 'What did it matter? Someone would phone them, I knew that. It didn't have to be me.'

'You went out by the pedestrian gates, I suppose.' Burden remembered Archie Greaves' evidence, the running 'boy' he had taken for a scared shoplifter. And he remembered what Wexford had said about the sound of feet pounding down the car park stairs. That had been Wexford in the lift. 'Did you run all the way home? It's getting on for three miles.'

'Of course I did.' The voice held a tinge of contempt.

Burden left it. 'Did you know Mrs Robson?'

The blank look was back, the colour returned to normal – a clay pallor. Clifford had never once smiled; it was hard to imagine what his smile would be like. 'Who's Mrs Robson?' he said.

'Come now, Mr Sanders. You know better than that. Mrs Robson is the woman who was killed.'

'I told you I thought it was my mother.'

'Yes, but when you realized it couldn't be?'

He looked Burden in the eyes for the first time. 'I didn't

think any more.' It was a devastating remark. 'I told you, I didn't think, I panicked.'

'What did you mean just now by your "shadow"?'

Was it a pitying look Clifford Sanders gave him? 'It's the negative side of personality, isn't it? It's the sum of the bad characteristics in us we want to hide.'

Not at all satisfied with what he had been told, finding the whole of this man's behaviour and much of his talk incomprehensible and even sinister, Burden resolved just the same to pursue it no further until the next day. It was at this point, though, that his determination began to take shape, a decision to get to the bottom of Clifford's disturbed mind and whatever motives had their source there. His behaviour was immensely suspicious; and more than that – disingenuous. The man was trying to make him, Burden, look a fool; he thought himself the possessor of an intellect superior to a policeman's. Burden was familiar with this attitude and the reaction it produced in himself – the chip on his shoulder, as Wexford called it – but he could not be persuaded that it was unjustified.

In the living room now, he talked to a rigid and sullen Dorothy Sanders, getting nowhere in his attempts to discover if Mrs Robson had been known to the family. Clifford brought in a basket of coal, fed a fire which did little to raise the temperature in the room, went away and returned with soap-smelling hands. Both mother and son insisted Mrs Robson had been unknown to them, but Burden had the curious feeling that though Dorothy Sanders' ignorance was genuine, her son was lying, or at least evading the truth for some obscure reason of his own. On the other hand, Clifford might have killed without motivation, or without the kind of motivation that would be understandable to a rational man. For instance, suppose he had not found a dead body and thought it was his mother's, but had seen a woman who had suggested to him his mother in her worst aspects and for this reason had himself killed her?

After leaving them, Burden drove further down the

narrow road which he now remembered – though there was nothing to show it – was called Ash Lane. The Sanders' house therefore was very likely Ash Farm. But as this passed through his mind and as he was thinking that they seemed to have no neighbours, he came to a bungalow set a little way back from the road which proclaimed itself as Ash Farm Lodge on a rustic board attached to wrought-iron gates. This he could see in his headlights. The bungalow itself was in darkness but as he paused, the engine running and the headlights beam undipped, a light came on in the house and a man appeared at the window.

Burden reversed and began turning the car, a lengthy process in that narrow defile. When he was once more pointing in the direction of Kingsmarkham he glanced to his right and with a start – more a jolt than an actual shock – he saw that the man had come outside and was standing on the doorstep looking at the car, his hand clutching the collar of a cowed-looking retriever. By now the whole place – with the two barns and tall silo behind it, plainly the present farmhouse – blazed with light. Burden drove off. He wouldn't have been surprised to hear a shotgun let off behind him, or to see the dog frenziedly pursuing the car. But nothing happened, there was only darkness and silence and an owl calling.

The news about Wexford reached Burden in a peculiarly horrible way. It was due to his own haste and keenness, he afterwards realized, behaving like some young ambitious copper instead of enjoying his day of rest. Of course, the point was that it would hardly have been a day of rest with Jenny's demanding mother and the Ireland aunts, and Jenny running up and down stairs. Even if he had glanced at the Sunday paper before he left Myringford, he would only have read commentaries on the latest dramatic developments in the Israeli Embassy trial; there would have been nothing in it about the car bomb. The explosion had happened too late in the evening for that.

And because the house was full of guests, no one had looked at television on Saturday night.

He phoned Ralph Robson before he left, but it was Lesley Arbel who answered, who agreed to his coming though telling him she couldn't think why as they had absolutely nothing more to tell him. Driving up the hill to Highlands, he told himself it was a pointless interview he had ahead of him, as the obvious thing was to wait until the next day and consult the Social Services department of Kingsmarkham Council. They might keep no records of those for whom their past home helps had worked, but they were more likely to put forward ideas and suggestions than Ralph Robson was.

The invalidism his niece fostered still kept the widower in his dressing gown. He seemed to have aged even in this short time, to hobble more painfully and be more bent. He sat by the gas fire with on his lap a little circular tray fancifully printed with wild birds in improbable colours, on which reposed a cup of tea and a plate of sugar-frosted biscuits. Burden had hardly been taken into the room by the girl – who this morning was dressed in a pink silk outfit, a kind of trouser suit with sarong top and harem pants, and very high-heeled pink shoes – when there came a ring at the doorbell and another visitor arrived. Lesley Arbel had no scruples about showing in the newcomer, though he must have been aware that Burden expected a private interview with her uncle. It was the neighbour opposite he and Wexford had seen from the window who had called, a Mrs Jago as far as Burden could gather from the mumbled introduction Robson made.

The reason for the visit seemed to be the usual one at a time of bereavement. She had come to see if there was anything she could do – any shopping, for instance, that she could get on the following day when Lesley Arbel had gone. Burden wasn't much interested in her, noticing only that she was a large stout woman, puffily overweight, dark and florid, and with a strong accent that suggested Central Europe to him. At least she seemed to have the tact or the good sense to realize Burden wanted privacy, and she left again as soon as Robson had said he would take up her offer and would she mind coming in again on the following morning?

The front door had scarcely closed and Lesley Arbel passed the hall mirror with an inevitable glance into it, when Robson said, 'It's time they did something for us. It's their turn, the lot of them. When you consider what my wife did for everyone in this blessed street, never spared herself, nothing was too much trouble. She'd only to hear someone was a bit under the weather and she'd be round seeing what she could do. Especially the old folks. I reckon she did more good on her own than all those so-called social services people. Isn't that right, Lesley?'

'She did a lot more good than my agony aunt,' Lesley said. 'Well, she was a sort of agony aunt herself, wasn't she? I used to call her that – joking, of course.'

Mystified, Burden echoed her words. 'Your agony aunt?'

'People brought her their troubles, didn't they?' It was Robson who answered for her. 'She works,' he said in a rather proud way, 'for the agony aunt on the magazine. For *Kim*. It's the problem page – you know, all those letters from readers about their troubles that the agony aunt answers. Lesley's her assistant.'

'Secretary, Uncle.'

'A bit more than a blessed secretary to my way of thinking. More a right hand. I thought you knew all that,' he said to Burden.

'No,' Burden shook his head. 'No, I didn't know. Your aunt – I mean your real aunt, Mrs Robson – I understand she'd been a council home help. Can you remember the names of some of the people she worked for?'

He addressed this question as much to Robson as his niece and Robson immediately took exception to it. 'Home helps don't work for people. They don't have employers, they have clients. They're more civil servants really.'

With an effort at patience Burden accepted this. He had to listen while Robson made out a case for his wife's

64

having carried out her civil servant's function in the home of (it sounded like) every elderly, sick or deprived person in greater Kingsmarkham. Individual names, though, he couldn't recall. He enumerated the tasks his wife had performed gratuitously for the neighbours, and by association this recalled shopping to him and from here the two bags of groceries which the police still retained. With a slightly scathing edge to his voice, he said, 'I suppose you'll say you've got too much on your plates with last night's trouble to worry about a minor matter like that.'

'Last night's trouble?'

'The car bomb. One of your blokes got blown up, didn't he?'

Lesley Arbel said, 'The one that was here with you – or that's how I understood it from the TV. I'm sure it was his name they said.'

Practice at not showing one's feelings comes in useful. And it is true that shock stuns. Burden remembered now the dull and distant explosion he had heard on the previous evening while standing up against the french windows in the Sanders' dining room. Some sense of dignity, some knowledge that it would be wrong and a matter for later regret to do so, stopped him enquiring any more from Robson and his niece. But he was numbed with shock too, getting up almost mechanically, making routine remarks, the replies to which he found afterwards that he had totally forgotten. He was aware too – and this he did remember – of their faces looking at him curiously and with a mild, perhaps only imagined, malice.

Robson said something more about his groceries, something about wanting them before he gave his neighbour Mrs Jago a shopping list, and then Burden had made his escape, was keeping himself from running to his car until the door had closed on Lesley Arbel's pink silk and high heels. He ran then.

Wexford's house was about as far from Highlands as it was possible to be, yet still be situated in Kingsmarkham. It wasn't wasting time, it was to calm himself, to make him a safer driver, that he went first into the phone box

65

at the foot of the hill only to find it vandalized and the lead pulled from the wall. The second phone box he tried was the kind which, along with its fellows in the railway-station entrance, could only be operated with a Telecom card. Burden got back into the car, the palms of his hands damp and sliding on the steering wheel. He turned into Wexford's street with the feeling that he hadn't really breathed for five minutes; he seemed to have been holding his breath until his throat closed up. Yet all the time he was clinging to the hope that Robson and his niece might somehow be mistaken. Now he 'found the difference' as Wexford could have quoted to him, 'between the expectation of an unpleasant event, however certain the mind may be told to consider it, and certainty itself.'

The sight of Wexford's house came as a second shock, and one not dulled by the first.

The garage was no longer there. The room over the garage was no longer there. The whole area between what remained of Wexford's house – the basic three-bedroomed structure – and the open ground next door was a heap of rubble, bits of car body, branches and twigs, shreds of fabric, twisted metal, broken glass. The side of the house from which the garage and the room above it had been torn was open to the weather – fortunately this morning mild and dry – and no attempt had yet been made to shroud in tarpaulins the gaping rooms in one of which a bed could be seen, in the other a picture hanging crooked on blue wallpaper. Burden sat in his car with the window down and stared at it. He stared in horror at the devastation and at the garden now revealed beyond, where fruit trees held leafless boughs against a tranquil pale blue sky.

In the middle of the front lawn the stout cherry tree still retained its branches – even, incredibly, some of its frostbitten leaves. And the lavender hedge which Wexford had so frequently in the past weeks promised to trim back as soon as he had the time was mostly still there, while looking as if the passage through it of a heavy missile had crushed some of it to the ground. The front wall was still there and undamaged, a child's woollen glove lying on one of the piers; Burden couldn't imagine how it came to be there. He looked back again at the wreck of the house, at what seemed to him only half or less of a house remaining. Then, slowly, he got out of the car and walked towards the front door, though he knew there could be no one living there now. If either of them survived, there could be no one there now . . .

He found himself numbed where he stood, paralysed and quite unable to think how next to act, when a man came out of the house next door, the house Wexford called next door though it was separated from his by a narrow open space that no one had ever been able to decide was large enough for a building site.

He said to Burden, 'How is he? Is he . . .?'

'I know nothing. I didn't even know . . .'

It was as if the street had been watching for him, took him necessarily for the bringer of news. A woman came out from opposite, a couple with a small child from further down on the same side.

The man next door said, 'He was in the car, his daughter's car. Sheila, you know. It was a hell of a bang, like the bombs in the war. I can just remember the war. My wife and I, we came out and there was smoke and you couldn't see a thing. I said to phone the police first thing and I did, but someone else had done it already. The ambulance got here like a shot. I must hand it to them, they didn't waste time. But we couldn't see what happened, only that they took someone away on a stretcher and then it was on the late-night news on telly about Mr Wexford and a car bomb, but they didn't know much, they couldn't tell you much.'

'He was lying on the lawn there,' said the woman with the child. 'He was lying there unconscious.'

'He was blown out of the car,' said her husband. 'It was the most amazing thing. We were watching Sheila in her serial and we heard this terrific bang and it was here, it was her car . . .'

'Where are they now, Sheila and her mother?' Burden asked.

'Someone said they went to the other daughter, wherever she lives.'

Burden said no more. Shaking his head, aware that he held one hand pressed against it as if it ached, he went back to his car and started the engine.

6

HIS dream was of cherry trees, notably the one George Washington was said to have chopped down and then been unable to tell a lie about when questioned by his father. A white cherry though, presumably that was, like the ones he had seen in a picture somewhere that were planted along the shores of the Potomac. Because of Washington's particular affinity with cherry trees? It must be. Probably those pink double cherries whose flowers looked as if made from crêpe paper weren't invented then. The one in his garden had been given him a year after he moved into the house by his father-in-law and he had never liked its papery blossoms and unnatural weeping branches, though he had liked his father-in-law very much. The tree was pretty for one week of the year, around the end of April . . .

He wasn't dreaming any more; this was more in the nature of a reverie. In some cherry-growing areas they put scarecrows in the trees, and in others sewed together sheets of netting large enough to protect the fruit from birds. Not that his tree was the kind that ever bore fruit but was sterile, those bright fluffy blossoms falling and leaving not a trace behind. He was aware now of a dull ache in his head above the forehead, a pain unaccountably associated with cherry trees. And yet not unaccountably . . . no. He opened his eyes, said to anyone who might be there, though for all he knew no one was, 'Did I hit my head on the cherry tree?'

'Yes, darling.'

Dora was sitting at his bedside and round the two of them the curtains were drawn. He tried to sit up but she shook her head, putting out her hand.

'What time is it?'

'About eleven. About eleven on Sunday morning.' She

69

read what was passing through his mind. 'You haven't been unconscious all this time; you came round in the ambulance on the way here. You've been asleep.'

'I don't seem to remember anything except hitting my head on the cherry tree. Oh, and taking a sort of flying leap for some unknown reason . . . maybe from the front doorstep? I can't think why.'

'There was a bomb,' she said, 'underneath the car. It wasn't our car, it was Sheila's. Something you did set it off – I mean, whoever had driven it would have set it off.'

Wexford digested that. He couldn't remember; he wondered if he ever would. Dora and Sheila had been watching television and he came into the front garden for something and leapt into the darkness as a man who flies in a dream might, but the tree was in his way . . . Dora, though, was saying he was in a car, Sheila's car.

'I was in a car?'

'You went out to move Sheila's car and put ours away.'

'The bomb was meant for Sheila?'

She said unhappily, 'It looks like that. Well, it must have been. You mustn't distress yourself, you're supposed to rest.'

'I'm all right. I've only had a bang on the head.'

'You've got cuts and bruises all over you.'

'It was meant for Sheila,' he said. 'Oh God, thank God I drove it. Oh, thank God! I don't remember, but I must have driven it. Am I in the Infirmary? In Stowerton?'

'Where else? The Chief Constable's downstairs and he wants to see you. And Mike's dying to see you; he thought you were dead. It was on television about you. Lots of people thought you were dead, darling.'

Wexford was silent, digesting it. He wouldn't think about Sheila at the moment and how near she had been to death, he wouldn't think of that yet. A sense of humour began creeping back.

'One thing, we shan't have to have the fence done,' he said and then he went on, 'A bomb. Yes, a bomb. Have we got any house left?'

70

'Well, you mustn't distress yourself. A bit more than half a house.'

Burden was temporarily in charge of the Robson case. It was his belief that Wexford would be off for at least a fortnight, though Wexford himself said that a day or two would do it. That was what he said to Colonel Griswold, the Chief Constable, whose sympathy was conveyed in incredulity that Wexford could remember nothing about the bomb and unreasonable anger against Burden for going away for the night without telling anyone.

'I'll make them let me go home tomorrow,' he told Burden.

'I shouldn't – not if I'd got your home to go to.'

'Yes. Dora says there's only about half of it left. I never liked that garage extension; I said it was jerry-built. No doubt that's why it fell down. I understand that people in our sort of situation usually go and live in a caravan.'

He had a large bandage round his head. Cuts on his left cheek were dressed with a white plaster. The other side of his face was turning black – before Burden's very eyes, it seemed. Sheila came in while he was still there and threw her arms round her father until he groaned in pain. And then the bomb expert from the Myringham Division of the Serious Crimes Squad came to question him and he and Sheila were obliged to leave. Now Burden, with Sumner-Quist's medical report in front of him, had to make up his mind whether it would be good for Wexford to be shown it later in the day. He would probably ask for it anyway, thus taking the power of showing it or withholding it out of Burden's hands.

In fact, there wasn't much in it Burden didn't already know. The time of Mrs Robson's death was as firmly fixed as it ever could be at between five-thirty-five and five-fifty-five. And death had taken place on the spot where the body was found. She had died of asphyxiation as the result of a ligature being applied to her neck. Sumner-Quist went on to suggest that the ligature – he never once here

71

used the term 'garrote' – was of wire probably in some kind of plastic coating, minute particles of such a substance having being found in the neck wound. This substance, presently being subjected to lab analysis, was most likely flexible polyvinyl chloride or polyvinyl chloride in combination with one of the polymers such as styrene acrylonitrile.

Burden winced a bit at these names, though he had a pretty good idea of the kind of stuff meant; no doubt it was much like the substance that insulated the lead on his desk lamp. It was suggested that the ligature had a handle at each end which the perpetrator must have grasped in order to secure a purchase on it and avoid cutting his or her own hands.

Gwen Robson had been a strong and healthy woman, five feet one inch tall, weight one hundred and ten pounds. Sumner-Quist estimated her age at three years less than what it had been in fact. She had never borne a child, suffered surgery of any sort. Her heart and other major organs of the body were in sound condition. She had lost her wisdom teeth and three other molars, but otherwise her teeth were present and healthy. If someone hadn't come up behind her in a car park with a garrote, thought Burden, she would very likely have lived another thirty years; she would long have outlived that arthritic, prematurely aged husband.

The Home Help Service was administered by the County Council, not the local authority, Burden soon discovered. It functioned from one of those bungalow buildings that house administrative offices in the grounds of once great private houses all over England. The great house in question was called Sundays on the Forby Road near the junction with Ash Lane. It had until recently been in private hands and, approaching it, Burden remembered the pop festival which had been held there back in the seventies and the murder of a girl during that festival. A huge sum had been spent on the purchase, causing anger among local ratepayers. But Sundays had been bought and these ugly single-storey buildings soon put up in the environs of the house. The mansion itself, though in part offices, was also available as a conference centre and for courses. Burden noted that a course in word processing was due to begin that day. His appointment was with the Home Help Supervisor, but it was her deputy who met him and began by telling him pessimistically that they could give him very little help. Their records went back only three years and Mrs Robson had been gone for two. The Deputy Supervisor could remember her, but the Supervisor herself had been in her present post less than two years. She produced for Burden a list of names, with addresses, of those men and women who had been Gwen Robson's 'clients'.

'What does a cross after a name indicate?'

'It means they've died,' she said.

Burden saw that there were more crosses than otherwise. On an initial glance no name or address leaped out significantly.

'What did you think of Mrs Robson?' he asked. This was Wexford's technique and although Burden did not altogether approve of it, he thought he might as well give it a go.

The reply came slowly, as if a good deal of thought and calculation was going into it. 'She was efficient and very reliable. A great one for phoning in, if you know what I mean. She'd warn you by phone if she was going to be even ten minutes late.'

Burden, irrepressibly, saw again the resemblance between the dead woman and Dorothy Sanders. Here was a new point of similarity – a shared obsession with time – but what he wanted was a meeting point, a location at which she and Clifford Sanders might have come into collision.

'I don't want to speak ill of her. That was a dreadful way to die.'

'It won't go any further,' said Burden, hope springing. 'What you say to me will be treated in confidence.'

'Well, then, she was a terrible gossip. Of course I didn't have that much to do with her, and to tell you the truth I used to avoid having much contact with her, but it seemed to me sometimes that she liked nothing better than finding out some poor old dear's private trouble or secret or whatever and spreading it round this place. Starting off always of course with that old one about it being within these four walls and she wouldn't say it to anyone else and so forth. I don't say there was any harm in it, mind, I don't say there was malice. As a matter of fact it was all done quite sympathetically, though she was a bit moralistic. You know the kind of thing – how wicked it was to have a baby without being married, how unfair on the child, and people living together not knowing the rewards of a happy marriage.'

'There doesn't seem much in that,' Burden said.

'Probably not. She was a great talker, she never stopped talking, and I don't suppose there's much in that either. I'll give her one thing, she was devoted to her husband. She was one of those women who are married to perfectly ordinary men and go about saying how wonderful they are – one in a million – and how lucky they are to have got a man like that. I don't know whether it's sincere, or if they're trying to make out they've got an exceptional marriage or what. I remember her going on in here one day about someone she knew who'd had a Premium Bond come up. If that happened to her, she said, the first thing she'd do would be to buy her husband some special kind of car – I don't know what, a Jaguar maybe – and then she'd take him on holiday to the Caribbean. Anyway, you've got your list; it's the best I can do, and I hope it's of some help.'

Burden was disappointed. He wasn't sure what he had expected – some name on the list, perhaps, to tally with that of a witness in the case or with someone he had talked to in connection with it. As it was, because he had gone so far, everyone whose name was here would have to be seen. Archbold or Davidson could do that. Among those whose names were followed by a cross Burden noted that of a man who had lived in the sheltered housing at Highlands opposite the Robsons' own home: Eric

Swallow, 12 Berry Close, Highlands. But what could that signify? The only difference between Eric Swallow and the others was that he was a 'client' who happened to have lived on the other side of the street from his home help.

The alibi of Clifford Sanders was the next important question of Burden's day. He saw from his notes that Clifford had told him he had left the psychotherapist Serge Olson at six p.m. Queen Street, where Olson had his premises in the flat over the hairdressers, was metered and except on Saturday mornings there were usually meters available. Burden, due to see Olson at half-past noon, stood in Queen Street observing that now, late on a Monday morning, three of the twelve meters were vacant. Clifford could easily have been in his car and away by two minutes past six if he left Olson at six. The worst of the Kingsmarkham rush traffic would have been over by then and he could have got into the Barringdean Shopping Centre car park with ease by ten-past six. But there was no way, if he was telling the truth, that he could have been there before five minutes to six.

Briefly calling in at the police station, Burden had phoned Stowerton Royal Infirmary to be told that Wexford was 'satisfactory and comfortable', a formula that conveys to the nervous caller the imminence of death. Burden had wasted no more time on the Infirmary, but phoned Dora at her elder daughter's. They had said that if Wexford continued to make good progress he could leave the hospital on Thursday. Wexford said he was going out tomorrow. Bomb experts were at the house, sifting through rubble, and until they were finished nothing could be done about clearing up the mess. Burden was early for his appointment and he walked up and down looking in the windows of the newly refurbished Midland Bank, the shoe boutique and the toy-shop, but thinking about the bomb and wondering if it had really been meant for Sheila. Why would anyone want to blow up Sheila? Because she had cut the wire round a Ministry of Defence air base?

Burden strongly disapproved of the Campaign for Nuclear Disarmament and Greenpeace and Friends of the Earth and 'all those people'. This was one of the few issues on which he and his wife disagreed, or on which his wife had not won him over to her point of view. He thought they were all cranks and anarchists, either misguided or in the pay of the Russians. But it was quite feasible that other cranks, equally if not more reprehensible, might try to blow them up. Such a thing had been attempted – and indeed had succeeded – in the case of the Greenpeace vessel in the South Pacific. On the other hand, suppose some enemy of Wexford's – even if it were not too far-fetched, someone involved in the Robson case – knew that when Sheila stayed with him he was always in the habit of moving her car in order to put his own away? Whether or not this was true Burden was unsure but he thought it likely, knowing his chief. It had been a dark, misty evening. Would it have been possible to creep unseen across the wasteland and fasten that bomb to the underside of the Porsche? Burden found he knew very little about bombs.

The hairdressers was called Pelage which Wexford, who had looked it up out of curiosity, said was a collective noun for the fur, hair or pelt of a mammal. It had been open only six months and the interior décor was very hi-tech, resembling nothing so much as the inside of a computer. But the building in which it was housed was as ancient as anything in this part of Kingsmarkham High Street and the narrow steep staircase up which Burden made his way was a good hundred and fifty years old. By the look of the worm-holes in the treads, it wouldn't endure much longer. If the woman descending hadn't been as thin as Burden they would have had difficulty in passing one another, for neither had been prepared to retreat. At the top a door was slightly ajar. There was no bell, so Burden pushed open the door and walked in, calling out, 'Hallo!'

He was in an ante-room, unfurnished but for floor cushions and something folded up to large suitcase size which reminded him of a mobile bench he had once borrowed for pasting wallpaper on, but was more likely to be a massage table. The ceiling was painted rather ineptly with signs of the zodiac and on the walls hung strange posters – one of a pair of boots with no legs in them but with distinctly separate toes and toenails, which Wexford could have told him was from a Magritte painting, and another of cats in cloaks and boots riding white horses. Burden remembered what Clifford Sanders had told him about his feelings and thought that this was what he felt here; he felt threatened.

A door at the opposite end of the room opened and a man came out in a very unhurried way. He stood just outside the door with his arms folded. He was a short man and extremely thickset without being fat; great breadth of shoulder and width of hip and thigh were not matched by a big belly. His hair – 'pelage', Burden could not help thinking – was dark and curly, long and thick as a woman's, growing low over his forehead, linked by brown curly sideburns to his round bushy beard which itself was linked to a dense and rather more gingery moustache. Very little face showed, no more than a surprisingly fine-pointed nose, thin lips and a pair of dark eyes like those of a fierce animal.

On the phone Burden had given his full name, but Olson extended his hand and said, 'Come in here, Michael – or is it Mike?'

Burden had an old-fashioned and (his wife said) ridiculous antipathy to being called by his christian name except by friends. But he was aware too of how foolish it made him look to stand on his dignity with a contemporary, so he merely shrugged and followed Olson into . . . what? A consulting room? A therapy room? There was a couch and it was so much like the famous one in the Freud museum in London that Burden and Jenny had been to, even to the scattered oriental rugs, that he was sure a deliberate attempt at duplication had been made. Apart from the couch the room was cluttered with cheap ugly furniture and hung with posters, including an anti-nuclear one which pictured a devastated globe and above it a quote from Einstein: 'The unleashed power of the atom has changed everything except our modes of thinking and thus we drift towards unparalleled catastrophe.' This obscurely reminded Burden of Wexford and recalled to him with how much more of an open mind his chief would have approached this man . . . yet, how could you, at his age, conquer your prejudices?

Olson had sat down at the head of the couch, no doubt a customary position for him. He gazed at Burden in silence, again probably a habitual pose.

Burden began, 'I understand Mr Clifford Sanders is a patient of yours, Dr Olson.'

'A client, yes.' There it was again, that word. Patients, customers, guests – all in his contemporary world had become clients. 'And I'm not a doctor,' Olson went on.

This immediately recalled to Burden indignant articles he had read about purveyors of various forms of psychiatry being permitted to practise without medical degrees. 'But you have some sort of qualification?'

'A psychology degree.' Olson spoke with a kind of calm economy. It was as if he would attempt to justify nothing, explain nothing; there he was, to be taken or left. Such a manner always gives an impression of transparent honesty and therefore made Burden suspicious. It was time for Olson to ask him precisely what it was that Burden wanted to see him about – they always did ask at this point – but Olson didn't ask, he merely sat. He sat and looked at Burden with a calm, mild almost compassionate interest.

'I am sure you have your own code of professional conduct,' Burden said, 'so I won't – at any rate, at this stage – ask you to divulge anything you may have diagnosed in Mr Sanders' . . . personality.' He frankly thought he was being magnanimous and rather resented Olson's faint smile and inclination of the head. 'It's a more practical matter I'm concerned with – the times of Mr Sanders' last appointment with you, in fact. Now as I understand it, he had a five o'clock appointment for a one-hour session and left you at six?'

'No,' said Olson.

'No? That isn't so?'

Shifting his gaze with what seemed perfect control, Olson turned his eyes on to the grey and cratered globe and the Einstein prediction. 'Clifford,' he said, 'comes at five as a general rule, but sometimes I've had to ask him to change and I did that last Thursday. I was giving a lecture in London at seven-thirty and I wanted to allow myself more time.'

'Do you mean to say Mr Sanders didn't come to you last Thursday?'

Olson was perhaps a man who would always smile indulgently at needless consternation. His smile was slight and a little sad. 'He came. I asked him to come half an hour earlier and in fact he came about twenty minutes earlier. And he left me at five-thirty.'

'Do you mean five-thirty, Mr Olson? Or with time for various parting remarks and fresh appointments and so on, would that be nearer twenty to six, say?'

Olson took off his watch, laid it on the table beside him and, indicating it, said, 'At five-thirty I pick up my watch and tell the client – in this case, Clifford – that time's up and I'll see him next week. There are no parting remarks.'

Jenny, Burden's wife, had been in analysis during her pregnancy. Had it been like this? Burden realized he had never exactly asked her. If you lay on that couch – did you? or wasn't it for lying on? – if you talked to this man, then, and opened your heart and spoke of your inmost secrets, he would be like an enormous impersonal ear ... Burden, without liking or trusting him, suddenly understood that this of course was what was required.

'So Clifford Sanders left here at five-thirty sharp?'

Olson nodded indifferently; there was no question of Burden's disbelieving him. He said, 'You went to London? Where were you ... lecturing?'

'I left here at six and walked to the station to get the six-sixteen train that arrives at Victoria at ten-past seven. My talk was on projection-making factors and I gave it

79

before an audience of members of MAPT – that is, the Metropolitan Association of Psychotherapists – at the Association's premises in Pimlico. I went there by taxi.'

The man seemed to have perfect assurance. Burden looked closely at him and said, 'Can you think of any reason, Mr Olson, why Clifford Sanders should have told us that his appointment with you was from five until six and that he left here at six?'

He's going to tell me he was threatened, Burden thought. He's going to talk about threats and defensiveness and projection. Instead, Olson got up and, moving to a very untidy desk which had perhaps once been a kitchen table, slowly turned the pages of an appointment book. He seemed to be examining some particular entry with care. Then he glanced at his watch and some inner reflection made him smile. He closed the book and still standing up, turned to face Burden.

'You may not know this, Michael. You may never have considered what a powerful figure time is in the human psyche. It might not be too presumptuous to suggest he could be another Jungian archetype in the collective unconscious. Certainly for some he can be an aspect of the Shadow.'

Burden stared at him with a failure of understanding as deep as disgust.

'Let's call him Time with a capital T,' said Olson. 'He has been depicted as a god in a chariot with wings and even been given a personification as Old Father Time – I expect you've come across that. Some people seem to be enslaved by time, by this old man with a skull for a face and a scythe in his hand, by this god in the winged chariot hurrying by behind them. They are his servants and they become very worried – very anguished, indeed – if they are not there, all present and correct, to bow down to him and do his bidding. But there are others, Michael, who hate time. They fear him and because this dread is so great and so omnipresent, they have no recourse but to drive him back into the unconscious. He is too frightening and so they banish him. The result of course is a total lack of knowledge of him, a world in which he is absent. His hours and half-hours for them pass uncounted. These are the people – and we all know them – who can never get up in the morning and at night are always astonished that it should be three or four by the time they get to bed. To be on time for a date entails for them an almost superhuman effort. Their friends get to know this and invite them to come half an hour earlier than the party begins. As for a memory of time – to ask them to have any kind of accurate record is almost an act of violence.'

Burden blinked a little. He had seized on a point though.

'Are you telling me that these regular five o'clock appointments with Clifford Sanders were in fact made for four-thirty?'

Olson nodded, smiling.

'But I thought you said he had the five p.m. appointment?'

'I said that he *comes* at five; that isn't quite the same thing.'

'So last Thursday when you phoned him you must have asked him to come at four?'

'And he came about ten minutes late. That is, as I said, he came at about four-forty.' A genuinely good-humoured smile now broke across Olson's face. 'You're thinking I'm dishonest with my poor clients, aren't you, Michael? I'm pandering to their neurosis in a way perhaps that robs them of their basic human dignity – is that it? But I have to live, too, you see, and I have to recognize Time as a figure in my life. I can't afford to waste half an hour of him any more than one of his most abject slaves.'

Neither can I, thought Burden, getting up to take his leave. To his dismay, as he showed him out Olson laid an almost affectionate arm across his shoulder.

'You won't resent a lesson, I'm sure, Mike.'

Burden looked at him, then at the couch, and recovered some of his aplomb. He said with an edge of sarcasm, 'I expect it makes a change for you to talk.'

At first Olson frowned, then his face cleared. 'That's for the Freudians, the silent listening therapist. I talk quite

81

a lot; I help them along.' He had the happy man's simple, unclouded smile.

It looks very much as if it was intended for your daughter, the Serious Crimes Squad man from Myringham said. You say your daughter hadn't given you any prior warning of her intention to visit you? She hadn't given me any prior warning, Wexford said. I don't know about my wife, I didn't ask. You'll have to ask my wife. We have asked her, Mr Wexford, and no – your daughter's visit was a complete surprise to her.

What made the bomb go off?

You were about to back the car, weren't you? You were going to back it out of the garage drive in order to put your own car in, your wife says. We think it was activated by the reverse gear – triggered off by putting the gear into reverse. You see, your daughter says she never had the Porsche in reverse between getting into it outside her London flat and arriving at your home about an hour and a half later. And one can see, sir, that there would have been no occasion for her to use the reverse gear.

The bomber wasn't bothered, you can see that. It didn't bother him whether the bomb went off five minutes after she started and outside the Great Ormond Street Hospital for Sick Children, for instance, or down here on Sunday afternoon when she was backing out to go off home. It was all the same to him as long as she was in the driving-seat.

As long as she was in the driving-seat . . . Wexford lay in bed thinking about it. They got him up at four and made him have his tea with a lot of other men seated round a table in the middle of the ward. Some bomber had tried to kill Sheila and had failed – but he wouldn't stop, would he, because he had failed once? He would try again and again. It might be because of her anti-nuclear activities, but on the other hand it might not. Freaks and oddballs were envious of the famous, the successful, the beautiful. There were even people who equated actors with the parts they played and who were capable of seeing Sheila as Lady Audley, a bigamist and murderess. For that she must be punished, for her beauty and her success and her lack of morals; for acting a treacherous wife and for being one . . .

How was he going to live and go about his daily work with that ever-present fear of an assassin stalking Sheila? The newspapers were full of it; he had three daily papers lying on his bed, all of them speculating with a kind of merry cynicism as to what particular terrorists might have it in for Sheila. How was he going to stand all that?

Sylvia came after she had fetched her son Robin from his choir practice and then Burden came at evening visiting, full of the Robson medical report, his theories about Clifford Sanders as perpetrator, Gwen Robson as arch-gossip and ferreter out of secrets in the home help sorority and a curious interview he had had with a psychiatrist.

'This stuff about some people being unpunctual – because that's really what it amounts to – doesn't really effect the issue. Sumner-Quist gives the latest time at which Mrs Robson could have been killed as five to six. Clifford could easily have got there before five to six. Without hurrying he could have got there by a quarter to.'

Wexford made an effort. 'Intending to meet Mrs Robson there? You're saying it was premeditated? Because to keep in with your theory he certainly couldn't have encountered her by chance. He wouldn't have gone to that dreary car park to sit there for half an hour and wait for his mother. Or are you saying he was so lost to time that he didn't know whether it was a quarter to or half-past?'

'Not me,' said Burden, 'Olson the shrink. Anyway, I don't go along with that. I think Clifford has a perfectly normal attitude to time when he wants to have. And why shouldn't it have been premeditated? I don't believe Clifford thought or imagined or fancied or however you like to put it that Gwen Robson was his mother. Anyone would have to be a total banana truck to do that. And if he wanted to kill his mother, he could do that at home.

No, the motive is likely to be a good deal more practical than that, as motives usually are.' He looked defiantly at Wexford, waiting for argument, and when none came went on, 'Suppose Gwen Robson was blackmailing him? Suppose she found out some secret about him and was holding it over him?'

'Like what?' said Wexford, and even to Burden his voice sounded weary and uninterested.

'He could be queer – I mean, gay – and afraid of Mum finding out. I mean, that's just a possibility since you ask.'

'But you haven't established any sort of link between them, have you? There's no evidence they knew each other. It's the kind of situation in which a son would only know a woman of her age if she were a friend of his mother's – and she wasn't. It's not as if Clifford has ever been in the market for a home help; he's not a housebound octogenarian or some bedridden invalid. And while Mrs Robson *may* have been a blackmailer, have you any actual evidence that she was?'

'I will have,' Burden said confidently. 'Inquest in the morning. I'll give you a complete run-down on what's happened this time tomorrow.'

But Wexford seemed no longer to be following what he said – to be distracted by some action of his neighbour in the next bed, and then by the arrival of a nurse with a drugs trolley – and Burden, looking at him with slightly exasperated sympathy, thought how true it was that patients in hospital rapidly lose all interest in the outside world. The ward and its inmates, what they had for lunch and what sister said, these things are their microcosm.

The inquest opened and was adjourned, as Burden had expected. It could hardly have been otherwise. Evidence was taken from Dr Sumner-Quist, who was again making very free with the term 'garrote'. And a lab expert was able to treat the coroner to some very abstruse stuff about polymers and long-chain linear polyesters and a substance called polyethylene terephthalate. It was all by way of discovering what the wire of the garrote had been coated in and Burden wasn't much wiser when the expert had finished, though he gathered it all amounted to grey plastic.

Robson was not in court. There was no reason for him to have attended. Clifford Sanders and his mother were both there; Clifford due for a drubbing from the coroner, Burden thought, for his curious action in covering up the body and running away. But the first witness of all was Dorothy Sanders, who went into the box with deliberate self-assured deportment – having dressed herself, no doubt by chance, in clothes very like those found on the dead woman, even to the lacy brown stockings.

The man who had evidently come with them and who now sat beside Clifford he recognized as the farmer he had seen in Ash Lane, and who had come out on to the doorstep with his dog to stare after Burden's departing car.

7

HOUSES without women – Burden could always recognize them. It was not that such places were particularly dirty or uncared-for, but rather that the absence of a woman's hand showed in an asymmetry, a placing of objects in bizarre ways, clumsy makeshifts. The kitchen of Ash Farm Lodge – a large kitchen, since the bungalow had obviously been purpose-built for a farmer – was like that: the table littered with account books and pamphlets, a pair of boots standing on a magazine on top of the oven, a dishcloth spread out to dry on the back of a Windsor chair, a twelve-bore shotgun suspended from what was originally a saucepan rack.

The man Burden had seen in court said his name was Roy Carroll. He looked about fifty, perhaps more. His hands were particularly large, red and calloused, and the skin of his face was a darkly-veined red. The dog lay curled up not in a basket but a large drawer. Burden had the feeling that before it dared wake up it would have to indicate in some canine way a request for permission to do so.

Carroll was brusque and uncouth. He had admitted Burden to the house in a grudging fashion and his replies to questions were hardly fulsome, a 'Yes' and a 'No' and a 'Yes' and other grunted monosyllables. He knew 'Dodo' Sanders, he knew Clifford Sanders; he had lived in this house since it was built. When was that? Twenty-one years ago.

'Dodo?' Burden queried.

'That's what they called her, her husband and that. His mum. Dodo they called her, that's what I call her.'

'You're friends?'

'What does that mean? I know her, I've done odd jobs for her.'

Burden asked him if he was married.

'Never you mind that,' Carroll said. 'I'm not now.'

Gwen Robson? He had never heard of her until her death was on television. He had never had a home help in the house. Where was he on the previous Thursday afternoon? Carroll looked incredulous at being asked. Out shooting, he said, getting a rabbit for the pot. This time of the year he was out shooting most days at dusk. Burden noticed something that was interesting but surely of no importance. The magazine the boots stood on was a copy of *Kim*, the last kind of reading matter to associate with a man of Carroll's sort. It brought to mind the poster in Olson's room, the one with the boots that had five toenailed toes but no legs in them, and unaccountably he shuddered.

A weekday morning and Clifford very likely at work. Burden phoned Munster's, the school which ran crash courses for A levels, and asked to speak to Mr Sanders. He wasn't even sure Clifford worked there, but it turned out to have been an intelligent guess. Mr Sanders was teaching. Could they take a message? Wexford would have treated this more delicately, Burden knew that, but he didn't see why he should be tender towards the feelings of someone who was probably a layabout and certainly a liar, who was very probably homosexual, who had mixed-up feelings of confusion between his mother and dead women and was a psychopath anyway. He asked the woman who answered the phone to give Clifford Sanders a message that Detective Inspector Burden had called and would like him to come to the police station and ask for him as soon as his class was finished.

In the meantime, he made an application for a warrant to search the Sanders' house in the expectation of finding something in the nature of a garrote somewhere. Of course he could simply have asked Mrs Sanders' permission to search, most people don't refuse this request, but he felt that she would. While he was waiting for Clifford he suddenly remembered Robson's shopping bags, so he summoned DC Davidson to find them, locate their contents and have the lot taken round to Highlands. The bags were red Tesco carriers and Burden had had intensive enquiries made at the Tesco store in the Barringdean Shopping Centre. Dressed in brown clothes similar to those worn by Mrs Robson, Marian Bayliss had retraced her possible steps through the centre. One of the checkout assistants remembered her passing through on the previous Thursday and put the time at about five-thirty. Burden began re-reading DC Archbold's report.

Linda Naseem knew Mrs Robson by sight, indeed knew her well enough to comment on the weather and ask after her husband. Gwen Robson was a regular shopper in the store and almost always came in on a Thursday afternoon, but what most interested Burden about this evidence was that Linda Naseem claimed to have seen Mrs Robson in conversation with a girl. This encounter, she said, took place immediately after Mrs Robson had paid and received her change, and when she was standing at the end of the checkout counter putting the goods she had bought into a carrier.

Describe the girl? She had been attending to her next customer and she hadn't taken much notice. Indeed, she hadn't seen the girl's face at all, only her back and the back of her head. She had been wearing a beret or some sort of hat. When Mrs Robson finished packing her bag, she and this girl went off together. At least, they went off. Linda Naseem couldn't absolutely say they went together.

Clifford came to the police station about half an hour after Burden had made his phone call; Munster's School was only about two hundred yards down the High Street. Burden's own office was rather a pleasant, comfortable place where any visitor might have felt he was paying a social call, so Burden didn't take him in there but into one of the interview rooms at the back on the ground floor.

The walls were bare, painted the colour of scrambled eggs, and the floor was of grey vinyl tiles. Burden motioned Clifford into one of the grey metal chairs and himself sat down opposite him at the plastic-topped yellow table.

Almost without preamble, he began, 'You told me you didn't know Mrs Robson. That wasn't true, was it?'

Clifford looked truculent to Burden, his dull face sullen. He wasn't showing any obvious symptoms of fear as he spoke in his slow, monotonous voice. 'I didn't know her.'

There was a point in any interrogation or enquiry when Burden simply changed from using a suspect's surname and style to his or her first name. Wexford asked permission before he did this, but Burden never did. Using people's surnames and styles, in his opinion, was very tied up with feeling respect for them. This was why he needed to be called 'Mr' himself. He would have said he reached a stage when he lost respect for the person he was questioning and therefore pushed them a few rungs down the ladder of his esteem. If we had a language – where you could tutoyer and vouvoyer, said Wexford, you'd start thouing them.

'Now, Clifford, I'll be honest with you. Frankly, I don't yet know where you met her or how you knew her, but I know you did. Why not tell me and save me the trouble of finding out?'

'But I didn't know her.'

'When you say that, you're not helping yourself or deceiving me. All you're doing is wasting time.'

Clifford repeated doggedly now, 'I did not know Mrs Robson.' He laid his hands on the table and contemplated them. The nails were closely bitten, Burden noticed for the first time, this gave them the look of a child's hands, pink and pudgy.

'All right, I can wait. You'll tell me in your own good time.'

Did he really take that phrase literally or is he sending

me up? Burden wondered. Not a gleam of humour showed on the round blank face when Clifford said, 'I don't have my own good time.'

A change of subject and Burden said, 'You must have been in that car park well before six. Mr Olson has told me you left him not at six but at five-thirty. You must have been there by five-forty-five at the latest. Would you like to know when Mrs Robson died? It was between five-thirty-five and five-fifty-five.'

'I don't know what time I got there,' Clifford said, speaking very slowly. 'It's no use asking me about times. I don't wear a watch, perhaps you've noticed.' He raised his arms in what Burden saw as an effeminate gesture, exposing plump white wrists. 'I don't think I went straight to the car park. I sat in the car and thought about what I'd been saying to Serge. We'd been talking about my mother; hardly anyone calls my mother by her first name any more, not now, but when they did they called her Dodo. It's short for Dorothy, of course.'

Burden said nothing, perplexed as to whether he was being teased or whether Clifford generally talked to strangers like this.

'Dodos are large flightless birds, now extinct. They were all killed by Portuguese sailors on Mauritius. My mother isn't a bit like that. Serge and I talked about a man's anima being shaped by his mother and my mother having a negative influence on me. That can express itself in the man having irritable depressed moods, and when I was sitting in the car I thought about that and went back over it all. I like to do that sometimes. The car was on a meter and there was ten minutes to run. And I got out and fed the meter some more.'

'So you do take note of time sometimes, Clifford?'

He looked up and turned on Burden a troubled gaze. 'Why are you asking me questions? What do you suspect me of?'

'Suppose I said you went straight to the shopping centre, Clifford. Isn't that what you did? You parked the car in the car park and then you went in to the shopping centre and ran into Mrs Robson, didn't you?'

'I've told you the truth. I sat in the car in Queen Street. You ought to tell me what you suspect me of doing.'

'Perhaps you'd better go and sit in your car and think about that one,' said Burden, and he let him go.

Such mock naïvety angered him. Dodos, indeed, flightless birds! What was an anima anyway, or come to that a negative influence? Grown men didn't naturally behave and talk like children, not men who were teachers and had been to universities. He was suspicious of the childlike stare, the puzzled ingenuousness. If Clifford was sending him up, he would be made to regret it. In the morning they would search that house. Burden couldn't help thinking how satisfying it would be to have the case all wrapped up before Wexford was back at work.

Sheila, Wexford discovered on being driven from hospital to his other daughter's house, was staying at the Olive and Dove, Kingsmarkham's principal hostelry. There was no room for her as well at Sylvia's, where her parents now occupied the only spare room.

'Anyway, I expect she feels it's easier to have her boy-friend there.'

There was rivalry between the two sisters of a never-quite-expressed kind. Sylvia cloaked her envy under the complacency of a happily married mother of sons. If she would have liked what her sister had – success, fame, the adoration of a good many people, lovers past and in the future – her covetousness was never explicit. But comments were made; a virtue was made of necessity. There was a tendency to talk about fame and money not bringing happiness and show-business people seldom having stable relationships. Married at eighteen, Sylvia would perhaps have liked at least a memory of lovers and the consciousness of something attempted, something done. Sheila, more open about her views, frankly said how nice it must be to have no worries, no fear of the future, reading in a leisurely way for an Open University degree, to be dependent on a loving husband. She meant she would have liked the children, Wexford sometimes thought. Sylvia was waiting for him to ask for enlightenment, but he kept his enquiry to himself until she had gone to fetch the boys from school.

'I know there's someone,' Dora said. 'She was phoning someone she called Ned just before you went out and set that bomb off.'

'Thanks very much,' said Wexford. 'You make it sound as if I put a match to a fuse.'

'You know what I mean. When she comes over this evening, we can ask her about him.'

'I wouldn't ask her,' said Wexford.

But Sheila phoned to say she wasn't coming, that she was postponing her visit to her father until the following morning. Something had come up.

'Come down, I should say,' Sylvia said. 'Come down on the London train. I suppose he's an actor or a Friend of the Earth or both.'

'"Those who find ugly meanings in beautiful things,"' said her father austerely, '"are corrupt without being charming."' He returned to the copy of *Kim* magazine he had found lying about.

Sylvia had told him she took it occasionally and had supplied the little defensive explanation people in Jane Austen's day thought they had to give for reading novels. It was something to pass the time; you could pick it up and put it down; some of the stories were of a really high standard. Wexford liked the name of the magazine which seemed to him very avant-garde and appealing, for he confessed to himself that a part of him still lived in a world of *Home Knits* and *Modern Mother*. He turned to the page of enquiries from worried readers.

The 'agony aunt' Lesley worked for was a woman of the name, or alias, of Sandra Dale. At the head of the page was a photograph of her, a plump, middle-aged woman with fair curly hair and a sympathetic expression. Two of the letters were featured in bold-face type. One didn't appear at all, only the answer to it: 'T. M., Basingstoke: Practices like this may seem fun and I can understand they please your boyfriend, but is it worth risking your whole future sexual happiness? One day when you are married or in a permanent relationship, you may bitterly regret habits you can't break but which are keeping you from true fulfilment.'

Wexford wondered if the purpose of this sort of thing was simply the titillation of readers. It would be a very strong-minded or deeply inhibited *Kim* reader who didn't speculate as to the nature of T. M.'s unbreakable habits. Very likely it was Robson's niece who had typed all these replies, having taken them down at Sandra Dale's dictation.

'There's a piece in there about Sheila,' Sylvia said, 'and some quite nice photos from the TV series.'

He turned to look at pictures of Sheila in a white ball-gown, in her Victorian lady's black street dress and bonnet. The last instalment of *Lady Audley's Secret* was showing that evening; it would be repeated on Saturday, but who knew where they would be on Saturday? Neil wanted to watch a programme about finance on another channel and his elder son Robin was trying to persuade his mother to let him stay up and see Auntie Sheila. Rather surprisingly, Sylvia came down on her mother's side and in favour of watching this final episode. Had Neil forgotten they wouldn't be able to see the repeat because they were going out to dinner on Saturday night?

Neil lost and Robin lost. The little boy had come down for the third time in his pyjamas and was standing wistfully in the doorway. Wexford suddenly knew he wasn't going to be able to watch; he had re-read the novel while Sheila was rehearsing for the television adaptation, and he knew very well what was to happen to Lady Audley tonight: she was to be cast into the continental insane asylum. The way he felt, he would be unable to bear seeing Sheila even acting that stuff, to see her manhandled and screaming . . .

His head ached and he was tired. He got up and took the little boy's hand and said he was going to bed, too, so he would come up with Robin. The introductory music, melancholy-sweet, followed them softly up the stairs and then someone closed the door.

It was a dangerous feeling, this excitement born of hunting down a quarry – or born, rather, of creating a quarry fit to be hunted. Burden knew he was doing this and that it would be wise to pause and take stock. He did pause, briefly, and reminded himself how important it was not to tailor facts to fit a theory. On the other hand, he was growing very sure that Clifford Sanders was guilty of this crime. All he must be careful to do was to avoid pushing witnesses. Guide them, yes, but not give them enthusiastic shoves. In a frame of mind he told himself was cool and unbiased, he went very early in the morning to Highlands. There he got a surprise; as he turned into Hastings Road, he saw Lesley Arbel come out of Robson's house and approach his car, the silver Escort which was parked at the kerb. Burden pulled up behind the Escort.

'Not back at work, Miss Arbel?' he asked.

She was dressed with extreme severe formality in a black suit, white tie-necked blouse, black transparent seamed stockings and very high-heeled black patent shoes. With her glistening chestnut-coloured hair and painted eggshell face, she reminded Burden of one of those 'grown-up' dolls little girls have for birthday presents and which come with their own fashionable wardrobe.

'I'm not at work this week. I'm doing a course in word processors.'

'Ah,' said Burden. 'That would be the one at Sundays.'

'The Sundays Conference Centre, yes. The company have given me two weeks off to take the course and it happened to be very convenient to stay with Uncle.' She put a hand in a sleek black glove on the car door, remembered something. 'Uncle's got a bone to pick with you. Those bags of stuff you sent over, he said the piece of beef had gone off. It smelt disgusting, he said. I never saw it – he'd wrapped it up and put it in the bin before I ever got home.'

Taken aback, Burden had no rejoinder, but at that moment another car drew up and parked on the opposite side of the street. The woman called Mrs Jago came down to her front gate as a little girl of about three and a young woman got out of the car; there appeared to be another, bigger child sitting in the passenger seat. The visitor, though thin as a reed, was sufficiently like Mrs Jago as to leave no doubt this was a daughter. A mass of dark curly hair, rather resembling Serge Olson's but longer and glossier, covered half her back. The child, who also had long curly hair, ran to her grandmother and was taken up in her arms, where she clung to the massive bosom like a limpet to a domed, shiny, seaweed-clothed rock.

Ralph Robson was a long time coming to the front door. Burden could hear his stick making muffled thuds on the carpet. By the time the door opened, the two little girls and their mother had once more driven off. Robson was more than ever owl-like this morning, his nose apparently beakier, his mouth pursed, his eyes round and cross. A sports jacket of brindled brown tweed enhanced the effect and the hand on the stick gripped like a bird's claw round a twig. Burden was prepared for an exchange of courtesies, but Robson plunged straight into the bone-picking of which Lesley Arbel had forewarned him: he wanted compensation, he wanted reimbursement to the amount of four pounds fifty-two which was the price of the piece of spoiled sirloin.

Burden told him to put it all in writing and where to send his complaint. As soon as Robson had switched off that particular diatribe, he got on to the subject of his hip. The pain had intensified since his wife's death, it was ten times as bad as it had been a week ago and he could hear the joint grinding when he so much as shifted his position in a chair. Of course he was having to move about a lot more now that his wife was gone, she had saved him all that. There were areas in this country, he said, where you could get a hip replacement on the National Health Service in a matter of weeks. And he had heard that if you lived elsewhere they could transfer you to one of those places, but his doctor wouldn't have that – his doctor had said it couldn't be done. He had got himself to the surgery the day before, and that was what the doctor had said. It would have been different, he was sure, if he had had his wife to speak up for him.

'Gwen would have got things moving. Gwen would have told him what's what. If she'd known they could get me into some hospital on the other side of the country, she'd never have rested until she got some sense out of him. What's the use of talking now she's gone? I'm stuck with this for years maybe, until I can't stick another blessed day of it and take an overdose.'

It crossed Burden's mind that Robson was rather more than naturally obsessive about his arthritic hip. On the other hand, if you had a thing like that perhaps it would tend to exclude everything else from your existence. That physical pain might even distract you from the mental pain of losing your wife. Intent on not leading Robson (as the judges say), he asked him, once they were seated in front of the realistic blue flames, if he could remember any comments his wife might have made about her past 'clients'. Robson, as expected, immediately said it was a long time ago. Burden pressed him, which only had the effect of making him return to the subject of his hip and Gwen's remarks on what had brought it about and why he should have had arthritis when she didn't. This time Burden said he thought Robson was being obstructive and presumably he did want his wife's killer found.

'You've no business talking to me like that,' Robson said, thumping his stick on the floor and wincing.

'Then cast your mind back and try to remember what your wife said to you about these people. She was a

96

talkative woman, I'm told; she was interested in people. You're not going to tell me she'd come home at lunchtime or in the evening and not say a word to you about the old people she'd been working for? What, she never came back and said old Mrs So-and-So kept all her money in a stocking under the bed, or old Mr Whatever had a lady-friend? Nothing like that, ever?'

Burden need not have worried about leading Robson. These examples, far from stimulating him to invention or recall, seemed to provoke a truculent bewilderment. 'She never said about any old lady keeping money under the bed.'

'All right, Mr Robson,' Burden said, keeping his temper with difficulty, 'what did she talk about?'

An effort was made, as of a disused engine sparking into life with rusty wheels turning. 'There was that old boy over the road – Gwen was very good to him. She went on popping in there day after day long after she stopped working for the council. A daughter couldn't have done more.'

Eric Swallow of 12, Berry Close, Highlands, Burden thought, nodding encouragingly at Robson.

'Mrs Goodrich – that was the name. She wasn't so old, but she was crippled with one of those things they just give letters to, MS or MT or something. She'd been a lovely woman, a concert pianist Gwen said. She said she'd got some beautiful furniture in her place – valuable pieces, Gwen thought, worth a fair bit.'

Julia Goodrich of Paston Avenue, since moved from the district.

'I can't remember the rest of them; there was dozens and I can't remember them by name. I mean, there was one as told Gwen she'd had three kids by three different fathers and not married to any of them. That really upset Gwen. And there was an old boy as hadn't nothing but his pension, and used to give Gwen five-pound notes just for cutting his blessed toenails. She gave him a lot of her time, she'd be a good hour with him . . .'

'Someone gave your wife five pounds to cut his toenails?'

Burden was intrigued and imagined Wexford's reaction to this bizarre picture. Was some sexual titillation or even satisfaction involved? Surely there must have been.

'There was nothing wrong in it,' Robson said, on the defensive at once. 'He just took his socks off and sat there and she did his nails with clippers. He never touched her, she wasn't that sort. His feet were spotless, she said, clean as a baby's. And there was someone else – I can't remember names – as she gave a regular bath to. He was getting over some illness; he wasn't old, but he couldn't stand the district nurses bathing him and he said Gwen was as gentle as his own nanny when he was a little kid.'

Don't lead him, Burden said to himself. You must take your chance.

'Wait a minute, I've thought of a name: an old spinster called Miss Mac-something.'

'Miss McPhail,' said Burden, thinking this justified. Robson didn't seem interested in how he knew; like a lot of people, he took a degree of omniscience in the police for granted. They only asked questions to catch you out or for their own amusement. 'Miss McPhail of Forest Park.'

'That's her. She was wealthy, had a big house that was going to rack and ruin for want of looking after, and a blessed great garden. This young boy used to come in and do a bit to the garden in his college holidays. She wanted Gwen to come and work full-time for her. No thanks, Gwen said, I've got a husband to see to. I'll give you a hundred pounds a week, she said, and this was four years ago. You're joking, Gwen said, but she said no, that's what she'd give her to be her full-time cook and companion . . . and I reckon Gwen was tempted, only I put my foot down.'

Robson shifted his weight in the armchair and this time Burden thought he heard the hip joint grind. He heard something and saw Robson's face contort. Then Robson said, 'Is that all, then? Got enough, have you?'

Burden didn't answer but got up to go. Miss McPhail was dead now, he reflected as he was leaving, hers was one of the names on the list with a cross after it. Passing his own home, he went in to use the phone and check up on Wexford's recovery, then continued to Ash Farm where a search had been in progress for the past two hours. Clifford wasn't there. Burden hadn't expected him to be, but Dorothy Sanders was waiting for him, her face tragic with woe, her eyes staring.

'They said two hours was the maximum. They said two hours at the outside, and they started at nine.'

'It's only ten-past eleven, Mrs Sanders,' said Burden, who should have known better.

'Why do people say these things and not stick to them?'

'They won't be long now. They'll put everything back as they found it; we do make a point of that.'

He made his way upstairs to Davidson and Archbold on the first floor. Archbold pointed up the narrow flight of stairs which led to the top storey and said the rooms up there were stuffed with old furniture – rubbish, junk, the accumulation of years. Going through all that had delayed them. Burden decided to investigate outside, where Diana Pettit had gone to search the garage and a kind of toolshed attached to the rear fence. He made his way along the passage that must lead to a kitchen and a back way out. Dorothy Sanders had her face pressed against the window, watching the search. Her back was rigid and her arms flexed and she was perfectly still, reacting to his arrival with not the faintest twitch of her body. Burden went out by the back door.

Beyond the Ash Farm ground – you could hardly call it a garden – farmland, drowned in rain, stretched away in all directions. There was no other house in sight. A hill shaped like a camel's hump cut off the view of Kingsmarkham and heavy clouds rested on the ridge of it.

Diana looked round when Burden came in and said, 'There's nothing here, sir.'

'That depends on what you're looking for, Diana. I suppose you've been told what you're looking for?'

'A garrote, though I'm not very sure what that is.'

Burden put his hands into the box of tools. It was one

of those metal boxes divided into sections on two levels, in which the upper drawers can be drawn outwards by a kind of concertina motion. He picked out two objects, saying, 'These would answer the purpose very well.'

8

IANA PETTIT and DS Martin both told Burden these were the kinds of things to be found in every toolbox in every garden shed. You might as well find a hammer or screwdriver in such a place and call it an offensive weapon. Everybody had a spool of plastic-covered wire and a great many people a garden line for making straight edges. Burden said he didn't; he had never even seen a garden line before. Was DC Pettit sure that's what it was?

Two metal pegs, ring-headed, were linked by a length of twine. The twine was merely knotted on to the pegs and a piece of the plastic wire might well have temporarily replaced it, thus making a serviceable garrote. He took the things away, getting Diana to give Dorothy Sanders a receipt for them. The wire went to the lab for analysis and comparison with the particles of plastic found in Gwen Robson's neck wound. With a similar length of plastic wire which he had been out to buy tied to the iron pegs, Burden shut himself up in his office and practised garroting first the angled lamp and then one of the legs of his desk. Neither was the right size for a human neck.

Next morning Linda Naseem, who had Wednesdays off, was back on her checkout. Burden went to talk to her himself. It was exactly a week today since Gwen Robson had come in here, having parked her car underground on the second level, and walked under the glazed covered way to the Barringdean Shopping Centre, arriving inside at about four-forty. The next three-quarters of an hour were easily accounted for: a little window-gazing and the purchase of two items from Boots where an assistant remembered her. The toothpaste and talcum powder had been in one of the carriers with the groceries and the light-bulbs from British Home Stores. No one remembered

101

her in there, but that was to be expected. She had probably entered Tesco at about ten-past five, taken a trolley or perhaps only a basket and begun walking round the store picking out items from her list. Clifford Sanders at that time had certainly still been with Olson. Burden saw that he was putting Gwen Robson's visit to the store too early; it was far more likely that she had not gone into Tesco until twenty-past five. That way she wouldn't have reached the checkout until five-thirty-five or maybe a little later.

There were five girls on the Tesco checkouts. Burden was looking for an Indian and three of the girls appeared to be of vaguely Indian origin. He went up to one of them and she pointed down the line to where a small, slight girl of ethereal fairness, white-skinned and flaxen-haired, was changing the spool in her till. As he approached her, he noticed her wedding ring. Of course she was called Naseem because she was married to a Moslem from the East or Middle East. Burden reprimanded himself for jumping to conclusions as he knew Wexford would have admonished him. It was inexcusable in someone of his experience.

She took him into a side room or office marked 'Private' on the door.

'You knew Mrs Robson by sight, I think?' he began.

She nodded, looking slightly apprehensive.

'What time did you say she passed through your check-out last Thursday?'

She hesitated. 'I know I did tell the other policeman five-fifteen, but I've thought about it since and it could have been later. I remember looking at my watch and seeing twenty to six and thinking good, only half an hour to go. We close at six, but they're still going through after that.'

'How much later?' Burden asked.

'Pardon?'

'How long after you had seen Mrs Robson did you look at your watch and see five-forty?'

'I don't know. It's ever so hard to say, isn't it? Ten minutes?'

Ten minutes or five minutes, thought Burden, or even two minutes. He asked her about the girl she had seen Mrs Robson talking to – was she quite sure it was a girl?'

'Pardon,' she said again.

'If you only saw the back of this person, who was in any case wearing a hat and presumably a coat or jacket as well, how did you know it was a girl and not a boy – a man, that is?'

She said slowly, as if reorganizing impressions and conclusions, 'Well, I just sort of knew – I mean I think it was. Oh, yes, of course it was. She had a hat on – a beret, I think.'

'It could have been a man, couldn't it, Mrs Naseem?'

'That just wasn't the impression I got,' said Linda Naseem.

Burden didn't ask her any more. Looking back on the interview, he felt he had been in the role of counsel who breaks down a witness's evidence by subtle questioning, leaving the jury to draw very firm conclusions from her uncertain replies. There had been no jury in Tesco's, but if there had been he had no doubt its members would have been thoroughly convinced of this fact: that on the previous Thursday Gwen Robson had been seen in the store talking to a young man at twenty minutes to six. He wandered back into the wide gallery of the lower level and stood in the Mandala concourse. It was all red and white poinsettias today and some sort of dark blue flower. Why these signs of patriotism on November 26? Probably those were simply the flowers the florist had most of.

Burden had a look in Boots, paused to examine the window of Knits 'n' Kits which today was full of tapestry canvases printed with dog and cat faces, glanced across at Demeter with its display of water filters and air ionizers. None of the assistants in any of these shops remembered seeing Gwen Robson. The fountain was playing, shooting up its jets of water to splash the lowest prisms of the chandelier. Burden went out through the main car-park exit, from the dry warmth and air freshener smell of the place into a cutting wind.

How long was he going to have to wait for a result from the lab? Several days probably. A phone call to Wexford's daughter's home obtained the engaged signal. Burden took his improvised garrote out of the desk drawer and practised flexing his hands round the pegs. One possibly got a better purchase by putting one's fingers through the rings and gripping the handles that way. He needed something more closely resembling a human neck than the desk leg. Into his mind's eye came an urn-shaped plant-pot container made of white polystyrene cunningly contrived to look like marble. DC Polly Davies had left it behind, with instructions as to the proper care of the cyclamen it contained, when she took her maternity leave and it had ended up in Wexford's office, the cyclamen long perished. The stem of that urn would be just about the right size and with a similar flexibility.

Still holding his garrote, Burden went up in the lift and along the corridor. The office door was slightly ajar and he pushed it open and went in. Wexford was sitting behind the desk, hunched up, wrapped in his old tweed overcoat. His head was plastered up and the bruises on his face had turned a sickly yellow-green. The small grey eyes that turned on Burden and his improvised weapon had a glassy look, atypically apprehensive, but his opening remark wasn't uncharacteristic.

'So it was you all along.'

Burden grinned. 'I've made this up and I was going to try it out on your plant-pot. Don't look like that; it's quite a reasonable idea.'

'If you say so, Mike.'

'What are you doing here, anyway? You're supposed to be off till the end of the week.'

'This is the end of the week.' Wexford said, shifting in his seat and flexing bruised hands. 'I've been reading all this stuff.' Every report made on the case so far had been sent up and lay on the desk in front of him. Burden, who loved reporting every interview in detail and even recording his own thoughts, had typed screeds. 'There are some quite interesting bits. I like Mrs Robson getting five quid for cutting the old boy's toenails.'

'I thought you would.'

'It makes me wonder how much of that sort of thing there was. This bath business, for instance. It's a fascinating line of enquiry.' Burden raised an eyebrow. Not quite certain what Wexford meant and somewhat repelled by the image, he picked the mock-marble urn off the window-sill and set about strangling it with his garrote. Wexford watched him speculatively. 'There are a lot of things I'd like to know which no one seems to have bothered with much,' he said. 'Lesley Arbel, for instance. Where was she last Thursday afternoon? We don't seem to know, though we do know that Gwen Robson was seen talking to a girl at five-thirty.'

'That was a man and it was five-forty,' said Burden, pulling on his handles, feeling the polystyrene crack and split, the wire digging into the spongy white flesh-like substance.

'I see. It would be a help to know why she was always down here and what she found so compelling about that not very exciting couple.' Wexford had picked up the only photograph they had of Gwen Robson – the snapshot, much blown-up, which the *Kingsmarkham Courier* had used. '"One of those characteristic British faces,"' he quoted, '"that once seen are never remembered."'

'Those Sanderses say they don't remember her; both of them say they never saw her before. But I just know Clifford knew her, I feel it in my bones.'

'For God's sake give over doing that, Mike. I'm not squeamish, but it turns me up. Her home help visits are another interesting thing. You note how she never seems to have spent much time with those who had little or nothing to give. I wonder what old Mr Swallow had on offer, the one who lived opposite. Did she cut his toenails too – and did she perhaps have some particularly erotic technique with the scissors?'

'It's rather disgusting, isn't it?'

Wexford grinned, lifted his shoulders.

'Is it important?' Burden put the garrote into his pocket and came to sit on the edge of the rosewood desk. When Wexford made no reply to this but only sat there looking bemused, he said, 'You don't look well, you know. I doubt if you should be here.'

'I'm going to have a quiet day,' Wexford told him. 'I'm going to see how many cups of tea I can drink between two and five this afternoon.' Enlightening Burden, he added, 'it seems to me we haven't chatted up Robson's neighbours nearly enough.'

But he went on sitting there after Burden had gone. If he hadn't put out his hand to the radiator and felt it almost too hot to handle, he could have sworn the central heating had gone wrong. Without the comfort of his old overcoat, he would have been freezing. Sheila was back in London; he hadn't wanted her to go, but of course he hadn't said a word. What he would have liked was to shut her up somewhere for ever and stand guard over the door. But she had gone back to London in a rented car, back to the flat by Coram Fields that those people — whoever they were, those bombers, terrorists, fanatics — very well knew she occupied. Sylvia had the radio on most of the day, so Wexford got to hear every news bulletin, and every time he braced himself to hear the sentence that would start, 'An explosion . . .' That was why he had come back to work so soon really.

Bomb experts from Scotland Yard had come down to talk to him and the Myringham man had been back. Wexford had wanted to know what they were doing to protect Sheila and they had given him plenty of sturdy reassurance, only he wasn't reassured. He knew he wouldn't have felt so frightened if Sheila had been living with her husband, though that was illogical enough. If anyone had told him he would actually be glad to hear that his daughter was living with a man while married to someone else, he wouldn't have believed them. But that was how he felt now. It would comfort him to know that Sheila had that man Ned, whoever he might be, around night and day. What would comfort him most, of course, was what his son-in-law Neil advocated.

'Get her to stop doing acts of criminal damage. Take away her wire-cutters, or better still get her to make a public statement of guilt and her intention not to do it again.'

Surprisingly, it was Dora who countered, 'Would you have much respect for her if she did a thing like that?'

'Being alive's more important than respect, I should say.'

'Of course she won't do that,' Wexford had said. He was almost cross. 'She can't deny her principles, can she? She doesn't think she's guilty; she thinks the law's wrong – the law itself is guilty, if you like.'

Sylvia looked askance. 'Rather a strange commentary from a policeman, surely, Dad?'

He hadn't said any more. Apart from finding some way out of this anxiety, of making Sheila safe, he wanted more than anything to avoid a flaming row with Sylvia and Neil. The Chief Constable had said something to him on the phone yesterday about the loan of a police house until his own was repaired – well, largely rebuilt, and at the pace at which builders worked nowadays that would be a year hence.

At any rate it was peaceful here. It was quiet and the cold he felt wasn't real. He had to 'struggle against a great tendency to lowness', as he put it to himself, and he went up to the canteen to get some lunch. Working his way through hot soup, hamburger and chips, comforting if not healthy food, he faced the prospect of getting into a car again and driving it. Neil had brought him to work and dropped him outside the gates. Donaldson, his driver, would take him up to Highlands. But sooner or later he was going to have to overcome the great barrier of inhibition that reared up between him and the driving-seat and wheel of a car. He would have to conquer the paralysis he felt would descend upon his left hand as it tried to close over a gear shift, even in his case an automatic shift. Last night he had relived in a dream the explosion

107

he thought he had no memory of, but had said nothing about it to anyone, not even Dora.

Patterns of life had changed subtly but radically during the years since Wexford had first become a policeman interviewing witnesses. In those early days all the men were out at work and all the women at home. Split-shift working, the advance in women's education and freedom, self-employment and of course unemployment had changed all that. He was not much surprised, at the first house where he called after leaving the car and Donaldson, to be admitted by a young man with a baby in his arms and a child of about three clinging to the legs of his jeans.

This was John Whitton, student and father of two, whose wife was a systems analyst in a full-time job. It was she who had spent time with Ralph Robson while he awaited the arrival of his niece. The house inside had that curious faint smell which all who have themselves been parents recognize – that of a compound of milk, infants' digestive processes, ammonia and talcum powder. This young parent had lived next door but one to Gwen Robson for the three years since his marriage when the local authority had allocated him and his wife a house at Highlands, but he assured Wexford that their acquaintance had been slight. Knowing her to be a council home help and with a reputation for philanthropy (his own word), they had once ventured to ask her if she would baby-sit for them.

'Our regular sitter had let us down and it was a special occasion. As a matter of fact it was our third wedding anniversary, and Rosemary was expecting this one any day. We knew it would be months before we got out in the evening again. I asked Mrs Robson and it wasn't that she wouldn't do it; it was the amount she wanted paying. We couldn't run to that, living on one salary; we couldn't give her three pounds an hour. It wasn't as if Scott ever wakes in the evening – it would have been twelve quid for just sitting about watching telly.'

108

It was a long shot but Wexford thought he might as well try it, and he asked John Whitton about the previous Thursday. Had he seen Ralph Robson during the course of the afternoon, preferably after four-thirty? But Whitton shook his head. He had been at home, for his wife had the car that day, but it was a busy time for him with the children's tea to get and both of them to be bathed. He couldn't even recall having seen Gwen Robson go out.

Next door, between the Whittons and Ralph Robson, lived the couple Mrs Robson had so disapproved of, Trevor Morrison and Nicola Resnick. They were both in the house from which they ran a mail-order secondhand-book business which Wexford guessed was of a rather precarious kind. Here the first of that anticipated tea was offered, though of the herbal sort — crimson liquid with a floral-labelled bag floating in it. Wexford accepted a coarse, dark brown crunchy biscuit. Nicola Resnick, though young and liberated-looking in jeans and boots and Guernsey, turned out as much of a gossip as ever her grandmother could have been.

'She tried to get that old boy opposite to make his will in her favour. He used to tell everybody about the money he'd got in the bank. He was about a hundred, wasn't he, Trev?'

'He was eighty-eight when he died,' Trevor Morrison said.

'Yes, well, ancient. You see, he was always whingeing about not being able to manage, especially his fuel bills in the winter. And he liked to use his phone. He'd got this daughter in Ireland or somewhere and he liked to phone her; no good waiting for her to phone him, he used to say. Well, I said to him you ought to apply for supplementary benefit. Why not? You've got a right to it and I believe in getting everything you're entitled to. These old people are proud but it's just pointless, that sort of pride. You work all your life, you've got a right to anything the state will let you have. But it wasn't that with him. It's no good me applying, he said to me, I've got money in the bank and I'll have to tell them; I've got more than three thousand

109

in the Trustee Savings Bank and when I let on about that, no way are they giving me benefit. And it was true.'

'This is Mr Eric Swallow we're talking about?' Wexford asked, making a valiant effort to drink his hibiscus tea.

'Old Eric, yes. I don't think I ever knew his other name, did you, Trev? Anyway, he used to tell everyone about this three thousand in the bank; he used to boast about it. And I heard him say his daughter was counting on getting that but she mustn't think it was automatic; it was his money to do as he liked with. Mind you, he was whingeing about her at the time, he hadn't had a word from her for weeks.'

'What was this about a will?'

'It must have been a year ago or more – at least that. She'd just given up being a home help, but she was in and out over the road every day. I was sitting here working on our catalogue and Trev was here too when she came to the door and asked if we would witness some document old Eric had got. It was quite a surprise – I mean, I'd hardly spoken to her before that and she'd ignore me if she saw me in the street. She said he had to sign this form and he needed two witnesses. And then do you know what she said? That we'd be better not being married, not being connected with each other! I was amazed. Well, I thought maybe it was something to do with this supplementary benefit and I was going to go, but Trevor asked Gwen what it was and all she said was it was nothing we need worry about, just a form. Well, naturally, that wasn't good enough for Trev and he said we had to know what we were signing before we went over there, and then she said it was Eric's will.'

'And that put me off quite a bit, as you can imagine,' said Trevor. 'It smelt, if you know what I mean.'

'That's absolutely right, it smelt. Anyway, I just said we were a bit busy and to count us out. Gwen said that was OK; she'd soon find someone and anyway her niece would be down the next night. I expect you know that niece, don't you, the one that looks like she was modelling clothes?'

It was all interesting enough, and would have been useful if Gwen Robson had been suspected of murder and Eric Swallow and any of these other old people her victims. But it was she who had been the victim. Wexford asked his question about Ralph Robson's movements and Nicola Resnick was able to tell him that she had heard sounds from next door late on the Thursday afternoon. The wall between the houses was thin and you could hear the click of lights being switched on and off, the thump-thump of Robson's stick and of course the television.

How could she particularly remember last Thursday?

Robson had had the children's programme *Blue Peter* on, she told him. That began at five-past five and was followed by a health programme about trace elements as food supplements. Nicola Resnick was interested in that and she had switched on her own set though Robson had his so loud she need scarcely have bothered.

Thursday afternoon once more, a week since the killing. Seven days ago Clifford Sanders had entered Queen Street from the High Street in his mother's car and parked it on the left-hand side on a meter, inserting into the slot, if he were to be believed, the forty pence that would ensure him one hour's parking. But it was already twenty minutes to five when he arrived, so that when he left Olson ten minutes on the meter still remained to run. And he had sat out those ten minutes, brooding on the things he had talked about to Olson, all that Dodo rubbish. Not that Burden believed that for a moment.

He went into all the shops on both sides of this part of Queen Street, the grocer's, a fishmonger, a fruiterer, a wine-shop, two cheap clothes boutiques and Pelage the hairdressers. No one remembered seeing Clifford Sanders sitting in a car on the meter outside Pelage. The difficulty was that the red Metro was regularly parked on one of those meters on a Thursday afternoon, so it was hard to sort out when it had been there and when it hadn't, and when Clifford had been seen sitting in it and when he had not. One of the stylists at Pelage was very definite about having sometimes seen him sitting in the car in the driving-seat, just sitting there as if lost in thought, not reading or looking out of the window or anything.

From the cover of the wine supermarket window, Burden watched Clifford arrive at ten minutes to five. There was no meter free and he drove as far as where Castle Street cut across, then turned and came slowly back. By now someone was pulling out so Clifford waited, moved the Metro into the space, got out of the car and locked it. The day was damp and very cold and he wore a grey tweed overcoat and grey knitted hat pulled down well over his ears. From a distance, Burden had to admit, he looked not so much like a girl as an old woman. He put a couple of coins into the meter, which must still have had time to run from the previous insertion. Then he came quite slowly across the road as if he had all the time in the world instead of being, as was in fact the case, nearly twenty-five minutes late for his appointment. Burden felt a sneaking admiration for Serge Olson's technique in deliberately naming a time for this client half an hour in advance of the five o'clock when he knew he would arrive.

After Clifford had disappeared into the entrance at the side of Pelage, Burden went off along Castle Street to have a cautionary word with a jeweller he suspected of being a fence. Then into a call box to phone his wife and say he might be late but not very late – say around eight-thirty. A cup of tea and a cake in the Queen's Café and it was two minutes to six when he came back down Queen Street. An icy rain had begun to fall and the dark was the darkness of midnight, though brightly illuminated here by dripping, fuzzy yellow and white lights that turned the pavements a gleaming dirty gold and silver. Snowflakes started appearing among the silvery rods of rain.

Clifford came out of Olson's door at two minutes past six. He wasn't hurryng, but he was moving a good deal faster than when he had arrived. Burden sheltered from the rain and Clifford's view in the doorway of the green-grocer's; they were closing up and people kept pushing past him to carry in trays of chicory and aubergines. Clifford got into the car without even glancing at the meter; he started up and was away as the hands of Burden's watch moved to five-past six.

Wexford had read and heard about people seeing on someone else's arm the brand mark of the concentration camps, but he had not had that experience himself; and he didn't have it now – Dita Jago on this cold afternoon having her arms covered by a woolly garment that was itself a work of art: a knitted tapestry of greens and purples, rich reds and jewel blues. But when he glanced enquiringly at the great pile of manuscript which lay on the table in this strange cluttered room, the perhaps orderly muddle of notebooks and loose leaves, scrawled-on envelopes and works of reference, she had nodded to him.

'My great work,' she said. A smile made the remark a modest one. 'My memoirs of Oswiecim.'

'Auschwitz?' he said.

She nodded and, lifting up the topmost sheet of manuscript, turned it over so that only a blank side showed.

9

THE room was of the same size and shape as the one in which he had talked to Robson and his niece; as the room Trevor Morrison and Nicola Resnick used as their office; as John Whitton's nursery. It was on the other side of the street and faced the opposite way, but the main difference from all those others lay in its rich clutter, the abundance of curious interesting things, the piles of books and papers and the adornment of its walls which was like nothing Wexford had ever seen before.

Unless you looked out of the window – seeing the trim little roadway, the trees in the pavement grass plots, the semi-detached houses – you might have believed yourself anywhere but on a local authority housing estate outside an English country town. What the walls were papered or painted with it was impossible to say, for they were covered all over with hangings which to Wexford had at first looked like lavish and elaborate embroideries but which, on examining them more closely, he saw to be knitted. Dora's efforts at what has been called 'the common art', resulting in jumpers for grandsons, at least told him that much. But this knitting was in all colours of the spectrum, those colours subtly matched and contrasted, creating abstract designs of immense complexity as well as pictures that in the execution of their strong primitive imagery reminded him of the paintings of Rousseau. In one a tiger crept through a jungle of green fronds and dark fruit-laden branches: in another a girl in a sarong walked with peacocks. The biggest, which covered the whole of one wall and had evidently been constructed in panels, was Chinese rather than tropical and showed a green landscape with little temples on the summits of hills and a herd of deer browsing between the woodland and the lake.

She was smiling at his wonderment. He only knew she was the creator of all this by the piece of work now in progress, another jungle picture taking shape from a circular needle, which lay on a round table beside Venetian glass animals and painted porcelain eggs. She had completed perhaps half of it.

'You're a busy woman, Mrs Jago,' he observed.

'I like to keep occupied.' Her accent was a rather unfamiliar guttural, Polish perhaps or Czech, but the English itself was grammatically and syntactically flawless. 'I have been writing my book for two years now and it's nearly done. God only knows if anyone will ever publish such a book, but I wrote it for my own satisfaction, to get it all down on paper. And it's true what they say.' She smiled at him again. 'Get it down, write it out and it's no longer such a terrible thing to remember. It doesn't cure but it helps.'

'The writer is the only free man, as someone said.'

'Whoever that someone was knew what he was talking about.'

She sat down facing him and picked up her knitting. Supplied with hibiscus tea by Nicola Resnick and Earl Grey by a Miss Margaret Anderson – who claimed never to have spoken to Mrs Robson or heard of her until she was dead – Wexford was rather relieved that Mrs Jago offered him no refreshment. Her fingers worked skilfully, moving with assurance a complex mass of coloured threads, selecting one, taking two or three stitches with it, abandoning this first shade and joining in another. Plump and tapering these fingers were, the wedding ring cutting deeply into the flesh. She was a mountain of a woman, yet somehow neither gross nor ungainly, her legs shapely with fine ankles and small feet in tiny black pumps. Remains of a gipsyish beauty showed in her full, pink-cheeked face. Her eyes were black, bright and in their cobweb wrinkles like jewels in a fibrous nest. Hair that was still dark was drawn back with combs into a large glossy bun.

'You came in and offered to do some shopping for Mr

Robson,' he began. 'That makes me think you must have known them fairly well.'

She looked up at him and the fingers were momentarily stilled. 'I didn't know them at all. I wouldn't be far wrong if I said that was only the second time I'd ever spoken to him except to say good morning.'

Wexford was disappointed. His hopes of this woman, though quite unjustifiable, had been high. Something about her made him feel she was essentially truthful.

'He was a neighbour,' she said. 'He'd lost his wife. She had been killed in a horrible way and it was the least I could do.' She remembered his name, though she had only briefly seen his warrant card. 'It was no trouble to me, Mr Wexford. I'm no Good Samaritan. My daughter takes me shopping or does it for me.'

'You may not have known him but you knew her, didn't you?'

She came to the end of her row, turned the linked needles. 'Hardly. Will you believe me if I tell you that was the first time I'd ever been in their house? Let me tell you something. I don't want you to waste your time on someone who can tell you very little. When I came out of the camp, they put me in a hospital the army ran. There was a man there, a soldier who was a ward orderly, and he fell in love with me. God knows why, for I was a skeleton and my hair had all fallen out.' She smiled. 'You wouldn't think that to see me now, would you? And I used to long and long to put on weight like they said I must. Well, this man – Corporal Jago, Arthur Jago – he married me and made me an Englishwoman.' She pointed to the pile of manuscript. 'It is all in the book!' Her knitting resumed, she said, 'But though I have tried I have never become very English, Mr Wexford. I have never quite learned to get on with the English way of always pretending everything in the garden is lovely. Do you understand what I mean? Everything in the garden is *not* lovely. There is a snake in the bush and worms under the stones and half the plants are poisonous . . .'

He smiled at the image she created.

116

'For example, Mr Robson – that poor man – he will say that what is to be will be; perhaps it is all for the best, life must go on. And Miss Anderson down the street who found a man who wanted to marry her at last when she was sixty years old . . . when he died a week before the wedding, what does she say? Maybe it was too late, maybe they'd both have regretted it. I cannot do with this.'

'But these are the tenets of survival, Mrs Jago.'

'Perhaps. But I cannot see that you survive any less if first you cry and rage and show your feelings. At least, it isn't my way and I am not comfortable with it.'

Wexford, who would have been quite happy to continue with this exploration of English emotion or lack of it, nevertheless thought it was time to move on. Weariness had come to take hold of him and his headache was back, a tight band wound around above the eyes. It was a piece of luck, sheer serendipity, that made him speak the name of the old man who had lived a few houses away in Berry Close.

'Eric Swallow,' he said. 'Did you have the same slight acquaintance with him?'

'I know who you mean,' she said, laying the knitting in her lap. 'That was rather amusing, but nothing to do with poor Mrs Robson being killed. I mean it couldn't be anything, really.'

'All right. But if it's amusing I'd like to hear it. There's little enough in this business to make us laugh.'

'The poor old man was dying. That isn't funny, of course. If I were English I would say maybe it was a merciful release, wouldn't I?'

'Was it?'

'Well, he was very old, nearly ninety. He had a daughter but she was in Ireland and she wasn't young, naturally. Mrs Robson used to do a lot for him; I mean, after she stopped being a home help and getting paid for it, she still went in there nearly every day. In the end when he got so that he couldn't get out of bed, they took him away and he died in the hospital . . .'

Wexford had had his eyes on the great landscape

tapestry, but the sound of a car door slamming made him turn his head and then almost immediately the doorbell rang. Mrs Jago got up, excused herself and went out into the hall with a surprisingly light, springy tread. Voices could be heard, the clamorous treble of children. Then the front door closed again and Mrs Jago came back with two little girls: the younger of them, though too big to be carried, was in her arms; the other, who looked about five or six and who wore a school uniform of navy coat, yellow and navy scarf and felt hat with stripey band, walking by her side.

'These are my granddaughters, Melanie and Hannah Quincy. They live in Down Road, but sometimes their mummy brings them to me for an hour or two and we have a nice tea, don't we, girls?' The children said nothing, appearing shy. Dita Jago put Hannah down. 'Tea is all ready and we shall have it at five sharp. You can tell me when it is three minutes to five, Melanie; Mummy says you can tell the time now.'

Hannah went immediately to the table where the painted eggs and glass animals were. And though the older child had a book to read and had opened it, she was keeping a sharp cautionary eye on her sister's handling of the fragile things. Wexford, from personal experience, knew only too well the advantages and the pitfalls of that particular relationship, the stresses created in infancy that lasted a lifetime.

Dita Jago was placidly knitting once more. 'I was telling you about old Mr Swallow. Well, one afternoon — a Thursday I think it was, a year ago or a bit more — the front-door bell rang and there was Mrs Robson. She wanted me to come into Mr Swallow's with her and be a witness to something. In fact, she wanted two people and she'd seen my daughter's car outside, so she knew Nina was here. I found out afterwards that she had already been to a couple who live on the other side. He's called Morrison, I don't know her name, but anyway for some reason they wouldn't do it.

'As I've said, I don't suppose I'd ever spoken more than

118

two words to her and she'd never met Nina. I had to introduce them. But that didn't stop her asking us both to go down there and witness this form.'

'Hannah, I'm going to be very cross if you break that little horse,' said Melanie.

A struggle ensued as the elder granddaughter did her best to prise from her sister's fingers a blue glass animal. Hannah stamped her foot.

'Grandma is going to be very unhappy if you break it. Grandma will cry.'

'No, she won't.'

'Give it to me, please, Hannah. Now do as you're told.'

'Hannah will cry! Hannah will scream!'

Shades of Sylvia and Sheila . . . Dita Jago intervened, drawing the younger child – who was by now carrying out her threat – on to her lap. Melanie looked mutinous, frowning darkly.

'Birds in their little nests should agree,' Mrs Jago said, not without irony, Wexford thought. She stroked the little girl's mane of dark curly hair. 'We thought it was something to do with the money he wanted to get from the what-do-you-call-it? DH-something – the supplementary benefit. There are always forms, aren't there? Anyway, we went down to Mr Swallow's with her and when we got there we found him asleep in bed. Mrs Robson was a little bit put out. My daughter said what was this form and had he already signed it? Well, you could see Mrs Robson didn't want to say. She said she'd wake Mr Swallow up; it was important and he'd want her to wake him.'

Hannah, her crying over, placed one thumb in her mouth and opening the other fist, showed her sister the blue glass horse, clenching her hand as soon as Melanie made a pounce for it.

Melanie turned away loftily. 'Five minutes to five, Grandma,' she said.

'All right. I said to tell me when it was three minutes to. Anyway, the piece of paper we had to sign was lying there on the table face-downwards. I mean we thought that's what it was and we were right. Nina just picked it up and took one look – and what do you think it was?'

Wexford had a pretty good idea, but he decided not to steal Mrs Jago's thunder and merely shrugged.

'It was a will, made out on a will form. Nina didn't get to read it because Mrs Robson snatched it away, but we could guess what was on it. It would have been leaving his money to Mrs Robson. Three thousand pounds, he used to boast he had; everyone here knew that. And she was after it – she liked money, there was no doubt about that. Well, we both shied away like anything. We told each other afterwards no way, absolutely not. Suppose that daughter had brought it up in court and we'd had to go there and say we'd signed it?'

'What was Mrs Robson's reaction to that?'

'Three minutes to five, Grandma,' Melanie said.

'I'm coming, darling. She didn't like it, but what could she do? I couldn't help having a laugh when we were outside. I heard later she went trying other people down the street, but she never struck lucky; she couldn't get anyone but her niece. It was only a few days after that they took Mr Swallow away and when he died there wasn't a will and his daughter got his money – being his real heir, you see, as was quite right. Now I must keep my promise to these children.'

Mrs Jago put the child on the floor and the knitting on the table and got up. 'You will stay for tea? We have Grandma's version of *sachertorte*.'

Wexford thanked her but shook his head. He had told Donaldson to come back for him at five and he thought of the deep pleasure of leaning back in the car and closing his eyes. Hannah had crept quietly to the table and replaced the little horse amongst the other animals with precision, with perfectly coordinated delicate fingers, her eyes all the while on her sister, her lips not quite smiling. It reminded him of Sheila playing all those years ago with a china ornament which Sylvia (though no one else) had forbidden her to touch. And Sheila had teased like this little one, peeping over a defiant shoulder with the faintest Gioconda smile.

'Of course, to do her justice she didn't want money for herself,' Dita Jago's voice interrupted his reverie. 'It was for him, it would have been all for him.' It was just as he was leaving, when they were out in the hall, that she said, 'Don't you want to know where I was last Thursday evening?'

He smiled. 'Tell me.'

'My daughter always goes shopping on Thursday after-noons and usually she takes me. But last week she dropped me off at the public library in the High Street and left the girls with me. She picked us up again at five-thirty.'

Why had she insisted on telling him that? he wondered. Perhaps merely to avoid a repetition of his visit. Or was he imagining things that the tone of her voice gave no hint of – reacting in a confused, almost fuddled, way because of the huge weariness which had overtaken him? Passing a wall mirror in the hall as he made his way out, he caught sight of his discoloured face, the bruised muzzle of a prize-fighter recovering from a bout, and turned quickly away. He was no narcissist, no lover of his own image.

The front door closed on him. Her grandchildren's demands had cut short any parting pleasantries Mrs Jago might have made. It was just before five, for her clock had been fast, and Wexford waited for the car with the anxiety of a disabled pensioner expecting an ambulance. He had to lower himself into a sitting position on the low wall, feeling his bruised body creak. Going back to work had not been a wise idea, yet it hadn't seemed like work, more a matter of paying social calls. Mike ought to be left to himself to handle this case; he was quite capable of doing so. Someone like Serge Olson would say that he, Wexford, was at fault – only probably he wouldn't use a word like 'fault' – in being unable to delegate, in refusing to yield authority to the younger man. It was very likely a sign of insecurity, fear of seeing Mike usurp his place, even his job. Psychology, he thought, and not for the first time, often just wasn't true.

Cars passed. With a strong inner shudder, an actual shrinking, he tried to contemplate what it would be like to sit at the wheel again, start the ignition, move the shift into gear. That, of course, he wouldn't quite have to do, just manipulate from 'park' to 'drive'. But the notion of putting his hand to that lever brought a darkness before his eyes and made him hear a sound he had no recollection of hearing: the roar of the bomb. He closed his eyes, opening them to see Donaldson draw up at the kerb.

A hunch he couldn't quite believe in – it all seemed behaviour of the crassest, most unfeeling kind – led Burden to assume that Clifford Sanders was heading for the Barringdean car park. He couldn't follow him: he hadn't a car immediately to hand and, making his way there on foot, he told himself he was wasting his time. No one would do that. No one would return to the scene of so horrific a crime precisely seven days to the hour later, and there go through the same prescribed ritual. With, that is, one notable exception . . .

He entered the shopping complex by the pedestrian entrance where, a week before, Dodo Sanders had stood rattling the gates and screaming for help. But first he went into the underground car park, descending to the second level in the lift. At least Clifford hadn't parked the car on precisely the spot where it had been the week before, but perhaps he had not done so only because that particular space and those next to it and opposite were already occupied. This time the Sanders' car was at the extreme opposite end to the lift and the stairs. It was empty which meant, presumably, that Clifford was somewhere in the shopping centre.

As he had been in the previous week, thought Burden, looking at his watch by the light of the glaring greenish strip-lights. Six-twenty-two, but he, of course, had walked here and taken some time to locate the car. Clifford's appointment had been at his normal time, five o'clock, so today his date to pick up his mother would be later. Six-thirty perhaps? With the centre closing at six and usually emptied by six-fifteen, would she be prepared to wait for him? But as he was speculating along these lines, watching the last cars backed out and driven away, he heard the clang of the descending lift. Clifford and his mother came out of it and Burden watched them walk towards their car, Clifford carrying two Tesco bags and a wicker basket. Burden thought he could easily be taken for a girl from the back; it was something to do with his plump hips and the rather short steps he took. He caught up with them as Clifford was lifting the boot-lid of the Metro.

Mrs Sanders turned and cast upon him a basilisk look. She was hatless, her hair set in a rather bouffant, cloudy way which didn't suit her. The red lipstick glistened in the pale face. He had wondered what that particular colour of skin reminded him of and now he knew: raw fish, a translucent, faintly pinkish white. She was perfectly calm and her voice was cold.

'I wish I'd never told anyone about finding that dead body. I wish I'd kept quiet,' Burden had an inkling then of the icy authority she exercised over her son and had no doubt exercised since he was an infant. There was an awful precision in that tone and it was backed by a great storehouse of nervous energy. 'I'm not usually a fool. I should have had the sense to stay out of it; I should have followed his example.'

'What example was that, Mrs Sanders?' Burden asked.

Her attention was on the time by her digital watch and that indicated on the clock in the Metro which she bent down to look at. Abstractedly, she said, 'He ran away, didn't he?'

'You tell me. I've got a very good idea what it was he did, and running away was only a small part of it.' While Clifford unlocked the driver's door, he said, 'You won't mind giving me a lift, will you? We can take your mother home first and then you and I will have another talk at the police station.'

123

Clifford didn't say anything. The only sign that he had heard was when he reached inside to release the lock on the passenger door. And on the way back to Ash Lane no one said a word. Half the carriageway of this end of the Forby Road was undergoing repairs, temporary traffic lights had been installed and a long queue of cars waited. Dodo Sanders, sitting in the front next to Clifford, pulled down her glove and lifted up her coat cuff to look at her digital watch. Why it should have been important to her to know the precise time they had left the car park and the precise time they began queueing at the lights, Burden couldn't guess. Perhaps, though, that wasn't the purpose of all this watch-gazing. It might be that she simply wanted to know the time, that all day long, every day, every five minutes, she had to know the time.

She spoke as Clifford drew up by the kerb. 'I can take the things in. There's no need to come with me.'

But he got out of the car, removed the bags from the boot and carried them up to the front door. He unlocked the door and stood back for her to pass in ahead of him. Burden understood it all. She was one of those people who say things like that but don't mean them. She was the sort who would say, 'Don't worry about me, I'll be all right on my own,' or 'Don't bother to write me a thank-you letter,' and then create hell when she got left alone or when no letter came. His mother-in-law was a bit like that, though Mrs Sanders was a thousand times worse.

Clifford got back into the driving-seat and Burden stayed where he was, in the back. He didn't care whether they talked or not; they would talk at the station. The driving was done with the slow care, the superfluous signals and excessive braking habitual to Clifford. He broke the silence as they turned in to find the last remaining parking space.

'What is it you suspect me of?'

Burden felt a reluctance to answer questions of that kind. They seemed to bring him down to Clifford's level of ingenuousness and simplicity. Simple-mindedness

124

expressed it better, perhaps. 'Let's leave that until we're inside, shall we?' he suggested.

He called up Diana Pettit and together they shepherded Clifford into that grey-tiled interview room. It was dark now, of course, had been dark for two hours, and the lights in this room were as grim and uncompromising as those in the Barringdean Centre car park, but much brighter. The central heating was on in here, though, just as it was all over the building. Police officers just as much as those they interviewed, as Burden had once told someone without irony, were often obliged to sit there for hours. The immediate warmth, a much greater heat than he enjoyed in his own home, made Clifford ask to take off his hat and coat. He was one who would ask permission before he did almost anything; no doubt asking for leave had been a requirement of right conduct dinned into him from his earliest years. He sat down and looked from Diana to Burden and Burden back to Diana, like a puzzled new boy whom school rules bewilder.

'I'd like you to tell me what you're accusing me of.'

'I'm not accusing you of anything yet,' Burden said.

'What you suspect me of, then.'

'Don't you know, Clifford? Haven't you got a clue? What do you think it is – helping yourself out of the collection in church?'

'I don't go to church.' He essayed a faint smile and it was the first Burden had ever seen him give. The smile seemed contrived with difficulty as if a mechanical process had to be set in motion, a series of button-pressing and lever-pulling only half-remembered. It irritated Burden.

'Perhaps you stole a car then. Or nicked a lady's handbag.'

'I'm sorry. I don't know what you're getting at.'

Burden said abruptly. 'Have you any objection if I record this interview? Tape it, I mean?'

'Would it make any difference if I had?'

'Certainly it would. This isn't a police state.'

'Do as you like,' Clifford said indifferently and he watched Diana begin recording. 'You were going to tell me what I'm supposed to have done.'

'Let me tell you what I think happened. I think you met Mrs Robson inside the shopping centre, in Tesco's. You hadn't seen her for quite a while, but you knew her and she knew you – and she knew something about you you'd like kept secret. I wonder what it was. I don't know yet, I honestly don't know, but you'll tell me. I hope you'll tell me tonight.'

Clifford said in an uneven voice, 'When I first saw Mrs Robson, she was dead. I never saw her before in my life.'

'What you saw, Clifford, was your opportunity. You and she were alone and you very much wanted her out of the way . . .'

He had to remind himself that this was a man, not a boy, not a teenager. And not simple-minded, not retarded. He was a teacher; he had a university degree. The blank, soft face looked even more spongy, but a spark showed in each dull eye. Clifford's voice squeaked. Fear or guilt or God-knows-what had done something to the vocal cords, leaving him with a eunuch's soprano.

'You don't mean you think I'd kill someone? Me? Is that what you mean?'

Not wanting to fall in with this play-acting, this vanity – for what else would explain it? – that made a man believe he could do as he pleased without fear of discovery, Burden said drily, 'He's cottoned on at last.'

Next moment he was on his feet and Diana too, stepping back from the table. Clifford had leapt up, face and lips white as if in genuine shock, his hands grasping the table edge and shaking it, vibrating it as his mother had shaken the wire gates.

'Me? Kill someone? You're mad! You're all crazy! Why've you picked on me? I never knew you meant that with all your questions, I never dreamed . . . I thought I was just a witness. Me kill someone? People like *me* don't kill people!'

126

'What kind do then, Clifford?' Burden spoke calmly as he lowered himself once more into his chair. 'Some say everyone's capable of murder.'

He met the other man's round staring eyes. A dew of sweat had appeared all over the putty-like skin, the pudgy features, and a drop trickled down his upper lip between the two wings of the moustache. Burden felt for him an impatient contempt. He wasn't even a good actor. It would be interesting to hear how all that would play back, that stuff about killing people. He'd play it to Wexford, see what he thought.

'Sit down, Cliff,' he said, his growing contempt making him accord the man less than the dignity of his unabridged Christian name. 'We're going to have a long talk.'

Exhausted when the car dropped him at Sylvia's, Wexford would have liked a home of his own to recover in, the sole companionship of his own wife. He had to settle for a drink, the whisky Dr Crocker strictly forbade. Someone had brought in an evening paper; a story on the front page was about a man who had all day been 'helping the police with their enquiries into the Kingsmarkham bomb outrage'. There was no picture and of course no name or description, nothing to make even tentatively possible the identification of this man who had wanted Sheila dead, who had conceived for her that particular brand of cold, impersonal, political hatred.

The boys were watching television, Sylvia trying to write an essay on the psychological abuse of the elderly.

'I know all about that,' Wexford said. 'Would you like to interview me?'

'You're not elderly, Dad.'

'I feel it.'

Dora came and sat beside him. 'I've been to look at our house,' she said. 'The builders have been in and weatherproofed it. At least the rain can't get in. Oh, and the Chief Constable phoned, something about a house we can have if we like. We do like, don't we, Reg?'

A leap of the heart before he started feeling ungrateful to Sylvia. 'Did he say where it is?'

'Up at Highlands, I think. I'm almost sure he said Highlands.'

10

REMORSE was perhaps too strong a word; it was distaste tempered with a hint of shame that Burden felt throughout that weekend. He said to himself, and he even said it to his wife who was home again with their son, that this was what the job was about, this was police work.

'The end justifies the means, Mike?' she said.

'It's the merest idealism to deny that. Every day in everything we do, it's implicit even if we don't come out and say it. When we were going through that bad patch with Mark and we decided the only way was to let him cry, that two nights of that would cure him, we were saying the end justifies the means.'

He took the child on his lap and Jenny smiled.

'Don't teach it to him though, will you?'

He spared himself half an hour to play with Mark and eat his lunch and then he was back at the police station in that interview room, confronting Clifford Sanders once more. But on the way the task behind him and the task ahead goaded him, made him wrinkle up his nose at the nastiness of it. How far removed from torture was it, after all? Clifford had to sit there in that comfortless room, left alone for part of the time for as much as an hour, food brought to him on trays by an indifferent police constable. And it would not have been quite so bad if Clifford had been tougher, less like a child. He looked like a big child, a kind of fined-down Billy Bunter. A stoicism had succeeded his bewilderment, an air of being a brave boy and sticking it out a little longer. But here Burden told himself he was being a fool. The man was a man, educated, neurotic perhaps but sane, simply lacking character and strength of mind. And look what he had done. The facts spoke for themselves. Clifford had been in the shopping centre, had been seen with Mrs Robson, had a garrote in his possession, had run away.

Was it likely that he had found the body, covered it up because it looked like his mother and then fled? Nobody behaved like that outside the pages of popular psychiatry. All that stuff which Serge Olson no doubt dispensed – about neurotics choosing girlfriends because they were looking for a mother, or employers as father-figures, or being put off sex because you'd seen your mother in her underwear – that was strictly for the books and the couch as far as Burden was concerned. And he was a fool to let himself feel a sneaking pity for Clifford Sanders. The man had meant to kill Mrs Robson and had succeeded. Hadn't he gone specifically to meet her armed with a garrote?

Probably his self-doubt was due solely to his failure so far to find the link between Clifford and Gwen Robson. He knew there must be a link and once he had found it, he would no longer be a prey to this unprofessional and certainly unfamiliar guilt. Facing Clifford again, with Archbold there to assist in this renewed interrogation and the tape recorder on, Burden reminded himself that the police had interviewed Sutcliffe the 'Yorkshire Ripper' nine times before he was arrested. And in the intervening time Sutcliffe had murdered his final victim. It would be a fine thing if Clifford Sanders were to kill again because he, Burden, had been squeamish.

He lowered himself slowly into the chair. Clifford, who had been gnawing at a fingernail, snatched his hand from his mouth as if he suddenly recalled nail-biting was something he must not do.

Burden began, 'Has your mother ever been ill, Clifford?'

An uncomprehending look. 'What do you mean?'

'Was she ever ill so that she had to stay in bed? When she needed someone to look after her?'

'She had what-do-you-call-it once. Like a kind of rash, but it aches.'

'He means shingles,' Archbold said.

'That's right, shingles. She had that once.'

'Did a home help come in to look after her, Clifford?'

But this approach led nowhere. Dodo Sanders had been confined to bed for no more than a few hours throughout the whole of Clifford's life. Burden abandoned this line of enquiry and carefully took Clifford through the sequence of events from the time he left Olson until he ran from the car park out of the pedestrian gates. Clifford got in a hopeless muddle with the times, saying he had got to the centre at five-thirty, later changing it to ten-past six. Burden knew he was lying. Everything was going according to his expectations and the only surprising thing which happened was when Clifford corrected him over the use of his name.

'Why have you stopped calling me Cliff? You can call me that if you like, I don't mind. I like it.'

Awaiting him in his office was a lab report on that spool of plastic-covered wire. There was a great deal of technical detail – Burden found himself back among the polymers – but the plain fact easily sorted out was that the shreds of substance found in Mrs Robson's neck wound were quite different from the stuff coating the wire in Clifford Sanders' tool-box. Well, he had been wrong. That might only mean, of course, that Clifford had disposed of the wire he used for his garrote – thrown it in the river or, more safely, stuck it in his own or someone else's dustbin. In the meantime Clifford could sweat for a day or two. Wexford was his immediate concern, Dr Crocker had strictly forbidden the Chief Inspector to return to work at the office and to see him Burden had to drive up to Sylvia's house.

'At any rate I shall be on the spot,' Wexford said. 'I'm going to be living up at Highlands. How about that?'

Burden grinned. 'That's right. There are two or three police houses. When are you moving in?'

'Don't know yet,' Wexford said, glancing through the paperwork Burden had brought him. 'I don't think the person – a useful genderless word – that the checkout girl saw talking to Mrs Robson was Clifford Sanders at all. I think maybe it was Lesley Arbel. But I'll tell you where I agree with you — when you say Mrs Robson was a blackmailer. I think so too.'

Burden nodded eagerly. He was always disproportionately pleased when Wexford approved some suggestion of his.

'She liked money,' he said. 'She was near enough prepared to do anything for money. Look at all that stuff you told me about the old man's will. She was running up and down the street searching for witnesses to a will under which she was to be the sole beneficiary. We may laugh about her bathing someone and cutting some other old man's toenails, but weren't those normally distasteful tasks undertaken for a very inflated payment? There's probably more of that sort of thing we haven't yet uncovered.'

'Mrs Jago says she did what she did all for her husband. There's an implication that this makes it all right, exonerates her. I imagine that was precisely the way Gwen Robson saw it herself.'

'Why did Ralph Robson specifically need money anyway?' Burden asked. 'Has anyone queried that one? I mean, if I said I needed money I'd really mean Jenny and Mark and me, my family. And you'd mean you and Dora, surely?'

Wexford shrugged. 'We've looked at her bank account at the TSB. She had rather a lot in it; I mean more than one would have expected. Robson has his own personal account and they've no joint savings. But Gwen Robson had something over sixteen hundred pounds and that could be the fruits of blackmail. Your idea is that Gwen Robson had evidence Clifford had done something reprehensible and was blackmailing him?'

Burden nodded. 'Something like that. And the worm finally turned. Clifford's pretty worm-like in most respects, I'd say, so why not in that one too?'

'What could Clifford have done? It would surely have to be an earlier murder. Nobody cares much about sexual irregularities these days.'

Burden's face indicated that he did. 'Gwen Robson cared about them.'

'Yes, but you can't imagine that the cramming school would – or Dodo Sanders, come to that. It would be hard to assign any sort of moral convictions to her. She strikes me as a person who has never heard of ethics, still less ever thought she needed views about them.'

Burden wasn't interested. 'I'll find out what it was,' he said. 'I'm working on it.' He studied Wexford's face: the bruises that were fading, the cut that might or might not leave a permanent scar. 'They had to let that chap go, the one they thought was your bomber. It was on the news this morning.'

Wexford nodded. He had had a phone call about it and a long talk had ensued, culminating in a request to take part in a conference at Scotland Yard. Dr Crocker had sanctioned this with the utmost reluctance and there was no way he would have agreed had he known Wexford intended to drive there. When Burden had gone, Wexford wrapped himself up, adding a scarf of Robin's that was hanging in the hall in case Dora or Sylvia should come home early and see him. His car was on the garage drive and he noticed for the first time – no one had told him – how scarred the bodywork was by chips of flying glass. He got into the driving-seat, feeling that this was unfamiliar, a strange thing to be doing, an act he hadn't performed for a long time.

Closing the door, he thought he would just rest for a moment or two, sit there holding the ignition key. Now if this were a thriller, he thought, a television drama maybe, and he an unimportant character or even a villain, he would put the key in and turn it and the car would blow up. He tried to laugh at that but couldn't, which was absurd, because he had no memory of the explosion and the bangs he thought he heard were not memory but the invention of his imagination. Go on, jump, he said, pushing himself along the plank, easing to the edge of the springboard. He took a breath, pushed the key in, turned it. Nothing happened; the engine didn't even start. Well, why would it? Dora had left it in 'drive'. He moved the automatic shift before he realized what he was doing, the terrible step that was going to be his crossing point.

Because there was nothing now but to go on, he turned the ignition key.

Burden was walking down the High Street, occasionally looking into shop windows already decorated for Christmas, when he saw Serge Olson coming towards him. The psychotherapist wore a check tweed jacket, its collar of mock fur turned up against the sharp east wind.

He greeted Burden as if they were old friends. 'Hallo, Mike, good to see you. How are you?'

Taken aback, Burden said he was fine and Serge Olson asked if he was making much progress. This wasn't a question Burden was accustomed to being asked by those he thought of as the public and he couldn't help thinking it a shade impertinent. But he made a non-committal, vaguely optimistic reply and then Olson surprised him very much by announcing that it was too cold to stand about and why didn't they go into the Queen's Café for a cup of tea? Burden realized at once that Olson must have something he at least thought important to tell him. Why else would be make such a suggestion? For all his use of Burden's Christian name, the two men had met only once before and then strictly on a policeman-and-witness basis.

But when they were seated at a table, instead of imparting secrets of the consulting room, Olson began to talk only of the recent Arab bombers' trial, the huge sentences meted out to the three guilty men and the threat made by some allied terrorist organization to 'get' the prosecuting counsel. Burden was at last moved to ask what it was in particular that Olson had wanted to talk to him about.

The fierce bright animal eyes gleamed. There was an incongruity here, for Olson's voice was always calm and leisurely and his manner placid. 'Talk to you about, Mike?'

134

'Well, you know, asking me in here for a cup of tea, I thought there must be some specific thing . . .'

Olson shook his head gently. 'Perhaps I might say Clifford Sanders could be a killer in certain circumstances? Or that his manner was very odd when he left me that evening? Or that men of twenty-three who live at home with their mothers must be psychotic by definition? No, I wasn't going to say any of those things. I was cold and I fancied some good hot tea I didn't have to brew up myself.'

Unwilling to let it go at that, Burden said, 'You really mean you weren't going to say any of that?' Olson's head shook more rapidly. 'Surely it is odd a man living with his mother, even if she's a widow. Mrs Sanders isn't what one would call old.'

Olson said nearly incomprehensibly, 'Have you ever heard of the Fallacy of Enkekalymmenos?'

'The what?'

'It means "the veiled one" and it goes something like this. "Can you recognize your mother?" "Yes." "Can you recognize this veiled one?" "No." "This veiled one is your mother. Hence you can recognize your mother and not recognize her."'

There was something veiled about Mrs Sanders. Her own face was a kind of veil, thought Burden, surprised by his own imagination. But in a brusque policeman-like way he said, 'What's that got to do with Clifford?'

'It's got something to do with all of us and our parents, and with knowing and unknowing. Over the entrance to the oracle at Delphi were the words "Know thyself" and I'm talking about a very long time ago. In the two or three thousand years since then, have we heeded that advice?' Olson smiled and, leaving a moment for his words to sink in, added, 'She's not a widow either.'

'She's not?' This was firmer, better charted terrain. Burden checked his sigh of relief. 'Clifford's father's still living, then?'

'She and her husband were divorced years ago when Clifford was a child. Charles Sanders' people were farmers

135

and that house had been in his family for generations. He was living there with his parents when he married. Putting it bluntly, his wife Dorothy was the family servant who came in daily to clean for them. It's not known what the parents thought about that. Obviously Clifford doesn't know. You needn't look like that, Mike, I'm not being a snob. It's not her menial status that set me wondering so much as – let's say her unattractive personality. I suppose she was good-looking and in my job I've learned that in nine cases out of ten that's enough. Five years later, he left them and he gave up the house to his wife and son.'

'What about the grandparents?' Burden asked.

Olson, who had eaten two elaborate iced cakes and a slice of fruit loaf, began brushing crumbs out of his beard with a green and yellow paper napkin. 'Clifford remembers them, but only just. He and his mother had his grandmother living with them when the father left. The grandfather had just died. There wasn't much money, and Charles Sanders doesn't seem to have supported them. It was a hard, lonely sort of life. I've never been to the house, but I imagine it's a bit grim and remote. She went out cleaning, did a bit of dressmaking and I'll give her credit where it's due; she insisted on Clifford's going to university – the University of the South, that is, at Myringham – though he had to live at home and take jobs in the holidays. I don't doubt she was lonely and fancied she needed him with her.'

Burden got up to pay. He felt curiously grateful that after his earlier incomprehensible remarks, Olson had managed to avoid jargon and Greek words and talk like anyone else. But something amongst what the psychotherapist had said touched a chord in his mind, set a vibration twanging.

'I invited you,' Olson said, 'but if you'll guarantee the ratepayers will foot the bill I'll give in gracefully.'

'What was that you said about Clifford taking holdiay jobs?'

'The usual sort of thing, Mike, only even that kind of

job is harder to come by these days. Unskilled labour, a bit of gardening, shop work.'

'Gardening?' Burden said.

'I believe he did have one job like that. He told me about it at some length – largely because he hated it, I suspect. He's not keen on an outdoor life and nor am I for that matter.'

There wasn't a chance, Burden thought. You didn't get your wishes coming true like that . . . 'You don't remember the name, I suppose?'

'No, I don't. But it was an old spinster woman in a big house in Forest Park.'

11

WAITING in reception, Wexford felt the guilt that
comes from disobeying a doctor's orders. It was
really a fear of being found out, of Dora or
Crocker or Burden discovering that he hadn't gone
straight to Scotland Yard. In fact, he probably wouldn't
have phoned this woman, have come here, if he hadn't
been buoyed up by his own success at starting that car, at
driving that car, at eventually driving himself to the station
in it. Better to think of this as his reason than his anxiety
over the slow progress which was being made on the
case. Curious looks were no longer levelled at his face;
the discoloration had nearly gone. The cut was one
he might have made while shaving – if he had been
drunk, for instance, or all his life up to now had worn
a beard. The Bomb Squad people, when he presented
himself, would hardly believe he had been the victim
of an explosion. But first there was this alibi to check
and some curiosity, perhaps pointlessly aroused, to
satisfy.

The brighter coloured of the two receptionists, the one
with orange curls, kept assuring him that Sandra Dale
wouldn't keep him a moment, then no more than one
minute, finally that she was on her way. Meanwhile Wexford contemplated *Kim* covers pinned up on the carpeted
walls, photographs recording various *Kim* functions, a
framed certificate or diploma commemorating the award
to *Kim* of something or other. Someone touched him
lightly on the shoulder.

'Mr Wexford?' He started easily but she didn't seem to
notice. She was a young girl, not in the least like the
picture in the magazine. 'I'm Rosie Unwin,' she said,
'Sandra Dale's assistant. Would you like to come this way,
please? I'm sorry to have kept you.'

They went down passages and up in a lift and then up a flight of stairs and along another passage. At least it wasn't open plan, one of those office complexes where it is impossible to shut oneself away. Rosie Unwin opened a door at the end of the corridor and Wexford saw a woman seated at a desk who was scarcely more like her own photograph than her assistant was. She got up and put out her hand.

'Sandra Dale.' She hesitated. 'It really is my name.'

'Good morning, Miss Dale.'

The photograph was purposely designed to make her look older, plumper, more motherly — or 'auntly'. Wexford didn't think this woman was much over thirty; to him she seemed a young girl, slender, long-legged, with a broad-browed round face and soft blonde hair. The picture made her into someone to be trusted, confided in, someone wise whose advice one could rely on. She asked him to sit down, herself retreating once more behind her desk. The other girl came into the room after him and stood looking not altogether confidently at a visual display unit where amber-coloured letters and geometric figures danced.

'Lesley's not here,' Sandra Dale said, 'but perhaps you knew that? She's away doing a course in working those things and I'm left to manage as best I can.'

'It's you I want to talk to,' Wexford said, 'and perhaps Miss Unwin too.'

The office was large and extremely untidy, though perhaps there was method underlying the apparent disorder. Letters lay all over Rosie Unwin's desk, face-upwards, and Wexford wondered if they could be of the kind he had read in Sylvia's copy of *Kim* but decided not. He wasn't able to read any of them and those he could see were nearly all handwritten. Another pile filled Sandra Dale's in-tray. She read his mind — or rather, misread it.

'We average about two hundred letters a week.'

He nodded. There was a little library of works of reference and two shelves of books: a medical dictionary and an encyclopaedia of alternative medicine, a dictionary of psychology, Eric Berne's *A Layman's Guide to Psychiatry and Psychoanalysis*. Rosie Unwin pressed a key and the screen emptied of its dancing figures.

'Would you like coffee?' Wexford had accepted before she added, 'It'll be instant and it comes in Styrofoam.'

He said to Sandra Dale. 'You'll have heard about the woman who was murdered in Kingsmarkham – you know she was Lesley Arbel's aunt?'

'I haven't seen Lesley since it happened. I know about it of course. Lesley's been very brave, I think – very gallant, carrying on with the course – considering Mrs Robson was more like a mother to her.'

'Didn't she have a mother of her own?'

She looked sideways at him, not slyly but perhaps rather mysteriously. 'You'll say she was only my secretary, but I know a lot about her. We all know a lot about each other in here. Sometimes I think the way we work is a bit like a kind of ongoing encounter group. It must be the effect of our ... our clients.' There it was, that word again. 'Their problems – they bring things up in our own lives, I guess. Lesley wouldn't mind my telling you that her mother abandoned her when she was twelve and her aunt and uncle just took her over. She was already at boarding school so they didn't adopt her, but she was almost as much their daughter as if they had.' The phone on her desk whistled and she picked up the receiver, murmured into it, 'Yes, yes ... right,' and said to Wexford, 'Excuse me just one moment. Rosie will be with you right away.'

But for a few minutes he was left alone. Curiosity that had nothing much to do with the case in hand impelled him to read the topmost letter on Rosie Unwin's desk. He didn't even have to get out of his chair, only lean to one side. Eyesight lengthens as age comes on and Wexford thought his had become about as long as anyone's could. Holding a book at arm's length was no longer any use to him. His arms were too short.

'Dear Sandra Dale,' he read, 'I know this is awful and

horrible and I am disgusted with myself, but I can't pretend about it any longer. The fact is that I am experiencing very powerful sexual feelings towards my own teenage son. I think I am in love with him. All the time I struggle against these feelings of which I assure you I am deeply ashamed, but just the same . . .'

He had to stop and sit up straight again as Rosie Unwin came in with the coffee, but not before he had noticed that there was an address on the letter and it was signed. Strange. He had somehow assumed most letters would be anonymous.

'About point nought-nought-one per cent,' she said when he spoke these thoughts aloud. 'And most people send us a stamped addressed envelope too.'

'How do you make your selection? The ones you decide to print, I mean?'

'We don't pick the most bizarre,' she said. 'That one you were reading, that wasn't typical. You *were* reading it, weren't you? Everyone who comes in here reads the letters; they can't resist it.'

'Well, I admit I was. You wouldn't print that, though?'

'Probably not. That's for Sandra to decide, and then if there's any query it would be the editor's decision – I mean the editor of *Kim*.'

'Like going to a higher court,' Wexford murmured.

'Sandra picks out those she thinks will have the widest appeal or impact – let's say common problems, the most human if you like. We'd only print the reply to that one from the woman who fancies her own son. We'd say, "To W. D., Wiltshire," and then write our reply. I mean we do draw the line. Can you believe it, we had a letter last week from someone asking us what the protein content of semen was . . . it's about somewhere.'

Wexford was saved from replying by the return of Sandra Dale. He waited until she was seated again, then asked her, 'So you last saw Lesley when? On Thursday November 19?'

'That's right. She didn't come in on the Friday, she phoned in and told me about her aunt, though I knew then,

141

mind you: I recognized the name. And on the Monday –
Monday the twenty-third, that is – she started the computer course. It was a bit of luck, if you can call it luck in
the circumstances, that the course happened to be in the
same town where her uncle lives.'

'She left here on Thursday afternoon, did she? What
time would that have been – five? Five-thirty?'

Sandra Dale looked surprised. 'No, no, she took the
afternoon off. I thought you knew.'

Wexford smiled neutrally.

'She finished at one. It was something about having to
go down to Kingsmarkham to register for the course.
She'd filled in one of the forms wrongly, something like
that; she tried to phone the place, but their phone was out
of order. Well, according to her it was. I'll be frank with
you: I wasn't terribly pleased. I mean, I'd got to do without my secretary for a fortnight as it was, and all for the
sake of doing our page on a word processor instead
of a typewriter which had always suited us perfectly
well.'

Wexford thanked her. This was not at all what he had
expected to hear. He had hoped only to pick up from the
agony aunt's department some useful pointers to Lesley
Arbel's character. Instead he had been handed a smashed
alibi.

Rosie Unwin said as he was leaving, 'I hope you won't
mind my asking, but are you any relation to Sheila Wexford?'

He was always being asked that, so he ought not to
have experienced that clutch at the heart. 'Why do you
ask?' he responded rather too quickly.

She was taken aback. 'Only that I admire her very
much. I mean, I think she's beautiful and a great actress.'

Not that she had heard something awful on the news,
or been told of Sheila's fatal injuries . . . death . . . on
breakfast television . . .

'She's my daughter,' he said.

They liked him now, they were all over him. He should

142

have told them the minute he came in, he thought. He waited for one of them – the younger, surely – to tell him as most people sooner or later did that Sheila didn't look much like him, inferring really not so much lack of resemblance as the discrepancy between her beauty and his . . . well, lack of it. But they were tactful. They didn't say anything about wire-cutting either. He went off through the labyrinthine building with Rosie escorting him, talking of Sheila all the way, then they were taking his identification disc from him and signing him out. In half an hour's time he had an appointment at Scotland Yard for another session with the Bomb Squad, and he thought he might as well walk at least part of the distance. So he made his way across Waterloo Bridge, beneath which the river lay sluggish as oil and above him not only the sun but the sky itself was invisible.

It was three days since he had last seen Clifford Sanders and in that time Burden's enquiries had confirmed most satisfactorily that he had indeed worked as a gardener for Miss Elizabeth McPhail at Forest House, Forest Park, Kingsmarkham. Her neighbours remembered him and one of them also remembered Gwen Robson's visits. What he would have liked was to have found someone who had seen them together, talking to each other. Perhaps this was a lot to expect. Beyond a doubt, Gwen Robson had received her offer of employment as Miss McPhail's full-time housekeeper four years ago. Clifford was twenty-three and four years previously would have been a year into his university course. Burden considered his strategy. Clifford would be at work now, at Munster's; he worked all day on Tuesdays until five. He would be tired when he got home and it would do no harm for him to find Burden there waiting for him, anxious for another talk either there in the back of beyond or down at the police station once more.

Davidson drove the two of them down the long lane that went past Sundays Park. At ten to five it was already dark and pockets of fog made very slow, cautious driving essential. The ivy-clad façade of the house loomed up out of the misty dark, looking alive, looking like a gigantic square bush or a surrealist nightmare of a tree. All the leaves hung limp and gleaming, dewed with water-drops. The car headlamps alone showed him the dark glistening mass, for not a light was showing amongst the coat of foliage. What did Dorothy Sanders do there all day — her son having taken the car and no bus stop nearer than Forby or Kingsmarkham, both at least two miles distant? Once a week Clifford took her to the Barringdean Shopping Centre, had his hour-long session with Olson, went to pick up his mother. What friends did she have, if any? How well did she really know Carroll the farmer? Each, it would seem, had been deserted by a partner; they were not far removed from each other in age . . .

The door opened and she was standing there. 'You back again? My son's not here.'

Burden remembered what Wexford had said about it being hard to associate her with ethics, with any moral sense. He was aware of something else, too, something he would never have thought of himself as sufficiently sensitive to feel — a coldness emanating from her. It was hard to think of her as having a normal body temperature, warm blood. And as he reflected these things, the whole passing rapidly through his mind as he stood on the doorstep, he felt also how very much he would hate to have to touch her, as if her living flesh would feel like rigor mortis.

She would think it was the icy air that made him shiver. He said, 'We'd like a few words with you, Mrs Sanders.'

'Shut the door, then, or the fog will get in.' She spoke of the fog as if it were some sort of elemental or ghost, always waiting outside for a chance unwise invitation.

Her face was thickly and whitely powdered, the lips

painted a waxy red, her head tied up tightly in a brown-patterned scarf so that no hair showed. She was dressed in her favourite brown, jumper and skirt, ribbed tights, flat tan-coloured shoes. Following her into the living room, Burden noticed how thin and upright she was – her hips narrow, her back flat – so that it was something of a shock to see her frontal aspect reflected in the big mahogany-framed mirror, her stringy neck and the deep lines on her forehead. It was cold in there and, whatever she had said about keeping the fog out, it seemed already to have penetrated. A damp chill touched Burden's skin, the only heat in the room concentrated in the few feet around the coal fire. He glanced at the empty mantelpiece of dark grey flecked marble, the chest of drawers and cabinet in a rather dull dark wood, their surfaces equally bare.

'May we sit down?' She nodded. 'Your son worked as a gardener for a Miss McPhail of Forest Park, I believe. That would have been while he was at university?'

She detected criticism Burden had not meant to imply. 'He was a grown man. Men should work. I couldn't keep him; the grant he got didn't cover everything.'

Burden said simply, 'Mrs Robson worked as a home help for Miss McPhail.'

The words were hardly out of his mouth before he realized Dodo Sanders was going to do it again. Once more she was going to register incomprehension at the name of Robson. Robson? Who's Mrs Robson? Oh, that woman, that one who was murdered, the one whose body I found, that one. Oh yes, of course. She said none of these things but she looked them all, nodding when Burden reminded her as if recollection had come tardily.

'He didn't know her,' she said evenly in her robot's mechanical voice.

'If you didn't know her, or know she worked there, how can you know that?'

She showed no sign of awareness at having betrayed herself or her son. 'She was in the house and he was in the garden; you said that. She wouldn't go into the garden and he wouldn't go into the house. Why would he? It was a big garden.'

Burden left it and allowed a silence to fall before saying, 'Have you ever let the upstairs rooms in this house?' He asked because the idea of the furniture up there intrigued him in an awesome kind of way. He remembered Diana Pettit talking about all that furniture impeding them in their search.

'Why do you ask?' The robot was talking again, its micro-chip tone giving each word equal weight.

'Frankly, Mrs Sanders, the place is barely furnished down here and cluttered upstairs — or so I understand.'

'You're welcome to look at it if you want.' It was a cordial turn of phrase she used, but not uttered in a cordial way. So might the wolf in Red Riding Hood have said that its teeth were all the better to eat you with. The dome-like bluish eyelids half closed once more, the head went back and Dodo Sanders said, 'My son is coming now.'

Light from the Metro turning in at the gates trickled across the ceiling and down the walls. The woman didn't speak again; she seemed to be listening, to be straining in fact to hear something. There came the distant sound of a wooden door closing, a bolt being shot. Visibly she relaxed, sinking a little from the waist. Clifford's key in the lock was succeeded by the sound of Clifford's feet being vigorously wiped. He must have known by the presence of the car that Burden was here and he didn't hurry; he even pushed the door open very slowly. He entered the room, looked at Burden and Davidson without giving any sign of recognition, without speaking, and walked towards the single empty chair like someone under hypnosis.

But before he had sat down his mother did an astonishing thing. She spoke Clifford's name, just the bare Christian name, and when he turned to look slowly in her direction she leaned her head to one side and lifted her cheek. He moved towards her, bent down and planted an obedient kiss on the floury white skin.

'Can we have a talk, Cliff?' Burden found himself speaking with undue heartiness, as he might have done to a boy of ten or so who has had a fright, who requires jollying along. 'I'd like to talk to you about Miss McPhail. But first we're going upstairs to take a look round the attics.'

Clifford's head turned, his eyes rested momentarily on his mother and moved away. It wasn't exactly a glance requesting permission, more a look of incredulity that such a step might be allowed, had apparently already been sanctioned. Dodo Sanders got to her feet and they went upstairs – all four of them went. It had been a farmhouse once, so the first flight of stairs was handsome and wide, the second which led to the attics narrow and too steep to climb without grasping at banisters. At the top Burden saw closed doors all around him, smelt a cold mustiness, the smell of neglect, and an uncomfortable memory of past dreams came to him – of secrets and things hidden in lofts, of a hand coming out of a cupboard and a disembodied smiling face. But he wasn't imaginative as Wexford was. He put his hand up to a wall switch and a light of low wattage came on; then he opened the first door.

Mother and son stood behind him, Davidson behind them. The room was crammed with furniture and pictures and ornaments, but these were not arranged in any sort of order and the framed paintings were all stacked against walls. Pieces of china and books lay on the seats of chairs, cushions in a heap in the corner. None of it looked valuable, certainly not antique or even of curiosity value but dating from the twenties and thirties, a few pieces older and with turned legs and piecrust edges. Downstairs everything was clean and any assessment of Dodo Sanders' character must have included her housewifely qualities, but up here there had been no sweeping and dusting. No vacuum cleaner had been lugged up the narrow stairs. Cobwebs hung from the ceilings and gathered in the corners in fly-filled traps. Because this was in the country, in a quiet place not much frequented by motor vehicles, the dust was not thick and flocculant, but dust there was: a thin, soft powdering on every surface.

The next room was the same, except that there were two bedsteads in there and two flock mattresses and feather-beds, bundles of pink satin eiderdowns and counterpanes tied up with string, sausage-shaped bolsters covered in ticking, rolled blankets, home-made wool rugs in geometric patterns and home-made rag rugs in concentric circles of faded colours. And there were more pictures, but this time they were photographs in gilt frames.

Burden took a few steps inside this room, picked up one of the photographs and looked at it. A tall man in tweed suit and trilby hat; a woman also wearing a hat, her dress shawl-collared and with a long flared skirt; a boy between them in a school cap, short trousers, knee socks, the group redolent of the mid-thirties. Man and boy closely resembled each other; it might have been Clifford's face he was looking at, the same pudginess, the same thick lips and even the same moustache, the same inexpressive eyes. But there was something in those people that Clifford lacked, an air in all of them of . . . what? Superiority was to put it too strongly. A consciousness of social position and social duties? Still carrying the framed picture, Burden looked into the other two attics while Davidson and Clifford and his mother silently followed him. Here was more furniture, more rolled-up rugs and watercolours mounted on gold paper framed in gilt, more books and china animals, but gilded pink Lloyd Loom chairs as well and a Susie Cooper teaset tumbled on a pile of cushions embroidered with flower gardens and country cottages. It was all rather dirty and shabby and practically valueless, but none of it was sinister or suggestive of the supernatural, none of it was the stuff nightmares are made of.

What had happened? Why was it all up here? He asked himself this as they descended. It wasn't as if the furnishings downstairs were superior to this or newer; nor that there was so much furniture downstairs that the surplus had found its way up here. Indeed, it was inadequate and Burden had come to the conclusion that mother and son must eat their meals from plates on their laps. He could imagine them with TV dinners or dehydrated messes, bought to save trouble. What he couldn't picture was this woman cooking the sort of food anyone would want to eat.

'Those are my grandparents and my father,' Clifford said, putting out his hand for the photograph.

Dorothy Sanders issued an order to him as if he were a schoolboy like the one in the picture. 'Take it upstairs, Clifford; put it back where it's kept.' Burden would have been more astonished to witness a protest on Clifford's part, a hesitation even, than to see what in fact happened – automatic obedience as he went immediately up to the attics.

'I'd like you to tell me a bit about your relationship with Mrs Robson, Cliff,' Burden said when they were all downstairs once more.

'His name's Clifford. It was my name . . . and he doesn't have relationships,' his mother said.

'I'll rephrase that. Tell me about when you first met her and what you talked about. It was at Miss McPhail's, wasn't it?'

Dorothy Sanders had withdrawn down the passage towards the kitchen regions. Clifford looked rather blankly at Burden and said he had once done gardening for Miss McPhail. He too seemed to have forgotten who Mrs Robson was; Burden reminded him and asked him if he ever went inside the Forest Park house – to have a cup of tea or coffee for instance, or to bring flowers in.

'There was a cleaning lady used to give me tea, yes.'

'That was Mrs Robson, wasn't it?'

'No, it wasn't. I don't remember her name; I never heard her name. It wasn't Mrs Robson.'

His mother came back and Clifford looked at her, childlike, as if for help. She had been washing her hands and reeked of disinfectant. To rid herself of contamination from all that furniture, or from that of the two policemen?

She said, 'I've already told you she was in the house

149

and he was in the garden. I've told you he didn't know her. You people don't seem to understand plain English.'

'All right, Mrs Sanders, you've made your point,' Burden said. He wasted no more time on her and looked away. 'I'd like you to come back to the police station with me, Clifford. We can get a clearer picture of things there.'

Clifford went with them in his docile way and they drove back to town. He sat at the table in the interview room and looked across it first at Burden and then at DC Marian Bayliss. His eyes went back to Burden, then were lowered towards the tiny geometric pattern on the table-top. In a low voice, not much more than a mumble, he said, 'You're accusing me of murdering someone. It's incredible, I still can't accept what's happening to me.'

Much of the skill of a policeman in interrogation lies in knowing what to ignore as well as what to seize on. Burden said quietly, 'Tell me what happened when you first got to the shopping centre and met Mrs Robson.'

'I've already told you,' Clifford said. 'I didn't meet her, I saw her dead body. I've told you over and over. I drove down into the car park on to the second level and I was going to park the car when I saw this person lying there, this dead person.'

'How did you know she was dead?' Marian asked.

Clifford leaned forward on his elbows, holding on to his temples. 'Her face was blue, she wasn't breathing. You're beginning to make me feel what happened isn't true, that it wasn't that way. You're changing the truth with all this until I don't know any more what happened and what didn't. Maybe I did know her and I forgot. Maybe I'm mad and I killed her and forgot. Is that what you want me to say?'

'I want you to tell me the truth, Clifford.'

'I've told you the truth,' he said and then, looking away for a moment, twisting in his chair, he directed a curiously appealing gaze on Burden. His voice was the same, a fairly resonant adult male voice, but the tone was that of a child of seven. 'You used to call me Cliff. What stopped you? Was it Dodo stopped you?'

Afterwards, when he looked back, Burden thought it was at this point that he abandoned his theory of Clifford's being as sane as he and understood that he was mad.

12

LEANING over the garden gate, the new resident of Highlands surveyed the estate that would be his home for at least the next six months. It was one of those days that sometimes occur even in December, a clear sunny day of cloudless skies and a gradually falling temperature. The frost to come that night would silver all the little grass verges and turn everyone's miniature conifers into Christmas trees. On the hill behind Wexford's new home Barringdean Ring sat like a black velvet hat on a green cushion. The sky blazed silvery azure. At the bottom of Battle Lane he could see where Hastings Road turned off and make out the roof of Robson's house and the Whittons' and Dita Jago's. It was high up here, the highest point of Highlands, so that he could even see the cluster of latter-day almshouses that made up Berry Close.

The removal van, newly arrived with half the furniture from the bombed house, blocked any view he might have had of the town. Sylvia had taken the boys to school, then come with the van driver to help her mother move in. Wexford thought he would walk to work and then if he couldn't face walking home Donaldson could bring him. Dora would need their car. He went back in and said goodbye to her, looking round the bare, bleak little house, trying not to prejudge what living in these cramped quarters would be like, the neighbours and their noisy children separated from these rooms only by thin dividing walls, the strips of gardens partitioned by wire fences. More wire fences! Never mind, they were lucky to have somewhere, lucky not to have to go on living with Sylvia . . . and he reproached himself for the ungrateful thought as his kind, busy daughter came in carrying a crate of his favourite books.

The air was nippy and the sunshine warm, but sun hung low on the horizon and the shadows were long. His route down into the town took him along Hastings Road and into Eastbourne Drive. There was no one about, the streets empty of people and nearly empty of cars. This was the last day of Lesley Arbel's word-processor course, but no doubt she would spend the weekend with her uncle. It was more than two weeks since Gwen Robson's death, nearly as long since someone had tried to kill Sheila. His cuts and bruises were nearly healed, his strength returning. He had several times driven his car, felt quite calm and assured at the wheel. The bomb experts kept on coming to him or getting him to go to them, pursuing their interminable questions. Try to remember. What exactly happened after you got into the car? Who are your enemies? Who are your daughter's enemies? Why did you jump out of the car? What warned you? He could recall none of it and believed those lost five minutes lost for ever. It was only in the night-time, in dreams, that he relived the explosion – or rather, instead of reliving what he couldn't remember, conjured up new versions for himself in some of which he died or Sheila died or the world itself disappeared and he hung suspended in a dark void. But last night, instead of the roar of the bomb he had heard thin reedy music and instead of Sheila's body, he had seen wheels spinning in the darkness, circles that shone and glittered and were filled with geometric patterns . . .

Striving to dispel these ideas and look at things rationally occupied his thoughts until he reached the police station. Once there, he somehow knew before he enquired that Burden had Clifford Sanders with him and Archbold in one of the interview rooms. Late in the morning Burden came out but kept Clifford there alone, sending in coffee and biscuits. Wexford couldn't tell what Clifford looked like after this continuous ordeal but Burden was haggard, his face pale and tense and his eyes exhausted.

'You were talking about the Inquisition,' Wexford said. 'About executioners taking payment to garrote the condemned before they were burnt at the stake.'

Burden nodded, slumped in his chair, his strained face rather ghastly in the pale, bright light from the sun.

'You said you'd read about it. Well, I've read of Inquisitors suffering as much as their victims, of the strain wearing them out and brainwashing them till they get like you. It's watching the torture that does it; you have to be a very special sort of person to be able to watch torture and not be affected by it.'

'Clifford Sanders isn't being tortured. I had doubts about that earlier on, but I don't any more. He's being put through a fairly heavy interrogation but not tortured.'

'Not physically perhaps, but I don't think you can separate mind and body like that.'

'He isn't kept awake artificially; he isn't under bright lights or kept on his feet or starved or denied a drink. He isn't even here all the time; he goes home to sleep. I'm going to send him home today, now; I've had enough for today.'

'You're wasting your time, Mike,' Wexford said mildly. 'You're wasting your time and his because he didn't do it.'

'Excuse me if I differ from you there. I differ from you most strongly.' Burden sat up revived, indignant. 'He had the motive and the means. He has strong psychopathic tendencies. Remember that book you lent me with that piece in it about psychopaths? The Stafford-Clark? "The outstanding feature is emotional instability in its broadest and most comprehensive sense . . ." Let me see, how does it go on? I haven't got your memory. ". . . prodigal of effort but utterly lacking in persistence, plausible but insincere, demanding but indifferent to appeals, dependent only in their constant unreliability . . ."'

'Mike,' Wexford interrupted him. 'You haven't got any evidence. You've trumped up what you've got to suit yourself. The single piece of evidence you do have is that he saw the body and instead of reporting it, ran away. That is absolutely all you've got. He didn't know Gwen Robson. He was a gardener in a place where she popped in sometimes in her home-help role, and he may once or twice have said hello to her. He wasn't seen talking to her in the shopping centre. He doesn't and didn't possess a garrote or anything that could be made into a garrote.'

'On the contrary, he has a hard and fast motive. I can't yet prove it, but I'm convinced he committed a crime in the past which Gwen Robson discovered and started blackmailing him over. Blackmailers don't succeed for long with psychopaths.'

'What crime?'

'Murder, obviously,' Burden said on a note of triumph. 'You suggested that yourself. You said no one would care about some sex thing, it had to be murder.' His voice grew tired again as he suppressed a yawn. 'Who, I don't know, but I'm working on it. I'm probing into his past. A grandmother maybe? Even Miss McPhail herself. I'm having Clifford's past looked into for signs of any remotely possible unexplained deaths.'

'You're wasting your time. Well, not your time – ours, the public's.'

This was an accusation to which Burden was particularly sensitive. He was beginning to look angry as well as tired and his face grew pinched as it always did when he was cross. He spoke coldly. 'He met her by chance in the shopping centre, she asked for more money and after he had followed her down into the car park, he killed her by strangling her with a length of electric lead he was carrying in the boot of the car along with that curtain. This he took with him and threw away on his way home.'

'Why cover the body and run away?'

'You can't account for inconsistencies of that sort in a psychopath, though probably he thought that if he covered the body it might not be found for a rather longer time than if he left it exposed. Linda Naseem saw him talking to Mrs Robson. Archie Greaves saw him running away.'

'Mike, we know he ran away, he admits that himself. And it was a girl with a hat on that Linda Naseem saw.'

Burden got up and walked the length of the room, then came back to lean on the edge of Wexford's desk. He had the air of someone who is bracing himself to say something unpleasant in the nicest possible way. 'Look, you've had a bad shock and you're still not well. You saw what happened when you came back to work too soon. And for God's sake, I know you're worried about Sheila.'

Wexford said dryly but as pleasantly as he could, 'OK, but my mind's not affected.'

'Well, isn't it? It would be only natural to think it was – temporarily, that is. All the evidence in this case points to Clifford and, moreover, not a shred to anyone else. Only for some reason you refuse to see that, and in my opinion the reason is that you're not right yet, you're not over the shock of that bomb. Frankly, you should have stayed at home longer.'

And left it all to you, Wexford thought, saying nothing but aware of a cold anger spreading through him rather like a draught of icy water trickling down his gullet.

'I shall break Clifford on my own. It's only a matter of time. Leave it to me, I'm not asking for help – or advice, come to that. I know what I'm doing. And as for torture, that's a laugh. I haven't even approached anything the Judges' Rules would object to.'

'Maybe not,' Wexford said. 'Perhaps you should remember the last lines of that passage you like so much defining a psychopath, the bit about the ruthless and determined pursuit of gratification.'

Burden looked hard at him, looked in near-disbelief, then walked out, slamming the door resoundingly.

A quarrel with Mike was something that had never happened before. Disagreements, yes, and tough arguments. There had been the time, for instance, when Mike had lost his first wife and gone to pieces and later had that peculiar love affair – Wexford had been angry with him then and perhaps paternalistic. But they had never come to hurling abuse at each other. Of course he hadn't meant to infer that Mike was a psychopath, or had psychopathic tendencies or anything of that sort, but he had to admit it must have sounded like that. What had he meant then?

156

As with most people in most quarrels, he had said the first hurtful, moderately clever thing that came into his head.

Some of the things Mike had said he was sure were right. In his assessment of the character of Gwen Robson he was right. She would do a great deal for money, almost anything, and what she had done had led to her death. He knew that and Burden knew it too. But he had chosen the wrong person from among her possible . . . what? Clients? Perhaps that was the best word even in this context. Clifford Sanders was not Gwen Robson's murderer.

Wexford looked out of the window and saw him being shepherded out to one of the cars. Davidson was about to drive him home. Clifford neither trudged nor shuffled, he didn't walk with his head bowed or his shoulders hunched, yet there was something of desperation in his bearing. He was like one caught in a recurring dream from which to awaken is to escape, but which will inexorably return the next night. Fanciful nonsense, Wexford told himself, but his thoughts persisted in dwelling on Burden's chosen perpetrator as Davidson drove out of the forecourt and on to the road, and all that could be seen of Clifford Sanders was his solid heavy-shouldered shape through the rear window, his round cropped skull. What would he go home to? That cold, dictatorial woman, that house which was big and bare and always chilly and where, according to Burden, everything that might have made it comfortable was stored away up in the attics. Useless to ask why he stayed. He was young and fit and educated; he could leave, make a life of his own. Wexford knew that so many people are their own prisoners, jailers of themselves, that the doors which to the outside world seem to stand open they have sealed with invisible bars. They have blocked off the tunnels to freedom, pulled down the blinds to keep out the light. Clifford, if asked, would no doubt say, 'I can't leave my mother, she's done everything for me, brought me up single-handed, devoted her life to me. I can't leave her, I must do my duty.' But perhaps it was something very different he said when alone with Serge Olson.

Wexford might not have gone to Sundays that day, might have sat on his office for a long time brooding over his quarrel with Burden, but a call came through from a man called Brook, Stephen Brook. The name meant nothing, then recall came with a recollection of the blue Lancia and a woman who had gone into labour while in the shopping centre. Brook said his wife had something to tell the police and Wexford's thoughts went at once to Clifford Sanders. Suppose this woman wanted to tell him something that would put Clifford entirely beyond suspicion? She might know him. It could, with some exaggeration, be said that in a place like Kingsmarkham everyone knew everyone else. It would bring him considerable satisfaction to have Clifford exonerated and might also heal the breach between himself and Burden – without if possible Burden's losing face.

The Brooks lived at the Forby Road end of town, their home a flat in the local authority housing area of the Sundays estate. From the window of their living room Sundays Park could be seen – its hornbeam avenue, its lawns and cedars, the cars of those taking the word-processor course parked at the side of the big white house. This small room was very warm and Mrs Brook's baby lay uncovered in a wicker cradle. The Brooks' furniture consisted of two battered chairs and a table and a great many small crates and boxes, all of them covered or draped with lengths of patterned material and shawls and coloured blankets. There were posters on the walls and dried grasses in stoneware mustard jars. It had all been done at the lowest possible cost and the effect was rather charming.

Mrs Brook was all in black. Dusty black knitted draperies was the way Wexford would have described her clothes if he had had to do so. She wore wrinkled black and white striped stockings and black trainers, and a very curious contemporary madonna she looked when she lifted the baby and, unbuttoning black cardigan and black shirt, presented one round white breast to its mouth. Her husband – in jeans, shirt and zipper-jacket uniform – would have appeared more conventional if he had not dyed his spiky hair to resemble the bird of paradise flower, a tropical blue and orange. Their modulated Myringham University accents came as a slight shock, though Wexford told himself he should have known better. Both of them were about the age of Clifford Sanders, but how different a life they had made for themselves!

'I didn't tell you before,' Helen Brook said, 'because I didn't know who she was. I mean, I was in hospital having Ashtoreth and I didn't really think much about all that.'

Ashtoreth. Well, it sounded pretty and was just another goddess like Diana.

'I mean, it was all a shock really. I meant to have her at home and I was all set to do that. Squatting, you know, not lying down which is so unnatural, and three of my friends were coming to perform the proper rites. The people at the hospital had been really angry at me for wanting to have her the natural way, but I knew I could prove to them my way was right. And then of course they caught me. It was almost as if they set a trap to get me into hospital, though Steve says not – they couldn't have.'

'Yeah, that's paranoia, love,' said Stephen Brook.

'Yes, I just started these labour pains – how about that? I was in Demeter and these pains just started.'

'In what?' Wexford said before he remembered this was the Barringdean Centre's health food shop. Briefly, it had sounded like some obstetrical condition.

'In Demeter,' she said again, 'getting my calendula capsules. And I sort of looked up and through the window and I saw her outside talking to this girl. And I thought I'll go out and show myself to her and I wonder what she'll think – the way she used to go on saying she hoped I'd never have children, that was all.'

'He doesn't know what you're on about, love.'

Wexford nodded his assent to this as Helen Brook shifted the child to her other breast, cupping the soft downy head in her hand. 'Saw whom?' he asked.

'That woman who got killed. Only I didn't know; I mean, I didn't know what her name was. I just knew I knew her, then when we read in the paper that she'd been a home help and where she lived I said to Steve, that's the woman who used to look after the lady next door to Mum. I was in Demeter and I recognized her, I hadn't seen her for yonks. You see, she'd heard about the way Steve and I got married and she was all peculiar about it.'

'The way you got married?'

'Well, Steve and I didn't go to a register office or a church or anything on account of our beliefs. We had a very beautiful ceremony at Stonehenge at dawn, with all our friends there. I mean, they won't let you go up into the stones like Mummy said you used to, but it was very beautiful just being able to see Stonehenge. Steve had a ring made of bone and I had a ring made of yew wood and we exchanged them, and our friend who's a musician played the sitar and everyone sang. Anyway, the council let you have a flat even if you don't get married the official way. Mum told the lady – what was she called, Gwen? – Mummy told her that, but she was still really sniffy and when she saw me that's what she said. She said I hope you don't have children, that's all. Well, that was two years ago and I hadn't seen her since and then I did see her talking to this girl outside Demeter. They went off into Tesco's together and I was going to follow them and kind of say, look, how about that? And then I had this terrific pain . . .'

She sat there, smiling blandly, the baby Ashtoreth now recumbent in her lap and subsiding into sleep. Wexford asked her to describe the girl.

'I'm not very good at describing people. I mean it's the way they are inside that counts, isn't it? She was older than me but not all that much, and she had dark hair that was quite long and she was wearing the most amazing clothes; that's what stuck in my memory, her amazing clothes.'

'Are you saying she was smartly dressed?' Wexford understood at once that he was using very outdated terms and Helen Brook looked puzzled. She leaned forward as if she had misheard. 'Her clothes were particularly elegant?' he corrected himself, and added, 'New? Beautiful? Fashionable?'

'Well, not specially new. Elegant — that might be the word. You know what I mean.'

'Was she wearing a hat?'

'A hat? No, she wasn't wearing a hat. She had lovely hair; she looked lovely.'

A young woman ought to be able to judge the style of a contemporary. What she had told him had confirmed Linda Naseem's evidence — or had it? Hats, after all, can be temporarily taken off. If this were the same girl both she and Helen Brook had seen, it meant that Gwen Robson had met her in one of the aisles of the shopping centre and presumably walked through the Tesco supermarket with her, the two of them then leaving together for the underground car park. If it was the same girl . . .

It is rare to recognize someone at the wheel of a car. Generally, it is the car we recognize, then look quickly to identify the driver. Silver Escorts attracted Wexford's attention at present, as did red Metros, and a closer look at the one approaching showed him Ralph Robson in the driving-seat. So Lesley Arbel was without transport today . . .

'Turn round,' he said to Donaldson. 'Take me to Sundays.'

When they arrived, people were coming down the steps of the Regency mansion; the course had come to an end. There were as many men as women and most of them were young. Lesley Arbel, emerging from the open double entrance doors, stood out conspicuously from the rest by her looks and her clothes. Wexford, who when he first met her had been reminded by her sleek dressing of actresses in the early days of the talking cinema, now again recollected those thirties' films. Only in them was it possible to capture such a scene, where there was no room for doubting who were extras and who the star. But because this was not a film and Lesley Arbel no confident movie queen swanning on celluloid, her appearance was a little ridiculous by contrast with all those in tweed coats and anoraks and jackets over tracksuits. She even came rather awkwardly down those steps, her heels so high as to throw her off-balance.

The Kingsmarkham bus passed along the Forby Road, stopping opposite the gates and Sundays Lodge, and it was no doubt this bus she meant to catch. But her heels and the long tight black skirt restricted her steps and she was making very slow strutting progress towards the avenue when Wexford put his head out of the car window and asked if they might give her a lift home. It was more than a surprise, it seemed a shock, and she jumped. He had a feeling that if more comfortably shod, she would have made a run for it. However she came cautiously up to the car. Wexford got out, opened the rear door for her and she got awkwardly in ahead of him, ducking her head and holding on to her small black grosgrain hat.

'I thought we might have a talk in private,' he said. 'Without your uncle, I mean.'

She was too nervous to speak and sat with her hands in her lap, staring at Donaldson's broad back. Wexford noticed that her nails – which had protruded a good half-inch from her fingertips – had been filed down and were unpainted. Donaldson began to drive slowly down the avenue, between the lines of leafless hornbeams. The sun had just set and all the trees made a black tracery against a spectacular crimson sky.

Wexford said quietly, 'You didn't tell me you were in Kingsmarkham on the day your aunt was killed.'

She responded quite quickly and it was as if the question had been of no great significance. So might she have replied if a friend had reproached her for failing to make a promised phone call.

'No, I was upset and I forgot.'

'Come now, Miss Arbel. You told me you left Orange-tree House early because you weren't feeling well.'

She muttered, 'I *wasn't* feeling well.'

'Your illness didn't prevent your coming to Kingsmark-ham.'

'I mean I forgot it might be important where I was.'

She had been frightened, but she wasn't frightened now; this must mean he had not asked the question she feared to hear. 'It's very important where you were. I understand you came here to check that you were on this course that was to start the following Monday?' She nodded, relaxing a little, her body less rigid under the stiffly padded shoulders of her pink and black striped jacket. 'That can be verified, you know, Miss Arbel.'

'I did check up on the course.'

'You could have done that by phone, couldn't you?'

'I did try but their phones were out of order.'

'And then you went to meet your aunt in the Barring-dean Centre.'

'No!' He couldn't tell if it was a cry of denial through fear of discovery or simple astonishment that such a meeting could have been suspected. 'I never saw her, I never did! Why would I go there?'

'You must tell me that. Suppose I told you that you were seen by at least one witness?'

'I'd say they were lying.'

'As you were lying when you told me you were ill on November 19 and went home early from work?'

'I wasn't lying. I thought it wasn't important just coming down here to look at a form and check up and then go back again. That's all I did. I never went near the Barringdean Centre.'

'You came and went by train?'

She gave an anxious nod, falling into his trap.

'You were very near the centre then, considering the pedestrian entrance is in the next street to Station Road. Wouldn't it be right to say you returned to the station from Sundays and, remembering your aunt would be in the Barringdean Centre at that time because she always was, you went in and met her in the central aisle?'

It was a vehement, tearful denial she made, but again

163

Wexford had the feeling that whatever she was afraid of it was not this; it was not fear of having been seen with her aunt half an hour before her death that frightened her. And to his astonishment she suddenly exclaimed miserably, 'I'll lose my job!'

This seemed almost an irrelevancy, at least a minor matter compared with the enormity of Gwen Robson's death. He let her go, opening the door for her when the car stopped in Highlands outside her uncle's house. For a few moments he stood there, watching the house. Behind drawn curtains the lights were already on. She had gone up the path at a hobbling run and was fumbling with her key when Robson opened the door to let her in. It was closed very rapidly. Now for the long evening, Wexford thought; the making of tea and perhaps scrambled eggs, the chat about the day she had passed and he had passed, complaints about his arthritis and sympathy from her, the relief of television. What had people in that situation done before television? It was unthinkable.

Was it all out of the kindness of her heart? Was it that she had truly loved her aunt and now loved and pitied her uncle? A saint, an angel of mercy – that she must be to remain here for yet another weekend when London and her own home and friends were available to her, when there were three trains an hour to take her there. But Wexford didn't think she was an angel of mercy; she hadn't impressed him even as being particularly kind-hearted. Vanity and self-absorption don't generally go with altruism – and what was the meaning of that final impassioned cry?

Dita Jago's daughter had called to collect her little girls and Wexford said to Donaldson, 'You can take the car back and knock off if you like. I'll walk home from here.'

A momentary surprise crossed Donaldson's face, then he remembered where home now was. Wexford strolled across the road. The Highlands lights were not the gentle amber lamps of the street where his own house was but the harsh white kind, glass vases full of glare borne on

164

concrete stilts. They stained the dark air with a livid fog and turned people and their clothes reptile colours, greenish and sour brown and sallow white. Melanie and Hannah – what was their name, Quincy? – looked tubercular, their lively dark eyes dulled and their red cheeks pallid. Their mother was wearing one of her own mother's brilliant knitted creations, a sweater that probably had as many colours as a Persian carpet, a skirt of thick gathered folds on which the intricate stripes, no doubt of rich and varied shades, undulated like shadows in the wind ... only it all looked brown and grey in that light.

Nina was her name? As Wexford asked himself that, he heard Mrs Jago call her by it and Nina Quincy, having settled her children in the back of the car, went up to her mother, put her arms round her and kissed her. Strange, Wexford thought; they see each other every day ... Mrs Jago waved as the car departed; a shawl wrapped her shoulders today, a tapestry-like square with a fringed border. It seemed to suit her monumental shape, the heavy-featured face with its load of bunched coils of hair, better than contemporary dress. She acknowledged Wexford calmly.

'You're living up here now, they tell me.'

He nodded. 'How are the memoirs?'

'I haven't been doing much writing.' She gave him that look peculiar to people who have something to confide but don't know if this is the right confidant. Should I? Shouldn't I? Will I regret it once the words are out? 'Come in a moment and have a drink.'

A chat with a neighbour on the way home. A sherry. Why not? But it wasn't sherry she gave him, far from it. A kind of schnapps probably, Wexford thought: icy-cold, sweetish and unbelievably strong. It made his eyebrows shoot up, it made him feel as if his hair stood on end.

'I needed that,' she said, though there had been no alteration in her pleasant friendly manner, no gasp of relief.

The pile of manuscript was precisely where it had been when he was last in this room, a hair lying across the top

165

of the title page. He was sure that hair had been there last time. If Mrs Jago had not been writing she had been knitting, and the jungle landscape had grown several more inches from the long curled needle, palm trees now sprouting fronds and a sky appearing. The germ of an idea pushed a shoot into his mind.

'Did Gwen Robson know you were writing this book?'

'Mrs Robson?' It sounded like a measure, if not of her indifference to her dead neighbour, of the degree of acquaintance she had had with her in life. A remoteness was implied that Wexford found himself not quite believing in. 'She was only once in this house; I don't suppose she noticed.' Wexford thought for a moment that she was going to sneer, to add that Gwen Robson wasn't the kind to read books or be interested in them. But instead she said, in such sudden contrast as to be shocking, 'My daughter and her husband have parted. "Split up" is what they say, isn't it? I hadn't any idea of it, I hadn't any warning. Nina just came in this afternoon and said their marriage was over. My son-in-law left this morning.'

'My daughter's parted from her husband too,' Wexford said.

She said, rather sharply for her but with some justice perhaps, 'That's different, though. A famous actress, rich, with a wealthy husband, always in the public eye . . .'

'Only to be expected, do you mean?'

She was too old and experienced to blush; it was more a wince she gave. 'I'm sorry, I didn't mean that. It's only that Nina's got the two girls and it's terrible for the children. And women left on their own to bring up children, they lead a miserable existence. She earns so little from her job, it's only part-time. He's leaving her the house, he'll have to support them, but – if only I could see why! I thought they were so happy.'

'Who knows what goes on in other people's marriages?' said Wexford.

Leaving her, he set off to walk up the hill. Wexford's Third Law, he thought, ought to be: always live at the foot of a hill, then you'll be fresh for climbing it in the morning. It was quite a steep haul up and all the way he could see his new home ahead of him, glowering uncompromisingly from the crown of the hill. There was no garage, so his car stood outside with Sylvia's behind it and behind that another unidentifiable one that might be a neighbour's. The removal van had gone. He wasn't out of breath as he opened the gate (wooden in the wire fence) and walked up to the front door. I must be quite fit, he was thinking as he turned his key in the lock, opened the door and had his ears at once assaulted by the voice of Sylvia – shrill, cross, loud, easily penetrating these thin walls: 'You ought to think of Dad! You ought to think how you're putting his life in danger with your heroics!'

13

THE other car must have been Sheila's, rented or else a replacement for the Porsche. Both sisters were standing up, glaring at each other along the length of the room. It was a very small room and they seemed almost to be shouting into each other's faces. There was a door into the hall and another door into the kitchen and as Wexford came in through one Dora entered by the other, accompanied by the two little boys.

Dora said, 'Stop it, stop shouting!'

But the boys were indifferent. They had come in to secure a pocket calculator (Robin) and a drawing block (Ben), and they proceeded to forage for these items in diminutive school briefcases, undeterred by the slanging match going on between their mother and their aunt. Their reaction would have been different if this had been parents quarrelling, Wexford thought.

He looked from one young woman to the other. 'What's going on?'

Sylvia's reply was to throw up her hands and cast herself into an armchair. Sheila – her face flushed and her hair looking wild and tangled, though this might have been by design – said, 'My case comes up on Tuesday week, in the magistrates' court. They want me to plead guilty.'

'Who's "they"?'

'Mother and Sylvia.'

'Excuse me,' Dora said. 'I didn't say I wanted you to do anything. I said you ought to think about it very seriously.'

'I have thought about it. I hardly think of anything else and I've discussed it with Ned exhaustively. I've discussed it with him because he's a lawyer as much as . . . well, my boyfriend, or whatever you call it. And it isn't doing our relationship a lot of good, to tell you the truth.'

Robin and Ben gave up the search and carried their cases outside to the kitchen. Tactfully, Ben closed the door behind him.

It was as if this freed Sylvia to speak openly and she said in a hard, unsympathetic way, 'What she does is her own business. If she wants to stand up in court and say she's not guilty, that governments are guilty for breaking international law or whatever – well, she can do that. And when she gets fined and refuses to pay the fine, she can go to prison if that's what she likes.'

Wexford interrupted her. 'Is that what you're going to do, Sheila?'

'I have to,' she said shortly. 'There's no point otherwise.'

'But it's not just her,' Sylvia continued. 'It's all the rest of us she involves. Everyone knows who she is, everyone knows she's your daughter and my sister. What's that going to do for you as a police officer, having a daughter go to prison? This is a democracy and if we want to change things we've each got a vote to do it with. Why can't she use her vote and change the government like the rest of us have to?'

Sheila said tiredly, 'That's the biggest cop-out of all. If you had a hundred votes all to yourself down in this neck of the woods you couldn't change anything, not with a sitting Member with a sixteen-thousand majority.'

'And that's not the worst,' Sylvia went on, ignoring this. 'The worst is that when those people who tried to bomb her know what she thinks, when she gets up and says it in court, they're going to have another go, aren't they? They nearly got you by accident last time and maybe this time they really will. Or maybe they'll get you on purpose – or one of my children!'

Wexford sighed. 'I've been drinking schnapps with a lady of my acquaintance.' He glanced at Dora and gave her the ghost of a wink. 'I rather wish I'd got the bottle with me.' How wrong of me it is, he thought, that I love one of my children more than the other. 'I suppose you've got to do what you've got to do, as the current phrase has it,' he said to Sheila, but as he got up and made for the

169

kitchen door – made for the beer he trusted was in the fridge – it was Sylvia on whose shoulder he laid a caressing hand.

'Not all that current, Pop,' said Sheila.

Things calmed down. At any rate, Sylvia soon left to take her sons home and cook her husband's supper. Then Sheila and her parents went out to eat, no one yet feeling comfortable in what Dora called 'this horrid little house'. Sheila talked moodily about Ned not wanting it known that someone in his position was consorting with someone in hers, though she didn't explain what his position was and Wexford, true to his principles, wouldn't ask.

'When peace is so beautiful,' Sheila said, 'and what everyone wants, why do they treat workers for peace like criminals?'

Passing the police station on their way back from the restaurant in Pomfret, Wexford saw a light on in one of the interview rooms. Of course there was no real reason to suppose that Burden was in there with Clifford Sanders, yet he did suppose it with a chilling sense of unease. Forgetting Sheila and her troubles for a moment, he thought: I shall be embarrassed when I next see Mike, I shall feel awkward and therefore shall postpone that meeting. What am I going to do?

Burden had not meant to recall Clifford to the police station. His intention had been to call off his dogs for the duration of the weekend and let his baited creature make a partial recovery. The metaphor was his wife's, not his, and he reacted with some anger to it. He now regretted discussing the case with Jenny and wished he had stuck to the principle (never much honoured in the observance) of not taking his work home.

'I've had the same sentimental rubbish at work,' he said. He would normally have said 'from Reg', but he was too angry with Wexford even to want to think of him by his Christian name. Burden had a Victorian attitude in this area, rather in the manner of those fictional heroines who called a man William while they were engaged to him and Mr Jones after they had broken it off. 'I don't understand all this sympathy with cold-blooded killers. People should try thinking of their victims for a change.'

'So you've said on numerous previous occasions,' said Jenny, not very pleasantly.

That did it. That sent him back to the police station after his dinner and Archbold to the Forby Road to fetch Clifford again. He used the other ground-floor interview room this time, the one at the front where the window gave on to the High Street, where the tiles were shabby black and tan (like an ageing spaniel, said Wexford) and the table had a brown-checked top with a metal rim.

For the first time Clifford didn't wait for Burden to begin. In a resigned but not unhappy voice, he said, 'I knew you'd fetch me back again today. I sensed it. That's why I didn't start watching TV; I knew I'd only be interrupted in the middle of a programme. My mother knew too; she's been watching me, waiting for the doorbell to ring.'

'Your mother's been asking you about this too, has she, Cliff?'

Again Burden reflected how much like an overgrown schoolboy he looked. The clothes were so much the conventional wear of a correct well-ordered teenager at a grammar school in, say, the fifties, as to seem either a mockery or a disguise. The grey flannel trousers had turn-ups and were well-pressed. He wore a grey shirt – so that it could be worn two or three days without washing? – striped tie, grey hand-knitted V-necked pullover. It was plainly hand-knitted, well but not expertly, the hand of the imperfectly skilled evident in the neck border and the sewing up. Somehow Burden knew it had to be Mrs Sanders' work. He already had an idea of her as a woman of many activities, but who did none of them well; she would not care enough to do things well.

Clifford's face was its usual blank, revealing no emotion even when he spoke those surely desperate sentences. He said, 'I may as well tell you. I tell you all the truth now, I don't hide anything, I hope you believe that. I may as well tell you that she says I wouldn't be questioned like this day after day, on and on, if there wasn't something in it. She says I must be that sort of person, or you wouldn't keep getting me down here.'

'What sort of person would that be, Cliff?'

'Someone who would kill a woman.'

'Your mother knows you're guilty then, does she?'

Clifford said with curious pedantry, 'You can't know something that isn't true; you can only believe it or suspect it. She says that's the sort of person I am, not that she thinks I killed anyone.' Pausing, he looked sideways at Burden in what the latter thought of as a mad way, an unbalanced way. It was a sly, crafty look. 'Perhaps I am. Perhaps I am that sort of person. How would you know till you did it?'

'You tell me, Cliff. Tell me about that sort of person.'

'He would be unhappy. He'd feel threatened by everyone. He'd want to escape from the life he had into something better, but that better would only be fantasy because he wouldn't be able to escape really. Like a rat in a cage. They do these psychological experiments; they put a piece of glass outside the open door of the cage and when the rat tries to get out it can't because it bumps into the glass. Then when they take the glass away it could really get out but it won't, because it knows it gets hurt bumping itself on the invisible thing outside.'

'Is that yourself you're describing?'

Clifford nodded. 'Talking to you has helped to show me what I am. It's done more for me than Serge can.' He looked into Burden's eyes. 'You ought to be a psychotherapist yourself.' To Burden's ears it was a slightly mad laugh that he gave. 'I thought you were stupid, but now I know you're not. You're not stupid; you've opened up places in my mind for me.'

Burden wasn't sure he knew what this meant. Like most people, he didn't like being called stupid even though the term was immediately revoked. But he had a feeling that Clifford would be even franker if they were alone and so

172

he sent Archbold away, ostensibly to fetch coffee from the canteen. Clifford was smiling again, though there was nothing pleased in that smile, nothing happy.

'Are you taping all this?' he asked.

Burden nodded.

'Good. You've shown me what I'm capable of. It's frightening. I'm not a rat and I know I can't break the invisible wall, but I can force the person who put it there to break it.' He paused and smiled, or at any rate bared his teeth. 'Dodo,' he said. 'Dodo, the big bird. Only she's not, she's a little pecking bird with claws and a beak. I'll tell you something; I wake up in the night and think what I'm capable of, what I could do, and I want to sit up and scream and yell – only I can't because I'd wake her up.'

'Yes,' said Burden, 'yes.' He didn't much care for this sudden feeling he had of being in waters that were too deep for him. He had had enough too and would have liked to send Clifford home. Not very vigorously he asked, 'What are you capable of?'

But Clifford made no answer to this. Archbold came in with the coffee and at a nod from Burden left the room again. Clifford went on, 'At my age I oughtn't to need my mother. But I do. In a lot of ways, I rely on her.'

'Go on,' said Burden.

But Clifford sidetracked, saying, 'I'd like to tell you about myself. I'd like to talk about me. Is that all right?'

For the first time Burden felt . . . not fear, he would never have admitted this was fear – but apprehensiveness perhaps, a tautening of muscles, the cautionary chill of being alone with a mad person.

However, he only said, 'Go on.'

Clifford spoke dreamily. 'When I was young – I mean really young, a little boy – we lived with my father's parents. The Sanders family had lived in our house since the late seventeen-hundreds. My grandfather died and then my father's and mother's marriage came to an end. My father just walked out on us and they were divorced and we were left with my father's mother. Mother put her into an old people's home and then she moved everything out of the house that reminded her of my father and his people; she moved all the furniture and the bed linen and the china upstairs into the attics.

'We hadn't any furniture, only mattresses on the floor and two chairs and a table. All the carpets and the comfortable chairs were upstairs, locked away. We never saw anyone, we hadn't any friends. My mother didn't want to send me to school, she was going to teach me herself at home. Dodo! Imagine! She'd been a cleaner before she got married – Dodo, the maid. She hadn't any qualifications to teach me and they caught her and at last they made her send me to school. She'd walk me into Kingsmarkham every morning and come and fetch me every afternoon. It's nearly three miles. When I grumbled about walking, do you know what she said? She said she'd push me in my old pushchair. I was six! Of course I walked after that; I didn't want the others to see me in a pushchair. There was a school bus, but I didn't know I could have gone on that: she didn't want me to, it was two years before I knew I could go on it and then I did. When she wanted to punish me she didn't hit me or anything; she shut me up in the attics with that furniture.'

'All right, Cliff,' said Burden, looking at his watch, 'that'll do for now.' He realized, when Clifford was silent and got up obediently, that he had spoken as a psychotherapist might: he had spoken in the manner of Serge Olson.

A confession was what he had expected from Clifford on the previous night. That confiding manner, that unprecedented free and open way of speaking, those discomfiting references to his mother's nickname had seemed to herald it. All the time they seemed on the brink of the final revelation, the ultimate admission, but it had not come and Clifford had digressed into that account of his early youth which was the last thing Burden wanted to hear. But one good thing had resulted; he no longer felt guilt or much unease. Jenny had been wrong and Wexford had been wrong. Clifford might be mad, might well be the psychopath Burden had designated him, but he was not being terrorized or pushed over some edge or driven to desperation. He had been almost cheerful, talkative, in command of himself, and he had seemed – odd though this was – actually to enjoy their talk and look forward to more.

It must only be a matter of time now. Burden would have liked to discuss all this with Wexford. Best of all he would have liked Wexford in on his next session with Clifford, sitting there at the table, listening and occasionally putting a question of his own. Burden didn't feel like an inquisitor or torturer any more, but he did feel the responsibility, that it weighed heavily on his own shoulders.

In the morning Sheila made amends.

'Sylvia wanted me to apologize in court,' she said. 'Can you imagine? I'm to stand there and make a public retraction and say I'm sorry to a bunch of terrorists, plead guilty and promise not to do it again.'

'She didn't mean that,' Dora put in.

'I think she did. Anyway, I'm not apologizing to anyone except you and Pop. I'm sorry I made a row in your . . . new home. Especially considering I'm kind of responsible for wrecking your old one.'

She kissed them goodbye and went off to Ned and Coram Fields. Half an hour after she had gone, Sylvia rang up to apologize for what she called 'that unnecessary scene'. Perhaps she should come over and explain what she really felt about the whole Sheila-wire-cutting situation?

'All right,' Wexford said, 'but only if you'll bring me every copy of *Kim* magazine you've got in the house.'

First of all she said she was sure she hadn't any copies; then when her father told her she was like her mother and never threw anything away, she said that she only kept them for the knitting patterns. In the afternoon she turned up with a stack too heavy to be fetched out of the car at one go and Wexford himself had to make two trips to carry them. There were more than two hundred, covering a period of something like four years. He knew that nothing except Sylvia's guilty feelings would have induced her to reveal to her father such a propensity for magazine-reading – and downmarket magazine reading at that. Dora said nothing when they were brought into the small living room, but her face registered a restrained dismay as Sylvia stacked them up into a kind of tower block between the bookcase and the television table.

Her explanation and a kind of manifesto of her views on the nuclear issue and the role of public figures in civil disobedience and non-violent direct action took a long while. Wexford listened sympathetically because he knew he would have listened to Sheila, and of course he bent over backwards to be fair to the daughter he loved less. Even thinking in those terms made him feel mean and rotten. And if she was really concerned that he might get blown up again, really worried about him and his life being in danger, he ought to go down on his knees to her in gratitude for caring that much for him. So he sat there hearing it all and nodding and agreeing or gently disagreeing, trying not to acknowledge the enormous relief, the leap of the heart when the doorbell rang and, looking out of the window, he saw Burden's car at the kerb. The odd thing was that he forgot all about being embarrassed.

Burden had Jenny with him and the little boy, Mark. If Sylvia's children had been girls – a comparable pair for instance with Melanie and Hannah Quincy – they would have immediately taken the two-year-old under their wing, talked to him and played with him with a precocious maternity. But being male they merely looked at him with bored indifference and, when adjured by Sylvia to show Mark their Lego, responded with, 'Do we *have* to?'

'I was going to ask you to come out for a drink,' Burden said, 'but Jenny says she won't have any of that sexist stuff.'

Sylvia said enthusiastically, 'Absolutely not! I quite agree.'

At the old house Wexford would have taken Burden into the dining room but there was no such place here, only a corner behind a strip of counter called a 'meals area'. But the kitchen, though small, had a table in it and two chairs which there was just room to sit in if you weren't overweight and were prepared to keep your elbows close to your sides. The big fridge dominated the room. Wexford took out two half-pint cans of Abbot.

'I'm sorry, Mike . . .' he was beginning as Burden simultaneously started to say, 'Look, I do regret saying those things yesterday . . .'

Their joint laughter was shamefaced as embarrassment gripped them.

'Oh, for Christ's sake,' Wexford said, nearly groaned it. 'Let's get it over with. I never meant you had psychopathic tendencies – I mean, would I say anything so daft?'

'No more than I meant that the accident had made you – well, lose your grip . . . or whatever it was I said. Why do we say these things? They just seem to come out before you think.'

They looked at each other, each one holding his green can of beer, each rejecting the actual use of the glasses Wexford had fetched from the cupboard. Burden was the first to break the eye contact which anyway had been only momentary. He looked down, busied himself with the can fastener and said in an uneven, hearty voice, 'Look, I want to talk to you about Clifford Sanders. I want to tell you everything he's told me and hear what you think. And then I want something I don't think you'll consent to do.'

'Try me.'

'To interview him with me – sit in at one of our sessions.'

'Your what?' said Wexford.

'Sorry, I mean interrogations.'

'Tell me what he's told you.'

'I could play you the tapes.'

'Not now. Just tell me.'

'He's been going on about his childhood, about that weird mother of his. He keeps calling her Dodo and laughing. I don't want to have to think him unbalanced

177

– that is, I don't care for the idea of him getting off on the grounds of diminished responsibility – but I reckon I have to.' And then Burden told him all that had taken place at the inteview of the night before, detailing what Clifford had said.

'You don't want me there,' said Wexford. 'He'll clam up if I'm there.'

'You've changed your mind, though, haven't you? You agree with me he's guilty?'

'No, I don't, Mike. Not at all. I just see that your believing it is more reasonable than I thought it was. You've no weapon that you can trace to his hand. However you may be deceiving yourself, you've no motive, and frankly I don't think you've even got opportunity. You'll never prove it; you haven't a hope unless you get him to confess.'

'That's just what I do hope for. I'm going to have another go at him on Monday.'

When they had all gone peace descended on the little house on Battle Hill, a peace however that was not entirely silent for through the thin dividing walls could be heard neighbours' noise: light-switches clicking, inane cackles of televised laughter, children's running feet, unidentifiable crashes. Wexford sat down with the new A. N. Wilson and was absorbed in it when the phone rang.

Dora went to answer it, 'If that's anyone else wanting to come and apologize, tell them I'm quite at leisure.'

But it was Sheila. He heard Dora speak her name and heard the deep concern and shock in her voice, then he was out of that chair at a bound.

She turned to him from the receiver. 'She's all right. She didn't want us to hear it on TV first. A letter-bomb . . .'

Wexford took the phone from her.

'It was there with the rest of my post. I don't know why, but I didn't like the look of it. The police came like a shot and they took it away and did I don't know what to it and it blew up . . .!'

She started sobbing, her words no longer comprehensible, and Wexford heard a man's voice murmuring comforting things.

14

'MY grandmother Sanders had some money, but she left it all to my father,' said Clifford. 'I never saw my father again. He went away when I was five; he didn't even say goodbye to me. I can remember it all quite well. He was there when I went to bed and in the morning when I woke up he was gone. My mother just said to me that my father had left us, but that I should see him quite often – that he would come to see me and take me out. But he never did come and I never saw him again. It's no wonder my mother didn't want anything about the place to remind her of him; it's no wonder she put all his family things up there in the attics.'

Involuntarily, Burden followed his glance upwards to the cracked and rather discoloured dining-room ceiling. Beyond the french windows a thin mist hung over the wintry garden, and the hill that hid the prospect of Kingsmarkham was a grey, treeless hump. It was Sunday afternoon and at a quarter-past three already growing dark. Burden had not intended to come here – had meant, as he told Wexford, to postpone any further interrogation of Clifford until the following day. But as he was finishing his lunch Clifford had phoned.

There was no reason why he shouldn't have found Burden's home number, it was there in the telephone directory for anyone to see, but Burden was astonished to get the call, astonished and encouraged. A confession was surely imminent, an intuition he had which was very much substantiated by the low, wary tone in which Clifford spoke – as if he feared being overheard – and the sudden haste with which he rang off as soon as Burden said he would come. The suspicion was inescapable that Dodo Sanders had come into the room; another word and she would have guessed what Clifford was up to and surely tried to stop him.

It was Clifford who had admitted him to the house. His mother put her head round the door of what was perhaps some kind of washroom and stared, saying nothing. Her head was swathed in a towel, obviously because she had just washed her hair in spite of visiting the hairdresser three days before. But this brought to Burden's mind what Olson had said about the fallacy of 'the veiled one'. Of course he had not meant anything of this sort, that particular veiling surely referring to hidden aspects of personality or nature. The turbanned head ducked back and the door closed. Burden looked at Clifford, whose appearance was much as usual. He wore his school uniform clothes, no concession to the casual having been made for Sunday. Yet there was a subtle change in his manner, something indefinable that Burden couldn't put his finger on. Up until yesterday, he had come into Burden's presence grudgingly or with injured outrage or even straight fear. This afternoon Clifford had admitted him to the house not as one might a friend, not that, but at least as some visitor whose call was a necessary and inevitable evil, a tax inspector perhaps. Of course it must be remembered that he had come at Clifford's personal invitation.

A fire had been lit in the dining room and it was fairly warm. Burden was sure Clifford had done this himself. He had even drawn up two of the dining chairs to the fireplace – hard upright chairs, but the best he could offer. Burden sat down and Clifford launched at once into this resumed story of his life.

'Children don't question what they live on, where the money comes from, I mean. I was a lot older when my mother told me that my father had never paid her a penny. She tried to force him to pay her through the court, but he couldn't be found; he'd just deserted her and disappeared. And he had a private income, you know; I mean he had investments of his own, just enough to live on without working. She had to go out cleaning to keep us and then she made things, sort of cottage industry things – bits she knitted and sewed. I was nearly grown-up before I knew any of this. She never told me before. I was at school while she was working and of course I never guessed.'

Burden didn't know what questions to ask, so he said nothing. He just listened, thinking of his confession, pinning faith on that. The recorder was on the dining table; Clifford had placed it there himself.

'I owe her everything,' Clifford went on. 'She sacrificed her whole life to me, wore herself out to keep me in comfort. Serge says I needn't think of it like that, that basically we all do what we want and that was what she wanted. But I don't know. I mean I do know intellectually, I know he's right, but that doesn't do away with my guilt. I feel guilty about her all the time. For example, when I left school at eighteen I could have got a job; someone I knew at school, his father actually offered me an office job, but my mother insisted on my going to university. She always wanted the best for me. Of course I got the maximum grant, but I was still a drag on her; I wasn't earning money except for a bit I got from gardening for people like Miss McPhail. When I got to Myringham University I never lived in; I came back home every night.' Clifford shifted his eyes, looking quickly into Burden's and then away. 'She can't be left alone at night, you see. Not in this house, at any rate, and she always is in this house. She hasn't anywhere else to go, has she?' He made the astounding statement with low-key carelessness, 'She's afraid of ghosts.'

Another little shiver exacerbated Burden's discomfort and he found himself nodding, murmuring, 'Yes, yes, I see.'

It was quite dark outside now. Clifford drew the brown velvet curtains, remained standing, holding the border of one of them rather too tightly and clutching it in a fist. 'I feel guilty all the time,' he said again. 'I ought to be grateful, and I am in a sort of way. I ought to love her, but I don't.' He lowered his voice, glanced at the closed door and then, bending towards Burden said in a near-whisper, 'I hate her!'

Burden just stared at him.

'My other grandmother died, the one called Clifford,' Clifford said, sitting down once more. He smiled in a slightly contemptuous way. 'My mother's mother, that was. My mother got her furniture and the money she had in the Post Office. It wasn't much, just enough to buy a secondhand car. We got that Metro and I learned to drive. I can learn things, I'm quite good at that. Not much good at earning my living though, and I feel guilty about that too, because there's a part of me knows that I ought to be able to pay my mother back for all she did for me. I ought to – well, buy her a flat to live in where she wouldn't be afraid of the ghosts and then I could stay on alone here, couldn't I? Actually, I think I'd like that. She'd take the glass wall with her and . . .'

The door was suddenly opened and Dodo Sanders stood there in her brown clothes, flat polished lace-up shoes, the white lined face on those trim shoulders always a shock, the scarlet mouth a clown's painted gash. A fresh turban concealed her hair which under the brown-patterned scarf was perhaps done up in curlers. She looked at her son, then slowly turned her head to fix her eyes on Burden. He tried to avoid meeting those eyes but he failed.

'You're wrong if you think he killed that woman.'

Burden thought of that machine voice on his tape, wondering if it would sound more or less metallic. 'Whatever I may think, Mrs Sanders,' he said mildly, 'I'm sure I'm not wrong.'

'It's impossible,' she said. 'I should know. My instincts would know. I know all about him.'

Clifford seemed about to bury his head in his hands, but instead he sighed and said to Burden, 'Could we talk some more tomorrow?'

Burden agreed, feeling confused and helpless.

Nothing had happened to her; she was all right. The letter had been sent to 'the occupier' and perhaps had not been meant for her or indeed anyone specific – was possibly a mere wanton arbitrary missive of destruction directed at whichever tenant of the flat might have the misfortune to open it. Wexford told himself all this as he descended Battle Hill, his umbrella up against the ferocious rain of Monday morning. But he didn't believe it. Coincidence had not that long an arm.

Next week she would appear in court to be charged, he supposed, under the Criminal Damage Act of 1971, and he repeated the charge over to himself: 'That you on Thursday, 19th November, at RAF Lossington in the County of Northamptonshire, had in your custody or under your control a pair of wire-cutters and did use them without lawful excuse to damage certain property, namely the perimeter fence belonging to the Ministry of Defence . . .' Something like that. Dora was right and Sylvia and Neil were right. She had only to make a statement in court to the effect that her action had been misguided – plead guilty, pay her fine, do no more. They would leave her alone then; they would let her live. He was tempted for a moment, seeing it briefly as such a small thing, such an easy thing to do in exchange for life and happiness, remarriage, children perhaps, a glorious career. But of course she couldn't do it. He almost laughed out loud at the idea, walking down there through the rain, and suddenly felt a lot better.

It wasn't Ralph Robson who admitted him to the house, but Dita Jago. Wexford furled his dripping umbrella and left it in the porch.

Mrs Jago said: 'We came in to see if we could get anything for him while we're out.'

Nina Quincy was sitting in that cheerful but somehow comfortless room, having taken her daughters to school, and Robson was in an armchair on the opposite side of the fireplace. He had taken up the hunched, lopsided attitude arthritic people adopt to minimize suffering, one leg stretched out, one shoulder raised. But even so his owl's face was sharp with pain. Dita Jago's daughter provided a cruel contrast to him, not only young and beautiful but blooming with beauty and health. Her face, innocent of make-up, was rosily flushed and her dark eyes bright; dark chestnut hair fell below her shoulders in a mass of waves. She had something of the appearance of a healthy Jane Morris, but Rossetti would have resisted painting anyone as fit and flourishing as she. Both women wore garments of unmistakable Jago manufacture, the younger a tunic of dark chenille patterned all over with stylized crimson and blue butterflies. In a stiff, rather formal way her mother introduced her to Wexford.

She held out her hand, said unexpectedly, 'I must tell you how I admire your daughter. We loved her in that serial. Not much like you, is she?'

It was a little meagre voice to emanate from so much rich, colourful beauty and momentarily he marvelled that someone could look so intelligent yet in a couple of sentences reveal she was not. He acknowledged her comment with a small, dry shake of the head and turned to Robson.

'Your niece has gone back to London, has she?'

'She went last evening,' Robson said. 'I shall miss her; I don't know what I'll do without her.'

Dita Jago said with unexpected briskness, 'Life must go on. She's got her living to earn, she can't stay here for ever.'

'She got down to it and spring-cleaned the whole blessed house for me while she was here.'

Spring-cleaning in December? It was an activity, anyway, which Wexford had imagined must be obsolete. Hard, too, to picture the exquisitely dressed and coiffed Lesley Arbel brushing ceilings and washing paint. His raised eyebrows elicited more information from Ralph Robson.

'She said she might as well give the place a complete turn-out while she was here. Not that it needed it; Gwen kept it like a new pin, as far as I could see. But Lesley insisted; she said she didn't know when I'd get it done again and she was right there. She had all the cupboards out, and the wardrobes, went through Gwen's clothes and took them off to Oxfam. Gwen has a good winter coat —

only bought it last year and I thought Lesley might have liked to keep that for herself, but maybe it wasn't smart enough for her.'

Wexford saw Nina Quincy's lips twitch, her eyes shift if not quite cast up as Robson went on, 'She even went up in the roof, but I said to leave that; I said you can't take the blessed Hoover up there. There was no need to lift up fitted carpets either. But when Lesley does a thing she does it thoroughly and the place is like a new pin, spotless. I shall miss her, I can tell you; I'll be lost without her.'

Nina Quincy got up. Her attitude, her look showed her as a woman easily and quickly bored, needing new sensations. She yawned and said, 'Shall we go if you've got that list?'

Wexford parted from the two women when they reached the gate. Again he marvelled at Mrs Jago's light, springy tread as she made for the car under the yellow and black golfing umbrella her daughter held up over them. For no reason apparent to him at that moment, he found himself thinking of Defoe who had written his *Journal of the Plague Year* as if it were autobiography, as if he had witnessed the plague's horrors instead of being an infant at the time.

Burden was in his office, awaiting the arrival of Clifford Sanders whom Davidson had gone to fetch. Clifford had asked on the previous day if they could talk again this morning and Burden was puzzled by the request, or had been for a while after it was made. But now his hopes had rallied and his expectation of a confession was restored.

When Wexford came in he said, 'I never thought I'd see the day when the hottest suspect in a murder case started asking to help us with our enquiries.'

It was delicate ground for Wexford and he put on a look of polite interest.

'He actually wants to come here this morning. I suppose it's one way of skiving off work.'

Wexford just looked at him. 'I'll tell you an interesting thing. Lesley Arbel's been spring-cleaning Robson's house,

186

turning out all the cupboards, been up in the roof pretending to want to vacuum-clean it, had the carpets up. What was she looking for?'

'Maybe she was just cleaning.'

'Not she. Why would she? The house was clean enough for any normal person not a fanatic already. Young girls these days aren't mad about cleaning, Mike. They don't know how to do it, or else they don't care. It would have been a different matter if she'd come down to be with Robson and found the place in a mess. Then she might have cleaned up – if she was exceptionally kind and thoughtful for her age . . . which she's not. And then there's the matter of her fingernails. Her nails were long and varnished earlier last week, but when I saw her last Friday they'd been cut short. That means she either broke a nail cleaning or thought it wiser to cut her nails before the cleaning started. And I should think she was the kind of girl who would be as proud of her long red nails as any Chinese emperor's concubine.'

'Maybe she had to cut them for the computer.'

Wexford shrugged. 'No different from a typewriter keyboard, is it? She'd been typing with long nails for years probably. No, she sacrificed her nails in order to perform the supremely generous task of cleaning her uncle's house.'

'What is it you're trying to say?'

'That she wasn't cleaning, or that the cleaning was incidental or an excuse to make to Robson. She was looking for something; she was turning the house upside down, lifting up the carpets, going up in the loft in search of something. I don't know what it was, though I've got a few ideas. I don't know if she found it, but I think the search was what brought her here and kept her here so long, not devotion to Robson. And I don't think we'll see her here again very much, either because she found what she was looking for or because she realizes she isn't going to find it. And that means it isn't in the house or that it was very cleverly hidden indeed.'

Instead of asking the obvious question, Burden said, 'We haven't searched the place ourselves. Should we?'

Wexford was hesitating when the phone rang and Burden picked up the receiver. Apparently Clifford had arrived.

'I'll have to go. What was she looking for, anyway?'

'The documentary evidence on which Gwen Robson based her blackmailing activities, of course.'

'Oh, there wasn't any of that,' Burden said breezily. 'It was all hearsay, all just what she'd heard or suspected.' He didn't wait for Wexford's reply, but went off down to the interview room on the ground floor, the one done up in shades of ancient spaniel. Rain was streaming down the window, making the glass opaque. Clifford sat at the table with a styrofoam beaker of coffee in front of him, Diana Pettit on the opposite side reading the legal page of the *Independent*. She got up and Burden gave her the sideways nod that meant to leave them with the tape recorder running. Clifford half rose and put out his hand; Burden was so surprised that he had shaken it almost before he knew what he was doing.

'Can we start?' Clifford asked eagerly.

It was difficult for Burden to handle this. For the first time in his career as a policeman he had the feeling that he had been insufficiently trained or that a branch of his training had been neglected. 'What is it you want to tell me?' he asked in a voice he knew sounded tentative and unsure.

'I'm telling you about the sort of person I am. I'm talking about my feelings.' Clifford's eyes moved and to Burden's astonishment a mischievous gleam appeared in them; it was so incongruous as to be shocking. He laughed gleefully. 'I'm trying to tell you what made me do it.'

'Do it?' Burden leaned forward across the table.

'Do what I do,' Clifford said blandly. 'Lead the life I do.' He laughed again. 'That was a joke. It was meant to make you think I was going to say "murder Mrs Robson". Sorry, it wasn't very funny.' Drawing a long breath, he made a throat-clearing sound. 'I am a prisoner. Did you know that?'

Burden said nothing. What was there to say?

188

'I am my own jailer, Dodo has seen to that. Why does she want that, you ask? Some are born to be jailers. It's for power. I am the first person she has really had in her power, you see – the only one. The others resisted, they got away. Shall I tell you how she met my father? My father was quite an upper class sort of person, you know; he had an uncle who was the High Sheriff of the county. I don't know what that really means, but it's very important. My grandfather was a gentleman farmer, he owned three hundred acres of land. It was all sold when my father was young so that they could keep on living in the style they were accustomed to. A lot of Kingsmarkham is actually built on my grandfather's land.'

Looking at him with mounting exasperation, Burden felt resentful at the stupid trick which Clifford had tried to play on him, pretending he was about to make a confession. And Clifford said, annoying him still further, 'Your own house, wherever that is, is probably on a bit of land that was my family's.'

Clifford drank his coffee, clasping the small beaker in both hands and affording Burden a close-up of his cruelly bitten nails. 'Dodo came to work for my father's parents as a cleaner. That surprises you, doesn't it? Not a maid – oh, no – but a daily cleaner they had to do the rough work. They had had maids, and a chauffeur, but that was before the war. After the war they had to make do with my mother. I don't know how she got my father to marry her. She says "love" but she would. I wasn't born till they'd been married two years, so it wasn't that. Once she was married, she wanted to own the place, to be the boss and the jailer.'

'How can you know that?' Burden found himself saying uncomfortably, for he was beginning to understand what Olson had meant with his fallacy of recognizing and not recognizing.

Clifford seemed to underline this when he went on, 'I know my mother. My grandfather died; he was very old and he'd been ill a long time. As soon as the funeral was over, my father left us – the very next day it was, I can remember all that. I was five, you see. I can remember going to the funeral with my mother and my father and my grandmother. I had to go; there wasn't anyone to leave me with, it was before I started school. My mother wore a bright red hat with a little veil and a bright red coat. It was new and she'd never had it on before and when I saw her in it I thought that was what women wore to funerals — bright red. I thought it must be the correct thing because I'd never seen her in that colour before. When my grandmother came down, she was in black and I said to her, "Why aren't you in red, Grandma?" and Dodo laughed.

'Now I'm grown-up, I've sometimes thought it was wrong of my father to abandon his mother. I mean, it was wrong of him to go anyway, but doubly wrong really to leave his mother with Dodo. Of course I didn't think about that when I was a child. I never thought much about my grandmother and what her feelings were. My mother put her into an old people's home; it wasn't long after my father left, only a few days. She didn't say goodbye either, just went out and never came back. I asked my mother how she managed it — I mean, I asked years later when I was in my teens. Somebody had said how hard it was to get old people into those council homes. My mother told me about it, she was proud of it. She had a hired car come round — it was when minicabs first started — and told my grandmother they were going for a drive. When they got to this home, she took her in and just said to the matron or whoever it was that she was leaving her there and they'd have to look after her. Dodo doesn't mind what she says to people, you see; that's one of the things that gives her power. People say to her, "I've never been spoken to like that in my life" or "How dare you?" but it doesn't bother her; she just looks at them and says something else awful. She's got through the inhibition barrier, you see, the inhibition on being rude.

'My grandmother lived another ten years, all the time in that home and then in a geriatric ward. The social services tried to get my mother to take her back but they couldn't force her to, could they? She just refused to let them in the house. But before that, as soon as the minicab brought her back in fact, she moved all the furniture upstairs. Mr Carroll, the farmer – he and his wife were the only people I remember we ever saw. They weren't friends but they were people we knew, the only people. My mother got him to help her take all that furniture up into the attics and then when –'

'What's all this leading up to, Clifford?' Burden put in.

Clifford ignored him, or appeared to ignore him. Perhaps he responded only to what he wanted to hear. His eyes were on the window. The rain had slackened and the streaming water separated into trickling droplets between which a green-grey blur could be seen and a lowering overcast. But perhaps he saw nothing and the sense of sight was shut. Burden felt uncomfortable and his discomfort increased with every sentence Clifford spoke. All the time he was expecting some sort of climax or explosion, expecting Clifford to jump up and begin screaming. But for the present the man on the other side of the table seemed locked in an unnatural calm.

He went on in a lighter, more conversational tone, 'When I was disobedient or offended her in some way, she'd lock me up in one of those attics. Sometimes it would be the one with all the photos in and sometimes with the beds and mattresses. But I got to know I'd always be let out before it got dark. She wouldn't go up there in the dark because she's afraid of ghosts. I think the supernatural is the only thing my mother *is* afraid of. There are bits of our garden she won't go near after dark – well, in the daytime, too, come to that. I used to sit in the attic looking at all those faces.'

'Faces?' repeated Burden in a hollow tone.

'In the photos,' Clifford said patiently. He was silent for a moment and the inspiration came to Burden to do as Serge Olson did, to take off his watch and lay it on the table in front of him. Clifford's eyes flickered as he observed the movement. 'I used to study the faces of my ancestors and think to myself, all those ladies in long skirts and big hats and all those men with dogs and guns, all of them had just ended up in me, that's all they'd come to in the end – me. I'd watch the light fade till I couldn't see the faces clearly any more and when that happened I knew she'd come. When she came it would be quite slowly, taking her time, and then the door would slide open and in a nice quiet pleasant sort of way, just as if nothing had happened, she'd tell me to come down and that my tea was ready.'

Burden said wearily, picking up the watch, 'Time's up, Clifford.'

He rose obediently. 'Shall I come back this afternoon?'

'You'll hear from us.' Burden almost said, 'Don't call us, we'll call you,' and then, standing alone in the room after Clifford had been taken away, asked himself with near-disbelief what he thought he was doing. Didn't he expect an admission of guilt? Wasn't that what it was all about? He went up to his own office and began looking through the reports which were the result of seemingly fruitless efforts on the part of Archbold and Marian Bayliss to find evidence of unsolved murder in Clifford's past. Both grandmothers had died natural deaths, or so it seemed. Old Mrs Sanders had died after a heart attack in the council home where her daughter-in-law had dumped her; old Mrs Clifford had been found by a neighbour dead in her bed at home. Elizabeth McPhail had died in hospital after months of incapacity caused by a stroke.

Still, he must keep on questioning him – that afternoon if necessary, and next day and the day after, every day until Clifford reached the present and finally told him in that monotonous voice that he had killed Gwen Robson.

Wexford was in the Midland Bank in Queen Street. It was four-thirty and the bank had been closed to customers for the past hour. The manager had been cooperative and answered all his questions without protest. Yes, Mr Robson had an account at the branch but no, Mrs Robson – who hadn't banked there anyway – had nothing on safe deposit. Wexford hadn't really expected it. Whatever Lesley Arbel had been searching for was hidden elsewhere – or Lesley had already found it. The manager was plainly unwilling to tell him anything about Mrs Sanders' account, also at the branch, presumably because she wasn't dead.

He came out into grey drizzle, into early dusk. The greengrocer's display looked glistening wet even though the awning was up, a sheen like dew on green leaves and citrus rind. Behind the bow window of the boutique skimpy clothes in fruit-salad colours shimmered. Into the tawny-lit warmth of the wine market Serge Olson was disappearing, passing in the doorway a man who was also known to Wexford: John Whitton, Ralph Robson's neighbour. His baby nestled fast asleep against his chest in a carrying sling; the older child, muffled to the eyes in knitted wraps and quilted nylon, grasped with a gloved hand the hem of his Barber jacket, for Whitton's arms were fully occupied with his two carrier bags of wine. He looked at Wexford without recognizing him and made for the Peugeot estate car parked at the kerb. The meter had no more than a couple of minutes to run and a traffic warden was already bearing down.

Whitton put the baby into a cot on the back seat, the wine on to the floor, and had no sooner straightened up than the crying began. The three-year-old clambered in, viewing its brother or sister with that dispassionate mild interest children often show towards a younger sibling in distress. Wexford watched because he was wondering how poor Whitton was going to extricate the car without touching the one in front or the one behind, though 'touching' was hardly the word for what had recently been done to the Peugeot; its offside headlamp had been smashed and the metal surround buckled. Nevertheless he would have turned away, knowing the dreadful irritation of being watched while one is manoeuvring a car, had Whitton – now in the driving-seat – not called out to him.

'I say, would you mind awfully telling me how near I am?'

Those people who stand in front of drivers, beckoning and holding up a warning hand – Wexford had often been exasperated by them, had long ago resolved never to join their number. It was different, though, when one was invited. The car crawled forward and he signalled to Whitton to stop when within an inch of the rear mudguard of the Mercedes in front.

'You ought to make it on the next lock,' he said as Whitton reversed.

And then Whitton did recognize him, speaking above the baby's frenetic yells: 'You came to talk to me about Mrs Robson.' The engine stalled and he swore, made an effort, smiled. 'I shouldn't lose my cool like that. That's what happens when you do.' A thumb cocked towards the left side of the car's bonnet indicated what he meant. 'My wife had a bit of a contretemps with a parking meter here three weeks ago.'

Wexford knew Whitton was telling him this because he was a policeman, because like so many of the public he thought all policemen, whatever branch of the force they belonged to and whatever their rank, were equally pre-occupied by traffic offences. In a moment he would be defending his wife lest Wexford whipped out a notebook . . .

'Mind you, she didn't so much as scratch another vehicle, which was a miracle considering the way this young fellow in a Metro got at her.'

A polite, 'Really?' and a short preamble to saying good-bye were on the tip of Wexford's tongue. Instead he said rather quickly, though knowing it was a long shot, 'When exactly was this, Mr Whitton?'

Whitton liked talking. Without being exactly garrulous, he liked a chance to talk and naturally he would, having taken over the role long assigned exclusively to women where he was locked into a daily relationship with children too young for conversation. First, however, he reached into the back of the car and picked up the baby off the back seat, its cries at once fading to whimpers. Amused, Wexford saw that he was settling down for a long, companionable talk . . . and then he wasn't amused any more, but excited.

'Three weeks ago, as I said. Well, as a matter of fact, it must have been the day Mrs Robson was killed. Yes, it was. Rosemary had the car that day and she was picking up our fruit and veg on the way home. A quarter-to-six maybe, ten-to . . .?'

15

IT was Burden's idea to have him up in his office rather than in either of the interview rooms. He couldn't stand any more of those vinyl tiles and the blank walls and the metal rim round the table. It wasn't any less warm down there than up here, but there was a sense of chill, a feeling that draughts crept in between plaster and window frame and under the unpanelled door with its corroded metal handle. So Clifford was brought upstairs and he came in as if paying a social call – smiling, hand outstretched. Burden wouldn't have been surprised if he had asked him how he was, but Clifford didn't do that.

The blinds were down and the lights were on. They were soft lights though, coming from an angled lamp on the desk and two spots on the ceiling. Burden sat down behind the desk and Clifford in front of it, in a chair with padded seat and wooden arms which Diana Pettit pulled out for him. She was still in the room, sitting near the door, but he seemed unaware of her presence. He was wearing a different grey shirt, this one with a button-down collar, and his pullover was of a darker grey with a cable pattern but errors had been made in the knitting of the cables. Burden found himself compulsively staring at one of these flaws up near the left shoulder, where the knitter in twisting the cable had passed the rib over instead of under the work.

'I'd like you to tell me about your relations with your other grandmother,' Burden began. 'Mrs Clifford, I mean, your mother's mother. Did you see much of her?'

Instead of answering, Clifford said, 'My mother's not all bad. I've given you a bad impression of her. She's really like everyone else, a mixture of bad and good, only her Shadow's very powerful. Can I tell you a story? It's a

196

romantic story really; my grandmother Clifford told it me.'

'Go on,' encouraged Burden.

'When my mother was a little girl they lived in Forbydean, her and her mother and father. She used to go to school past Ash Farm on her bicycle and she got to know my father, who was a bit younger. Well, they played together; they got to play together whenever they could, which was mostly in the holidays because my father was away at his prep school. When she was thirteen and my father was twelve, his parents found out about the friendship and put a stop to it. You see, they thought their son was a lot too good for my mother even to play with: they said a farm labourer's daughter wasn't good enough for their son. And my father didn't put up any sort of resistance; he agreed with them, he hadn't understood before, and when my mother came round next time he wouldn't speak to her, wouldn't even look at her. And then my grandmother came out and told my mother she must go home and not come any more.'

Burden nodded abstractedly, wondering how long all this was going to take. It wasn't an unusual story for this part of the world at that period. Similar things had happened to his own contemporaries, forbidden for reasons of social snobbery to 'play in the street'.

Clifford went on, 'I'm really telling you this to show you the good side of my mother. I said it was romantic. Later on, you see, she went to work for them and they didn't recognize the little girl they'd prevented from playing with their Charles. And *he* didn't until she told him after he'd married her. I wonder what they all thought then?'

Burden was not sufficiently interested to hazard guesses. 'Did your grandmother Clifford come to see you when you were a child? Did you visit her with your mother?'

Clifford sighed. Perhaps he would have preferred to continue his speculations about the romantic story. 'I sometimes think I spent my childhood walking. I walked through my childhood, if you know what I mean. It was the only way to get anywhere. I must have walked hundreds of miles, thousands. My mother doesn't walk that fast but I was always breathless, trying to keep up with her.'

'You walked to your grandmother's, then?'

Clifford sighed again. 'When we went, we walked. There was the bus, but my mother wouldn't pay bus fares. We didn't go to my grandmother's very much. You have to understand that my mother doesn't like people and she didn't particularly like her mother. You see, my grandfather died very suddenly, then when my father walked out and my grandmother Sanders went into a home we were left alone with the house to ourselves. I think she liked that.' He hesitated, looked down at his bitten nails, said half-slyly, 'And she likes me, so long as I'm obedient. She moulded me into a slave and a protector. She made me like Frankenstein made the monster, to go wrong.' A small shrill laugh, which might have moderated those words, somehow made them the more terrible.

Burden looked at him with a kind of uneasy impatience. He was framing a question about Mrs Sanders' mother, a wild idea coming to him of Gwen Robson possibly having once been to her as a home help, when Clifford went on: 'Once when I wouldn't do what she wanted, she locked me in the attic with the photographs and she lost the key to the room. I don't know how she lost it – she never told me, she wouldn't – but I expect she dropped it down the plughole or it fell down a crack in the floor or something. She's accident-prone, you see, because she doesn't think about what she's doing; her mind's always on something else. So I expect that's how she lost the key. She's very strong even though she's small and she tried to break down the door by putting her shoulder to it, but she couldn't. I was inside, listening to her crashing at the door. It was winter and starting to get dark and she was frightened; I know she was frightened, I could feel her fear through the door. Maybe the ghosts were creeping up the stairs after her.'

He smiled, then laughed on a high shrill note, wrinkling

up his nose as if in a mixture of pleasure and pain at the memory. 'She had to go and get help. I was scared when I heard her go away, because I thought I was going to be left there for ever. It was cold and I was only a little kid, in there in the half-dark with that old furniture and all those faces. She took the bulbs out of the sockets, you see, so that I couldn't put the light on. But that meant *she* couldn't put the light on either . . .' Another smile and rueful shake of the head. 'She went to get Mr Carroll and he came back with her and put his shoulder to the door and burst it open. I never got put in there again, because the door wouldn't lock after that. Mrs Carroll came with him and I remember what she said; she turned on my mother and said she'd a good mind to tell the prevention of cruelty to children people, but if she did they never did anything.

'Mrs Carroll went away six months ago. She ran away from her husband – with another man, my mother said. It was Dodo who had to tell Mr Carroll. She sort of hinted to him that there was this other man and then she told him straight out. I thought he was going to attack her but people don't attack her, or they never have yet. He broke down and sobbed and cried. Do you know what I thought? What I hoped? I thought, my father left my mother and now Mrs Carroll's left her husband. Suppose Mr Carroll was to marry Dodo? That would be the best escape, wouldn't it, the cleanest way to get free? I wonder if I'd be jealous, though, I wonder if I'd mind . . .?'

He was interrupted by a tap at the door, followed by the appearance of Archbold to tell Burden that Wexford would like to see him.

'Now, do you mean?'

'He said it was urgent.'

Burden left Clifford with Diana. Perhaps it was no bad thing to take a break here. He wasn't interested in Clifford's boyhood, but he valued the mood these reminiscences seemed to bring him to, a mood of open revelation and frankness. All these stories of his youth (which was precisely how Burden saw them) would lead

Clifford, though by a crazy path, to the final incriminating outburst.

Instead of taking the lift, he walked upstairs. The door to Wexford's office stood a little ajar. Wexford was nearly always to be found either behind his desk or standing at the window thinking, while apparently contemplating the High Street. But this morning he stood abstractedly looking at the plan of greater Kingsmarkham which hung on the left-hand wall. He turned his eyes as Burden came in.

'Oh, Mike . . .'

'You wanted to see me?'

'Yes. I apologize for the interruption, but perhaps you'll see it wasn't exactly an interruption, more a breaking-off. Clifford Sanders – he didn't do it, he couldn't have done. You may as well let him go.'

Hard-faced, immediate anger starting, Burden said, 'We've been through all this before.'

'No, Mike, listen. He was seen sitting in his mother's car in Queen Street at five-forty-five on November the nineteenth. A woman called Rosemary Whitton saw him; she spoke to him and he spoke to her.'

'She was trying to move her car,' Wexford said, 'and she hadn't much room, only a few inches each end to play with –'

With the sexism of the stand-up comic, but straight-faced and deadly serious, Burden interrupted him: 'Women drivers!'

'Oh, Mike, come on! Clifford was sitting in the car behind her and he had a couple of yards behind him. She asked him if he'd move and he told her to go away. "Leave me alone, go away," was what he said.'

'How does she know it was Clifford?'

'She gave me a good description. It was a red Metro. She's no fool, Mike; she's something rather high-powered, a systems analyst, though I confess I'm not sure what that is.'

'And she says it was at a quarter to six?'

'She was late, she was in a hurry. Women like her are always in a hurry – inevitably. She says she wanted to get home before the kids were put to bed at six. When she first got back into the car she looked at the clock – I always do that myself, I know what she means – and it was exactly five-forty-five. Which means it was a good few minutes after that by the time she'd had her slanging match with Clifford and crunched the headlight on a meter.'

'Is that what she did?' asked Burden ruminatively, his frown threatening a further attack on women at the wheel. 'Why didn't he tell me that?'

'Didn't notice, I daresay. She says he moved as soon as it was too late to matter.'

The woman's statement would now have to be checked, thoroughly investigated, and until that had been done Burden's interrogation of Clifford must be suspended. He didn't go back to the interview room. The anger and frustration which might more naturally have been vented on Wexford he wanted to splash furiously over the man downstairs. He could have put through a phone call to his own office but couldn't face explaining to Clifford, so he sent Archbold back with the message to let him go, to tell him he wouldn't be needed again.

'Where would you hide something, Mike, if you were Gwen Robson?'

Smarting from his defeat, not yet fully grasping what the result of exonerating Clifford would be, Burden said sullenly, 'What sort of something?'

'Papers. A few sheets of paper.'

'Letters, do you mean?'

'I don't know.' Wexford said. 'Lesley Arbel was looking for papers, but I don't think she found them. They're not in the bank and they're not with Kingsmarkham Safe Depository Limited – I've just tried there.'

'How do you know Lesley Arbel didn't find them?'

'When I spoke to her on Friday she was worried and unhappy. If she'd found what she turned the house out for, she'd have been over the moon.'

'I'm wondering if Clifford could have killed his other grandmother, his mother's mother. He's a very strange character altogether. He has all the salient features of the psychopath . . . What are you laughing at?'

'Leave it, Mike,' Wexford said. 'Just leave it. And leave the psychiatry to Serge Olson.'

Burden was to remember that last remark when Olson phoned him on the following morning. He had thought of very little apart from Clifford Sanders during the intervening time and everything he had done had been concerned with this new alibi. He had even interviewed Rosemary Whitton himself and, unable to shake her conviction of the relevant time, had questioned the Queen Street greengrocer. If no one in Queen Street remembered Clifford in the Metro, a good many shopkeepers recalled Mrs Whitton hitting the meter post. The manager of the wine market remembered the time: it was before he closed at six, but not much before. He had turned the door sign to 'Closed' immediately he returned from inspecting the damage. Unconvinced but obliged at any rate temporarily to yield, Burden turned his attention from Clifford Sanders to Clifford Sanders' father . . . As a temporary measure at any rate. He wouldn't speak to Clifford Sanders again for a week, and in the meantime he would root out Charles Sanders and begin a new line of enquiry there. But before he could begin, Serge Olson phoned him.

'Mike, I think you should know that I've just had a call from Clifford cancelling his Thursday appointment and, incidentally, all further appointments with me. I asked him why and he said he had no further need of my particular kind of treatment. So there you are.'

Burden said rather cautiously, 'Why are you telling me, Mr Olson – Serge?'

'Well, you're subjecting him to some fairly heavy interrogation, aren't you? Look, this is delicate ground – for me, at any rate. He's my client. I am anxious not to,

202

let's say, betray his confidences. But it's a serious matter when someone like Clifford abandons his therapy. Mike, Clifford needs his therapy. I'm not saying he necessarily needs what I can give him, but he needs help from someone.'

'Maybe,' said Burden, 'he's found another psychiatrist. You needn't worry about the possible effects of what you call heavy interrogation anyway. That's over, at any rate for the time being.'

'I'm glad to hear it, Mike, I'm very glad.'

Putting it into words, that he had given up questioning Clifford, put things into perspective. Burden suddenly realized how much he hated being closeted with Clifford and hearing all these revelations. He would have no more of it – not until, that is, he had another positive lead. His mind made up, he looked out of the window to where they were putting lights in the branches of the tree that grew on the edge of the police station forecourt. It wasn't a Christmas tree or even a conifer, come to that, but an ash whose only distinction was in its size. Burden watched the two men at work. Putting coloured lights in the tree was his idea, later backed up by the Chief Constable, in the interest of promoting jollier relations with the public. Wexford's comment had been a derisive laugh. But surely you couldn't go on feeling antagonistic towards or afraid of or suspicious about a friendly body that hung fairy-lights in a tree in its front garden? This morning he felt neither jolly nor friendly, in the mood rather to snap at anyone who made jokes about the tree. Diana Pettit had already had the rough side of his tongue for suggesting that all the little lamps should be blue. When the phone rang again he picked up the receiver and said, 'Yes?' testily.

It was Clifford Sanders. 'Can I come and see you?'

'What about?' asked Burden.

'To talk.' No time was mentioned and Burden knew what Clifford was like about time. 'You made me finish early yesterday and I'd a lot more to say. I just wondered when we could start again.'

In my own good time, my lad, Burden thought. Next week maybe, next month. But what he said was, 'No, that's it. That's all. You can get back to work, get on with your life – OK?' He didn't wait for an answer, but put the phone down.

It rang again ten minutes later. By that time the younger and more intrepid of the two men had climbed to the top of the ladder and threaded the lead with bulbs on it through some of the highest branches. Burden thought how disastrous it would be, and what the media would make of it, if the man fell and got hurt. He spoke a milder 'Yes?' into the phone and got Clifford's voice suggesting in an eager, urgent tone that previously they had been cut off. Burden said that as far as he knew they hadn't been cut off. All that needed to be said had been said, hadn't it?

'I'd like to come and see you this afternoon if that's all right.'

'It's not all right,' Burden said, aware that he was back into an earlier mode of addressing Clifford – talking as if he were a child, but unable to do otherwise. 'I'm busy this afternoon.'

'I can come tomorrow morning then.'

'Clifford, I'm going to ring off now. OK, is that understood? We're not being cut off, I've finished, I can't discuss this any more. Goodbye.'

For some reason this second call disturbed Burden. It gave him a curious feeling very much like that experienced by those who, having had little to do with the handicapped, are brought into unexpected contact with someone who lolls and drools and paws at them with spastic hands. Their recoil and gasp are unforgivable, are outrageous, and Burden felt a little ashamed of himself as he put the phone down sharply, as he stepped back, looking at the phone as if Clifford or something of Clifford actually lived inside the brown plastic instrument. What a fool! What was the matter with him? He lifted the receiver once more and gave instructions to the switchboard to put no more calls from Clifford Sanders through to him; furthermore, to monitor all calls that came.

It would be useless to search the house. Lesley Arbel had had two weeks in which to do that and she might be less experienced at searching than Wexford's officers were, but she had had more time and presumably a personal interest in what she was seeking – whatever that was. A will? Gwen Robson had had nothing to leave. Something that would incriminate a guilty, frightened person? Wexford couldn't imagine her blackmailing her own, surely loved, niece. And yet Lesley had been desperate to find those papers, if it was papers.

'I'll lose my job!' she had cried out to him.

It seemed quite inconsequential. At one moment he had been asking her why she had not told him she was in Kingsmarkham that Thursday; the next, she was bewailing her threatened job. He walked up the path to Mrs Jago's house and rang the bell. She came quickly to the door – large, smiling, light-footed. The smile looked a little forced but not, he thought, because he as a policeman was unwelcome.

'All alone today?' he asked.

'Nina doesn't work on Tuesday or go shopping. I saw her yesterday.' They were in the living room now, in the jungle of knitted flowers and trees, but the manuscript was no longer on the table. Dita Jago followed the direction of his eyes. 'I didn't want to see her today. I'd had enough, I didn't feel I could take any more.'

The miseries of a deserted wife, did she mean? The plaints of a young woman abandoned to bring up two children on her own? He didn't enquire. He asked her where she thought Gwen Robson would have hidden whatever it was she had to hide, but as he did so he remembered how she had disclaimed all but a bare acquaintance with the dead woman. She picked up the circular needle from which the great tropical landscape hung and he saw that she had reached the sky, a blue expanse with tiny clouds. But instead of resuming her work, she sat clasping the two reinforced points of the needle in her hands. She looked at him and away.

'I knew her so little. How can I say?'

'I don't know,' he said. 'The house is the same as this one. I was thinking there might be some peculiarity, some feature of the house well known to residents but absolutely unknown to outsiders?'

'A secret panel?'

'Not exactly that.'

'Perhaps the murderer took this mysterious thing away, whatever it was. Would you like a drink?'

He shook his head rather too quickly and her eyebrows rose.

'What's become of the book?' he asked for something to say. 'You've finished it and sent it to a publisher?'

'I haven't finished it and I never will. I nearly burned it last night and then I thought – who needs emotional gestures, dramas? Just put it away in a drawer – so I did. I had such a day yesterday, it upset me so. It's a funny thing, but I'd like to tell you about it. May I? There doesn't seem to be anyone else I could tell.'

'It makes a change,' he said, 'someone wanting to tell me things.'

'I like you,' she said, and it wasn't naïve or disingenuous; it sounded simply sincere. 'I like you, but I don't really know you and you don't know me, and I doubt if we shall ever know each other much better.' A glance levelled at him seemed to ask for confirmation and he nodded. 'Maybe that's an ideal set-up for confiding.' She was silent, but her hands were still and they no longer held the needle.

'My daughter told me that she had an affair with a man – no, not an affair, not so much as that, a one-night stand, I think it's called – and she was silly enough to tell her husband about it. Not at once; she waited a long while. She should have forgotten it, put it behind her. He confessed something of his own to her, some peccadillo, and she came out with this thing of hers and instead of being as forgiving as she was, he said that changed everything – it changed all his feelings about her.'

'Like *Tess of the d'Urbervilles*, Wexford murmured, 'and we think times have changed. She didn't say anything of all this to you till yesterday?'

'That's right. I'd asked her if there was any hope of a reconciliation. Well, I went so far as to ask her what was the basic trouble between them. You're a parent, so you know what I mean by "went so far". They don't like questioning even when it . . . well, springs from one's real concern.'

'No,' said Wexford, 'they don't.' He considered. 'May I . . .?' He was unusually tentative. 'Would it be possible for me . . . to read your manuscript?'

She had picked up her knitting, but now she let it fall into her lap once more. 'Why on earth . . .?' A sudden eagerness in her voice nearly told him he was on the wrong tack, pursuing the wrong course altogether. 'You don't know any publishers, do you?'

He did, of course. Burden's brother-in-law Amyas Ireland had become a friend over the years, but he wasn't going to encourage false hopes there. Nor to tell the whole truth at this stage. 'I'm simply curious to read it.' He observed how her attitude towards the manuscript had changed since she had taken heart from confiding in him. 'Will you let me?'

Thus it was that he found himself making his way up a hill which seemed steeper than it had the evening before, carrying what felt like ten pounds' weight of paper in one of Tesco's red plastic bags. He had planned on finishing the A. N. Wilson that evening and longed to know how it ended – but this, this was important.

It was too early yet to switch on the Christmas lights in the tree, Burden thought, only December 8. However, no one showed any signs of wanting to switch them on and to passers-by they must be invisible. The evening was dark and misty. How long was it since they had seen the sun by day or, come to that, the moon by night?

There were the usual cars on the forecourt where the lamps made everything look like an out-of-focus sepia photograph. Someone had just driven up in a Metro which could have been of any colour. It meant nothing to Burden and he took his raincoat off the hook and went down in the lift. Home early for once! His little boy would still be up, bathed and powdered, running around in pyjamas; the radio on because Jenny preferred it to television; a smell of something exotic but not too exotic, one of the few examples of foreign cuisine he liked – pesto sauce, for instance, or five spices in a stir-fry being prepared for his dinner; Jenny harassed but happy in a blue tracksuit. Burden took a yearning, sensuous delight in these things. The clutter, the pretty paraphernalia of domestic life which are the aspects of marriage many married men dislike gave him intense pleasure. He never got enough of them.

He crossed the black and white checkerboard floor of the foyer and someone got up from a chair and came over to him. It was Clifford Sanders.

Clifford said, 'I've been trying to get hold of you all the afternoon. They kept saying you were busy.'

Burden's initial reaction was to turn on Sergeant Camb who stood behind the reception counter, but as he took a step towards him he remembered he had said nothing to the sergeant, or indeed to anyone, about not admitting Clifford to the police station. It hadn't occurred to him that Clifford would actually come here. Had he the right, come to that, to exclude him? He didn't know. He didn't know if he could legally keep innocent, law-abiding members of the public out. Anger against Clifford must be kept under control.

He said stiffly, 'I was busy. I'm busy now. You must excuse me, I'm in a hurry.'

The otherwise blank, childlike, pasty face seemed to have only one expression – puzzlement. A deep bewilderment left the eyes unclouded, puckered the skin of Clifford's forehead into a concentrated frown. 'But I've got a lot more to say. I've only just started; I have to talk to you.'

Not for the first time, Burden thought that if he had seen this man in the street and not known who he was, he would have thought him retarded. These were deep waters, muddied and with strange things in their depths – but was it possible to be retarded not in the body or the brain but somewhere else? In the soul, the psyche? A horribly uncomfortable feeling took hold of Burden and he seemed to shrink away from the touch of his own clothes on his skin. He could no longer look into those infant's eyes, watch the working of thick, uncontrolled lips.

'I've told you, we've nothing more to say to one another.' God, he sounded like someone ending a love affair! 'You've helped us with our enquiries, thank you very much. I assure you we shan't want you again.'

With that he escaped. He would have liked to run, but dignity forbade it, that and self-respect. He was aware as he walked with deliberately measured tread towards the swing doors that Camb was watching him curiously, that Marian Bayliss who had just come in had paused to stare and that Clifford still stood in the centre of the floor, his lips moving silently and his hands held up in front of him.

Burden opened the door and, once outside, ran to his car. The red Metro he had seen come in but whose colour the yellow lamps had altered was parked beside it. Impossible to draw any conclusion but that Clifford had done this purposely.

And as Burden switched on the ignition, he saw Clifford come out. He ran up, calling, 'Mike, Mike . . .!'

Burden didn't have to back. He drove straight out through the gates.

16

'HE'S made a transference,' Serge Olson said. 'It's a very clearly defined example of transference.'

'I don't know what that means,' Burden said.

They were in Wexford's office, the three of them. The psychotherapist's face amid surrounding and intervening bushes of hair was like that of an extremely intelligent vole peering out from a frondy sanctuary. And the bright beady eyes had their fierce animal look. Burden had expected to go to him, but Olson had said he would come to the police station as he had no clients on a Thursday morning. Throughout the previous day Clifford Sanders had pursued his course of trying to speak to Burden. None of his phone calls had been put through but Burden was told, to his considerable dismay, that fifteen had been made. And Clifford had returned to the police station in time to repeat his intercepting tactic as Burden left for home.

But it was his presence on the forecourt this morning – the red Metro parked just inside the gates and Clifford patiently seated at the wheel – which had really rattled Burden. He had had enough. No sooner was he inside than he was on the phone to Olson, and Olson had been there within fifteen minutes.

'I'll try to explain, Mike,' he said. 'Transference is the term employed by psychoanalysts to describe an emotional attitude the subject develops towards his or her analyst. It can be positive or negative, it can be love or hate. I've often experienced it with clients – though not really with Clifford.' Burden's puzzled face seemed to give him pause and he looked at Wexford. 'I think you know what I mean, don't you, Reg?'

Wexford nodded. 'It's not a difficult concept. It seems natural when you think about it.'

'You mean he's got to like me? He's kind of come to depend on me?'

'Absolutely, Mike.'

Burden said almost wildly, 'But what did I do? What in God's name did I do to set something like this up? I only put him through a routine interrogation; I only questioned him the way I must have questioned thousands of suspects. No one ever did this before, they were only too glad to get shut of me and this place.'

Wexford was at the window. The red Metro was still down there, its bonnet a few inches from the trunk of the tree decorated with the lights. Clifford sat in the driving-seat, not reading, not looking out of the window, just sitting with bent head.

'People are different,' Olson was saying. 'People are individuals, Mike. You can't say that because no one ever made the transference before, no one ever would. Were you particularly gentle with him? Paternal? I don't mean paternalistic. Sensitive in your approach?' The expression in those gleaming dark eyes rather indicated Olson's doubts of such a possibility.

'I don't think so. I don't know. I just listened, I let him talk; I thought I'd be more likely to get somewhere that way.'

'Ah.' Olson gave a reflective smile. 'Listening, letting the client talk – you did what the Freudians do. Maybe he prefers a Freudian therapist.'

Suddenly it began to rain. In straight glistening rods the rain bore down on the tarmac, the roofs of the parked cars, the roof of the Metro, hard enough to create immediate puddles. Wexford turned from the streaming glass with a quick, repudiating shake of the head.

'What's to be done then?' he asked.

'It's a good rule, Reg, not to yield to the subject's wishes. Part of his problem, you see, is the way in which he wants to fashion his world. But the world he makes isn't conducive to his happiness, to his adjustment. It doesn't tally with reality; it just looks easier to him. Do you understand that, Mike? If you see Clifford now, you'll be

211

allowing him to make his world in the shape he wants and people it with the people he wants. For instance, because he's lost his own father he wants to put you in his world as his father. I'd say sure, do that, if it would be best for him, but I don't think it would be. It would deepen the transference and create even greater divergencies from reality.'

'Are you suggesting I simply have someone go out there and send him home?' asked Wexford. 'I don't know why but it seems . . . irresponsible.'

Olson got up. Taking no risks with the weather, he had arrived wrapped in yellow oilskins and these be fastened and zipped round himself once more, his sharp nose sticking out from under the canary-coloured hood.

'He's a very badly disturbed human being, Reg,' he said. 'You're right there. But you and Mike, you have to understand I'm a professional. You, Mike, were kind enough to call me "doctor" when we first met and though I'm not that, I have to have professional ethics. I can't go up to Clifford and tell him to come back to me. I can't go and tell him he's got his usual appointment at five today and mind not to be late. All I can do is go and get in that car beside him, sit there as his friend and try to persuade him to confront what he sees as his relationship with you and maybe get it into a more . . . reasonable perspective.'

They both watched from the window. The increasing torrent of rain made it difficult to see. Olson's figure looked like a bright yellow bird hopping and flapping its way to a dry nest. The Metro's door shut on him and once more the rain enclosed the car in walls of water like reeded glass.

'I suppose it's sound,' Wexford said, 'that stuff about not letting him create his own world, about not giving away to him. I must confess to feeling a bit apprehensive.'

'Of what?' Burden asked almost rudely.

A car driven recklessly, a fatal accident that was only partly accident, a handful of pills washed down with brandy, a rope slung over the beam of an outhouse . . . Wexford put none of this into words. He saw the Metro begin to back, sliding slowly through sheets of water and sending up jets of spray. It turned and headed for the gates, Olson still inside.

'That's fixed him for a bit,' and Burden. 'Thank God for it! Now perhaps we can get on with some work.'

He shut the door rather too hard behind him. Wexford turned his back on the window and the rain and thought about the dreams he kept having of wheels spinning in space, of circles with squares inside them. Had they anything to do with the fact that the evening before and the evening before that he had been reading the manuscript of Dita Jago's concentration camp experiences? It was with him in the office today, Donaldson having come for him that morning in the car.

'Is it any good?' Dora had asked.

'I don't think I'd answer that question if anyone else had asked it. But "as an offering to conjugal unreserve", frankly, not much. As a writer, she makes a fine knitter.'

'Reg, that's unkind.'

'Not when it isn't heard outside these four flimsy walls. Who am I to judge, anyway? What do I know? I'm a policeman, not a publisher's reader. It's not for its style or atmosphere that I'm reading the thing.'

In her discreet way she hadn't asked why he was reading it, any more than she had asked why he always had his nose in *Kim* magazine. She knew better than that. He turned to where he had placed a marker between the sheets. It was at a point about half-way through and the young Dita Kowiak had begun work in the Auschwitz Krankenbau – the hospital – as an orderly. Wexford should have been moved by the descriptions of emaciated patients, the administering of intracardiac injections of toxic substances, the hurling of naked corpses into trucks. Dita had survived because for a time at any rate the hospital workers were regularly fed, even if the diet of turnip soup and mouldy bread was inadequate. She told of Russian prisoners-of-war poisoned with Cyclon-B gas, the burning of five hundred corpses in the space of one hour. But instead of being affected, he felt only that he

213

had heard all this before. She had no gift for delineating place or bringing a character to life. Her prose was wooden and repetitious and there was no impression of her own sufferings permeating the text. She might never have been there; she might have copied all this piecemeal from the concentration camp autobiographies which, after all, were legion. And perhaps she had . . .

Several times he had come to points in the narrative where pages were missing, but up till now those pages had always turned up later on. The lack of numbering made things difficult. Here, however, the narrative stopped abruptly in mid-sentence, in the middle of an anecdote about a doctor at the hospital called Dehring. Wexford carefully scrutinized all the remaining pages of the manuscript, but could find no further mention of Dehring's name. There was at least one page missing, perhaps two.

But would Dita Jago have let him take the manuscript if it contained – or conspicuously did not contain – something incriminating? It would have been easy to refuse. 'I couldn't bear to have anyone read it,' would have done the trick. Or when he asked where the manuscript was, she need only have said that she had sent it away to be typed or had even, as she threatened, burned it.

Whatever efforts Serge Olson had made, they failed to have any effect on Clifford Sanders. He made five phone calls to Kingsmarkham police station in the course of the afternoon, though none of these was actually put through to Burden. Next morning there was a letter for him, sent to his home. At the police station someone else might very likely have opened any missive that came, but here Burden naturally opened his own post. This brown envelope he had at first supposed to contain the bill for fitting a new carpet in the dining room.

Clifford addressed him as Mike. This was probably Olson's doing, Burden thought. The letter began 'Dear Mike'. The writing was a child's – or a teacher's – a round, neat, admirably legible hand, upright but with the slightest tendency to a backward slope. 'Dear Mike, I have a lot I want to say to you and I think you would be interested to hear it. I know you want me to think of you as my friend, and that is how I do think of you. In fact, I don't find it easy to confide in people, but you are an exception to this rule. We really get on well together, as I am sure you will agree.' Here Burden laid down the letter for a moment and sighed. 'I do understand that other people, those in authority over you I mean, are doing everything in their power to stop our meeting, and I expect you feel threatened with the loss of your job. Therefore I suggest we arrange to meet outside your working hours. Even employers like the police surely cannot object to their officers having their own personal friends. I will phone you tomorrow . . .' Burden noticed that he mentioned no precise hour and recalled what Olson had said about Clifford's attitude towards time. 'Please tell them you expect a call from me so that if you are out they can take a message. My idea is to call on you at your house this evening perhaps or during the weekend. With best wishes. Yours ever, Cliff.'

Burden's little boy had climbed on to his lap and he stroked his hair, held him close for a moment. Suppose his Mark should grow up into such a one? How could you tell? Clifford had looked like this once, been as endearing, inspired perhaps the same breath-catching love. Only I shan't walk out on him when he's five, thought Burden. But when he tried to summon up pity for Clifford, he failed and felt only exasperation.

'I'm taking no calls from this man,' he said when he got to the police station, 'and I'd like him to be told that no message he leaves will reach me. Right?'

After that he concentrated on the quest of the moment, finding the whereabouts of Charles Sanders. If Sanders had never paid maintenance to the wife he had deserted and she, presumably, had been too proud to ask for it, he could not be traced through the courts or social services. It wasn't an uncommon combination of names. Telephone directories and electoral registers yielded a number for Archbold, Davidson, Marian Bayliss and Diana Pettit to call on, and Archold had run to earth a likely-sounding Charles Sanders in Manchester. Burden had plans to go up there and see him, though he wanted to get the man on the phone first, and as yet he hadn't even managed to hear the sound of his voice. Engaged signals alternated with ringing tones as if Sanders unplugged his phone between answering calls. However, he never answered Burden's.

Later in the morning when he saw the red Metro come on to the forecourt, Burden had to suppress a feeling that was not too far from panic. He was being hounded, persecuted. The anxious fears which had been building up inside him had the effect which such an accumulation sometimes does, that of heightening the powers of his imagination. He found himself envisaging a future in which Clifford Sanders dogged his footsteps, in which every time he lifted a phone receiver he heard Clifford's voice at the other end of the line, in which – worst of all – when he looked in a mirror he saw Clifford's face over his shoulder. You are a hardened, tough police officer, he told himself fiercely. Why do you let this boy shake you? Why are you rattled by it? You can keep him off, others will keep him off. Calm yourself. Ignorant as he acknowledged himself to be of the workings of the psyche, he nevertheless recognized the evidences of paranoia in Clifford's letter and now he saw them in himself. And then he recalled the precise moment when he had first recognized Clifford's madness.

A memory came to him of something he had been told by his historian wife: how going to look at the mad people in Bedlam was as popular a pastime in the late eighteenth century as safari park visiting was today. How could they? His instinct was to put himself as far from the mad as he could, to pretend they didn't exist, to build walls between them and him. Yet Clifford wasn't mad in a padded cell, straitjacket way; he was only disturbed, deprived, lonely, his thought processes somehow askew. Burden picked up the phone, arranged for Sergeant Martin to go out there and tell Clifford to leave, to tell him he was trespassing or something.

He wondered if Wexford had seen him and felt a sudden need to talk to Wexford about it, to be franker on the subject of his feelings in respect of Clifford than he had been up to now. But as he was going down, had got so far as entering the lift, he remembered that Wexford – for some mysterious reason of his own – had gone to the Barringdean Shopping Centre. Burden thought he would like a drink or even a Valium, though he hated the things and feared them. Instead he sat at his desk and briefly put his head in his hands.

The sandwich, according to the claims of Grub 'n' Grains, was 'American style', pastrami and cream cheese on rye. If he hadn't been told that it was pastrami, which he had never tasted before, Wexford would have sworn he was eating corned beef of the well-known Fray Bentos type. He had been doing a bit of crime reconstruction, mostly in his head, but the true scene of the crime seemed the right place in which to do it.

The fountain played in the left-hand concourse, its jets of spray concealing the ascending and descending escalators and the entrance to British Home Stores. But opposite him Wexford could see the several clothes shops and between them and Boots the Chemist the wools and crafts shop called Knits 'n' Kits. Next door to the café was Demeter with its bakery adjacent, then a travel agent, then W. H. Smith. Wexford drank his tropical fruit cocktail, paid for his lunch and made his way up to Demeter.

The health foods store kept its herbal remedies on shelves immediately to the left of the window and Wexford soon found the calendula capsules. It was these which Helen Brook had been looking for when she saw Gwen Robson outside in the aisle between the shops in

217

conversation with a very well-dressed girl. And here she had been taken with the first of those early labour pains which prevented her from going up to Mrs Robson and speaking to her. Wexford bent down, took a jar of capsules from the shelf and dropped it into his wire basket. Then he straightened up and looked out of the window. Boots the Chemist could be seen and, this side of it, the wools and crafts shop, with the Mandala – circles of chrysanthemums and cherry-fruited solanum today – cutting off sight of the entrances to Tesco. Gwen Robson had shopped in Boots, bought her toothpaste and talcum powder, paused to look at the Mandala flowers perhaps, and there encountered the girl Helen Brook had seen her speaking to. It must have been Lesley Arbel, Wexford thought, who – perhaps having time to spare before the departure of the London train – had come in here specifically to meet her aunt. He imagined a conversation, surprise expressed by Mrs Robson, a brief explanation from Lesley about the word-processing course, a promise perhaps that she would see her aunt on the following night. Or had it all been more sinister?

It must have been on this side of the Mandala that they had stood, for Helen Brook to have seen them. And somehow Wexford knew that if the girl were Lesley she would not have been looking at flowers but, even while talking to her aunt, would have had her eyes fixed on those shop windows to the left of her with their window displays of clothes and shoes. He looked at them himself, at the space Dora's sweater had occupied which was now filled by an extraordinary red and black frilled corselette; on to the next window which was a medley of red and black and green and white shoes and boots, to the window of Knits 'n' Kits. Here a loom with a half-completed piece of work on it – a wall-hanging or rug – predominated. He thought inescapably of Dita Jago. Did she use this shop? Making his way to the door with the basket over his arm, his thoughts miles away from herbal remedies and packets of nuts, he was jolted to attention by an indignant voice.

218

'Excuse me, but you haven't paid for your tablets!'

Wexford grinned. That would be a fine thing, a turn-up for the book, a detective chief inspector getting done for shoplifting. As bad as, or worse than, his daughter going to prison. But he didn't want to think about that, he wouldn't think of it. Under the resentful gaze of the shop assistant, he replaced the calendula capsules on the shelf, leaving the wire basket on the floor.

It had been there in his mind, lying under a level of consciousness, for days now...well, weeks. Gwen Robson had been dead three weeks. It drew him to that window. Of course he had already dimly glimpsed it, half-noticing it as he came into Demeter. The pairs of knitting needles were hung in a sort of zig-zag pattern all down the right-hand side of the window, hanks of wool on the left and the loom with its half-completed achievement in between. But they weren't, strictly speaking, all pairs. Wexford went in. Better not attack the window display, he thought, not yet.

Men didn't come in here much. There were two women at the counter, one leafing through a book of patterns. Wexford found a metal stand, the kind of thing that used to be called a 'tree', with packets of needles hung all over it. He unhooked the one he wanted. Lesley Arbel might have come in here before she met her aunt. Why not? She would have known the shop was here and known what she wanted. Dita Jago too, seeking only a replacement perhaps and later finding another use . . .

With a sharp tug he pulled the circular knitting needle out of its plastic pack and held it up as one might hold a divining rod, each hand clasping the thick metal pins at each end, the long wire hanging slack between and then pulled taut. Wire and pins were coated in a pale grey plastic substance. His eye caught sight of the obvious victim to experiment on – a torso in styrofoam wearing a lilac lacy jumper, with an extravagantly elongated neck on which the head was poised at an unnatural angle. Approaching it with the garrote at the ready, he was aware of a hush in the shop, then of the three pairs of eyes fixed on him and following his moves.

Hastily, he replaced the circular needle in its packet. He had found his weapon.

17

CLIFFORD SANDERS came to Burden's house at nine in the evening. It was no surprise to Burden; he had been expecting this from the moment he got home and thinking of various ways to handle it so as to avoid a confrontation. He considered getting his wife to answer the door or asking his elder son John, who had come to eat supper with them, to answer it; he thought of taking the whole family, including little Mark, out to eat. In a wild moment he even had an idea of going away for the night, booking a room in an hotel. But when the time came, he answered the door himself.

It was the first time for days that he had actually faced Clifford and spoken to him. Clifford wore a raincoat, navy blue, very like a policeman's. His face was pale, but that might have been due to the light from overhead in the porch. Behind him hung a thin greenish fog. He put out his hand.

Burden didn't take it but said, 'I'm sorry you've come all this way for nothing, but I have explained I've no more questions to ask you at present.'

'Please let me talk to you.'

The foot in the door – Clifford had taken a step forward, but Burden planted himself firmly between door and architrave. 'I have to insist you understand you can give us no more help with our enquiries. It's over. Thank you for your help, but there's nothing more you can do.' Every parent knows the expression on a child's face just before it cries: the swelling of tissues, the seeming collapse of muscles, the trembling. Burden couldn't bear it, but he couldn't cope with it either. 'I'll say good night, then,' he said absurdly. 'Good night.' And stepping back, he closed the door hard.

Retreating across the hall, standing and listening, he waited for Clifford to ring the bell. He was bound to do that – or try the knocker. Nothing happened. Burden was sweating; he felt a trickle of sweat run down his forehead and one side of his nose. Mark was in bed, Jenny and John still in the dining room at the back of the house. Burden went into the living room which was in darkness, made his way stealthily to the window and looked out. The red Metro was parked at the kerb and Clifford was sitting in the driving-seat in that accustomed pose of his, the way he perhaps passed several hours of each day. Burden was still standing there watching when the phone rang. He answered it in the dark, still looking out of the window.

It was Dorothy Sanders.

Burden was obliged to recognize the voice, for she did not identify herself or ask if she were speaking to Inspector Burden. 'Are you going to arrest my son?'

In other circumstances Burden would have made some discreet and non-committal reply. Now he was beyond that. 'No, Mrs Sanders, I'm not. There's no question of that.' A mean, despicable kind of hope took hold of him that he could get this woman on his side, enlist her aid even. But he only said, 'I don't want to see him, I've no more enquiries to make of him.'

'Then why do you keep getting him down there? Why don't you leave him alone? He's never here, I never see him. His place is at home with me.'

'I quite agree,' said Burden. 'I couldn't agree more.' As he spoke the car door opened, Clifford got out and once more came up the path towards the house. The bell ringing made a searing sound in Burden's ears, almost pain. He found himself gripping the phone receiver in a wet palm as the doorbell rang again. 'He'll be back home with you in ten minutes,' he said, screwing up his nerve, feeling anger bring a fresh flood of sweat.

'I can complain to the proper authorities, you know. I can complain to the Chief Constable – and I will.' Her tone changed and she said in a slow deliberate way,

222

pausing between the words, 'He didn't do anything to that woman. He didn't know her and he hasn't anything to tell you.'

'Then you'd better lock him up, Mrs Sanders,' Burden said indiscreetly. He put the receiver back, heard John go to the door, a murmured exchange and then John, who had been primed, said firmly, 'Good night.'

In the dark there, Burden thought wildly of an injunction to restrain Clifford from persecuting him, of seeking out a judge in chambers, of arresting and imprisoning Clifford when he broke the order. He heard the Metro door close and listened, holding his breath, for the engine to start up. The silence seemed to endure a long time and the eventual sound of the motor turning and firing was a glorious relief. Burden didn't watch the departure of the Metro but when next he looked out of the window it was gone, the street empty, the fog thick and still and opaque as muddy water.

Returning the manuscript, he asked about the missing pages, but there were no guilty reactions and no evasions.

'I realized as soon as you'd gone,' Dita Jago said. 'I took two pages out to check something on them at the public library.' She looked at him steadily – too steadily? 'You remember I told you I was at the library on the day Mrs Robson was killed? I was checking up something about a man called Dehring.' She didn't ask if he had enjoyed reading the manuscript or what his impression was, commenting only, 'You read that far!'

While she was out of the room fetching the pages, he examined quickly the circular needle from which the great wall hanging depended. The pins at each end of the wire were of a much finer gauge than the one he had handled in the Barringdean Centre and would not have stood up to excessive pressure. But that meant nothing. Mrs Jago would have other circular needles, probably in every available size. He glanced at the sheets of paper she showed

223

him, noting corrections made in red ballpoint. She made no comment on his interest, but as he walked down the path and glanced back he saw her watching him from the window, her expression one of benign mystification.

Ralph Robson was cleaning his car, a popular Saturday afternoon pastime at Highlands. Out here he managed without his stick, holding on to the bodywork of the car for support. Wexford said good afternoon to him and suggested that the task on which he was engaged was not perhaps the wisest activity for someone in his condition.

'Who's going to do it if I don't?' Robson said belligerently. 'Who's going to give me a helping hand? Oh, it's one thing when anything like that first happens. They're all coming round. Can I do this and can I do that? That soon cools off. Even Lesley. You wouldn't credit it, would you, but I haven't seen Lesley for a whole blessed week. She hasn't so much as phoned.'

Nor will she, Wexford thought. You've seen the last of her. She either got what she wanted or knows there's nothing in it for her.

'There's one bright spot though.' Robson winced as he straightened up from rinsing out his cloth in the bucket of water. 'I'm getting my hip done. Doctor's transferring me to another what they call health area the week after next. Sunderland. I'll be getting my replacement up in Sunderland.'

The Saab passed Wexford as he began the climb up the hill, passed him and drew into the kerb ahead. His thoughts had shifted, as they mostly did these days, from the Robson case to Sheila. She was coming to stay the night; it was years since they had seen so much of her as they had in these past few weeks, and inevitably he speculated as to why this was. Because she understood and sympathized with his anxieties for her safety? Or because she was sorry for her parents having to live in this poky, uncomfortable little house? A bit of both, maybe. She got out of the passenger side of the Saab and his heart leapt with the usual old relief.

'Pop, this is Ned.'

The man in the driving-seat was young, dark, distinguished-looking. Wexford knew at once that he had seen him somewhere before. They shook hands over the seats and Wexford got into the back of the car.

'Ned's not staying, he's on the way to Brighton. He's just going to drop me off.'

'That sounds like an early warning in case we start evincing our well-known lack of hospitality.'

Ned laughed, and there was a bit of an edge to the sound. Because Wexford had said 'early warning' which had another, quite separate, significance?

'Oh, Pop,' said Sheila, 'I didn't mean that.'

'At least I hope he'll stay for a cup of tea,' Dora said when they reached the house.

'Of course I will. I'd like to.'

They had rather taken it for granted that with both daughters married all this sort of thing would be over. There would be no more suitors brought home, the sight of whom aroused dismay or resignation or hope. Sylvia indeed had married so young that before Neil there had been no more than a couple of casual boyfriends. But Sheila's men had come in a constantly changing series until at last the chosen one, Andrew Thorverton, had surely put an end to this parade. Or so it had seemed to those naïve parents who, because of their age, inevitably regarded marriage – at any rate in their own family – as an institution of permanence. Was this Ned a prospective second husband? Sheila seemed to treat him in a rather cavalier fashion.

He was gone on his way to Brighton before Wexford found out his surname. She could go back on the train; he wasn't to trouble himself about her – that was Sheila's airy parting shot as she and her father stood in the flowerbed sized front garden watching him go.

'Nice car,' Wexford said tactfully.

'Well, I suppose. It's always having to have things done to it. I mean, that last weekend you were in the old house

225

and I came down, it was in being seen to. I offered to lend him mine as a matter of fact, but considering what happened it was just as well he hired a car instead.'

They went back into the house. With the coming of early dusk the fog was returning. Wexford closed the front door on the dank chill outside. 'I've seen him somewhere, him or his picture.'

'Of course you have, Pop. His photograph was all over the papers when he was prosecuting those Arab terrorists.'

'Do you mean to say he's Edmund Hope? Your "Ned" is Edmund Hope the barrister?'

'Of course he is. I thought you knew.'

'I don't quite know how you could have thought we knew,' said Dora, 'considering you never introduced him. "This is Ned" doesn't convey much information.'

Sheila shrugged her shoulders. Her hair was tied back in a ponytail with a length of red ribbon. 'He's not "my" Ned. We're not together any more – just friends, as they say. We actually lived together for four whole days.' Her laugh had a hint of bitterness in it. 'It's all very well these brave statements: "I don't agree with what you say, but I'd die for your right to say it." That sort of thing doesn't amount to much when it comes to the crunch. He's like the rest of you – well, not Dad – who don't want to know me if I go to jail.'

'That's not fair, Sheila. That's very unkind and unjust. I'll never not want to know you.'

'I'm sorry, Mother – not you either, then. But Ned didn't even want other people to know he knew me. And I went along with it – can you imagine?' She came up to Wexford, who had been silent and staring. 'Pop . . .?' Her arms were on his shoulders, her face lifted up to his. She had always been uninhibited, demonstrative, a 'touching' person. 'Is this nasty house haunted? Have you seen a ghost?'

'You actually offered to lend Edmund Hope your car for the weekend while he was in the middle of prosecuting those terrorists?'

'Don't be cross, Pop. Why not?' She made a face at him, lips protruding, nose wrinkled up.

'I'm not cross. Tell me the circumstances. Tell me exactly when and how you offered to lend him the Porsche.'

Extreme surprise made her step back and hold out actressy hands in a wide sweep. 'Goodness, I'm glad I'm not one of your criminals! Well, he'd stayed the night and when he tried to start his car in the morning it wouldn't start, so I drove him to court – the Old Bailey it was. And before I dropped him I said he could borrow my car if he wanted.'

'Could anyone have heard you say it?'

'Oh, yes, I expect so. He was standing on the pavement and I called it out after him; it was a sort of afterthought. I said something like, "You can have this car for the weekend if you like," because I knew he was supposed to be staying with some friends in Wales, and he called back thanks and he'd take me up on that. Only after that I remembered I'd said I'd come down here, and I was quite glad when he rang up in the evening and said his own car would be ready in the morning.' Realization came to her quite suddenly and drained the colour from her face. The white stood out round the blue irises of her eyes. 'Oh, Pop, why did I never think of that? Oh God, how awful!'

'The bomb was meant for him,' Wexford said.

'And the letter bomb too? That was during our – er, four-day honeymoon.'

'I think we'd better tell someone, don't you?' He picked up the phone, feeling an unlooked-for, absurd happiness.

The night had passed without disturbance or dreams. Burden lay awake for a long time thinking about Charles Sanders One – the Manchester one, who had eventually answered his phone and turned out to be twenty-seven years old – and Charles Sanders Two, from Portsmouth, with children of Clifford's age, a young wife and an Australian accent. But his mind was not fraught with anxieties and soon he slept heavily and uninterruptedly. The dense fog which enveloped town and countryside brought its own kind of silence, the muffled sensation less of there being no sound to hear than of deafness. Jenny was up and Mark was up on Sunday morning before he awoke to see the bedroom curtains drawn back and a fluffy whiteness pressing against the windowpanes. It was the phone ringing which had awakened him and in spite of his peaceful night, the first possible caller that occurred to him was Clifford.

Jenny must have answered it on the other phone, for the ringing stopped. Burden picked up the receiver at his bedside and to his enormous relief heard Wexford's voice. It was Wexford wanting to tell him the solution to the bomb puzzle; wanting also to come round later in the day with another solution, the answer to the mystery of the weapon Gwen Robson's killer had used. Burden said nothing about Clifford or Clifford's mother's phone call. That could wait till later, till he saw Wexford – or perhaps might never need to be told.

The morning passed with no more phone calls and no more visits. There was usually considerable traffic in Tabard Road, which was a through road, but today it was quiet, the fog keeping people at home. Was it also keeping Clifford at home, or was there another reason for his absence? Burden wondered how much his mother's power and influence over him would enable her, at her level of necessarily far less physical strength, to be his jailer.

The fog did not dissipate as it had on the preceding days, but seemed to thicken as afternoon came on. His sister-in-law Grace and her husband came to lunch, also Jenny's brother. Burden thought how awkward it would have been if the red Metro had arrived and Clifford presented himself once more at the front door, but nothing like that happened. His guests went at about four, when the fog darkened and the yellow gleams of streetlights faintly penetrated it. None of them lived far away and they had all come on foot. Watching the departure from the front window, he saw Amyas encounter Wexford just outside the gate. This was about as far as it was possible to see, and even so the figures of the two men seemed as if swathed in lightly swaying pennants of gauze.

'It was a huge relief,' Wexford said, taking off his coat in the hall. 'Yet when you come to think of it, what does that amount to? Aren't I really saying I'm glad it's someone else's child and not mine that's threatened? There but for the grace of God, in fact – which is only another way of saying, "I'm all right, Jack".'

'Edmund Hope may be all right too. It's likely they've found another target by this time. After all, it's more than three weeks ago.'

'Yes, and more than three weeks since Gwen Robson's death. How's this for a garrote, Mike?' Wexford drew from his pocket the circular needle he had bought at the Barringdean Centre; the pins at each end were a quarter of an inch in diameter, forming tough, strong handles to hold on to. 'You're the plastics expert,' he said. 'Would this be the right sort of stuff?'

'It's the right colour. I should say it's pretty obvious a thing like this was used. Does that necessarily make it a woman who used it?'

They went into Burden's living room, where a fire had been lighted; the blaze from it lit the room with flickering yellow. Burden put up the fireguard in case Mark came in.

'This was a premeditated crime,' Wexford said, 'only in the sense, I believe, that the perpetrator had had an idea of killing for some time and was waiting only for opportunity. But I don't think he or she went into that car park with the weapon at the ready. It's more likely it had just been bought in the shop where I got this one, and that means the prospective user might have bought it or someone else purchased it *for* the prospective user. In other words, it was on a shopping list, so the purchaser could have been a man or a woman.'

'And he or she,' Burden went on, 'came up into the car park looking at it perhaps? I mean, perhaps it came loose from its packaging and the purchaser was curling it up and replacing it?'

'Or the purchaser, who wasn't the prospective user and maybe had never seen such a thing before, was fascinated by such a peculiar thing. It *is* a peculiar-looking thing, Mike. The purchaser might have just been standing there unwinding it and looking at it when Mrs Robson came along.'

A car drew up outside. Its progress sounded slow, as it would necessarily have had to be in the dense fog. Burden jumped up a bit too quickly and went to the window – not Clifford, but Burden's next-door neighbour whom he could see getting out to open his garage drive gates.

'It's not too early to draw the curtains, is it?'

'I didn't know there was any prescribed time for it,' Wexford said, eyeing him speculatively.

'It seems a pity to lose the last of the light.'

The impenetrable greyness outside made nonsense of this remark. It was now impossible to see across the street, in fact to see much beyond the pavement and kerb on this side. Burden pulled the curtains across the window and was switching on a table lamp when the phone rang. He gave a nervous start which he knew Wexford had seen.

'Hallo?'

His mother-in-law's voice and his wife's intermingled as Jenny picked up the bedroom extension. He couldn't control the little gasp of relief. Wexford said with quick intuition, 'Has Clifford Sanders been hounding you?'

Burden nodded. 'I think it's stopped though. He hasn't phoned or been here all day.'

'Been here?'

'Oh, yes. He was here last night, came to the door twice, but I do think it's over now. Anyway,' Burden lied, 'it's not important, it's not a problem. Your Mrs Jago – do you see her as . . .?'

Instead of answering directly, Wexford said, 'Dita Jago might very well have been one of Gwen Robson's black-mailees. She had the means to kill her. Of everyone in this case, she was the most likely to have been buying a circular knitting needle in the shopping centre that afternoon. On the other hand, she says she was in the public library, the central branch in the High Street, with her grand-daughters. I jib a bit at asking those two little girls to alibi or not alibi the grandmother they're obviously fond of; I won't do it if I can avoid it, but . . .

'Anyway, the papers Lesley Arbel was looking for — and ransacked or spring-cleaned her uncle's house in the process of so doing — weren't sheets from Dita Jago's manuscript. They were photocopies of letters.'

Burden said, 'Do you mean letters Gwen Robson took or borrowed from the homes of her clients? Incriminating letters she then had copied?'

'Not quite, her niece got these letters for her. It was Lesley Arbel who made the copies to show to her aunt. Not because she thought they could be used for any criminal purpose, certainly not that, but to amuse her, I think — to entertain someone who loved gossip and took the same kind of pleasure in sexual irregularities as some of our Sunday newspapers do — gloating over matters that ostensibly they deplore.'

'Are you talking about letters to the agony aunt?'

'Of course. Lesley Arbel had easy access to them and a photocopier in the office where she worked. Some of the letters would appear in *Kim* — my God, Mike, the amount of *Kim* I've grubbed through in the past week — but most wouldn't and some, even in these days of licence, would be considered unfit for publication. And even though there's an unwritten law in the agony aunt's department that staff preserve discretion — lip ser-vice to a kind of poor woman's Official Secrets Act — it must have seemed harmless enough, what she was do-ing. None of it would go beyond the four walls of the house in Hastings Road . . . What is it, Mike? What's wrong?'

Burden had jumped up and stood with head lifted. 'Did you hear a car?'

Drily Wexford said, 'I hear a car every minute of my life when I'm not asleep. How do you escape it in this world?'

The door opened and Mark came in, followed by his mother. But Burden continued to stand transfixed, only holding out an absent hand to the child. Mark wasn't shy; he went up to Wexford, wanting the pencil he held in his hand, then the pad on which notes had been made, finally climbing on to Wexford's knees. Burden went to the window and parted the curtains with both hands. His knuckles had whitened and his shoulders drooped a little.

'Oh, not again?' Jenny said. 'He's not back again?'

'I'm afraid he is.' Burden turned back into the room and faced Wexford. 'Am I overreacting when I say I'm seriously thinking of applying for an injunction?'

Instead of answering directly, Wexford said, 'Let me go.' He lifted the little boy on to the floor, sacrificed pad and pencil to him. 'Don't get it on the carpet, or your Mum'll be after me.'

As he came out into the hall, the bell rang. Wexford let it ring again. Burden had joined him, was standing just behind him. The letter-box lid started flapping as fingers pushed at it and then the other hand pounded on the knocker. The fingers appeared under the opened letter-box lid and there was something about them and the smear marks they left on pale paintwork that made Burden draw in his breath with a rough hiss. Wexford crossed the hall and opened the door.

Clifford took a step back when he saw him. He was looking beyond Wexford's bulk and when he saw Burden he smiled. Wexford eyed him in a kind of stricken silence, for Clifford was covered with blood. His grey shirt and knitted pullover and the zipper-jacket he wore, his grey flannel trousers, his striped tie and grey socks and lace-up shoes – all were thick with blood, matted and plastered with it, and in places the blood was damp still, glistening still. And Clifford, smiling, stepped over the threshold into the hall with no one to impede him until the little boy came out of the living room and Burden, sweeping him up in his arms, shouted, 'Don't let him see. For God's sake, don't let him see!'

18

THE driving-seat of his mother's car which had always been a curious place of refuge for Clifford, a sanctuary and scene of unimaginable cogitations, was bloodied from his clothes. Easy to make an analogy here with wombs, but Wexford shied away from that one. Though it was dark and foggy, he had the seat of the car and the blood-encrusted steering wheel covered up before it was towed away. Now they sat in the first of a convoy of police vehicles, Clifford between him and Burden, crawling through the fog. Donaldson's headlights made two green bars of radiance that petered out into the wool-like greyness after a few feet. Behind them another driver clung to Donaldson's rear lights and a third followed, all moving at about fifteen miles an hour.

Clifford had Burden to himself now, a captive therapist, and his face wore an expression that was at the same time serene and insane. At appalling cost he had got what he wanted. He talked. He spoke uninterruptedly, sometimes lifting up his bloody hands which had smeared Burden's door with stains, the bitten nails blackened with blood, turning them over and looking at them with wondering pleasure. Already he had told Burden what he had done and – insofar as his conscious mind understood this – why he had done it. But he repeated himself as if he enjoyed the sound of his own monotonous, now measured and almost complacent voice.

'She sent me up into the attic, Mike. She thought she could shut me in like she did when I was little. I was to go up there and fetch her down a lamp. The one in the dining room had got broken, there was a fault in the connection, and she said to fetch her one of the lamps that had belonged to my grandparents. But I'm cunning, Mike, I'm cleverer than she is basically, I've got a better brain. I knew she would rather sit in the dark than use anything from up there. She wouldn't use a lamp my father's mother had used.'

Burden was returning his gaze with what looked like blankness unless you knew Burden as Wexford did and then you understood it was controlled desperation.

'The truth was she wanted to keep me from seeing you. When she told me she'd phoned you to complain about our seeing each other – when she told me that, I saw red. But I didn't show my feelings, I kept everything suppressed, I didn't even answer her. I went upstairs like an obedient little boy. Of course I couldn't be sure what she was up to then; I wondered what she was at. I knew she was following me up, though, and I said to myself, why is she following me when she's asked me to fetch her something? If she's going to come up too, why couldn't she have fetched it herself?'

Forcing the words out in a voice that sounded unlike his own, Burden said, 'So what . . . what did you do, Clifford?' He had already cautioned him. It had been a bizarre ritual taking place in the hall of Burden's own house, Clifford pleasurably pointing out individual bloodstains on his jacket, his shirt, his trousers, beginning on a confession whose utterance held a childlike innocence, while Burden mouthed in that same strangled tone the words of the caution: 'You are not obliged to say anything in answer to the charge but anything you do say . . .'

Now Clifford continued in the same blithe, confiding way, 'It wasn't the attic where Mr Carroll had to break the door down. We'd never had that door mended. The photographs were in there. It was the one with the bedroom furniture.' He brought his face closer to Burden's – said in an intimate way, as to one familiar with the secrets of all hearts, 'You know what I mean.'

Donaldson braked hard as they came suddenly up against the headlights of a huge truck. It was carrying earth-moving equipment, cranes and scoops that loomed dinosaur-like out of the rolling mist. Slowly the convoy edged past it; they were beyond Sundays now, in the narrow lane that led nowhere but to the Sanders' house and the farmer's bungalow. Fog filled the channel between high hedges, hung overhead like dark fallen cloud. They weren't far from the entrance now. Donaldson crept along, stopped the car once or twice – like a dog sniffing, scenting its way to the familiar ground. And it seemed that down here in the least likely place, a low place still in the river valley, the fog had lifted a little, for a high wall of hedge was visible and a tree like a great figure with arms upraised.

Clifford hadn't once looked out of the window; Burden's face seemed the only view he required. He said conversationally, 'All those mattresses were in there, and blankets and things. I expect you remember that time I showed you. And there was a lamp there too, like she said there was. She's clever, she knows about getting her details right. But there was something she forgot. It was the wrong sort of plug, the old-fashioned sort with no earth, an old ten-amp plug with no earth. It was so absurd I could have laughed out loud, only I didn't feel like laughing then, Mike . . .'

The gap in the hedge was found and Donaldson turned in carefully. Tyres crunched on the gravel. The leafy wall of the house, a great square of dark, still, hanging foliage, reared before them. Clifford turned his head at last, gave his home an indifferent look.

'She came up behind me. She was quiet enough, but I was prepared for her. Strange, isn't it, Mike? She's a mystery, she's hidden behind a mask, and she's slow and gliding like all mysterious people. But I know her and I knew what she was going to do; it was so obvious. Her hand went down to the door handle to pull out the key and I was standing there with that old lamp in my hands –'

'Come on, Clifford,' Burden said, 'we're here.'

The air felt wet; it was just as if a cold, wet hand wiped their faces as Wexford walked up to the front door. Dr Crocker was getting out of the car behind with Prentiss, the Scene-of-Crimes man, and there was a new photographer he didn't recognize. Clifford wouldn't separate himself from Burden but stayed close to him, nearly but not quite touching him. If he had actually touched him, Burden thought he might have cried out in horror, though he would have exerted all the control he was capable of to avoid this. It was bad enough knowing some of the blood adhered to his own clothes after that nightmare car journey. He knew he would have to burn everything it had touched.

Wexford asked Clifford for the front-door key and Clifford's answer was to pull out his pockets, the pockets of his jacket and trousers. They were all quite empty. He had left his ignition key in the Metro. As to the others . . .

'I must have dropped them somewhere. I've lost them. They may be somewhere in the garden here.'

Under the wet grass, among the blackened weeds beaded with waterdrops, or on the road in the gutter outside Burden's house. Wexford made the decision quickly.

'We'll force the door. Not this one, it's too heavy. A door at the back.'

It was a slow, grim procession that made its way round the side of the house to the back regions where the rear wall and shed were just visible in the light of Archbold's and Davidson's torches, but nothing beyond. The beam of light played on a back door that looked solid enough, but was less weighty than the massive studded oak barrier whose key Clifford had lost. Davidson was the biggest of them after Wexford and he was also the youngest, but it was Burden who pushed forward and put his shoulder to the door. He had energy which must be released, some act of violence he needed to perform.

Two hard runs at it and the door went down. The crash it made set Clifford laughing; he laughed merrily as they stepped over the shattered boards, the broken glass. Olson would have said, Wexford thought, that it was more than a citadel of bricks and mortar they had broken into and laid open. The flooding of the place with light brought a kind of relief, not that a really bright illumination was possible for Mrs Sanders had been mean with the electricity. It was colder in here even than outside. A little of the fog seemed to have got in as Burden recalled the woman had once warned him it would, waiting ghost-like on the threshold to slip in. The damp chill seemed to penetrate clothes and prick skin with icicles.

'Stop that laughing,' he said roughly.

His voice wiped Clifford's face clean of all amusement. It was at once grave and rueful. 'Sorry, Mike . . .'

They went upstairs, Wexford leading the way. Through some lunatic quirk of meanness or indifference, it was impossible to turn upstairs lights on from downstairs, so that one walked out of light into a yawning darkness before a hand could reach out for a switch. The comparatively elegant staircase gave way to the steep attic flight. Wexford could see nothing at the top, only deep blackness. He put out his hand for Archbold's torch and the thin beam of light showed him a half-open door at the head of the stairs.

The light switch wasn't even on the staircase wall but up in the passage. He deliberately averted his eyes from the open door and the room until the light was on. Then he entered the room with Burden and Clifford at his heels, the others close behind. Wexford put the attic light on and then he looked.

Dorothy Sanders lay half on her back, half-sideways on one of the mattresses. A small, thin woman, composed of wire only in metaphor and fancy, she had had as much blood in her as anyone else and most of it seemed to have spilled from that fragile frame. Face and head were a mass of blood and tissue, cerebral matter and even bone chips. Her hair was lost in it, drowned in it. She lay in her own blood, dark as wine and clotted to a paste, on a mattress dyed crimson-black.

Beside the body, not flung down but set up precisely on a small round-topped bedside table, was a lamp in the art nouveau style, a sculptured lily growing from its heavy metal base, its shade composed of frayed and split pleated silk. It was a forensic scientist's ideal, this lamp, from the clots of blood and bloody hair which encrusted its base to the stain which transformed its now bent silk shade from green to an almost total dark brown.

Of them all only Clifford was unused to sights such as this, but he alone among them was smiling.

It was very late. They had done everything – what Sergeant Martin insisted on calling 'the formalities'. But the idea of going to their respective homes had scarcely entered Wexford's head, still less Burden's. Burden's face had that look of a man who has seen indelible horrors. They are stamped there, those sights, but showing themselves in the staring eyes and taut skin as the skull inside the flesh reveals itself, a symbol of what has been seen and a foreshadowing of a future.

Burden couldn't rest. He stood in Wexford's office. He just stood, keeping his eyes averted from Wexford's, then bending his head and pressing his fingers to his temples.

'You had better sit down, Mike.'

'You'll be saying it wasn't my fault in a minute.'

'I'm not a psychiatrist or a philosopher. How would I know?'

Burden moved. He held his hands behind his back, came over to a chair and stood in front of it. 'If I had left him alone . . .' He didn't finish the sentence.

'Strictly speaking, it was he who wouldn't leave you alone. You had to question him in the first place; you couldn't be expected to foresee the turn things would take.'

'Well, if I hadn't . . . rejected him then, when he wanted to talk to me. It's ironical, isn't it? First he didn't want me and then I didn't want him. Reg, could I have averted this by letting him come and talk to me?'

'I wish you'd sit down. I don't know what it is you want, Mike. Do you want the hard truth or something to comfort you?'

'Of course I want the truth.'

'Then the truth probably is – and I realize it's hard to take – that when you in your own words rejected Clifford,

239

he felt he had to do something to draw your attention to him. And the best way to draw a policeman's attention to someone is to become a murderer. Clifford, after all, isn't sane; he doesn't have sane reactions. Of course he attacked his mother to prevent her locking him in that room, but he could have achieved that without killing her. He could have overpowered her and locked her in there himself. He killed her to attract your attention.'

'I know, I see that. I realized it when we were there . . . in that room. But he was a murderer already. Why couldn't he have admitted killing Mrs Robson? That would have attracted my attention all right. Do you think —' Burden drew in his breath, expelled it with a sigh. He was sitting down now, leaning forward and holding on to the edge of Wexford's desk with both hands. 'Do you think that's what he wanted to talk to me about when he kept on trying to see me? Do you think he wanted to confess?'

'No,' Wexford said shortly. 'No, I don't.'

He was anxious now to bring this conversation to a close. The question he was sure Burden was going to ask would be far better postponed till the morning. Burden was in a bad enough state as it was without this further addition to his guilty feelings. For this would be the ultimate guilt. Of course he would have to know tomorrow, he would have to know as soon as possible in the morning . . . before the special court sat. 'Mike, would you like a drink? I've got some whisky in the cupboard. Don't look like that, I don't tipple the stuff secretly — or even un-secretly, come to that. One of our . . . clients offered it to me as a bribe and because I thought it would be handy to have, I took it and gave him the current Tesco price for it. Six pounds forty-eight, I think it was.' He was talking for the sake of talking as, burbling on. 'I won't have one, though. Let me have the Clifford tapes, will you, and then I'm going to drive you home. I'll give you a stiff one and then take you home.'

'I don't want anything to drink. I shall feel like hell in the morning. If I could justify what I did, I'd feel better. If I could tell myself the only possible way we could have nailed this man was by waiting for him to commit another murder – giving him enough rope, so to speak. You say you don't think he wanted to confess?'

'I don't think he wanted to confess, Mike. Let's go home.'

'What time is it?'

'Nearly two.'

They closed the office door and walked down the corridor under the pale, steady, bleaching lights. Clifford was downstairs, at the back, in one of the cells. Kingsmarkham police station cells were more comfortable than most prisons, with a bit of rug on the floor, two blankets on the bunk and a blue slip on the pillow, a cubicle with loo and basin opening off the tiny room. Burden cast a backward glance in that direction as they came out of the lift. Sergeant Bray was on duty behind the desk with PC Savitt beside him, looking at something in a file. Wexford said good night but Burden said nothing.

For the first time, the Christmas lights were on in the tree. Burden had noticed them as something unreal in the fog, a kind of mockery, as they returned from Ash Farm bringing Clifford with them. Either they were on a time clock which had failed to work, or someone had forgotten to switch them off. The reds and blues and whites came on for fifteen seconds, then the yellows and greens and pinks, then the lot, winking hard before the reds and blues and whites returned alone. By now the fog had almost lifted and the colours glimmered in a thin mist.

'Wicked waste of the taxpayers' money,' Burden growled.

'I haven't got my car,' Wexford said. 'It seems so long ago that I'd forgotten. I suppose I meant to drive you in your car.'

'I'll drive you.'

A town that slept, a town that might have been emptied of its folk that silent night – inhabitants who had fled, leaving a light on here and there.

Burden said, climbing up to Highlands, turning into Eastbourne Road, 'I still can't see how he did it – killed

241

Gwen Robson, I mean. He must have been in that car park by a quarter to six, met her as she came in to get her car and killed her. He would have been getting out of his mother's car and she walking up to hers. That must have been the way of it – unpremeditated, a frenzied act on the spur of the moment. He'll tell us now, no doubt.'

Wexford began to say something about the grotesqueness, the incongruity, of a young man stepping out of a car and happening by chance to be holding a circular knitting needle. They passed Robson's house – dark, all the curtains drawn – and Dita Jago's where a light was on, a red glow behind drawn crimson curtains. A cat came out of the Whittons', streaked across the road. Burden braked hard as it leapt clear, on to a wall, up a tree.

'Damned things,' said Burden. 'One shouldn't brake, one shouldn't give way to one's reflexes like that. Suppose there'd been someone behind me? It was only a cat. Look, Reg, that woman Rosemary Whitton has to be wrong. I mean, it's pretty hard for me to have to face that, because it means I was irresponsible in not consenting to talk to Clifford when he wanted me to. I took her word, of course I did. But we never really confirmed it.'

Wexford sighed. 'I did.'

'What? Took her word? I know. But she was wrong. And the wine-market manager was wrong too. Rosemary Whitton must have seen Clifford ten minutes earlier and he'd gone before she hit the meter. It was a genuine mistake, but it was a mistake.'

Up Battle Hill to stop outside his gate. The house was dark; Dora had gone to bed long ago.

Wexford unclipped the seat belt. 'Wait till the morning, shall we?'

He said good night, dragged himself upstairs and fell exhausted into bed – then awoke immediately, energetically, into a prospect of sleepless hours. When they were past and he was back down there, preparing for Clifford's appearance before the magistrates, he was going to have to tell Burden the facts: that he had checked and double-checked Rosemary Whitton's statement; that he had not only checked with the wine-market manager and three occupants of flats above the wine market, but had also found the traffic warden who, arriving on the scene to examine the damaged meter, had – while talking to Rosemary Whitton – seen Clifford drive away. It had been five to six.

19

DOROTHY SANDERS had never been divorced;
Davidson's investigation of records had established
that. Nor had she needed to keep herself by the
humble sewing and knitting – traditional occupations of
the poor virtuous woman she had once read about in
some historical romance? – which she told her son had
supported them in his childhood. For during those years
she had been regularly drawing on the joint bank account
that was in her name and her husband's. Now that she
was dead, access to that account was no longer denied to
the police.

It had been fed by the interest on Charles Sanders'
investments, mostly unit trusts. Over a period of eighteen
years since their separation, only she had drawn on it.
From the bank manager's slightly defensive manner, Wexford gathered that this perhaps curious fact had never
been noticed. He was a man opposed to new technology
and blamed the fault, if fault it was, on the fact that
in recent years the administration of the account had
been by computer. Wexford marvelled at Mrs Sanders'
capacity for lying and sustained secretiveness. It made
him wonder if she had ever been married to Sanders,
even if Clifford was her own child, but these facts
were soon established. Dorothy Clifford and Charles
Sanders had been married at St Peter's, Kingsmarkham
in October 1963 and Clifford born to her in February
1966.

Wexford had himself driven back to Ash Farm and he
took Burden with him, insisted on it. Burden had accepted
Clifford's innocence of the first crime at first with reservations and arguments, then with a deep and bitter self-
reproach. It was clear to him, and this Wexford was
unable to deny, that the death of Dorothy Sanders had

come about as the direct result of his refusal to continue the sessions with Clifford.

Burden was silent for a while. Then he said, 'I think I shall have to resign.'

'For God's sake, why?'

'If it's true that I could drive a man to murder – and it is, I did do that – I'm not fit to be a police officer. It's part of my duty to prevent crime, not provoke it.'

'So, logically, you should never have questioned Clifford in the first place. Suspecting him of the murder of Gwen Robson, you should nevertheless have ignored him because he appeared to be an unbalanced person with abnormal reactions.'

'I'm not saying that. I'm saying that having once questioned him I shouldn't have . . . well, abandoned him to his fate.'

'You should have gone on talking to him day after day, for hours on end, session after session? For how long? Weeks? Months? What about your work? Your own sanity, come to that? Am I my brother's keeper?'

Burden took that question which Wexford had meant rhetorically – which perhaps Cain had meant rhetorically – in a literal way. 'Well, yes, maybe I am. What was the answer to it, anyway? What did whoever it was – God, was it? – say?'

'Nothing,' said Wexford. 'Absolutely nothing. Come on, forget about resigning. You're not resigning, you're coming with me to the scene of the crime.'

In gloomy silence Burden sat beside him in the car. It was a passive sort of winter's day, neither cold nor mild, the sky pale grey and clotted like porridge. Sometimes the sun appeared low on the horizon, a shiny disc of plate showing through where the gruel thinned. The shop windows in the High Street were full of pre-Christmas glitter and a huge imported Christmas tree, gift from some town in Germany no one had previously heard of but which was twinned with Kingsmarkham, had been set up outside the Barringdean Centre. Burden remarked in a sour way about the amount it must cost to run that electronic

245

digital arrangement at the Tesco end which announced alternately that here were gifts for all the family and that nine shopping days remained until Christmas.

'What are we coming here for, anyway?'

He meant to Ash Farm, down long winding Ash Lane, where the grass verges were grey with splashed mud and dead elms with peeling trunks awaited the axe. But the air was clear today and in the distance the outline of the hummocky hill that hid the town could be seen. Ivy-clad Ash Farm slid into view, its many eyes peeping from amongst the evergreen growth. Two police cars were parked in front of it and a policeman in uniform was on duty at the foot of the flight of steps.

'I hadn't thought of going inside,' Wexford said.

'You said we were visiting the scene of the crime.'

Wexford made no reply but nodded to PC Leonard who saluted him and said, 'Good afternoon, sir.' In spite of what he had seen on the previous evening he found it hard to realize that Dorothy Sanders, so strong and upright and confident, was dead, the metallic voice silenced for ever. And when he looked through the dark gleaming glass into the thinly furnished room where the ashes of a fire lay in the grate, he half-expected to see her there, moving across the uncarpeted floor, issuing her orders with a pointing finger. A ghost, that would have to be, and she had been afraid of ghosts, afraid of the dark and of letting fog enter the house . . .

With Burden following him and Donaldson, he walked round the house into the back garden. It was new to him, but Burden had been out there before on the day of the search, triumphantly discovering garrotes in the shed attached to the rear wall. A curious place to put a shed, wasn't it? In order to reach it, a considerable area of damp grass had to be crossed. Earth, whether turfed or not, is always wet in winter, even during dry spells. He felt his shoes sink into the squelchy softness.

Dorothy Sanders had paid less attention to her garden than to her house, but had nevertheless achieved out here a similar kind of barren neatness. There were few plants

246

that looked cultivated, though it was hard to tell at this time of the year, and even fewer weeds. It looked as if Mrs Sanders – or Clifford, on her instructions – had watered the flowerbed areas with the kind of toxic stuff that destroys broad-leaved plants. It looked as if at some point during her life in this house she had set about destroying the garden as it must once have existed. The few trees had been savagely lopped, so that from the stumps of amputated branches new twigs grew out at strange angles. A faint pinkness had appeared in the sky, sign of sunset. It would be dusk very soon, then deeply dark. Nine shopping days to Christmas, seven long nights and seven short days to the Solstice. One day to Sheila's court appearance . . .

These short days, cut off in mid-afternoon, hindered his progress. Nature still had the upper hand . . . just. Or, rather, he couldn't be absolutely sure the expense of using powerful lights was warranted. He padded through the wet grass to the furthermost corner of the garden and there, up against the back fence, he could just make out in the distance the low roof of what must be Ash Farm Lodge, rising above screens of Leyland cypress.

'Would you like to introduce me to Mr Carroll?'

They drove down the lane in the sunset light, the last of the light. With a rattling cry, a cock pheasant rose out of the hedge on seldom-used cumbersome wings. There was the sound of a shot and then another.

'It's only Carroll,' said Burden. 'The way Kingsmarkham's become urbanized, we forget we live in the country sometimes.'

Carroll's dog came timidly to meet them. Perhaps, though, it wasn't timid – perhaps it was slyly creeping up preparatory to an attack. Wexford put out his hand to the dog and a harsh voice shouted, 'Don't touch him!'

The farmer appeared with a dead hare slung round his neck, in his left hand a pair of redleg partridges he was holding by their tail feathers.

Wexford said mildly, 'Mr Carroll? Chief Inspector

Wexford, Kingsmarkham CID. I believe you've met my colleague, Inspector Burden.'

'He was this way before, yes.'

'Can we go inside?'

'What for?' Carroll asked.

'I want to talk to you. If you'd rather we didn't go into your house, you can come back to the police station with us. That will suit us just as well. It's up to you, one or the other.'

'You can come in if you want,' Carroll said.

The dog preceded them in, head down and tail between its legs. Carroll made a growling noise at it, a remarkable animal noise which might have been expected to come from the dog, not its master. This was apparently the signal for it to go into its basket which it did like a hypnotic subject, curling itself into a circle and putting its head on its paws. Carroll hung up the twelve-bore, took off his boots and put them on the now stained and corrugated magazine on the oven top which was still just recognizable as a copy of *Kim*. The hare and the birds trailed bloody heads into the sink. The table was a mass of papers, chequebook and paying-in book from the Midland Bank, a VAT ledger, crumpled invoices. Wexford knew the chances of his being asked to sit down were around a hundred to one, so he had seated himself and motioned to Burden to do the same before Carroll had got his slippers on.

'Where's your wife, Mr Carroll?' Wexford began.

'What's that to you?' He didn't sit down, he stood over them. 'It's her up the road that's dead, and her boy that's potty did it. You stick to that, you see he's put away for life; that'll keep you lot busy, not coming poking into my business.'

'Rumour has it that your wife has left you,' Wexford observed.

For a moment he thought the farmer was going to strike him. Unpleasant as that would be, it would at least provide a reason for arresting him. But Carroll, having clenched his fists and put them up, stepped back, setting his teeth.

248

Wexford decided just the same that he might feel more at an advantage on his feet. He was a bigger man than Carroll, though older.

The kitchen was rapidly growing dark. He reached for the only switch in the room and unexpectedly bright light poured from the central bulb in its incongruous shade: pink frilled cotton in the shape of a mob-cap. There were other such touches in that grim place: a battery-operated wall clock, its face a sunflower, a calendar that pictured a kitten in a basket, the date May of this year. In the bright light Carroll blinked.

'It was about six months ago that she left, wasn't it? End of June?' If Carroll wouldn't answer, there wasn't much he could do. He changed tack a little. 'Tell me about your neighbour, Charles Sanders? Did you know him? Were you here when he was living here?'

Carroll growled. It was the same language he used when issuing commands to his dog, but succeeded by reasonably comprehensible English. 'His dad died. Day after the funeral he upped and left. What do you want to know that for?'

'You don't ask the police questions, Carroll,' said Burden. 'We ask you. Right?'

Another growl. It was almost funny.

Wexford said, 'He never came back. He never came back to see his son, he never contributed to his wife's support or his son's. He left his old mother in his wife's care and she dumped her in an old people's home. I'm being very frank with you, Mr Carroll, and I'd like you to do the same by us. It's eighteen years since Sanders left. You were newly married, newly arrived here. I don't think he left, I think he's dead. What do you think?'

'How should I know? It's no business of mine.'

'What did your wife think, Mr Carroll? She knew, didn't she? Somehow or other she found out about Sanders. Did she tell you what she knew, or did she keep it to herself? Maybe she told only one person?'

'What person?'

By that remark Wexford had meant to infer nothing that

249

could in fact be of momentous significance to Carroll, but the farmer read into it more than was implied and his face grew red and seemed to swell. Although he made no immediate move, a change had come over him – a kind of concentration, a gathering and intensifying of power, enough to make Burden spring to his feet and push back the chair. It was that which did it. Carroll reached behind him for the gun on the wall, unhooked it and, stepping back, levelled it at them from a distance of about four feet.

'Put that down,' Wexford said. 'Don't be a fool.'

'I'm giving you one minute to get out of here.'

At least now they would be able to arrest him, Wexford thought. The farmer could look at them and keep his eye on the sunflower clock at the same time. One eye open, the dog watched from his basket. This was something it understood – a gun aimed, a helpless quarry. When I double up full of shot, Wexford thought ridiculously, maybe it will come and retrieve me.

Burden said, his head cocked towards the door, 'There's Donaldson coming now,' as if he heard footsteps.

It was a trick and it worked. Carroll turned his head and Wexford's fist shot out to catch him on the jaw. The gun went off as he fell, and in that low-ceilinged bungalow room it made an enormous noise, a noise like a bomb, a noise like the bomb in his front garden which Wexford couldn't remember hearing. The farmer rolled over and the gun dropped from his hands to clatter away across the tiles. Bits of plaster dropped from the ceiling where shot had peppered it. Smoke and a stench of gunpowder and the bewildered dog looking from side to side, beginning a helpless, forbidden barking. And then Donaldson did come, pounding up the path and throwing open the back door.

'Are you OK, sir? What happened?'

'I don't know my own strength,' said Wexford. He considered poking at Carroll with his toe, but thought better of it and heaved the man up by the shoulders. Carroll groaned, his head sagging. 'I don't suppose we've got any handcuffs in the car, have we?'

'I don't think so, sir.'

'Then we must do without, but I don't think he'll give much trouble.'

Carroll was a big man and it took the three of them to get him into the car. They shut up the dog in the kitchen and Donaldson, who was fond of dogs, gave him a bowl of water and the hare.

'That's the way to undo years of training in half an hour,' he said cheerfully.

The artifacts that lay all over the surfaces in Wexford's office – in court they would have been called 'exhibits' – included Carroll's twelve-bore, a muddied copy of *Kim* magazine, a circular knitting needle, size six, and some of the contents of the dead woman's coat pockets. There was something distressing, though scarcely pathetic, about that lipstick in its shiny gilt case, the red of a fire engine. The almost white face powder with its faint iridescence had been marketed for someone young and fair, someone like Lesley Arbel. The chequebook for the joint account was in the names of C. L. Sanders and D. K. Sanders and – at least during the lifetime of this particular book it had been used only to draw sums of cash. A hundred pounds a month was what Dorothy Sanders had drawn during the past two years. It wasn't much, it was modest, but for the past two years her income had been supplemented by Clifford's earnings.

That morning Kingsmarkham magistrates had committed him for trial on a charge of murder and remanded him in custody until the trial was due. Even Burden could see now that there could be no other murder charge for him to face, that it was impossible for him to have been guilty of the death of Gwen Robson. He had seen Clifford driven away to the remand prison at Myringham before he and Wexford left for Ash Farm and had not mentioned him since. But now he came into Wexford's office and spoke abruptly.

'I felt I should have stood up before the magistrates and

said I wanted to make a statement. I should have admitted my responsibility – well, my share in what that poor little guy did.'

'"Poor little guy", is it now? What's become of your much-vaunted principle of reserving pity for the victim?' Wexford was reading a letter, nodding from time to time as if what he read brought him a long-awaited satisfaction. He winced at the sounds that were coming from the depths of the building, a steady crash-crash-crash, and looked up at Burden irritably.

'I've let him down all along the line. I should have publicly admitted my part in what he did.'

'You'd make yourself a laughing-stock. Imagine what used to be called the press, and are now for some daft reason called the media, would make of that. Excuse me.' Wexford's phone was ringing and he picked up the receiver. 'Yes, yes, thanks,' he said. 'You've a record of that on your computer, have you? Is it possible for me to have some sort of print-out? Yes . . . yes. Someone will come down for it before the library closes. When do you close? Six-thirty tonight? That's just about an hour. All right. Thanks for your help.'

'What's that noise?' Burden opened the door a crack the better to hear the banging. When Wexford shrugged, he asked in a tone of minimal interest, 'What was all that about?'

'A woman's alibi. And another one has just fallen neatly into place. Just a matter of clearing things up really, eliminating remote possibilities. Do you remember that gale we had in the middle of last month? It blew down the phone lines at Sundays and Ash Lane.'

'You think I'm a maundering idiot, don't you? It's all hot air and bullying with me, but underneath I'm weak as water. I was scared of Clifford, do you know that? When he came to my house, I was afraid to answer the door.'

'You did answer it though.'

'Why was I so set on it? Why did I make up my mind it had to be him when all the evidence was against it?'

'At any rate you admit that now.' Wexford sounded bored, languid. 'What can I say? Anything I say sounds like saying I told you so. Well, no, I might tell you to let it be a lesson to you. You'd like that, wouldn't you?' He got up and looked out of the window at the tree with its winking lights, the red, blue and white sequence, the yellow, green and pink sequence. The sky was dark but clear, a dome of deepening blue with stars. 'Mike, I truly think that if he hadn't killed her then, he would have killed her one day. Tomorrow or next week or next year. Murder's infectious too. Have you ever thought of that? Clifford killed his mother because she was there and because she was restraining him and . . . to draw your attention to him. But perhaps he also killed her because the idea had been put into his head, because he knew, if you like, that it was possible to kill people. He had seen a murdered woman he thought at first was his mother. Hoped it was his mother? Maybe. But the idea was planted, wasn't it? Others could do it, so he could do it. It infected him.'

'Do you really think so?' Burden's face was desperately hopeful, the face of a man who may drown if the flung hand can find nothing stronger than a straw. 'Do you honestly think that?'

'Ask Olson, he'll tell you. Let's go home, Mike, and make a few enquiries about our prisoner on the way.'

The phone rang again as they reached the door and Wexford went back and picked it up. The voice at the other end was so clear that even Burden heard from three yards away, 'I have Sandra Dale on the line.'

Wexford said into the phone, 'It doesn't matter, I don't need it any longer,' and after listening for a moment, 'that doesn't surprise me. You won't find it now.'

He thanked her and said goodbye and they went downstairs. PC Savitt told them that Carroll, who had been put in the cell previously occupied by Clifford, was quiet now. Dr Crocker had seen him and offered him a sedative, which Carroll had surprisingly accepted. Before that he had threatened to break the place up, though had got no further than a regular lifting up of two of the legs of the iron bedstead prior to letting them crash on to the floor.

'Could you hear him, sir?'

'I should think they could hear him in the Barringdean Centre.'

Burden stood on the steps outside the swing doors. 'It's a funny thing the way you can do something, take a determined course of action over a length of time and be absolutely sure you're right, not have a shadow of doubt. And a week later you can look back amazed at what you did, hardly able to realize it was you who did it, and wonder if anyone like that can actually be sane. I mean, I wonder if anyone like *me* can be.'

'I'm cold,' said Wexford. 'I don't want to stand about here.'

'Yes, all right, sorry. What was that you were reading?'

Wexford got into his car. 'It was the letter Lesley Arbel was searching for and Sandra Dale has been searching for, which I have been searching for and have at last found.'

'Aren't you going to tell me what was in it?'

'No,' said Wexford and he shut the car door. Rolling down the window half-way, he said, 'I would have done but you're too late, you've missed the boat. I'll tell you in the morning.' He grinned. 'I'll tell you everything in the morning.'

And he drove away, leaving Burden standing there watching the car depart, not sure if he understood quite what 'everything' implied.

20

B URDEN drove the car down to the second level and
parked as near as he could to where Gwen Robson's
body had lain nearly a month before. Every space
on the level was now full and would be all day, every day,
up until Christmas and beyond during the end-of-the-year
sales.

Serge Olson was the first to get out of the car. He had
come into the police station just as they were leaving to
enquire when and how he would be permitted to visit
Clifford Sanders in the remand prison, and Wexford had
invited him to go with them. An Opel Kadett and a Ford
Granada were now parked where Gwen Robson's Escort
and the Brooks' blue Lancia had been. A Vauxhall came
nosing round looking for a space and proceeded down
the ramp towards the third level. But apart from themselves there were no people. It was car world, an area of
car life where bodies were cars and people their brains or
moving spirits. Oil and water lay in pools, car excrement,
and the place smelt of car sweat.

Wexford shook himself out of fanciful imaginings
and said, 'Lately we seem to have lost sight somewhat
of our victim, of Gwen Robson. But if she wasn't the
first to be murdered, she was at any rate the first we
knew of – the first to draw our attention to this case.'
Burden looked enquiringly at him, but he only shook his
head.

'She brought her death on herself; she was a blackmailer. But like a lot of blackmailers she was – I won't
say innocent, she was naïve. She tangled with the wrong
person. And I think she justified what she was doing by
the reason for which she wanted the money, which was
to pay for her husband's hip replacement. If he was to
have this operation on the National Health service, it was

possible he would have had to wait up to three years, by which time she feared he might be totally crippled. Three or four thousand pounds would pay for the replacement to be done privately and for hospitalization. At the time of her death, she had accumulated about sixteen hundred.'

Wexford's glance took in Olson and his driver. 'Let's go into the centre, shall we?'

It was one of those freak December days that are like April; all that was missing were the leaf buds on the trees. The flags on the turrets of the Barringdean building fluttered in a light breeze and the sky was milky-blue with clouds like shreds of foam. They came out of the metal lift with its graffiti into mild sunshine.

'"This castle hath a pleasant seat,"' Wexford said dryly. And if you half-closed your eyes the centre's medieval fortress look was compounded by the trolleys tumbled about the car-park entrance and across the roadway like siege-engines abandoned by their users. 'I've already discussed this with you, Mike. We know that Lesley Arbel brought her aunt photocopies of letters received by the agony aunt at *Kim*, the magazine she worked for, in disregard of the undertaking she had given when she got the job not to divulge or discuss the contents of such letters. Nevertheless, she did make photocopies of certain letters and she did show them to Gwen Robson. Now Gwen Robson, being a salacious woman, was interested in a general way in what she was shown, but she was far more deeply interested in letters coming from people who lived in this neighbourhood.'

Walking along the covered way that would bring them to the doors in the middle of the central gallery, Wexford went on, 'I don't know what gave her the idea of blackmail, but it was an idea both obvious and clever. True, she might have picked up information of a damaging kind about her clients while she was working, but it was unlikely she would have been able to acquire documentary evidence. She had tried other ways of raising money, but these ways had either ceased – the old people who paid for special indulgences had died, for example – or failed, as in the case of Eric Swallow whom she was unable to induce to make a will in her favour. Blackmail remained, the blackmail of women whose secrets they dared only divulge to a more or less anonymous oracle, an agony aunt.

'Two letters particularly interested Gwen Robson both because of their sensational content and the addresses of the women who had written them. One was from a Mrs Margaret Carroll of Ash Farm Lodge, Ash Lane, Forbydean, and the other . . . well, here we are half-way between Tesco and British Home Stores. Shall we go into the café for coffee, or a healthful veggie juice in Demeter?'

The dissenting voice was Olson's, who would have preferred the vegetable juice. But he gave way gracefully, only stipulating decaffeinated coffee.

'I believe,' Wexford went on, 'that Gwen Robson's blackmailing efforts had been successful up to a point, that is, her two women victims had been paying her for her silence over a period of weeks or months. No doubt because, poor things, they couldn't raise a lump sum. Let us come to the day in question, November 19, a Thursday and four-thirty in the afternoon, the time when more of the residents of Kingsmarkham seem to be in here than at any other. Gwen Robson arrived at four-forty, parked her car in the second level and came in most probably by the way we did, under the covered way and through the central door. Now we know what shopping she did, though not the order in which she did it, and we have no way of knowing how much window-shopping she indulged in. But we can make an intelligent guess that she started at British Home Stores where she bought her light bulbs and went on to Boots for her toothpaste and talcum powder. Let us say that brings us to five o'clock.

'Helen Brook is in Demeter next door here, buying calendula capsules. She sees Mrs Robson out of the window and at once recognizes her as the busybody home help who criticized her lifestyle and said she hoped she would never have children – this presumably because she feared they would be illegitimate. Helen Brook intends to show herself to Mrs Robson as ample proof that she is indeed about to have a child, but before she can do this she actually goes into labour, or has her first labour pain. However, she has already noticed that Mrs Robson is in conversation with a very well-dressed girl. Whom do we know that we should describe like that? Lesley Arbel. The Robsons' niece Lesley Arbel, whom we know to have been in Kingsmarkham that afternoon.'

The coffee came and with it a slice of Black Forest cake for Burden. He must be eating for comfort. Not for the first time Wexford marvelled at the manifest untruth expressed by healthy eating experts: that if you give up sweet things, you soon lose your sweet tooth. He turned his eyes from the chocolate cake, the cream and the cherries, and looked out at the concourse where in time for Christmas a sub-aqueous arrangement of coloured lights turned the fountain jets to red and blue and rose.

'The killer had in his or her possession, or so we have supposed,' he went on, ' a circular knitting needle of some high-numbered gauge – that is with thicker pins at each end of the wire. But suppose it was Mrs Robson herself who had it, and her killer took it from her? This is possible if in her innocence she showed it to her killer. She might have been into the wool and crafts shop immediately prior to her meeting with the well-dressed girl. Why did Lesley Arbel come in here when she knew she would see her aunt on the following day anyway? She wanted the photocopies of those letters back; she was starting to regret ever leaving them in Gwen Robson's possession.

'Lesley Arbel is a narcissist, entirely self-absorbed, interested only in her appearance and the impression she makes on others. You'll have to tell me if this is a sound description, Serge?'

'Near enough,' said Olson. 'Narcissism is extreme self-love. The soul-image is not projected and a relatively unadapted state develops. A narcissist would be suspended in an early phase of psychosexual development where the sexual object is the self. This girl, does she have friends? Boyfriends?'

'We never heard of any. The only person she seems really to have liked was her aunt. How do you account for that if they don't care for others?'

'The aunt might simply be a mirror. I mean – it's Gwen Robson you're talking about, isn't it? – if Gwen Robson was much older than she and nothing much to look at, but really admired Lesley and flattered her and showed her off, that would be the only kind of "friend" Lesley could tolerate. Her function would be to reflect the most flattering kind of Lesley-image. A lot of girls have that kind of relationship with their mothers – and we call those good relationships!'

'I think that was it,' said Wexford. 'I think she also liked and valued her job and was very much afraid of losing it. Not only are jobs hard to come by anyway, but she feared that if she lost her job on *Kim* for this particular reason, a flagrant breach of confidence, she would in some way be blacklisted among magazines – and for all I know she was right. She wanted those letter copies back and she wanted to be sure they had not been copied in their turn.'

'Why would she kill Gwen Robson for that?' Olson asked, his frown deepening, his eyes very bright.

'She wouldn't. She didn't. It was only after she knew her aunt was dead that she became afraid about the photocopies and took the place apart trying to find them. As far as we know Gwen Robson didn't knit: there was no evidence of her knitting in the house. And I am sure Lesley Arbel didn't. Neither of them bought a circular knitting needle on the afternoon in question. Lesley, anyway, wasn't even there. It is true, as she said, that she came to Kingsmarkham, but she came for the purpose she said she did – to make certain she was properly registered for her word-processor course. According to British Telecom the phones at Sundays were out of order all that day, the cables having been damaged by wind on the previous night. Lesley was unable to get through on the phone, so down she came. All quite clear and reasonable. Far from entering the Barringdean Centre, she went straight to the station and was on a train before her aunt left home.'

Burden objected. 'But Helen What's-her-name saw her.'

'She saw a well-dressed girl, Mike. The well-dressed girl was talking to Gwen Robson out in the Mandala concourse and the time was about five. Clifford Sanders was half-way through his session with you, Serge. Where was Dita Jago? Now from the first, I was very interested in Dita Jago. She of all possible suspects possessed the weapon – or versions and repeats of the weapon: she had in her house probably half a dozen circular knitting needles in various sizes, of small and large gauge. She is a heavily-built woman, but strong and light on her feet. Suppose she was another of Gwen Robson's blackmailees – the hold which her neighbour had over her being the fact that far from being on the receiving end, so to speak, in Auschwitz, she had in fact assisted the authorities? That afternoon we know that her daughter took her own two daughters and Dita Jago shopping, dropping her mother off at the public library and presumably leaving the two children with her. But perhaps that is only an alibi concocted by the two women. Perhaps Dita went with her daughter but instead of going into the centre, preferred to sit and wait for her inside the car in the car park.'

'Would anyone prefer sitting in that car park?'

'Someone like Dita Jago might, Mike, if she had something to knit or to read – both quite likely occupations in her case. Let us say that Gwen Robson parted from the very well-dressed girl, whoever she may be, and entered the Tesco supermarket on her own where she helped herself to a trolley and began her shopping. Now your Linda Naseem, Mike, says she saw her at about five-twenty but it might have been a bit after that. Most probably it was a little before five-thirty. Again she was observed talking to a girl, but this time only the girl's back was seen. It may have been the same girl and it may not. All we know of her was that she was a girl, was slim and wearing some kind of hat. By now, Serge, Clifford is just about taking his leave of you prior to beginning his meditations in the car in Queen Street.

'If you've finished, shall we pay the bill and take a walk? You've got chocolate icing on your chin, Mike.'

'Ratepayers?' queried Olson, eyeing the chit.

'I don't see why not.' Wexford led them out into the I-shaped gallery, crossed the wide area between the line of seats and moved towards the concentric circles of flowers: poinsettias again today, fleshy-leaved kalinchoe and the Christmas cactus with spiky vermilion blossoms.

'The Mandala,' said Olson. 'Schizophrenics and people in states of conflict dream of these things. In Sanskrit, the word means a circle. In Tibetan Buddhism, it has the significance of a ritual instrument or mantra.'

Looking at the flowers but taking in Olson's words, Wexford couldn't help seeing the instrument, also circular when so manipulated, that had killed Gwen Robson. And then he remembered his own dreams after the bomb – the circular images full of patterns, kaleidoscopic designs of extreme and severe symmetry. And there was comfort in what Olson was saying: 'Its order compensates for the disorder and confusion of the psychic state. It can be an attempt at self-healing.'

They paused outside the window and the wool and crafts shop. Today the display was of canvases for tapestry work; the hanks of wool and needles had disappeared.

'Go on, Reg,' said Olson.

'Gwen Robson talks to the girl in the hat, packs her shopping into two carrier bags and leaves the centre by the Tesco supermarket exit which brings her out some two hundred yards or so to the left of the covered way. She follows the path through the car park, probably pushing her two bags in a trolley which she abandons in the trolley park at the lift-head, then goes down in the lift to the second level. It is still full of cars, the time being no more than five-forty.

'Dita Jago, sitting in her daughter's car knitting, sees her come in and also sees her opportunity. She pulls the circular needle out from her work, leaves the car, goes up behind Gwen Robson on her light feet, and, as Gwen Robson is unlocking the door of the Escort, strangles her with this highly efficient garrote.'

'Is that really what you think happened?' asked Burden as they entered Tesco. He took a wire basket, having always in such places an uneasy feeling that to walk through without one might not be illegal but was suspect and reprehensible behaviour, likely to lead store detectives to the belief that you were up to no good. He even helped himself to a can of aerosol shoe polish. 'You really think she is our perpetrator?'

'You'll destroy the ozone layer,' Wexford said. 'You'll coat the earth in black froth — and all for the sake of shiny shoes, you narcissist. No, I don't think Dita's our perpetrator; I know she isn't. The librarian at the High Street branch of the library remembers her being there with the two little girls from somewhere around four-fifty until about five-thirty, when her daughter came back to collect her. She was checking up on facts for this book she's writing, we now know. The librarian remembers because the little girls kept asking the time; they were supposed to be reading, but they kept asking their grandmother if it was half-past five yet and then they asked other people and had to be hushed. Dita Jago took out three books and the date is on the library's computer.'

Burden took his aerosol to Linda Naseem's checkout. If she recognized him she gave no sign of it, but as they passed on he looked back and saw her chattering in whispers to the girl next to her. The main exit doors slid open to let them pass through into the sunshine. There was a seat out there, just outside, with a strip of turf

262

dividing the centre from the biggest above-ground car park. Wexford sat down in the middle of it with Olson on his left and Burden – after examining his purchase, scrutinizing the label to see if what Wexford had said of it might be true – on his right.

Wexford said, 'We'll return to those letters. Now I knew that these particular letters would have to be out of the common run, not quite of the my-boyfriend-keeps-pressurizing-me-to-go-all-the-way genre. They were going to be of the kind that even in these days *Kim* wouldn't care to print. The agony aunt's assistant gave me an example of this type when she said someone had enquired about the protein content of semen.'

'You don't mean it?' said Burden, horrified. 'You're joking.'

'I only wish I had that much imagination, Mike.' Wexford grinned. 'One thing I did understand – where the letter copies had gone. The killer took them out of Gwen Robson's handbag after the deed was done, that much seemed obvious. The killer's own letter and the other. One of the writers was Mrs Margaret Carroll, but Gwen Robson never blackmailed her; she had nothing to blackmail her about. So we come to the other.

'My daughter Sylvia brought me copies of *Kim* magazine covering four years, about two hundred copies therefore. When I read through the agony aunt's pages I wasn't looking for a letter. I was looking for an answer, only because I was hoping against hope that this would be one of those appeals considered too . . . well, what? Obscene, indecent – hardly. Too open and revealing perhaps to print. But the agony aunt's reply would be printed under a heading with enough information to give me more than a clue as to who the writer was.

'There a₁. ⁿmmon initials to have and highly unusual ones. I'd say n ₂, RW are pretty ordinary – and yours too, Mike, MB. And your wife and your elder son both with JB even more so. "JB, Kingsmarkham" wouldn't convey much, would it? But your initials, Serge, are something else; SO isn't a usual combination at all. And the combination I was looking for must be even rarer.

'Well, I found it. Take a look at this.'

He had made a copy of the relevant back page of *Kim* and he passed the original to Burden and the copy to Olson.

Burden read his aloud: ' "NQ, Sussex: I understand and sympathize with you in your dilemma. Yours is certainly a difficult and potentially tragic situation. But if there is the slightest possibility that the man you mention could be an AIDS carrier, you must see your doctor at once. Tests can be easily and quickly carried out and your mind set at rest once and for all. Feeling guilty and ashamed is pointless. Better realize that by delaying you are putting your husband, your marriage and your family life in danger. Sandra Dale." '

'Nina Quincy?' said Burden when he had finished. 'Mrs Jago's daughter?'

'The letter that was never printed was photocopied by Lesley Arbel and shown to Gwen Robson. The full name and address were on that, of course. And Gwen Robson knew at once who it was; she had met Nina Quincy in Mrs Jago's house when she was hunting for two people to witness Eric Swallow's will. She was introduced to her and noted the unusual name. Nina Quincy lives in a big house in Down Road, she has her own car. To someone like Gwen, she would appear rich and a fine potential subject for blackmail.

'And for a time, I believe, she paid up. She has a part-time job of her own, and the likelihood is that for some weeks she was giving a considerable part of her salary to Gwen. You must understand that she was worried sick. Picture what it must have been like. Her husband had been away abroad on business and she had gone to a party, drunk too much, spent the night with a man she afterwards discovered to be bisexual and actually living with someone dying of Aids. She was afraid to go

264

to a doctor, especially as by the time she made her discovery her husband had been home for some time and they had been leading a normal sex life. Or so I suppose. I haven't seen this letter because the copy of it no longer exists and *Kim*, who claim to keep all letters sent to them for a three-year-period, are unable to find either this or the Carroll letter.

'On November the nineteenth, Nina Quincy – who still had not consulted her doctor or said anything of this to her husband, though the reply to the letter appeared in *Kim* last May – went as usual to the Barringdean Centre, having dropped off her mother and the two children at the library, entering here at about five to five. The first shop she went to was the wool and crafts place where she bought the first item on her mother's shopping list, a circular knitting needle gauge number eight – that is, a length of plastic-covered wire with a stout peg at each end measuring perhaps a quarter of an inch in diameter. This, or something similar, would be a purchase she had often made in the past for her mother.

'Coming out of the shop, she encountered Gwen Robson by the Mandala. It wasn't very imaginative of us to conclude that someone Helen Brook thought well-dressed would also appear well-dressed to us – at least to Mike and me, a couple of conventional coppers. Helen Brook would have turned her nose up at Lesley Arbel's pencil skirts and high heels. But Nina Quincy was dressed in just the way Helen admired: elaborate tapestry knits, a patterned beret and her hair down her back, a fringed shawl no doubt, a peasant-style skirt, jacquard socks. You see how I've worked on getting my terms right. Anyway, that's well-dressed in Ashtoreth's mother's book. What did she have to say to Gwen Robson? I think she pleaded with her to ask for no more. I think she told her that it was impossible to go on paying her at this rate – fifty pounds a week or perhaps more? And we must conclude that Gwen Robson did not relent, but said something to the effect of her need being greater than Nina's and perhaps that Nina shouldn't have done what she did if she didn't expect to pay for it. She was that sort of woman, was Gwen.

'If you've sunned yourselves enough we may as well take a look at their Christmas tree, see if it's as good as ours, then we'll go underground once more.'

'Are you going to tell us,' said Olson, 'that Nina followed her while she was shopping? That sounds grotesque.'

'Not necessarily; they may have encountered each other again at the checkout. After all, whatever trouble she was in Nina did continue to lead the life of a housewife and mother; she did do her own shopping and her mother's. She had to do it and then she had her mother and her daughters to pick up at five-thirty. So, yes, we'll say they met again at the checkout and more words passed between them, only a back view of Nina and her beret being visible to Linda Naseem. But they left the Tesco separately, meeting for the third time that afternoon only when they were both in the car park.

'Those white lights look a bit stark, don't you think? I prefer our rainbow effect.'

The three of them stood underneath the Norway spruce which towered to a height of thirty feet. A notice at its foot announced that Father Christmas would be in the centre to meet children every day from Tuesday December 22. The date reminded Wexford of what today's was, one week before that, and raised into the forefront of his mind Sheila's court appearance. She would have left the court some hours ago and the waiting photographers and television cameras would have departed. By now it would be in the papers. Not for her the angry hand pushed against the lens, the averted head or coat held up like a yashmak, the veil to inhibit recognition. She would want to be seen, want the whole nation to know . . . He made one of those shifts that are much a remarkable feature of man's mental processes, as if a lever were lifted and a new picture dropped into place, or a kaleidoscope shaken. With the

266

others following, he stepped into the shade and cold of the covered way.

'We can't tell exactly what happened next,' he said, 'but Nina Quincy – having settled matters at last, having taken action and perhaps feeling relief – had got into her car and driven away. She picked up her mother and her children and took them home. The blackmail was over; Gwen Robson would never menace her again. She, however, had something left to do. Now that this particular threat was past, she had to go to her doctor and arrange to have that test.

'Well, eventually she did and the test was negative. She had nothing to fear and she knew her husband was an unforgiving man. Yet when he confessed to her some indiscretion of his own which he'd committed while he was in America, she was silly enough to tell him the whole story . . . and he left her.'

Beyond the open gates, across Pomeroy Road in his window sat Archie Greaves. Wexford put up his hand in a salute, though sure the old man wouldn't be able to see him, certainly wouldn't recognize him. But there was an answering wave from beyond the glass, the wave Archie would give to any friendly customer in the Barringdean Centre. They went down in the lift and stepped out at the second level. A car went round rather too fast, splashing oil from a puddle – a red car, of course.

'You didn't say anything about her taking the letter copies from Mrs Robson's bag,' said Burden.

'She didn't take them.'

'But someone –'

'Once she had made her decision, she had nothing to fear from that letter. She had already told Gwen Robson while they were in the centre that blackmail was pointless as she intended to go to her doctor and confess to her husband.'

There was a space now where the Robson Escort had been parked, and the space where the blue Lancia had been was empty too. Burden stood in the middle holding out his arms in rather a dramatic way, a foot

on either side of the dividing white line. And in a voice
made shrill by exasperated bewilderment, he demanded
to know why it was then that Nina Quincy had done
murder.

21

THEY stood for a while on the spot where Gwen Robson had died.

'You know, Mike,' Wexford said, 'I don't think we've considered sufficiently what a horrible crime this was. We've accepted it, not put it into perspective. Only a very few people would be capable of committing such a crime. What – approach a woman either from behind or face-to-face and garrote her with a wire? Imagine the horror of it, the helpless thrashings of the victim, her struggles . . . who but one of those psychopaths you're so keen on could stand it?'

'I must say,' Olson put in, 'I wouldn't have thought a . . . well, fairly sheltered ordinary middle-class sort of girl like Nina Quincy with a conventional lifestyle capable of it. But I'm not a policeman, I don't know. The affectivity might be there, but it's just that a young mother – that's the last category you'd pick on for this kind of crime. In my game, that is.'

'And in mine,' said Wexford. 'When I said that Nina Quincy felt satisfied because she had taken action, I meant only that the action she had taken was her defiance of Gwen Robson, her decision to get medical help at last. Of course she didn't kill her, though I daresay she sometimes would have liked to, which is what I think you mean. But she didn't kill her. In order to be back in the High Street and at the library by five-thirty, she must have left the Barringdean Centre by five-twenty at the latest, and we know the earliest time at which Gwen Robson could have died was five-thirty-five.'

The acrid stench of petrol made Wexford wrinkle up his nose. 'If we want to save our lungs, we'd better get back in the car,' he said. 'Before we go into the next sequence of events, perhaps we should take a look at the couple called Roy and Margaret Carroll. We already know that the writer of the other letter was Margaret Carroll – a woman with something of a social conscience, a woman who was upset when she discovered that her neighbour was in the habit of punishing her little boy by shutting him up in cold, dark attics.'

'Do you know who they are?' Burden said to Olson. 'Neighbours of Clifford and the late Dodo Sanders? Does it mean anything to you?'

'Clifford mentioned her,' Olson said carefully. 'He said she once threatened his mother with the cruelty-to-children people.'

'That's right. She was also concerned about another aspect of the Sanders' life, though this was something she didn't begin to suspect until last summer. Strange, isn't it, how all these things erupted last summer around May and June? Her own life was none too easy, I suspect, with a husband of a kind usually called a brute – a Cold Comfort Farm kind of character, only grimly for real. He was going to have a go at us last night with a twelve-bore. Did Mike tell you?'

Olson raised his brown tufty eyebrows. 'Where is he now?'

'In custody, where I hope he'll remain for quite a while.'

'And the wife? What's happened to her?'

'She left him last summer – something else that happened then, about June, I think. The wonder was that she didn't go years ago. Well, no, I'm deceiving you and I don't want to do that. Let's say only that she seems to have left him; at any rate she disappeared. Clifford believes there was a man friend and Carroll gives the impression of believing that too. I don't. I think Margaret Carroll is dead, just as Charles Sanders is dead. A year after Roy Carroll and his wife came to live at Ash Farm Lodge, Charles Sanders died. That was why he never came back to see his little boy, why he seemed to abandon his old mother, why he contributed nothing to his son's support, why his wife was obliged to live on what she drew from their joint account – an account steadily though meagrely fed from Charles Sanders' investments – and incidentally why Mike hasn't been able to find him.

'Let's go back, shall we? We've renewed our acquaintance with the place; we can hold what we need to in our mind's eye.'

Burden reversed the car and circled slowly towards the upward ramp. 'Is that what they're doing up there at Ash Lane, searching for Charles Sanders' body?'

'Well, the remains of it, Mike. It's eighteen years past and there won't be much left. Frankly, I don't know where to begin the search for Mrs Carroll, but there are ways of help open to us.

'You see, Mrs Carroll suspected Sanders was dead when she was in her branch of the Midland Bank and saw Dorothy Sanders drawing a cheque on a joint account. She happened to stand next to her and quite innocently saw this over her shoulder. At any rate I think so; it's an intelligent enough guess. Did other others then begin to fall into place? The sudden and quite unexpected death of Charles Sanders' father? This death immediately followed by the departure of Charles? The memory soon after of secret digging? Not enough for her to come to us – or perhaps she couldn't bring herself to the enormity of such a step. It was a pity she didn't; she might be alive today if she had.'

When the car turned into the High Street something recalled Wexford's mind to Sheila and the tribulations of her day. She or someone representing her would have phoned Dora by now. What had happened to her – an account of what had happened with pictures – would be in the evening paper. It would be on the streets by now; the London evening papers were always on Kingsmarkham streets by three and it was nearly four. The sun was setting, dyeing the sky a gold that would fade to pink and darken to dusky purple. He caught sight of a newsboard with something on it about missile treaty talks and felt a

271

ridiculous relief because Sheila's name wasn't there. As if Sheila's court appearance, Sheila's fate must as a matter of course be the lead story.

'Mike,' he said, 'put the car on one of those meters in Queen Street, will you? I have to buy a paper.'

Her face looked at him, framed in newsprint, not smiling nor laughing, no raised hand waving at cameras. She looked frightened; her expression was grave and big-eyed. She was leaving the court and even without reading the caption it didn't take a policeman's knowledge to recognize where she was going and with whom. The headline he couldn't help reading, though he forced himself to postpone further elucidation until he was at home: 'Sheila Goes to Jail', the picture caption said. '*Lady Audley's Secret* star gets a week inside.'

The man behind the counter, an obliging, nothing-is-too-much-trouble Indian, smiled patiently at this apparently stupefied customer who didn't know you had to pay for an evening paper. He coughed discreetly. Wexford put two ten-pence pieces on the counter and crushed the paper clumsily into his pocket.

Olson and Burden were out of the car, standing outside Pelage.

'Come up to my place,' Olson said. 'I'll make you a cup of tea.'

The steep narrow staircase was a bit like the attic stairs at Ash Farm, Burden thought. But there was something cosy, something sane for all its bizarreness, about what awaited them at the top. He remembered how it had once felt threatening and now he wondered why. What had he meant? He had become a therapist himself since then — with disastrous results. His own, sometimes timid, psyche suddenly seemed less important. Wexford, who had never been up here before, saw the poster with the globe and its ruined continents, with Einstein's ominous words, and it brought home to him Sheila's fate so that he flinched. He wondered if the others had seen, decided they hadn't and anyway, so what? Olson was using spoonfuls of powdered stuff called instant tea. Inwardly Wexford laughed at himself for minding, for caring about trivia in the midst of . . . all this. He said:

'Thanks to your tapes, Mike, I know exactly what Clifford told you. Whether those tapes could be admitted now, whether you were strictly correct to make them, doesn't matter. Clifford told you he hoped his mother and Roy Carroll might get together – might even possibly marry – and he told you how all the information about Margaret Carroll having a lover, another man in her life, came to Carroll from Dorothy Sanders. It was Dorothy Sanders, the neighbour, who was in a position to see who visited Ash Farm Lodge while Carroll was out in the fields and perhaps also to see whom he went out to meet. Or so Carroll could be made to believe.

'Carroll is a jealous, possessive man. She inflamed his jealousy and terribly damaged his pride, but for her own sake she had to do it. Clifford was wrong when he guessed Carroll might be attracted by his mother or enjoyed her company; all he got from her was information about his wife's infidelity. When his wife disappeared he thought he knew why and who with, but the last thing he wanted was for the rest of the world to know. That was why he never reported her as missing when she disappeared last June. He preferred to keep her disappearance dark but if anyone suggested to him, as we did, that his wife might be somewhere living with another man, he went out of his mind with rage.'

Burden drank his tea as if it were the real stuff brewed from leaves in a hot, dry pot, as if the milk in it had come yesterday from a cow. 'So Carroll didn't kill her?'

'There was only one person in this case capable of committing these crimes, and that person is beyond our reach now. Retribution, if you like, or chance or misfortune has caught up with her. Only Dorothy Sanders could have killed a husband, depriving a child of its father and a mother of her son. Only Dorothy Sanders could have gone up to her victim and garroted her with a length of wire.

'Here's the letter Margaret Carroll wrote to *Kim* last

273

spring,' Wexford went on, holding out the photocopy to Burden. 'I went back to Ash Farm last night and found it slipped into the back of a photograph frame in one of those attic rooms. The picture, incidentally, was of a family group I take to be Charles and his parents. I wonder why she didn't burn the letter? Because something she had done murder for must be precious? Or one day to have it to show to Clifford or Carroll if a defence was needed? We shall never know. The original would have been kept by *Kim* for two years, except that Lesley Arbel saw to that when she couldn't find the copy. She destroyed both those letters as soon as she got back after her Sundays course.'

Burden read it aloud: '"Dear Sandra Dale, I am in a terrible dilemma and cannot decide what to do. I am so worried it is stopping me from sleeping. I have good reason to believe that a neighbour of mine killed a person close to her nearly twenty years ago. The person was her husband. I won't go into what made me think this after so long, but the new evidence I got made me remember certain suspicious things happening all that time ago. Her father-in-law died too and he was a healthy strong man, not old. My husband does not like the police and would be very upset I think if I had to explain all this to them, if we had police here questioning me etc. I cannot mention names here. It has taken months to screw myself up to write this. I would appreciate your advice . . ."' He looked at Wexford. 'Did this Sandra Dale reply?'

'Oh, yes. She didn't print the letter, of course, or the reply. She wrote back very properly advising Margaret Carroll to come to us and lose no time in doing so. But Margaret Carroll didn't — too frightened of the husband, no doubt. And by then Gwen Robson had got hold of the letter through Lesley.'

Olson put in, 'But how did she know who Margaret Carroll meant by her "neighbour"?'

'She was a Kingsmarkham woman: she knew the area and knew Mrs Carroll only had one neighbour. I daresay she remembered Clifford from the Miss McPhail days. Anyway, she took herself down to Ash Farm and asked

Dorothy Sanders for money — weekly payments if she liked, she didn't mind instalments — not to tell the police about the contents of the letter. By that time she was already successfully extracting payment from Nina Quincy, stashing it away for her husband's expensive op.

'She wasn't concerned with Margaret Carroll. It wouldn't have excited her interest if she had known that Margaret Carroll had disappeared soon after Dorothy Sanders made the first payment. Besides, it was in her interest to steer clear of Mrs Carroll who, had she dreamed of what was going on, probably would have been stirred into coming to us, would have saved her own life and killed one of the geese that laid golden eggs. Dorothy Sanders made no second payment. A second payment was asked for when Gwen Robson encountered her by chance in the Barringdean Centre that Thursday afternoon, but Dodo saw to it that it was never paid.'

Burden objected. 'But look, didn't you say you saw her come into the car park as you were leaving it at ten-past six? Gwen Robson was dead by five-to.'

'I saw her come back a second time, Mike. She had been there before.'

'She went back?' Olson said. 'When she'd committed murder? Why didn't she just leave, go home, anything?'

'She's not like other people, is she? We've already agreed on that. She didn't have their responses, their reactions, their emotions. This is what I think happened, all we'll ever know now of what did happen. First of all, it was she that Linda Naseem saw from the back talking to Gwen Robson. She had a girl's figure, we've commented on that: she looked like a girl from the back, or when you couldn't see her face and hair. Either she went with Gwen Robson into the car park — arguing perhaps, threatening even, trying to make her change her mind — or else she followed her. I lean rather towards the alternative and think she followed. You see, by then — it wasn't yet five-thirty — she hadn't finished her shopping.

'So they entered the car park more or less together. While Gwen Robson was unlocking her car Dodo went up to her and garroted her with the circular knitting needle she had bought in the centre after she had had her hair done. Remember, we know she had been in there because she had bought the grey knitting wool which she put into the boot of the Escort in the absence of her own car. The job done, she returned to the centre.'

'But why? If she was going to report the death to us, why not do it then? Why not pretend, as she later did, that she'd discovered the body?'

'She had her shopping to finish, Mike. She only came to the centre once a week and she wasn't going to upset her routine. There was still her fish to buy and her groceries to get. Didn't I say we aren't dealing with an ordinary normal woman here? Dodo was special, Dodo was different. She had probably killed her father-in-law, she had already killed a husband, very likely with a knitting needle garrote, and a neighbour also by the same means. Maybe she even used the garrote afterwards to knit Clifford's sweaters. Waste not, want not! She went back to get the rest of her shopping done. It was not yet a quarter to six. Possibly she thought some other car driver would see the body, for the car park at that time would still have been half-full. However, no one did. Only Clifford did, coming in at six o'clock. He thought it was his mother, he thought the body was Mother Dodo. And he did a mad thing, a typically Clifford thing. He covered it up with a curtain from the boot of the car and then he ran away, pounding down the stairs as I was coming up in the lift, bursting out through the pedestrian gates for Archie Greaves to see.

'Dodo came back at ten-past six, so that I was permitted a sight of her emerging from the covered way, and she entered the car park as she truthfully told us at precisely twelve minutes past. One useful thing only came out of my being there, my seeing her. She was carrying two bags of shopping but not the grey knitting wool, which is how I know she had been in the car park earlier. Did she expect to find a crowd there, even the police there? By the time I saw her, she must have realized that wasn't happening. Only one thing had happened — someone had covered it

276

up. Who? A policeman? A car driver who had gone off to get help? What? One thing was clear; it wouldn't do for her just to do nothing. Her car was there but no Clifford. If he had been there perhaps they could just have driven off, taking no action. But he wasn't and she couldn't drive. Margaret Carroll wrote about her particular dilemma. Dodo's was worse. What was she to do?

'Wait. Think. What if the driver of the only other car on the second level turned up, the blue Lancia? Where was Clifford? Where was the man or woman who had covered up the body? At least she didn't realize at that time that it was her curtain which had been used – or rather a curtain from up in her attics. She went down by the stairs or in the lift, looking for Clifford, and that was the first time Archie Greaves saw her. The second time she was screaming and raving and shaking those gates. Her nerve had broken; it was all too much, the waiting and the not knowing and . . . the silence.'

Olson nodded. He offered more tea not seeming to notice the haste with which it was refused, then pushed his hands through the dense bush of curly hair. 'I suppose there was no real motive for those early murders? She was a true psychopath? Because if we're looking for self-interest, it was surely in her interest to keep her husband alive?'

'Oh, there was a motive,' said Wexford. 'Revenge.'

'Revenge for what?'

'Mike can tell you the story. He knows it, Clifford told him. Clifford thought it romantic; he couldn't see through the veil his mother wore. Her life had been dedicated to an act of revenge against the people who said she wasn't good enough for their son, and against the son who agreed with them.

'She was a multi-murderer who killed dispassionately but who was afraid of her victims after they were dead. She disinfected herself to be rid of their contamination and was frightened of their ghosts.'

Burden and Olson had begun a discussion on paranoia, on infantilism and transference, and Wexford listened to them for a moment or two, smiling to himself as Burden said, 'We live and learn.'

'We live at any rate,' said Wexford and he left them, walking the few hundred yards back to the police station when he got into his own car under the Christmas lights which were already winking away on the ash tree. There he sat and read about Sheila, read the statement she had made, her refusal to pay the fine demanded on conviction – her brave, foolhardy, defiant declaration that she would do it all again as soon as she came out.

'The Chief Constable rang,' Dora said as he came into the house. 'Darling, he wants to see you as soon as possible; he couldn't get you at the office. I suppose it's about this place.'

I don't suppose so for a moment, said Wexford but to himself, not aloud. He knew exactly what it would be about and felt the crackle of the evening paper in his raincoat pocket. For some reason, for no reason, he gave Dora a kiss and she looked a little surprised.

'I don't suppose I'll be long,' he said, knowing he would be.

Dusk, nearly dark, a little before five. His route to Middleton where the Chief Constable lived took him along his old road. It would be the first time he had been there since the bomb and he knew he had consciously avoided it, but he didn't now. The sky was jewel-blue and windows along the street were full of Christmas lights. Bracing himself for the shock of devastation, he slowed as he came to the strip of open ground, the empty site. He braked, pulled in and looked.

Three men were coming out of the gate, up to a van with ladders on its roof. He saw the contractors' board, the stack of bricks, the concrete-mixer covered up against the frost. He got out and stood looking, smiled to himself.

They had begun to rebuild his house.